The Glamorous Life

My studio specialized in fake—sorry, faux—finishes. I was a natural. I made new surfaces look old, wood look like marble, and plaster look like wood. Gradually I branched out into murals, portraits, and even antique reproductions, always taking pains to ensure they could not possibly be passed off as Old Masters. Now, at the age of thirty-one, I was the owner of a reasonably successful business, meaning that most months I brought in enough to support myself and to pay my assistant, Mary. It wasn't a lot, but I managed to keep my head above water.

As long as I dog-paddled furiously.

People loved to think of the art world as a mysterious and potentially dangerous milieu. The artistic life was fulfilling, exciting, and a whole lot of fun, but in my experience, at least, it was distinguished less by drama than by long hours, low pay, and plenty of grunt work. Provided, of course, that I stayed away from my grandfather's world of fakes, frauds, and felons.

But despite my best efforts, that world had a way of sneaking up and biting me in the butt when I least expected it. . . .

FEINT OF ART

AN ANNIE KINCAID MYSTERY

Hailey Lind

A SIGNET BOOK

SIGNET
Published by New American Library, a division of
Penguin Group (USA) Inc. 375 Hudson Street,
New York, New York 10014, USA
Penguin Group (Canada), 90 Eglinton Avenue East, Suite 700, Toronto,
Ontario M4P 2Y3, Canada (a division of Pearson Penguin Canada Inc.)
Penguin Books Ltd., 80 Strand, London WC2R 0RL, England
Penguin Ireland, 25 St. Stephen's Green, Dublin 2,
Ireland (a division of Penguin Books Ltd.)
Penguin Group (Australia), 250 Camberwell Road, Camberwell, Victoria 3124,
Australia (a division of Pearson Australia Group Pty. Ltd.)
Penguin Books India Pvt. Ltd., 11 Community Centre, Panchsheel Park,
New Delhi - 110 017, India
Penguin Group (NZ), cnr Airborne and Rosedale Roads, Albany,
Auckland 1310, New Zealand (a division of Pearson New Zealand Ltd.)
Penguin Books (South Africa) (Pty.) Ltd., 24 Sturdee Avenue,
Rosebank, Johannesburg 2196, South Africa

Penguin Books Ltd., Registered Offices:
80 Strand, London WC2R 0RL, England

First published by Signet, an imprint of New American Library,
a division of Penguin Group (USA) Inc.

First Printing, January 2006
10 9 8 7 6 5 4 3 2 1

To Mom and Dad

whose sage and practical advice to pursue careers in the
computer industry produced an artist, a historian,
and an art historian.

Acknowledgments

Many thanks to Mary Ann Roby of A-1 Editing Service, who helped to whip this baby into shape; to Kristin Lindstrom of Lindstrom Literary Group, for taking a chance on the unknown Hailey Lind; and to Martha Bushko of NAL/Signet, for her faith in art and for making it all happen.

Thanks as well to John, whose Medici-like patronage has made the artistic life possible for more than a few; to Jorge, Candida, Susan, Sandra, Karin, Steve, and Karen, for their thoughtful critiques and unflagging support; to J.C., for always believing, and for a lot of good scotch; to Shay and Suzanne, for food, friendship, and getting married; to Mary for being Mary; to Anna, for refusing to buy another book until this one was published; to the entire MVSC, for uncommon neighborliness . . . and above all to Malcolm and Sergio, for all the joy.

Prologue

"Georges, *please*—try to concentrate on what I'm saying," I persisted. "It is illegal and immoral to forge art."

"Ah, but my agent assures me that there's no law against *writing a book* about forging art, *cherie*. As to whether it is immoral, well . . ."

"You already have an agent?" I asked, momentarily distracted from my halfhearted moral outrage.

"But of course, Annie! It is a wonder, this book. It is the ultimate tool for the democratization of art, a way for me to spread the joys of . . ."

I stopped listening out of an instinct for self-preservation. Georges was spreading something, all right, but it sure wasn't joy. My hand tightened around the telephone as my mind reeled at what this might mean for me. For the past several years I had been working like a dog to establish myself as a legitimate artist and faux finisher in San Francisco, determined to distance myself from my grandfather Georges LeFleur's world of art felons, forgers, and fakes.

And now he was writing a "memoir" that would no doubt include so many professional secrets, not to mention scores of recipes for committing art fraud, that it might as well be a required textbook for "Forgery 101." In certain circles, what Grandfather was proposing was roughly akin to publishing instructions for how to build an atomic bomb using common household cleaners.

I was his beloved granddaughter.

I was trying to talk him out of it.

I didn't stand a chance.

"Answer me this, *cherie*. Just this one question, and I will agree not to publish this wonderful tome."

I perked up.

"Why should a painting that is considered exquisite on Monday, and is revealed as a fake on Tuesday, be reviled on Wednesday? Tell me: how has the painting changed? Is it any less beautiful? Any less a work of art?"

I sat back, deflated. I didn't know. That was a big part of my problem. In addition to inheriting my grandfather's artistic talent, I had also developed a tendency toward moral flexibility—at least when it came to art. I tried to stifle it, but it wasn't easy. Fighting genetics never was.

According to family lore, at the age of eighteen months I had toddled across the room, plucked the paintbrush from my grandfather's hand, and corrected the shading on a "Renoir" that Georges was painting for a financially strapped German baroness who had been forced to quietly sell the original.

At the age of ten, I won a California state Masters of Tomorrow competition with a brilliant copy of Leonardo da Vinci's *Mona Lisa,* was proclaimed a prodigy, and had my painting hung with great fanfare in the Governor's Mansion in Sacramento. When the artist is ten, the ability to paint a fake is considered adorable.

At the age of sixteen, I waged a three-month-long campaign to convince my skeptical parents to allow me to spend the summer in Paris with Georges, who insisted that arthritis had long since forced him to give up his life of crime. No, no, he swore, he would simply teach me French.

Grandfather was a man of his word about the language, if not the life of crime. I learned to say "I am afraid you are mistaken, good sir," "I am just a tourist," and "I must insist upon calling my attorney" in French as well as in five other European languages, plus Cantonese.

Most of what I actually learned, though, was how to forge art, as the only thing arthritic about Grandfather was his moral compass. By the end of that summer Georges and I had managed to flood the European art world with our forged sketches, temporarily causing a brief but devastating crash in the market for Old Master drawings.

The eve of my seventeenth birthday was spent in a dank Parisian jail, where those French phrases had come in handy. And where I vowed, as God was my witness, never to listen to my grandfather again.

"*Allô*, Annie? Are you there? What is your answer, *cherie*?"

I sighed.

"The only thing I know for sure, Grandfather, is this: genuine art is priceless and forgery gets you arrested. And that's enough of a difference for me."

It wasn't much of a comeback, but it was the best I had.

Chapter 1

The clever art forger has one decided advantage in any sticky legal situation: collectors, dealers, and museums do not wish to advertise their gullibility.

—*Georges LeFleur, "Gentleman's
Disagreement," unfinished manuscript,*
Reflections of a World-Class Art Forger

Our eyes met. I tried to keep a poker face. I failed.

"Ah, *hell*," Ernst swore softly.

"So don't tell anyone it's a fake. Who would know?" My voice echoed in the nearly empty vault.

"I will not be party to a fraud," he snapped. There was a sheen developing on Ernst's elegant brow, which I noted with guilty pleasure. It was kind of fun to see an ex-boyfriend sweat. Especially one who had dumped me so unceremoniously.

"Besides," Ernst added, "*you* knew."

"I could be wrong," I lied.

He shook his head and sighed. "You're never wrong about forgery. I had my doubts anyway. That's why I asked you to meet me here tonight."

That's why he *begged* me to meet him at the Brock

Museum in the middle of the night, to be more precise. I wasn't exactly welcome during regular business hours.

"In that case, I suggest you keep my name out of it when you go to the board. It won't help your case if I'm associated with this," I said, turning my attention back to the exquisite fake of Caravaggio's *The Magi*. I had to bite my tongue to refrain from praising the forger's skill in capturing the artist's unique blend of dramatic shading and rich, almost luminous colors. Upstanding art types usually found it hard to appreciate this kind of talent.

And Ernst Pettigrew was as upstanding as they came. The glamour boy of museum curators, Ernst had twinkling blue eyes, a charming European accent, and a sleek BMW convertible. As nurturing of the fine art in his care as he was of the egos of wealthy benefactors, he had won the coveted position of head curator at San Francisco's Brock Museum last year at the tender age of thirty-five.

Ernst and I enjoyed a brief fling six years ago, when I was happily working as one of the Brock's lowly, under-paid restoration interns and he had just arrived from Austria to catalogue the museum's substantial European art collection. He had broken off our nascent affair when I was "outed" by an old rival as having once been accused of art forgery. My assurances that the charges had been settled out of court placated no one at the Brock, including Ernst. Although I'd been upset by Ernst's lack of faith, what hurt the most was his public denunciation of me over a mediocre Waldorf salad and a watery iced tea at the annual Brock Frock Talk fashion show fund-raiser.

One does not know true humiliation until one has been shunned by the Ladies Who Lunch.

Ernst was now living in a plush condo in the Marina and dating an emaciated model named Quiana. I knew this because in moments of weakness and self-loathing, I read the *San Francisco Chronicle*'s society pages.

Now my damning assessment of the "Caravaggio" resting on the easel before me might well mean that Ernst's career was finished. No matter how you looked at it, fifteen million dollars was a lot of money to spend on a fake. And knowing the way museums such as the Brock reacted to these kinds of expensive mistakes, I was certain Ernst's vilification would be even more public than my own. I didn't wish that kind of professional humiliation on anyone, scummy ex-boyfriend or not.

"You could try to spread the blame," I suggested. "Didn't Sebastian run the usual tests to authenticate the age of the canvas and types of paint used?" Dr. Sebastian Pitts was the overrated and undertalented art authenticator who had ruined my chances in the legitimate art restoration field by digging up those old forgery charges. I would happily help Ernst feed Pitts to the Brock lions.

Nodding distractedly, Ernst walked out of the vault, past a long bank of archival storage drawers, and wordlessly smashed his fist through the wall.

I gawked at the gaping hole, impressed by both his temper and his strength.

"Who painted it?" Ernst demanded, the color mounting in his face as he struggled for control.

"How should I know?" I lied again. Of course I knew. How could I not?

Part of learning how to perpetrate fraud is learning how to recognize it. However, just as it takes true artistic talent to be a world-class forger, the ability to identify another artist's signature style is more inborn than acquired. And to my grandfather's delight, I had a real flair for aesthetic profiling.

"We should get her outta here."

I started at the sound of Dupont's raspy baritone. Under the spell of the fake Caravaggio I had forgotten that after sneaking me into the building, Dupont, the night custodian, had remained in the corridor as a look-out. My heart pounded. The Brock Museum was spooky in the dead of night. It was spooky in the broad of day, too. Belatedly, I wondered why I had agreed to this mid-night assignation in the first place.

Ernst nodded curtly at the stooped, balding janitor, then turned back to me. "Let me secure the Caravaggio in the vault," he said. "We have to talk."

"What is there to talk about?"

He gave me a pained look.

"Oh, all right," I said with a sigh. Normally I wouldn't indulge an ex-boyfriend like this, but Ernst was staring down the barrel of professional suicide. I glanced at the workroom clock, the one with large black numbers and a ticking second hand that always reminded me of elementary school. 12:30 A.M. "I need coffee," I said. "Meet me at Grounds for Suspicion, on Fillmore. Twenty minutes?"

Ernst nodded distractedly, staring at his pricey but worthless Caravaggio.

Dupont led the way out of the workroom and through the marble-floored galleries of the European art collection, his grim countenance betraying only his customary dissatisfaction with life. The custodian's crowded key ring clanked loudly as he unlocked a metal maintenance door tucked behind a gleaming white statue of Apollo. This sculpture was also a forgery, and not a very good one at that, but since it had been sculpted in 137 A.D., nobody was complaining. Funny how bad art plus a millennium or two added up to big money.

I followed Dupont into a labyrinth of relentlessly beige and gray utility corridors. We snaked our way past endless banks of archival drawers and storage lockers, our footsteps ringing on the linoleum, the unnatural silence broken by the occasional hiss of steam pipes. Despite the still-tender humiliation of my unceremonious dismissal six years ago, I breathed a sigh of relief that I was no longer trapped here in the Brock's vast grid of tunnels, just another timid art mouse in a dead-end maze.

At last we reached the exit to the rear employee parking lot. Dupont tapped in a security code and held the door open for me.

"Thanks, Dupont," I said brightly. "Nice chatting with you!"

He grunted.

The door slammed shut behind me.

I fled.

"Yo! Skinny latte, half the moo!" the pierced and tattooed barrista sang out.

Grounds for Suspicion Café was no more than a five-minute drive from the Brock and, open until two in the morning, it was a hangout for serious caffeine addicts. I ordered a nonfat latte easy on the milk, splurged on a chocolate chip cookie, and settled into what used to be my favorite spot by the greasy front window. When I worked at the museum, a group of us would come here to sip expensive coffee and debate the artistic merits of Cubism versus Expressionism. I regularly scandalized my colleagues by disdaining anything painted later than Picasso's Blue Period. I mean, really—even as a teenager, Picasso had demonstrated the talent of a Rembrandt, yet he became famous for a few squiggled lines and splashes of color. That was art?

Tonight there were five or six people haunting the café, most, by the look of them, angry young artists and angry young students: sleep-deprived, disgruntled, and dressed tip to toe in black.

I, too, was an artist, frequently sleep-deprived, occasionally disgruntled, and—I glanced down at my jeans, T-shirt, and jacket—yup, dressed in black. But I was not angry. I was my own boss, and my decorative painting business, True/Faux Studios, was finally enjoying the patronage of a steady clientele.

It hadn't been easy. Following my banishment from the Brock, I briefly considered a career as an adult phone sex operator (for eight dollars an hour and no benefits? no way), flirted with returning to a career of crime (with the possibility of ending up in a Parisian jail cell? no thanks), but instead wound up working a series of dead-end office jobs, surfing cable TV, and generally feeling like a loser. On the afternoon of my twenty-eighth birthday I was watching TV in bed, working my way through yet another pint of Double Fudge Chunk ice cream, when I saw an appallingly perky woman named Kitty apply a simple painting technique to a blank wall. Her efforts resulted in a moderately interesting mottled effect, but a wildly pleased studio audience.

Right then and there I had an epiphany: if the art world shunned me, so be it. I would offer my talents to a more appreciative audience, those creative souls seeking to add unique touches to their cookie-cutter homes and businesses.

My studio specialized in fake—sorry, faux—finishes. I was a natural. I made new surfaces look old, wood look like marble, and plaster look like wood. Gradually I branched out into murals, portraits, and even antique reproductions, always taking pains to ensure that they could not possibly be passed off as Old Masters. Now, at the age of thirty-one, I was the owner of a reasonably successful business, meaning that most months I brought in enough to support myself and to pay my assistant, Mary. It wasn't a lot, but I managed to keep my head above water.

As long as I dog-paddled furiously.

The bell on the café door tinkled. A rumpled, fiftyish

man with a bad case of bed head entered, wearing blue-and-white-striped pajamas and clutching a yapping bichon frise under one arm. He ordered hot chocolate for himself and steamed milk for Snowball, "my bestest fwend in the whole world." The barrista replied, "He want a scone with that?"

No sign of Ernst. I sighed. Patience was not among my virtues.

Bored with people-watching, I picked up one of San Francisco's many free newspapers and skimmed the cover story about a local art dealer and bon vivant who had suddenly dropped out of sight. Whether his disappearance was the result of design or foul play, no one seemed to know, but the paper hinted broadly that something nefarious was afoot.

I had to smile. People loved to think of the art world as a mysterious and potentially dangerous milieu. The artistic life was fulfilling, rewarding, and a whole lot of fun, but in my experience, at least, it was distinguished less by drama than by long hours, low pay, and plenty of grunt work. Provided, of course, that I stayed away from my grandfather's world of fakes, frauds, and felons.

Speaking of which . . . I pondered the fake Caravaggio. A number of intriguing questions presented themselves. What had happened to the real one? *Was* there a real one? A fundamental challenge in the art world was establishing a work's provenance: documenting when it was created, where, by whom, who had owned it, and what had happened to it over the years. A painting without a provenance was a painting whose authenticity was in doubt, precisely because of talented forgers such as my grandfather.

The Brock's new masterpiece, *The Magi,* painted in 1597 by the eccentric Italian artist Michelangelo Merisi da Caravaggio, was one such enigma. In 1637 the painting disappeared from the home of a Florentine nobleman and its whereabouts remained unknown for more than three hundred years. *The Magi*'s sudden reappearance last year on the gallery walls of a flamboyant New York City art collector, Roland Yablonski, was little short of miraculous, and had been the talk of the art world. The Italian government initiated a lawsuit to repatriate the masterpiece, but after a lengthy international court battle, Yablonski's claim was upheld, whereupon he promptly sold *The Magi* to the Brock Museum for an amount rumored to be in excess of fifteen million dollars. With its penchant for understatement, the Brock had immediately announced that its newest masterpiece would be unveiled in March at a gala reception, to which the City's movers and shakers had already received gilt-edged invitations.

Mine had apparently been lost in the mail.

Thinking about the Brock made my head ache, so I flipped through the paper until I found my favorite column, "Advice from the Sexpert." I was pondering the existence of what the Sexpert called "furries"—people who liked to have sex while dressed in full-body animal costumes—and trying not to conjure a mental image of that when I heard the barrista call out, "Last round." Glancing up, I saw that Snowball and his human friend had departed and only two of the Angry Ones remained. The ticking hands of the Elvis clock over the register indicated that forty minutes had passed.

Had I been stood up?

Outside, Fillmore Street was shrouded in darkness. The night was full of the sounds of the city. A faraway garbage truck labored noisily. A diminutive man in a baseball cap shouted what sounded like abuse in an unidentified Asian language. Sirens screamed in the distance. The keening of a car alarm was abruptly silenced.

More sirens.

A lot of sirens.

Where the hell was Ernst?

I fumbled through my bag until I found my tattered address book, an ancient one full of arrows and cross-cuts. My father kept trying to talk me into getting a Personal Data Assistant, but I resisted, believing that the solution to my lack of organization probably involved therapy, not another electronic gadget. Since I could scarcely remember to write numbers down on something that stood a reasonable chance of not being run through the washing machine, I figured the odds of my remembering to input data into a PDA were somewhere between zero and zilch.

Fishing around in my bag some more, I found four quarters, a dime, and a Canadian nickel. I owned a cell phone but usually forgot to bring it with me, or else neglected to recharge it, which meant that most of the time I didn't have it when I needed it, or if I did have it, it didn't work. Hoping that Ernst was better about these things, I went to the pay phone and called his cellular. Five rings and voice mail. I dialed the Brock's switchboard and punched in Ernst's office extension. Maybe he had decided to finish up some paperwork and fallen asleep at his desk. Or something.

No answer.

The sirens were now so close that the barrista and the remaining Angry Ones were crowding the front window, trying to catch a glimpse of what was going on and speculating with poorly concealed delight about what might be happening.

I could join them and speculate. I could waste more money calling Ernst. Or better yet, I could drive back to the museum and investigate.

A few minutes later everything looked peaceful as I approached the Brock's imposing granite façade. But when I turned the corner to park near the rear employee entrance I counted a dozen police cars, a paramedic unit, two fire trucks, and an ambulance, all with lights flashing. This was not a good sign.

My heart pounding in my chest, I stashed my truck on a side street and hurried back to the museum on foot. Half the neighborhood had poured out of their elegant houses, attracted by the noise and excitement, and were milling about in their nightclothes, chattering and craning their necks for a better look. A handful of uniformed police were setting up a barricade and politely asking the well-heeled crowd to "Step back. Just please step back." I automatically avoided the officers and tried to look innocent. Lessons learned in childhood run deep.

The museum's rear door banged open and the crowd fell silent. A stretcher rolled out. On the stretcher was a body bag. In the body bag appeared to be a body. The paramedics loaded it into the ambulance and drove away, lights on but sirens off. No need to hurry.

I swallowed hard. Maybe it wasn't as bad as I thought. Maybe some total stranger had had a heart attack. Or a stroke. Or choked to death on a peanut chewy. I once had a close call with a peanut chewy.

I spotted the tall, broad form of Carlos Jimenez, a security guard whom I'd met my first week at the Brock, when he had intervened to protect a malfunctioning soda machine from my wrath. We had commiserated about the slave wages we both received, and Carlos showed me how to get a free soda by jimmying the change slot. Our friendship was cemented by an exchange of confidences concerning our mutual disdain for the museum's moneyed matriarch, the insectlike Agnes Brock.

"Carlos!" I called out. "*Qué pasa?*"

"Annie! What are you doing here?" Carlos came over to the barricade.

"I was . . . just having a drink nearby and heard the commotion. What's going on?"

Carlos' wide, dark face looked bleak. He glanced around to see if anyone was eavesdropping, but the throng's attention was riveted on the museum's rear door, as if awaiting the start of Act II.

"There's been a murder," he whispered.

"*What?* Who?"

"Well, geez, Annie, I hate to be the one to tell you this . . ." Carlos hesitated.

"*Who?*" I demanded.

"Stan," Carlos whispered.

"Stan?" Who the heck was Stan?

"Stan, you know Stan, Annie," Carlos said gently. "The janitor."

"You mean Dupont? His first name is Stan?"

He nodded.

I was both relieved and appalled. Relieved that Ernst was alive but appalled that Dupont was not, especially when I recalled my flippancy to him earlier this evening. What had my parting remark been? "Nice chatting with you"? Had that been his last nonlethal human interaction? Remorse washed over me. This was why it was important not to be a smart-aleck. I had always known Miss Manners had her reasons.

"What happened?" I asked.

"Dunno. I was on a break. By the time I got back the cops were already here."

"What about Ernst Pettigrew?"

"What about him?"

"Is he—isn't he here?"

Carlos looked at me oddly. "Why would Ernst be here? It's the middle of the night."

A uniformed cop with a pronounced paunch called out

to Carlos, saving me from having to answer. I decided it was time to vamoose.

Then I hesitated. Although the very thought of talking to the police made me want to hyperventilate, I realized I should tell them what I knew about the evening's events. It was my civic duty. A man was dead. True, I had never liked Dupont—Stan—whatever—but that didn't mean it was okay for somebody to kill him.

I took a step forward and stopped. I didn't really know anything relevant. Dupont had been fine when I left him. Plus, I wasn't supposed to have been in the museum in the first place. How would I explain why I had been at the Brock at midnight without bringing up Ernst, the forged Caravaggio, and my own dubious past?

Still . . . Dupont was dead. And it seemed a little too coincidental that his murder had occurred on the heels of my having confirmed to Ernst Pettigrew that a massive art fraud had been committed. Had Dupont discovered the fraud and been killed to ensure his silence? That seemed far-fetched, not to mention illogical. Dupont didn't know about art. Dupont knew about cleaning. And . . . keys. Dupont knew about keys.

I considered the facts as I knew them. Fact One: Ernst Pettigrew was about to lose everything he'd worked for because *The Magi* was a fake. Fact Two: Stan Dupont was dead. Fact Three: Ernst was missing. So: what did Facts One, Two, and Three add up to? Had Dupont orchestrated some scheme to steal the original Caravaggio and replace it with the fake? Had Ernst stumbled across the scheme and struck out, enraged, killing Dupont? *Get a grip, Annie,* I scolded myself. Ernst was a lousy boyfriend, but he wasn't a murderer.

Clearly I wasn't ready to talk to the police. But I felt the need to do something constructive. Like what? Like . . . talking to the man who had forged *The Magi*.

I had recognized the artistic signature immediately: it was my grandfather's old friend and rival Anton Woznikowicz. Spelled just like it sounded. We had worked together years ago, Anton and Georges and I, just one big, happy, art-forging family. But in the past few years I had tried to cut off contact with Anton—and the rest of my grandfather's circle—in an effort to keep True/Faux Studios entirely legitimate. I knew from bitter experience that this world had a way of sneaking up and biting me on the butt when I least expected it.

Anton was a gifted artist, though not of Georges' caliber. But like Georges, he was likely to vanish the minute the police started poking around. And on top of everything else, I was worried about the old guy. If someone had been murdered in connection with his forged Caravaggio, Anton himself could be in danger. I hurried back to my truck, fired up the engine, and headed across the City to Noë Valley.

Unless I was gravely mistaken, I was about to be bitten on the butt.

Chapter 2

Why is the imitation of nature more sacred than the imitation of art? Are Michelangelo, Rembrandt, and Delacroix to be reviled? For each learned his trade by copying the masters who had come before, just as their students learned the trade by copying them. If the imitation provides as much pleasure as the original, who is to say it is less worthy?

—*Georges LeFleur, "Real or Fake: Who Decides?" unfinished manuscript,* Reflections of a World-Class Art Forger

I had embraced the Californian habit, sometimes called Zen navigation, of starting to drive before I'd fully decided where I was going. Tonight was no exception. I was in gear, with the truck in motion, before it occurred to me that I was heading out in search of an art forger who might be connected to this evening's homicide, at two in the morning, in a city of nearly three-quarters of a million people.

What was wrong with this picture?

I was not famous for my common sense, but this seemed like a bad idea even to me. I had burned up all my stored caffeine at the scene of the murder, and a sudden wave of fatigue washed over me. I had also spent a long, hard day at the studio. Time to pack it in. I turned the truck around and headed east for the Bay Bridge, Oakland, and home.

Twenty minutes later I was trudging up three flights of stairs to my apartment, stepping lightly to avoid the squeaky spots so as not to awaken my neighbors. I sighed with relief as I entered my own little slice of heaven.

My home was the top floor, formerly the maid's quarters, of a once-stately Victorian built in 1869 for a wealthy merchant. The plumbing and electrical systems were suspect, but rent was cheap, moldings were ornate, and if you stood on the toilet you could glimpse San Francisco Bay from the bathroom window. The place was a lot like me: a bit quirky, occasionally contrary, but with lots of character. Also like me, it had a good foundation but needed some aesthetic work.

I locked the dead bolt, slung my bag on the hat tree, shuffled down the short hallway to my bedroom, changed into an oversized T-shirt, and crawled into bed. The events of the night were sinking in, and I needed to think. I knew I had to talk to the police, and soon. But old loyalties ran deep, and I wanted to keep Anton Woznikowicz out of the picture if at all possible. I also hoped to make sure he was safe from whoever had killed Dupont—that is, if the killing was even connected to the forgery. And Anton might be able to give me the most important information of all: who had commissioned a forgery of *The Magi,* and why.

I had to admit that Ernst's sudden disappearance left me feeling more than a little unsettled. We had once savored good wine, laughed until we snorted over the asking price for the splattered art of Jackson Pollock, and talked late into the night about everything from Austrian architecture to zinc white oil color. I could not imagine

Ernst being involved with anything criminal. Then again, I never would have thought him capable of punching his fist through a wall.

As I was finally dropping off to sleep, I realized that two thirty in the morning was the perfect time to call Europe, which was eight hours ahead of California. Switching on the bedside lamp, I put a call through to Amsterdam, the last known whereabouts of my rogue of a grandfather, Georges LeFleur.

Anton had been my grandfather's protégé and closest friend until their affection was tested by a dispute over a beautiful woman named Gina, a Persian cat named Mina, and a fake Bernini statue. Now avowed enemies, Georges and Anton kept careful tabs on one another, in what I presumed was an enduring professional and personal rivalry. It seemed likely that Georges would know something about *The Magi* and the situation at the Brock, or would at least know where to find the Polish forger. I knew Anton had a studio in San Francisco, but after finishing a big commission like *The Magi* he might well have taken an extended vacation to a country without extradition treaties.

No one answered my first call to Amsterdam, but I left a message with the pleasant but guarded woman who answered when I phoned Milan. I tried a few other possibilities, first in Barcelona and, finally, in Paris, the city that had long ago captured my grandfather's heart. None of the numerous gallery owners, artists, or self-described FOGs—Friends of Georges or, as I preferred, Forgery's Old Guard—would admit to knowing his whereabouts. But that was typical; it was understood that they would pass the word along. My grandfather would call me when he was good and ready, and not one moment sooner. I switched off the light, slipped back under the covers, and fell fast asleep.

* * *

I awoke the next morning in a funk. Under the best of circumstances I wasn't a morning person, but today my grumpiness was worsened by a short night of fitful slumber. On top of everything else, I stumbled into the kitchen only to discover that I was out of coffee.

I recognized that compared to war, famine, or being murdered at the Brock, running out of coffee probably didn't qualify as a catastrophe. But those were not my choices. I was confronted with a morning sans coffee, and I didn't have time to stop at a café. An interior designer was coming by the studio to pick up a project this afternoon and I had a stack of paperwork waiting for me. I also hoped to track down Ernst, assure myself that he was safe, and demand a logical explanation for last night's events. Then I needed to either find Anton—or speak to the police. I might need some time for wrestling with my conscience over the latter.

I skipped the shower, pulled on a navy blue T-shirt and a pair of paint-splattered overalls, slipped into some socks and my trusty Birkenstocks, and hit the road. As I queued up to cross the Oakland Bay Bridge, I fiddled with the radio, hoping to glean information about last night's murder. Dupont's death rated only a fleeting mention, but the radio did say that the Brock had reported nothing missing.

That seemed odd. If I were going to sneak into an art museum to murder someone, I would take another moment or two to steal something valuable. Then again, I was a reformed art forger, not a thief or a murderer, so what did I know?

Preoccupied with these thoughts, I pulled into the parking lot at my studio building and inadvertently nudged the rear bumper of a large, expensive-looking car that was parked in my usual space.

I didn't mean to hit it. I didn't hit it hard. But I did hit it.

As far as I was concerned, bumpers were designed to bump things, thereby avoiding damage to the rest of the vehicle. Besides, dings on a bumper were par for the course in a big city. Unfortunately, the gentleman who stepped out of what I belatedly realized was a late-model Jaguar sedan did not agree with me on this point, a fact he soon made clear.

"It appears you have scratched my bumper," he said, straightening after a close inspection of the offended car part. He was tall—a tad over six feet—and broad-shouldered, and he filled out his fine gray Armani suit just about perfectly. It was hard not to notice.

I pulled into the next parking space and braced myself.

He approached my driver's-side window, taking in my scruffy overalls, jean jacket, and wild sleep hair with a sweeping glance.

"Sorry about that," I replied, hastily smoothing my snarled curls. "Who are you?"

As my mother often pointed out, I had been raised right, so it wasn't her fault.

"J. Frank DeBenton."

I was getting a sinking feeling that J. Frank DeBenton here was not going to be a sport about a scraped bumper. Reluctantly, I climbed out of my small green pickup and shuffled over to peer at the damage.

"That's not a scratch," I informed him.

"It most certainly is."

"It's more of a ding. See here?" I pointed to a minuscule divot in the bumper. "The surface of the paint isn't broken. I'm an artist. I know about these things." I thought I was being rather helpful, under the circumstances.

"Ding, scratch, whatever." He waved dismissively. "You have damaged my car."

Despite his obvious displeasure, Mr. DeBounty was kind of cute, what with his dark eyes flashing in exasperation and his sleek mahogany hair gleaming in the early-morning sunshine. If that hair were ruffled up a bit, and if he were, say, naked, I could see painting him as a smoldering faun in a bacchanalian fantasy, a garland of grape leaves on his head, a wineskin in his hand, mischievously menacing a trio of frolicking nymphs . . .

"What do you intend to do about it?" he continued, ruining the moment.

Really, I found his attitude a bit of a puzzle. The only thing keeping my annoyance in check was that I had, in fact, hit his car. I forced myself to set aside enticing images of mythical revelries and instead tried to assume the knowledgeable tone of the *San Francisco Chronicle*'s consumer adviser. "You do realize, don't you, that painted bumpers like these are little more than a rip-off by the auto industry to make money by convincing consumers they have to be maintained like the rest of the car. It's a *bumper,* Mr. DeBootis. It's *supposed* to be bumped."

"DeBenton," the man said through extraordinarily even, white, clenched teeth. "J. Frank DeBenton. And I—"

"How do you do?" I held out my hand. "I'm Annie Kincaid. I'm a faux finisher, decorative painter, portraitist—you name it. If it involves paint, I'm your gal. I have a studio upstairs."

From the stony look on his face and the reluctance with which he shook my hand, I surmised that he was unimpressed with my extemporaneous résumé.

"I'm very sorry about your car," I continued, hoping to wrap this up and get to work, since it seemed highly unlikely that this man would be posing nude for me anytime soon. "It's a very nice car, too. I should have been more careful, but nobody but me ever parks in that space, which, by the way, is *my* parking space. So you see, I could give you my insurance information and everything, but you're probably going to feel rather silly about all this later, so why don't we just forget the whole thing? You don't see me crying about *my* bumper, do you?"

DeBenton looked askance at my vehicle. "And how, precisely, would you be able to tell if it had been scratched?" he inquired acidly.

There was a moment of awkward silence.

"Oh, never mind, Ms. Kincaid," DeBenton said abruptly. "I won't pursue this any further. Do keep in mind, however, that this is *not* your parking space."

"Is that right?" Although relieved that he was not going to jack up my insurance rates, I felt proprietary about my parking space. And I was beginning to suffer severe caffeine withdrawal.

"Yes, that's right," he said smugly. "It belongs to me. All the parking spaces do. I am the new owner of this property, as I'm sure you read in the memo I sent to the building's tenants two weeks ago."

Hmm. Memo. I was a little behind on my paperwork.

"My office is right there," he continued, pointing to a prime ground-floor suite distinguished by an imposing oak door, which now sported a black lacquer sign with J. FRANK DEBENTON ENTERPRISES, SPECIALISTS IN SECURE TRANSPORT discreetly lettered in gold leaf. It was only then that my mind registered the presence of the six armored cars parked at the rear of the lot.

Mr. Enterprise adjusted his cuffs and straightened his tie. Pride of ownership exuded from the top of his Armani suit jacket to the tips of his Italian calfskin loafers. The slightest trace of a smile hovered on his well-formed lips.

Realization dawned.

On its heels came horror.

I had just rear-ended my new landlord.

"Oh," I blustered, eloquent as always. "Okay, then.

I'm really sorry about . . . I mean, I didn't mean to . . . Good to meet you, Mr. DeBoo—BENton. Sorry about the bumper and everything. Maybe we could do lunch sometime? My treat. So . . . See you 'round!"

And grabbing my canvas tote bag, the one with a faded image of *Mona Lisa* that my assistant, Mary, had "improved" one rainy afternoon by giving Mona several nose piercings and a truly impressive blue-and-green Mohawk, I fled up the exterior wooden staircase to my second-floor studio.

The building was a former chair factory, built in the days before electricity, when multipaned windows and tall ceilings were essential. The light-filled space was an ideal setting for artists' lofts, even though every year there were fewer real artists and more architects and computer designers, all of whom claimed to be artists in their own right. I wasn't buying it. As far as I was concerned, art involved getting messy and working with noxious chemicals like turpentine and horsehide glue. In my view, the architects and computer people were far too neat and much too comfortable to go anywhere near the label of "artist."

Yanking open the perennially stuck upstairs door, I walked halfway down the hall to my studio, number 206. As usual, I felt a thrill of pride when I spied my lavishly painted wooden sign:

TRUE/FAUX STUDIOS
ANNA KINCAID, PROPRIETOR
FAUX FINISHES—MURALS—TROMP L'OEIL
NOT FOR THE FEINT OF ART ALONE

The sounds of Sammy Davis Jr. and the aroma of French roast coffee assailed my senses as I opened the door. My assistant, Mary Grae, waved a piece of paper in my general direction.

"'J. Frank DeBenton'? Who the hell is J. Frank DeBenton?" she demanded without preamble, as if we were in the middle of an ongoing conversation.

I studied Mary's outfit du jour. The ensemble featured a black fishnet blouse worn over a shiny, vaguely scaly vinyl vest, which contrasted nicely with skintight black jeans and a silver key chain jangling from the belt loops. Her blue eyes were outlined in black kohl, her dark blond hair sported an assortment of black ribbons, and on her feet were the ever-present Doc Martens black boots. Nearly six feet tall and twenty-three years old, Mary was a scary symphony in black.

"I thought we agreed you wouldn't read my mail," I groused, dumping my jacket and books on the second-hand desk that Mary and I had painted a virulent shade of purple last spring in a fit of Impressionist angst. "And can we turn down the volume, please?"

Mary had recently become enamored of the Rat Pack, so the strains of Sammy, Ol' Blue Eyes, Dino, and That Other Guy now frequently filled the studio. Thanks to Grandfather's influence, I was more of an Edith Piaf fan myself.

"J. Frank DeBenton?" Mary repeated, though she obliged me by lowering the decibels to within reason. "What kind of name is that?"

"I don't know," I replied absentmindedly. "French? Maybe Swiss?"

Mary shrugged and tossed the letter onto the already cluttered desk. "Sounds like a prick," she said in the declarative tone reserved for the true believers and the truly young. Mary was only eight years my junior, so I probably should not have thought of her as all that young, but in my experience, the twenties were a very aging decade.

I retrieved the single sheet of cream-colored linen stationery, elegantly embossed with my new landlord's name and logo: a shield emblazoned with a roaring lion. I skimmed the letter quickly, my stomach lurching when I read the final paragraph. Great. Just great. Now what was I going to do?

I turned to Mary. "Did you read the part about the rent increase?"

"*What?*" Mary's blue eyes widened in outrage. Despite her tough-as-nails exterior, Mary was frequently shocked by the world's duplicity. "I told you he sounded like a prick."

"I'm afraid the distinguished J. Frank DeBenton is the new owner of the building," I said, rereading the letter. "He's reminding me that my lease expires April first and he intends to bring the rent up to 'market standards.' Translation: he's doubling the rent."

"What a bastard!" Mary exclaimed, watching me with concern. "What are we going to do?"

A surge of affection ran through me. Paying the rent wasn't Mary's worry, but trust her not to abandon me. I shook my head. "I don't know. There's no way I can afford double the rent."

"Who's doubling the rent?"

The deep voice resonated from behind the wooden partition I had built to hide the aluminum industrial sink, microwave oven, and mini-fridge from the rest of the studio. It was followed by the distinctive spitting sound of an espresso machine.

I felt my spirits lift. Pavlov's dogs had nothing on me.

"Pete!" I yelled over the noise. "Have I ever told you I love you?"

Pete poked his large head around the side of the partition. "No, you have never said this to me. No woman says this to me. How am I ever going to carry on my genetics if no woman ever says this to me? This is my problem, you know, because it takes two to tangle."

Mary and I shared a smile at Pete's take on the English language as he disappeared behind the partition. Pete was constantly looking for love and could not understand his lack of success. Neither could we: he was as sweet as they came, and handsome in a hulking, potato-like kind of way. Born in Bosnia, Pete now owned the stained-glass business across the parking lot, but made himself at home here. He was a good friend and, just as important, the only one in our circle who could coax foamy milk for cappuccino from my cranky, garage-sale espresso machine.

The spitting was replaced by muffled clinks and clanks, and Pete emerged carrying a tray bearing three cups of cappuccino, a sugar bowl, spoons, and enough paper napkins to supply a day care center. He was an incongruous waiter, his six-foot six-inch frame supporting beefy shoulders and a large, broad, flat face with stern brows and gentle brown eyes.

"Who's doubling the rent?" Pete repeated as he set the tray down on the wicker trunk that served as a coffee table in the sitting area where I entertained clients.

"Our landlord," Mary answered, flinging herself onto a large fake-leopard-skin floor pillow. A designer friend had been stuck with the pillow after the client who ordered it had a conversion experience at a PETA rally, became a vegan, and started wearing clothes woven from hemp. The client claimed she could no longer tolerate upholstery that reminded her of the slaughter of innocents, and since the pillow was kind of horrible looking, my designer friend gave it to me.

"It's truly a doggy dog world," Pete declared with a sad shake of his head. Last month I had given Pete a word-a-day calendar, hoping it would untangle some of his worst linguistic snarls, and it had been a success of sorts. Now he made twice as many mistakes, twice as enthusiastically. He lowered himself gracefully onto the old red velvet sofa and distributed the coffee. "You want me maybe to talk to him?"

"Yeah," Mary chimed in, her eyes narrowed. "Pete and I could *talk* to him."

"No thanks, guys," I said with a grateful smile. It was nice to have a loyal Bosnian and a Gothic Madonna ready to go to battle for me, no questions asked. "Unfortunately, he's within his rights. There's no rent control for business properties in San Francisco." I joined Pete on the sofa and sipped my cappuccino, momentarily achieving a state of bliss.

"So what's the Plan?" Mary inquired from the pillow on the floor. Mary always seemed to think I had a plan.

Mary was heartbreakingly young.

"Well, I might have considered throwing myself on his mercy and appealing to his aesthetic sensibilities, but I think I just blew it," I told them.

"Already?" Mary asked, sitting up and scooping copious amounts of sugar into her coffee. "Have you even met him yet?"

"I ran into him in the parking lot," I confessed. "Literally."

"You collisioned with our landlord?" asked Pete, aghast.

I propped my feet on the wicker trunk. "We call it a fender bender," I told him, and started to laugh.

Mary and Pete exchanged puzzled looks. I worked the joke harder.

"Fender Bender—Frank DeBenton. Get it?"

Pete reached over and pushed my cappuccino closer to me. "You should imbibe more, Annie," he said gently.

Annoyed now, I pointed out the obvious. "He's your landlord, too, Pete."

Pete's large brown eyes registered sympathy, but noth-

ing near my level of anxiety. That was Pete. Loyal to a
fault, eternally optimistic, but a bit slow on the uptake.

"Yes, but I have a five-year lease," he said.

Oh. Maybe Pete wasn't so slow. I had always liked the
freedom of a year-to-year lease, and it had never occurred
to me that the real estate fever that gripped the rest of the
city would turn this run-down factory district into a
sought-after neighborhood. But then the twentysome-
thing computer folk had caught on to the appeal of loft
spaces. Even the dot-com bust had not greatly eased San
Francisco's real estate market. Rents in former artists'
colonies were spiraling upward, and landlords had started
kicking the artists out into the streets or, worse, across the
Bay into Oakland.

Don't get me wrong. I was a true Oaktown booster.
But in my line of work, which involved persuading rich
people to part with their money in the name of art, a San
Francisco address had an undeniable cachet. Now, with
the prospect of penury staring me in the face, I wondered
for the umpteenth time if I shouldn't relocate my studio
to Oakland, where life was cheaper, the weather better,
and the people, perhaps not coincidentally, nicer.

After spending a few minutes chatting about the evils
of property ownership, the deplorable lack of rent control
in a city that seemed determined to run the hardworking
poor out of town, and whether one really could tell the
difference between VHS and DVD when viewed on a
television set manufactured in 1978, we decided we had
all better get to work.

I thought it best not to mention the previous night's incident at the Brock, since the last thing I needed right
now was one Goth and one Bosnian bodyguard. As soon
as Pete trotted off to his warehouse to receive a shipment
of stained glass from Germany, I called Ernst again and
left messages on both his cell phone and his office num-

bers. I also tried looking Anton up in the phone book; it had been years since I had been in his San Francisco studio. To my surprise, there were several Woznikowiczes in the directory, but none was an Anton. I checked the Yellow Pages. There was no professional listing for him under "Art Restoration," either.

Impatiently I decided that any further sleuthing would have to wait until after Mary and I finished up a project for Linda Fairbanks, an interior designer who wanted "old, aged, interesting but not crumbly" garden ornaments for a client's conservatory without—surprise!—paying for real ones. We had spent most of last week beating the mass-produced ornaments with hammers and bunches of keys, dousing them with acid, soaking them in tea baths, rubbing them with leaves, and splattering them with pigment suspended in a translucent oil glaze. The cheap cement garden cherubs and gnomes, a birdbath, and a small fountain now looked old, graceful, and expensive.

It had been a stretch with the gnomes.

Three hours later, Linda arrived on schedule and practically swooned with pleasure at our work. So many of the designers I knew were swooners that I figured it had to be a required course in design school. I wasn't much of a swooner myself, especially where concrete garden gnomes were concerned. Neither was Mary, who had explained to me, "Norwegians don't swoon. Swoon in a snowbank and see how long you last." But Linda was a well-respected designer with a large and affluent clientele, and as such she was my entrée to the kind of people who had a spare $250,000 to decorate the new town house. Best of all, Linda paid her bills on time and without haggling, so I was not above a little pandering.

Mary and I bundled the figures in bubble wrap and carried them, armful by heavy armful, carefully down the stairs. The building had no elevator, and after several trips lugging cement garden ornaments, I cursed my second-floor location. We loaded up Linda's silver SUV and sent her happily on her way, the gnomes waving bye-bye through the rear window. As Mary and I stood in the sunshine stretching our tired muscles, I made a mental note to cite the lack of an elevator in my negotiations with the new landlord.

Caught up in my strategizing, I almost backed into a dainty, well-dressed man with pronounced frown lines. I recognized him immediately, and not only because of his signature red bow tie. Anthony Brazil was one of San Francisco's foremost gallery owners, as well as one of my father's old friends. For a number of reasons, mostly having to do with my grandfather, Brazil had rarely deigned to speak to me over the years and had certainly never sought me out. For the second time that day I was conscious of my less-than-elegant attire. To add to the general louche atmosphere, by now I was sweaty and grimy to boot. I wiped my hands gracelessly on the seat of my overalls and stuck out my right one. He offered his after a moment's hesitation, shifting a large art portfolio from one hand to the other.

"What brings you to this neighborhood, Mr. Brazil?" I asked, eyeing the portfolio.

"Annie. It has been a while. Might I speak with you"— he glanced at Mary, who was openly eavesdropping—"in private?"

"No sweat, sweet cheeks," Mary piped up. "I can take a hint." She turned and loped off toward the bakery on the ground floor of our building.

I had planned to track down Anton after Linda Fairbanks left, but Brazil seemed so agitated that I took pity on him and led the way upstairs.

He followed, puffing slightly, then halted in my doorway and took in the scene: the wide wooden plank floor and exposed brick walls; the inviting sitting area with the faux fireplace I had painted on the wall; the skylights high overhead; the half-dead ficus tree; the jumble of easels, shelves of art supplies, and worktables piled with paintings and pictures and artifacts at various stages of completion; the smell of linseed oil and turpentine. I loved my studio, and most of my clients were thrilled to get a peek at a working artist's space. Brazil, in contrast, appeared decidedly underwhelmed.

"So what can I help you with?" I asked, annoyed.

"I spoke with your father recently, Annie. Needless to say, we are all counting on you to stifle your grand-father's most recent writing project . . ." He trailed off, and I remained silent, not wanting to encourage him in this particular line of thinking. "Anyway, I happened to mention a problem I was having, and your father recom-mended you, both for your talent and for your discretion."

I tried to keep the surprise off my face. I loved my fa-ther and he loved me, but our relationship was strained by history and temperament. It was hard to imagine him rec-ommending me to anyone, for anything. "Really," I man-aged.

"I wonder if I might prevail upon you to examine some drawings that were lent to a—colleague. I'd like your opinion as to whether they are genuine. This is a very del-icate matter—"

I held up my hand. When it came to appraising possi-ble forgeries, it was best not to know the particulars. "Let's see the drawings, shall we?"

I led Anthony to the worktable near the window, cleared a space, and spread out a clean cloth. I opened the portfolio carefully, feeling a familiar tingle of excitement.

There were ten sketches, sepia-toned studies of heads, whole seminude figures, and clouds of drapery. I'd seen thousands of such things. Sketches were to artists what rough drafts were to writers. For every painting executed, there might be dozens or even hundreds of preliminary drawings, careful studies of one aspect of the final painting: a hand, a head, a sleeve. Before the invention of photography, a quick sketch was also the only way to capture the details of a live scene for replication in the studio. Some of the Old Masters were more prolific sketchers than others, but all left at least some drawings. The ravages of fire, humidity, insects, and human carelessness meant, however, that only a small percentage had survived the passage of time.

As I knew only too well, much of the fraud perpetrated in the world of Old Master drawings was not out-and-out copying, for example, a pen-and-ink replica of a known Michelangelo sketch for the Sistine Chapel's *The Creation of Adam.* Instead, most forgers drew sketches of new subjects in the *style* of a particular artist. This occurred for several reasons. Most important, artists rarely duplicated sketches, so forgery was to be suspected if two identical drawings turned up. Second, it was much easier for a forger to replicate an artist's technique in a new sketch than it was to copy the exact lengths of lines and flow of ink of a known sketch.

Finally, an artist might draw thousands of sketches in the course of a lifetime, not all of which would have been catalogued by art dealers or art historians. This meant that the discovery of an unknown Leonardo da Vinci drawing in Great-aunt Nellie's attic, while not likely, was plausible, and the all-important provenance might be credibly established if it were documented that Great-aunt Nellie had once made a trip to Florence, where she'd bought some old drawings.

Sketches were also harder to authenticate than paintings, whose pigments, canvas, and occasional stray brush hairs could be sampled and tested for age. And because sketches were perfunctory by nature, they often revealed less of their creator's personality than paintings, which were labored over for months or years. Still, to a trained and discerning eye every stroke of an artist's pen or pencil was as individual as a signature. This is why I felt certain that none of the drawings fanned out before me matched the character of the artists who were supposed to have drawn them.

What's more, because the sketches were attributed to such well-known artists as Gianfrancesco Penni, Rembrandt van Rijn, and Peter Brueghel the Elder, I had the feeling they were that rarity in the world of art fraud: forgeries of known drawings. If I was right, these drawings were a pile of worthless fakes.

Loath to break the news to Brazil, who was pacing agitatedly behind me, I studied the drawings more closely to confirm my suspicions. At first glance the paper looked old enough, brown and brittle along the edges, with scattered wormholes and a few dark smudges marring the finish. Two of the drawings had been torn and repaired in the traditional manner, with rice paper glued to the back of the original like a patch. The watermarks appeared to be genuine. All in all, the forgeries were good enough to pass a casual inspection.

But when I placed the sketches on the light table and examined them under a magnifying glass, I confirmed that they were recent forgeries. Modern paper, made from wood pulp by machines, has an obvious "grain," which means that the paper fibers bend in a single direction. Paper made from linen in the traditional manner—the method in use before the nineteenth century—was shaken in the mold, causing the fibers to bend in many directions. Smart forgers got around this problem by scavenging paper from the endplates of antiquarian books, the backs of print mounts, or by drawing over bad—but genuinely old—sketches.

I also studied the watermarks. True watermarks exhibited fine, hatched lines caused when a wire was pressed into the paper as it was shaped by the mold. Fake watermarks—such as the ones I saw before me—mimicked this process with an application of colorless oil or were scratched into the paper with a sharp blade.

I sat back. These were the mistakes of an amateur—or those of a pro in a great big hurry. I was surprised that Brazil had not known how to verify this for himself. If all art dealers were schooled in the basics of forgery, it would save the art world a lot of grief.

What bothered me most, though, was not that these sketches were forgeries. What really troubled me was that all these sketches had been drawn by the same hand.

And, for the second time in two days, I was pretty sure I recognized that hand.

"Who did you say you lent these drawings to?" I asked Brazil, who was now lurking on the other side of the light table.

He hesitated. I raised an eyebrow.

"Harlan Coombs," he muttered.

"*The* Harlan Coombs?"

"Is there more than one?" Brazil replied tartly.

Harlan Coombs was the dealer I had read about last night at the café. The one who was missing. According to the article, he was the perfect San Francisco art dealer: open and friendly, laid-back yet knowledgeable. In the past few years he had made himself and his vendors a pile of money selling expensive artwork to newly minted computer millionaires.

"I thought he'd disappeared," I said stupidly, before realizing what this meant. Coombs must have fled with the original drawings and sent Brazil these forgeries in their place.

In brief: Brazil had been royally screwed.

He must have read my mind, because he looked even more constipated than when he'd arrived. "Yes," he said stiffly. "He has indeed . . . disappeared."

In many ways, the art world was a throwback to the olden days when a dealer's reputation was all-important and a gentleman's word was a point of pride. Brazil would not have asked for collateral from Coombs; it would not have been considered necessary. But, as a result, Brazil was now out big money and his reputation was going to take a hit. He was probably keeping the whole thing quiet, hoping to find a solution before anyone realized he'd been duped.

"I'm sorry, Anthony," I said. I didn't like the man, but he was obviously suffering. "These are, indeed, forgeries. Not even very good ones. Not that it matters," I added hastily.

"I see," he murmured, and moved to sit heavily on my velvet sofa. His face had lost its customary pink hue.

I switched off the light table and carefully replaced the forged drawings in the portfolio before going to the kitchen area and pouring two glasses of an inexpensive Merlot from my emergency wine stash. Anthony's natty self-assurance seemed to have deserted him, and he sagged as if he'd lost his stuffing. I sat in silence, savoring the warmth of the wine while I waited for him to gather himself.

Brazil took a sip and grimaced. Here in wine-soaked California, I always insisted, it was possible to find bottles of wine under seven dollars that were still drinkable. Apparently Brazil disagreed.

He set his nearly full glass on the wicker trunk, where it wobbled ominously. "I had no reason to doubt him, you know," Anthony said, wiping his face with a manicured hand. "Harlan and I have done business for years. Years! All of us sell to him. My God! This is unprecedented, calamitous, ruinous!" He tossed his silvered head melodramatically.

I felt for him, but after last night's events my sympathy was muted. We were talking forged drawings here, not life and death. On the other hand, I had just identified two major forgery jobs in as many days, which seemed more than a little coincidental. "I would like your help, Annie," he said confidentially. "This is your world. Perhaps you could find Harlan Coombs or the drawings."

My world indeed, I thought waspishly. Geez, make a little splash in the world of art forgery at the age of sixteen, and people couldn't stop bringing it up.

"I'm afraid I don't know anything about that world anymore," I began. "I—"

"I am not insinuating that you are in any way still involved with your grandfather's, shall we say, special occupation?" he said with an air of sincerity. I wasn't buying it. "But you *are* in contact with him, and perhaps some of his friends, yes?"

"Well, I . . ."

"Please, Annie. For old times' sake. For your father's old friend."

Nice try. Like I was sucker enough to think that helping Anthony Brazil would somehow earn me my father's esteem.

"I would, of course, make it worth your while," he added.

Now he had my interest. I hated to focus so much on money, but I was staring down the barrel of a major rent increase.

"How much are we talking about?"

"I could offer, oh, say ten percent of their market value."

"Twenty." I figured I had him on the ropes, and I knew he could afford it.

"Ten, and that's my final offer."

"Twenty, Anthony. It's a bargain at twice the price and you know it."

Brazil blanched. I was starting to think it was his version of a facial tic.

"Fine," he snapped, and stood up. "Twenty percent. I need those drawings and I need them soon. You have only one week and then the deal is off. Agreed?"

I nodded.

"Oh, and Annie," he added as he moved toward the door, "this must be done with the utmost discretion. The *utmost*. My reputation is on the line. I trust I can count on you?"

"Sure thing," I said, opening the door for him. "Don't get your knickers in a twist. I'm the soul of discretion."

Brazil grimaced one last time and was gone.

I leaned against the door, thinking. Years ago I had vowed never again to involve myself in the underworld of art fakes and forgers. Unfortunately, I now had to make some money and I had to make it quickly. I didn't see any way around it: just this once I would have to break my vow.

One week to catch a forger. Luckily, I knew who he was, and had already planned to ask him a few questions about a certain fifteen-million-dollar fake.

It looked like Anton had been a busy boy lately.

Chapter 3

"Repairing" your fake will add immeasurably to its worth. By painstakingly patching torn drawings and "touching up" flaking paint, you give the collector the impression that the artwork was cherished enough for its "previous owners" to pay for costly repairs.

—*Georges LeFleur, "How to Market Your Forgery,"*
unfinished manuscript, Reflections of a
World-Class Art Forger

I retrieved my assistant, a latte, and a gruyère cheese croissant from the bakery, asked Mary to continue working on a large fir dining table we were faux-finishing to resemble intricate inlaid stone, and set out to find Anton Woznikowicz.

As I headed across town I sipped my latte and reminisced about how patiently the paunchy, good-natured Pole had taught me to achieve the coveted Old Master crackle, back when I was a budding teenage forger and he was still working with my grandfather. I could not believe he would have willingly been involved in Dupont's demise. Anton had a hot temper, but he was not the violent type. He was more the sneaky, behind-the-scenes type.

Still, I was willing to bet Anton could shed some light on what had happened at the Brock. After all, the list of people with the money, knowledge, and connections to commission a high-quality forgery and arrange to swap it for a museum's original masterpiece was a short one. It was also possible that the Caravaggio forgery had no connection whatsoever with last night's events at the museum, in which case I could concentrate on shaking down Anton for Anthony Brazil's stolen drawings—thus securing my immediate financial future—without feeling compelled to mention the wily art forger when I spoke with the police.

Invigorated, I circled the hilly, clogged streets of San Francisco's Noë Valley and Bernal Heights neighborhoods, sure that I would recognize Anton's studio when I saw it. True, it had been several years since I'd last visited, but my memory was pretty good. After half an hour of fruitless searching I lost all confidence in my powers of recollection, took a deep breath, and tried to think of other ways—besides my grandfather—to find Anton's address. I had my cell phone in my pocket and fully charged in case Georges called me back, but I wasn't betting the family portfolio on it.

Who else might know where to find Anton? I angled the truck into a tiny parking space on Sixteenth in front of Mission Dolores and pulled out my phone. I stared at it, but it stared back mutely. Perhaps Anton had already been questioned by the police and fled the country with the genuine drawings and I was wasting my time. Maybe Ernst had finally turned up, the real Caravaggio had been recovered, and the murderer had been caught. But how would I find this out? The City's art community would know; its grapevine put the UN to shame. But unfortunately I was no longer part of that community.

I continued to stare at my cell phone, wondering what

was happening at the Brock. I decided to try calling Ernst again, figuring I had nothing to lose.

His voice mail picked up at both numbers.

Rats. Frustrated and at a loss for what to do next, I watched a young cassock-clad priest shepherd a group of teenagers into the mission's historic garden. I wondered what it would be like to be part of a religious order. I kinda liked the wardrobe . . .

Okay, Annie, focus. Who else did I know at the Brock? There was Naomi Gregorian, although that was iffy. Not because we didn't know each other well, but because we did.

The year after college, Naomi and I had been art interns at the Brock. We spent hours shoulder to shoulder under a fume hood, cleaning paintbrushes with noxious chemicals; wore itchy polyester uniforms while serving canapés at receptions to which we were not invited; and ran countless personal errands for the upper-echelon staffers. And we did all of this gladly, in exchange for the privilege of learning the ancient techniques of art restoration.

I was disappointed but not surprised when Naomi dumped me the moment I was bounced from the Brock. She had always known which way the wind was blowing. While I sweated to get my faux-finishing studio off the ground, Naomi grimly climbed the museum's steep ladder from intern to art restorer. From time to time our paths would cross at a gallery opening or at the Legion of Honor, and we would exchange nods and a few polite words. If I called her, Naomi probably wouldn't hang up on me.

Probably. The Brock's switchboard operator put me through.

"Naomi Chadwick Gregorian," a voice singsonged officiously. Chadwick was Naomi's middle name, which she had never used until she became a full-fledged art restorer and snob.

I found it all a little hard to swallow. Naomi and I had first met as freshmen in college, where we were both art majors. Our strained friendship took a turn for the worse our senior year, when I discovered that Naomi had fished through my studio scraps and included some of them in the portfolio she submitted to win a coveted slot as an intern at the Brock Museum. When I saw my sketches among hers during the celebratory art department reception, I debated raising a stink but ultimately decided against it. One of the many things my grandfather had taught me was to stockpile such information for future leverage.

"Naomi! It's Annie!" My voice rang with false cheer and bonhomie. "Annie Kincaid!"

Silence.

"Naomi? You there?"

"Hullo, Ann," Naomi replied stiffly.

My given name was Anna, though I preferred Annie. Either would do. Ann would not.

Naomi knew this.

"This is probably an odd question," I babbled on, as if Naomi weren't sending subliminal "drop dead" messages through the telephone line. "Or maybe not, considering what's going on there. And listen, about that, I don't really know, but it's bothering me, which is why I'm calling."

Hmm. Maybe I should have thought this out better before dialing.

"What do you want, Ann?" Naomi asked curtly. True to form, she was not going to make anything easy for me.

"I heard Stan Dupont was killed last night at the museum," I replied. I winced at my bluntness. Poor Stan.

"We've been asked not to discuss the matter with the public," she said frostily.

"I'm not 'the public,' Naomi. I'm your old friend. Remember, Nancy Fancy Pants?"

That should get her. "Nancy Fancy Pants" was Naomi's freshman-year dorm nickname. The students on our floor had bestowed it upon her because while everybody else wore patched jeans and faded T-shirts from Goodwill, Naomi wore matching separates from Burberry and Ann Taylor. The woman had an unhealthy relationship with monograms.

To be fair, Naomi was not singled out for this treatment. Everyone in our dorm had a nickname. Mine was "Kinky Pinky Kincaid," thanks to a brief and largely regrettable flirtation with fuchsia hair dye. But whereas everybody else outgrew their nicknames, Naomi's had stuck.

"You most certainly are the public, Miss Hoity Nose," she replied hotly.

It was my theory that Naomi had never forgiven me for being a better artist than she. I wasn't sure where the "Miss Hoity Nose" came from.

"Just tell me what happened," I said, remembering another pertinent fact about Naomi: she couldn't resist gossip.

"Well . . ." she said dramatically, "as long as you promise not to tell anyone . . ."

She was cracking. I checked the clock on my truck's dashboard. It had taken less than three minutes.

Naomi's voice fell to a whisper. "It was last night, after closing. The interns were gone by about ten, so it must have been after that. The museum was as silent as a tomb," she said, piling on the melodrama.

"And . . . ?"

"I'm trying to tell you, if you'd just listen," she whined.

"So tell me already."

"You don't have to be so rude, Ann."

I took a deep breath and counted to ten.

"It was Stanley Dupont, one of the janitors. He was shot. Murdered most foul."

"Was it a robbery? Was anything taken?"

"That's the weird thing," she replied. "The security tapes should have shown something, but they're missing. Apparently the alarms were shut down for a while just before midnight, and someone opened a side door. You know Stanley had been with the Brock *forever*—he had access to almost everything. Carlos in Security told Debbie in Accounting that he heard that Stanley had brought in a woman, but nobody knows for sure. It's hard to imagine him sneaking a woman in for a secret rendezvous. I mean, ick."

"Mmm?" I replied, distracted by the image of myself as Mystery Woman.

"The really odd part is, Stanley was found near the main vault, where *The Magi* is kept," Naomi continued, clearly delighted, as people often were, to be the bearer of bad news. "You know, the Brock's newest acquisition. But the vault was locked. If someone was trying to steal the Caravaggio, why kill Stanley before the vault was opened?"

"Surely Dupont didn't have access to the vault?"

"No, of course not, but a thief might have thought he was Security. Stanley always had a lot of keys. Or maybe he was just in the wrong place at the wrong time."

"So *The Magi* is still there?"

"Yes. Nothing was taken. And poor Stanley was doing so well. He just bought himself a new cherry red Miata and a time-share in Cancún. I saw pictures. Lots of thatched-roof huts on the beach. All for nothing. I mean, it just seems so senseless." For once, Naomi and I were in accord. "Maybe it was something personal. Maybe the woman was someone's wife. Can you imagine cheating on your husband with Stanley?"

Nope, sure couldn't.

"Does the name Anton Woznikowicz mean anything to you?" I asked her.

"Anton Wozni—whatsis?"

"Woznikowicz."

"Wooznookoowhich?" When it came to music and languages, Naomi had a tin ear. Where I'd aced French our freshman year, she'd flunked it, as well as Russian, Spanish, and Italian. By our senior year, she was desperate to fulfill the college's foreign language requirement. Fortunately for her, Latin was not a spoken language.

"No, Woz-ni-ko-wicz. Just like it's spelled."

"Doesn't sound familiar."

"How about Harlan Coombs?"

There was a long silence. "Don't tell me you're getting involved with that sort of thing again? Really, Ann, I thought you were trying to be an honest housepainter."

"Just answer the question, Naomi," I said through clenched teeth. Naomi was always primed to assume that I would slip back into criminality if given the chance. "I take it you've heard of him?"

"Who hasn't? He was only the city's foremost art dealer until he absconded with tens of thousands of dollars' worth of valuable drawings. You of all people should know that."

"I only know what I read in the papers, Naomi. Did the museum buy from him? I mean, before anyone knew what he was up to?"

There was another pause and I tried to figure out how these recent events were connected. What did Dupont's death, Ernst's absence, and the fake Caravaggio have to do with Harlan Coombs and the stolen drawings? And how in the world had Anton gotten himself mixed up in the whole mess?

"Coombs was here a few weeks ago," Naomi said slowly. "That was when, as far as we knew, he was still legitimate. Then the police were here asking about him. Before the murder, I mean. They were here again today, of course. It makes it so hard to get anything done—"

"What did Coombs want?" I interrupted.

"I presume he was meeting with Acquisitions. We've done business with him for years. No one had any reason to doubt his character. Well, listen, Ann—I've got to run. Things are pretty crazy around here. Can't yak all day on the phone like some folks."

I bit my tongue and reminded myself that Naomi wasn't evil, she was just clueless and self-absorbed. I was about to hang up when I remembered to ask about Ernst.

"Ernst Pettigrew?" she asked. "He hasn't come in today. Probably has that flu that's going around."

He seemed healthy enough last night at the Brock, I thought. Maybe it was a twenty-four-hour, avoid-the-police kind of flu. "Do you have his home number?"

She sighed. "Really, Ann. He's involved with a lovely woman. I know you've made some bad choices, but don't you think it's time to get on with your life?"

That did it. Maybe she *was* evil. The gloves were coming off.

"Thank you *so* much, Naomi, you've been *such* a help," I purred. "Do be sure to let me know if I can ever return the favor. I may have a few old drawings lying around."

I hung up on her shocked silence. Art restorer, my ass. I could out-restore Naomi with my hands tied behind my back and a paintbrush in my mouth. Speaking of which, I now had an idea for how to find Anton. My grandfather had once mentioned, in a tone suffused with contempt, that in addition to forgery Anton did legitimate art restoration for a number of local gallery owners and art dealers. I could remember the name of only one of those galleries, but it seemed like a good place to start.

I crawled across town toward the shopping mecca of Union Square, swearing at the midday traffic, and gratefully surrendered my truck to the parking garage at the intersection of Ellis and O'Farrell. Within several blocks of Union Square was a high concentration of art galleries, both small and large, alternative and mainstream. There were galleries sprinkled all over San Francisco, but it was not a true art-loving city in the style of New York or Paris, where entire city blocks were devoted to art. Here people were in pursuit of the artistic life more than the actual art itself.

As I marched past Macy's, eyes averted to prevent my lusting after things I didn't need and couldn't afford, I realized I was dreading doing the gallery hop alone. Like Hester and her scarlet *A,* I always felt as if I bore the mark of Georges LeFleur. Whenever I walked into an art gallery I half expected the owner to bolt from behind a desk, point a long, scrawny finger at me, and screech, "Forger's spawn! Forger's spawn!"

For today's mission I needed someone irreverent. Someone sassy. Someone who was a lot like me when I wasn't having a crisis of confidence caused by my unfortunate choice in grandfathers. Whipping out my cell phone, I called Mary, who as part of her commitment to being earth-friendly, traveled by bicycle. It would take her half an hour to get here. I signed off, relieved.

Still . . . thirty minutes was plenty of time to speak with at least one gallery owner. Why was I being so cowardly? Was I somehow less worthy because I had taken a brief walk on art's wild side?

I lifted my chin, squared my shoulders, and hiked a

few blocks to a building on California, where I took the elevator to the sixth floor and sauntered down the corridor, past several modern art galleries, until I reached Albert Mason's Fine Arts.

I moseyed through the gallery, perusing its offerings while an exotic-looking woman at the front desk went to fetch "Monsieur Mason" for me. Paintings in the Old Master style had become all the rage, forcing smaller galleries like this one to scramble to meet the demand. Mason had several quality eighteenth- and nineteenth-century pieces, but he also had a lot of bad art that just happened to be old. Evidently he was not immune to the pressure to fill his customers' orders regardless of artistry.

Albert Mason materialized, inquisitive yet sedate, pleasant yet distant, in the manner of gallery owners the world over. In his late fifties, with short salt-and-pepper hair, a stocky build, and the kind of complexion that reddened easily, he looked the type to take ballroom dancing lessons and dote on an overfed cat. He wore gray gabardine pants, a crisp pink Oxford shirt, a striped tie, and a blue blazer with brass buttons. Imported Italian leather loafers with tassels graced his dainty feet.

"Thank you for speaking with me, Mr. Mason," I began after introducing myself. "I'm looking for a mutual friend, Anton Woznikowicz—"

"In that case, you are not welcome in this gallery, young lady," he spat, turning a disturbing shade of scarlet. "I'll thank you to leave."

Pivoting on his heel, he disappeared behind a privacy wall. I followed.

"Mr. Mason, please," I pleaded to his blue serge back. "I need to know . . ."

His shoulders twitched, which I took to be an encouraging sign.

"How about Harlan Coombs?" I persisted. "Could we talk about him?"

That stopped him. He jerked his head toward his office.

"Who are you?" he demanded as he sank into a leather chair behind his desk.

"I'm, uh, well, as I said, I'm Annie Kincaid," I told him, following his example and taking a seat. "I worked in restoration with the Brock Museum," I said, twisting the truth a tad, "and now have my own business in China Basin. I'm trying to locate an old friend, Anton Woznikowicz. Coincidentally, I'm also trying to track down Harlan Coombs."

"Is Coombs an 'old friend' of yours as well?"

"Uh, no, not really." Why hadn't I worked out a story before I came here? Still, I supposed I could tell him what I was doing without naming names. "A . . . mutual friend asked me to look into some drawings that he'd lent to Harlan Coombs. I thought they might have been . . . um, shall we say, 'improved' by Anton, and I know Anton has done restoration work for you in the past, so I thought you might know where I could find him."

Now that wasn't so hard. I smiled at him brightly.

Mason glanced at the closed office door, as if worried that all of San Francisco was lurking outside to catch a whiff of scandal. Those of us in the art world tended to think that everyone was as passionate about art as we. In fact, most of the people in my life not only didn't know a Bronzino from an Alma-Tadema, they didn't much care. But because this man was an art dealer who clearly cared passionately, I scooted my chair closer.

"Listen, Ms., uh, Koolaid," he said, a pink tongue darting out and licking his lips. "If you do find Harlan, he's got a few things of mine, too. Bastard skipped town with all kinds of drawings."

"Why would he do that?" I asked, mentally filing "Koolaid" away for use in the future as a possible alias.

Mason leaned forward, his arms crossed on the desk, an eager look on his face. "I heard he was involved in day trading."

"Oh?"

He glanced about furtively, and I found myself doing it, too. Paranoia was contagious.

"You know," he said impatiently. "In the stock market. He apparently made a lot of money, but when tech stocks took a dive last fall *he* took a bath. I heard Harlan kept hoping that if he invested more, he'd recoup his losses. Even make a killing. That was when he took off with seven of my most valuable drawings, including a sketch of a mother and child by Mary Cassatt and a sketch for *Madonna del Baldacchino* by Raphael. He sent back two, but they were obvious forgeries. The rumor is it was because of a woman he was seeing, that she pushed him to live high on the hog."

Sure, I thought sourly, blame a man's bad behavior on a woman. Some things never seemed to change.

"Do you have any idea where Harlan might be?" I asked.

"If I knew that, I'd have my drawings, wouldn't I?" he snapped.

So much for our friendly gossip fest.

"What about Anton?" I asked.

"The last time I saw Anton, he was having a drink with Harlan at Vesuvio's, in North Beach. That was when Harlan was still playing the market. Then, when he disappeared with my drawings, Anton claimed he didn't know him." Mason snorted derisively. "Well, I know what I saw, Ms. Koolaid. I haven't heard from either of them since."

I mulled that over. "Do you have an address for Anton?"

"It won't do you any good. He's gone."

"Could I have it anyway, please? And Harlan Coombs' address as well."

Mason put on a pair of black-rimmed reading glasses and flipped through the giant Rolodex at his elbow. He scribbled the information on a piece of paper and shoved it across the desk.

"You said you were associated with the Brock Museum, Ms. Koolaid?" he asked as I was rising to leave.

"Mmm," I managed.

"Can you tell me anything about last night? Do they think the curator—Pettigrew—did it?"

"Did what?"

"The murder. Didn't you hear?" Mason asked with relish.

"Yes, but what does Ernst Pettigrew have to do with it?"

"He's only the most obvious suspect." Mason lowered his voice and leaned toward me conspiratorially. I leaned forward, too, so that our foreheads were almost touching. Frankly, it was kind of creepy.

"I heard that *The Magi* is a *fake* and Ernst killed the janitor to hush him up," Mason whispered.

I leaned back. That was absurd. Ernst was no killer. Moreover, if he were, and he wanted to silence anyone who knew the Caravaggio was a fake, I would have been the first to go. Last time I checked, I was still alive and kicking.

"Why would Ernst kill the janitor to cover up a crime and then disappear? Wouldn't that just make him look guilty?" I asked. "Besides, don't tell anyone, but *I* heard from a very good source at the Brock that Dupont was involved in a love triangle, and that Ernst was in Cabo San

Lucas wooing a wealthy donor, some old friend of Agnes Brock's."

This was how nasty rumors got started, and I was happy to do my part. I was, after all, a forger's spawn.

I thanked Mason for his time and started toward the door.

"By the way," he said, "I would be willing to offer a small reward in the event that my drawings were recovered."

I turned back to him and smiled. "I believe twenty percent of the market value is the going rate."

Mason looked as if he'd swallowed a bad oyster. "All right. Twenty percent."

Before I left I got it in writing.

As I wandered out of the gallery and rode the elevator down to the street, my mind was on Ernst. What in the world had happened last night? I kept imagining Ernst calling me up and amusing me with some long, involved tale, told in his cute Austrian accent. The scene ended with Ernst announcing that his model girlfriend, Quiana, was too skinny and too vapid. He had never realized how much he missed my idiosyncratic take on the world, until—

Get it together, Annie, I told myself. *Not only is that not going to happen, but deep down you* know *you don't want it to, anyway.*

Here's what else I knew: while I was at the café waiting for Ernst, somebody killed Stan Dupont and Ernst Pettigrew dropped off the radar screen.

Here's what I did not know: everything else.

No, wait. I also knew that Anton Woznikowicz had forged *The Magi* as well as a number of sketches that Harlan Coombs used to defraud gallery owners, such as Anthony Brazil and Albert Mason. And at some point before the murder, Harlan had disappeared.

So what did it all add up to?

Darned if I knew.

"Annie! Hey!" Mary called as I wandered onto the street.

Mary looked like an angel on steroids. For reasons known only to herself, she had donned a sparkly tuxedo jacket over her vinyl vest, put on fingerless black lace gloves, and exchanged her usual Doc Martens for leather motorcycle boots. The very outfit I would have chosen for a bike ride through inner-city traffic.

Now that I had Anton's address, I could call off the gallery walk in favor of dinner. But gossiping with Albert Mason had provided a lot of information, and a possible commission, for very little effort. I figured it couldn't hurt to shake down a few more artsy types. Somebody had to know something. In the art world, somebody always did.

"You want to grab something to eat first, or should we work up an appetite by assaulting some gallery owners?" I asked Mary.

"Assault and battery, by all means." Mary smiled, her big blue eyes blinking disingenuously.

"Let's hold off on the battery, shall we?" I said, not entirely sure she was kidding. Those boots looked like they could kick some serious butt.

We walked toward Chinatown, then turned down an alley crammed with small tables and umbrellas. Well-dressed San Franciscans lounged in the late-afternoon sunshine, enjoying colorful salads of tapenade-topped pan-seared tuna with endive, and watercress with blood oranges and cinnamon-infused almonds. My mouth watered as we headed for the next street over, where there was a clutch of small, understated, and very pricey galleries.

We went into the first one we came to, the Catharine

Chaffrey Gallery, and while Mary strode around ostenta-
tiously checking out the paintings and rolling her eyes, I
asked the curator about Anton and Harlan. Catherine
Chaffrey, a woman in her fifties who looked as if she'd
just been goosed by an electrical current, knew Anton
only by reputation. Her voice, dripping with acid, con-
veyed precisely what that reputation was. When it came
to Harlan Coombs, Chaffrey repeated much the same
gossip as Albert Mason had: Harlan played the stock market, got into debt, and disappeared with artwork that did
not belong to him, although she, at least, did not blame
Harlan's misdeeds on a mythical woman. But the local art
scene had clearly been stunned by the betrayal, and we
shared a moment of sadness that a system so dependent
upon professional ethics had broken down.

The moment ended when Chaffrey started dishing
about the murder at the Brock. Apparently the gossip
grapevine worked even faster than I thought, because she
speculated that Ernst had been having an affair with Stan
Dupont's wife, who was some sort of minor European
aristocrat, and that they had eloped with the money de-
rived from selling the original Caravaggio. I speculated
that her scenario was about as likely as Jasper Johns
learning how to paint. By her reaction, I gathered she was
a Jasper Johns fan.

We were interrupted by Mary, who had begun wondering loudly what kind of moron would buy this kind of
crap. Hustling her out the door, I led the way to the next
gallery, where folks claimed, improbably, not to have
heard of either Anton or Harlan but were dying to talk
about Ernst Pettigrew and the Brock. The next few galleries yielded the now-familiar responses: outrage at Harlan, wariness about Anton, and titillation over the murder.
No new information was forthcoming, but it was evident

that the respectable art-dealing world agreed on two things: Anton was a scoundrel and Harlan was a crook.

Oh, and Ernst Pettigrew had killed Stan Dupont in a fight over a deposed Bavarian princess' love child.

It was now well past six o'clock and my stomach was growling like the MGM lion. Since we were so close to Chinatown, Mary and I popped into a favorite family-run restaurant, made our way through the cacophonous kitchen, clattered up the rickety metal staircase, took a seat at a tiny table cheek by jowl with the other customers, and ordered an inexpensive meal of hot-and-sour soup, steamed eggrolls, and shrimp with pea pods in garlic sauce, only to end up, twenty minutes later, eating wonton soup, chicken lo mein, and beef with broccoli.

There may have been a language problem. When it came to things like dining in Chinatown, it was good to be flexible.

Chapter 4

*Who are these "experts" who spew such vitriol?
Have they labored to give birth to a work so magnificent as to make grown men weep? Have they
placed paint upon canvas in such a way as to make
believers of atheists, romantics of those of hardened
heart, or visionaries of the hopeless? Let them hold
their tongues until, godlike, they have created
beauty where once there was none.*

—Georges LeFleur, "Experts & Other Lower
Life Forms," unfinished manuscript,
Reflections of a World-Class Art Forger

The problem with running a business is that it never runs
itself. A corporate employee could take a personal day
every now and then without everything going to hell in a
handbasket. Not so a small-business owner. If I didn't do
the work, it didn't get done. Worse, I didn't get paid.

The rejuvenating powers of Chinese food caused me to
flirt with the idea of setting off after Anton again. But as
I pulled out my wallet to pay the check, I reconsidered. I
owed some faux finish samples to several clients, and I
had to teach Mary how to apply gold gilt so that she could
practice for a big job that was scheduled for next month.

And if that weren't enough, I had a commissioned portrait awaiting my attention. On the off chance that I wasn't cut out to be an art detective, I should probably keep my day job.

As I took a twenty-dollar bill out of my wallet, the piece of paper with Harlan Coombs' address fell out onto the table. Grant Street, near California. Hmmm. Right smack-dab in the middle of Chinatown, just a few blocks from where we were eating. It was an odd address for an art dealer who socialized with the crème de la crème of San Francisco society.

I glanced at Mary, who was watching me patiently.

Mary, who was almost six feet tall, wore scary leather boots, and was game to do anything.

"Listen . . ." I said. "Would you mind if we checked something out before heading back?"

I wasn't sure what I thought we might find at Harlan's place. The theft of the Old Master drawings left a number of outraged and politically well-connected art dealers holding the bag. It seemed doubtful that Harlan would be hanging around his apartment, doing a little housework and waiting for the police to show up. Unlikelier still that Anton would be relaxing there with him. And nearly impossible to imagine that upon seeing me they would hand over tens of thousands of dollars' worth of stolen sketches. But the address was so temptingly near . . .

"Somebody skip out on the bill?" she asked.

Realizing that I hadn't told Mary about my arrangement with Anthony Brazil and Albert Mason, I gave her a quick rundown on the Harlan Coombs mini-drama. I decided against discussing the murder, or my reason for being at the Brock last night.

"Sweet," she said. I took that as a yes.

We inched our way out of the jammed dining room and down to street level, where we pushed through the crowded sidewalks on Grant, passing countless bins piled high with cheap imported goods—bamboo backscratchers, plastic pop guns, painted rice paper fans, carved wooden chopsticks—before reaching the address Mason had given me.

A small doorway was sandwiched between a souvenir shop and a Chinese apothecary. Brass mailboxes lined the entrance, each with a tiny label. I peered closely. There, after CHAN, HENRY, and CHANG, MEI, was COOMBS, HARLAN. Apartment 3C.

Mary and I looked at each other. Either Harlan had already absconded or he was the world's worst fugitive.

"So push the buzzer," Mary said impatiently.

"I'm not going to push the buzzer," I said, reconsidering. "He might be dangerous."

"Push the buzzer, Annie. C'mon—how many art dealers do you know who can really kick ass?"

Albert Mason flashed into my mind. She had a point. "Well . . ."

"He's not gonna be here, anyway," Mary persisted, reaching around me and pushing the buzzer. "Not if he did what you said he did, and not if people are looking for him."

"Yes?" a woman's voice said after several seconds.

Mary and I gawked at each other.

"Say something," Mary hissed.

"Like *what*?" I was terrible at improvising, my heart was pounding, and I was beginning to sweat.

"Package for, um, Harlan Coombs!" Mary shouted into the speaker.

The door buzzed. Mary smirked and pushed her way inside. Where did she learn to do things like this? I wondered as I followed her up a dark, grubby staircase that smelled of cabbage and unfamiliar spices. Mary was

from a small town in Indiana. People from small towns in
Indiana were supposed to be cautious.

Then again, Mary had hitchhiked to San Francisco the
day she turned eighteen.

We reached the third-floor landing and paused to catch
our breath. A long, unremarkable hallway was painted a
dingy yellow and illuminated by a single bare bulb in the
ceiling. Muffled sounds from televisions and the clanking
of pots and pans drifted down the hall.

My enthusiasm for this undertaking was waning. What
if Coombs was the exception to the art-dealer-as-wimp
rule? What if he was a former-Navy-SEAL-turned-art-
dealer-turned-criminal? What was I going to say? "Heya,
Harlan—you don't know me, but I know you did some
bad things that will send you to San Quentin for a stretch,
so I'll tell you what. You give us the drawings you stole
and we won't rat you out. Oh, and by the way, nobody
knows we're here."

Sure, *that* should work.

I was about to sound the retreat when a door at the end
of the corridor slowly swung open and a tall, elegant
woman stepped into the hallway.

"You have a package for Harlan Coombs?" She spoke
coolly, her startling catlike eyes no doubt taking in the
fact that we had no package.

"Well, I—"

The woman said something over her shoulder and
stepped back into the apartment. I relaxed a bit. Maybe
Harlan really was home and willing to talk with us.

Mary and I took a cautious step down the hall but
stopped in our tracks when a very large man with no visible neck appeared in the doorway. He did not look happy
to see us. Nor did he look much like the grainy newspa-
per photo I had seen of Harlan Coombs. The identifica-

tion became irrelevant when the man started lumbering toward us, slowly at first, then gaining speed.

Moving as one, Mary and I sprinted the length of the hallway and back down the stairs, narrowly missing a large Chinese family from the second floor that crowded into the stairwell just in time to slow No Neck's progress. Flying down the last set of stairs, we threw ourselves across the minuscule foyer and out the front door. I looked around frantically, grabbed Mary's arm, and yanked her into the crowded souvenir shop next door, where we crouched behind a display of windup cable cars, on sale for ninety-nine cents.

After several minutes of heavy breathing I ventured a peek around the snow-globe-packed shelves. Plenty of tourists, but no man missing a neck. Still, there was no way to tell if he was lurking outside, waiting for us to emerge. Together we half crouched, half crawled to the rear of the shop, slipped through a beaded curtain decorated with a painting of the Buddha, and entered a storage room, where two women unpacking boxes of embroidered pink silk slippers started yelling at us in Vietnamese.

"Out?" I asked, breathless.

The women pointed in the direction of the front door. "Out! Out!" they cried in unison.

Ignoring them, we went the other way, only to find the rear exit partially blocked by packing boxes. We shoved and dragged the boxes aside, then Mary burst through the door, with me on her heels.

We turned right, then made a quick left into a small alley full of smelly trash and caged poultry, came out onto Jackson, where we skirted Union Square, then doubled back onto O'Farrell and jogged to the parking garage on Ellis, double-timing it so as to catch an open

elevator. We rode to the fourth level and dragged ourselves toward the truck.

We climbed into the cab, where all was silent but for
the sound of heavy breathing. I was drenched in sweat,
my nose was running, my hands were shaking, and I had
one hell of a stitch in my side. I was trying to decide
whether or not to throw up.

Several long minutes passed.

"I'm thinking faux finishing might be more your
speed, Annie," Mary said dryly.

I glared at her, unwilling to spare the oxygen for a
snide reply. Besides, she had a point. Maybe it was time
to return to Plan A: don't quit the day job. Teaching faux-
finishing courses for do-it-yourselfers was looking better
all the time.

I fired up the engine, paid a small ransom to the parking attendant, and swung by Mason's gallery to pick up
Mary's bike, which she had left chained to a lamppost in
flagrant violation of the posted signs.

We drove across Market and past the grimy blocks
south of Mission, weaving through the ubiquitous traffic
snarls caused by confused tourists, double-parked deliv-
ery vans, construction sites, and left-turning vehicles.
Mary was quiet until we passed under the freeway and
headed toward the warehouses of China Basin. Then she
started to giggle.

"It's not funny," I grumbled. "No Neck there looked
like he meant business."

"Maybe he just wanted the package we promised
him," she said, laughing. "You should have seen your
face! You looked scared to death!"

"Yeah, well, here's a news flash, Wonder Woman: I
was scared to death."

By the time we pulled into the parking lot at the studio, we were both a little high on adrenaline and relief.

My new landlord looked up from his desk and arched an eyebrow as Mary's boots beat a tattoo on the old wooden boards outside his office. We both waved at him cheerily, then climbed the outside stairs, struggled with the upstairs door, and clomped down the hall to the studio. I paused to straighten the TRUE/FAUX STUDIOS sign.

"You're such a Libra," Mary commented.

"What's that supposed to mean?" I asked, inexplicably offended. Libras are rather nice people, I thought. Not as stubborn as, say, Aries. My grandfather is an Aries.

"Because you can't pass that sign without straightening it. But you never nail the damned thing down so it won't happen again. Very Libran."

"Yeah, well . . . I painted it, didn't I . . . ?" I trailed off, thinking I'd made my point.

Mary, a meticulous Virgo, smiled.

I checked the message machine, but there was no call from Georges. I was still hoping my grandfather could tell me something about Anton's involvement—or lack thereof—in the Brock Museum murder, and perhaps his current whereabouts. Tomorrow I would check out the address for Anton that Albert Mason had given me, but I doubted the old forger had hung around any longer than Harlan Coombs. On the other hand, it was the only lead I had, and Brazil's reward money would go a long way toward paying my looming rent increase.

Then again, I did not enjoy running into—and away from—scary men with no necks. It made sense that Harlan would have a lot of people looking for him and the missing drawings. Thin Woman and No Neck didn't look like art dealers, but what did I know? In any case, they couldn't possibly have recognized us, so we were safe. I didn't exactly have a high profile in the City. Comforted by our anonymity, I put some water on for coffee and turned my thoughts to business.

First on the list was preparing sample boards. Sample boards were just what they sounded like, samples of a proposed faux finish, which I submitted to the client for approval. It was true that in case of error, misunderstanding, or changes of mind, faux finishes could be painted over. But faux-finishing techniques were complicated, painstaking, and very labor-intensive. I once faux-finished an entire living room four times, and by the time I had completed it to the client's satisfaction, she and I were ready to have it out with paintbrushes and toxic solvents at twenty paces.

Linda Fairbanks had asked for boards in shades of sage and ochre, which were among this year's favorite color schemes. Mary began by priming and painting the boards with an undercoat of Navajo white for the ochre sample, and pale gray green for the sage. When these were dry, we mixed dabs of artists' oil paint into a glaze medium, known as scumble, made of turpentine, linseed oil, and marble dust. I coated the boards liberally with this mixture, then created texture and pattern with rags, plastic wrap, and a badger-hair brush. The result was a "broken" paint surface that allowed the base color to shine through, creating a luminous, old European look.

I also owed Irene and Walter Foster two samples, one of a distressed harlequin pattern in two color combinations and the other of a mahogany wood grain. The Fosters had a home in the Richmond District that, to my mind, was an example of how to go overboard with the faux finishing, something Mary and I privately referred to as a "faux pas." But the Fosters loved it, and as long as they paid my bill, who was I to complain?

The work went quickly. Mary completed the boards and got her first lesson in gilding before leaving around ten for a night on the town. I stayed another hour, touching up the sample boards and faxing supply orders, then turned to the paperwork I'd been avoiding. When the words swam on the page, I worried that I had a brain tumor until I remembered that I was operating on about three hours' sleep. Cancel the call to the neurosurgeon. Looked like it was past time to pack it in. I left the studio windows open a crack to release any lingering toxic fumes, switched off the overhead fans, grabbed my stuff, flicked off the lights, locked the door, and headed downstairs.

When I got to the outside stair landing, I peeked over the railing. Sure enough, the lights still blazed in Fender Bender's office. What was wrong with that guy? Didn't he have a private life? He glanced up from some blueprints as I passed, and I waved, climbed into my truck, and roared off into the night.

The next morning, I hauled my lazy carcass out of bed, heated water, ground a coneful of Peet's French roast coffee beans that I had remembered to bring home from the studio last night, and inhaled as the aroma filled the kitchen. I plopped down at my "rustic country breakfast ensemble"—a cheap pine table and two chairs that I'd bought on clearance with the idea, not yet realized, of refinishing it as "French Country"—and stared intently into my mug.

I could no longer put off an encounter with the police. I hated the idea of trying to explain why I'd been at the Brock, from which I'd been banished years ago, for a secret midnight rendezvous. But a man had been murdered, and as far as I knew, Ernst was still missing. I might well know something that would help the police with their investigation.

I swung around in my chair and stared out the dormer window. Then again . . . If I could get Anton to tell me who had commissioned the forgery of *The Magi,* I could be of real assistance to the police. This would be harder to do if I were, say, in police custody.

I also wanted to ask Anton about Anthony Brazil's and Albert Mason's missing drawings. If Anton had some of them, I might be able to collect at least part of the reward and I wouldn't have to deal with the scary No Neck guy again.

So that's what I'd do today. I would attempt to track down my grandfather's old buddy Anton, who was larcenous but not scary, and I would do it first thing, before something came up to delay me. And when I got back I would call the cops. Really.

I had heard my downstairs neighbor's door slam half an hour ago, so I knew hot water was available. I showered with confidence, toweled off briskly, calmed my disheveled chestnut hair with plenty of hair goop, and pulled on a pair of worn jeans, a black tank top, and an oversized blue cotton shirt from the Gap that an old boyfriend had left behind. It had been one of the best things about that relationship.

One of the perks of being an artist was that people expected me to dress like one, which meant that just about anything was acceptable. A light swipe of lipstick and mascara was about as far as I usually went with the whole makeup thing. Black socks, black leather clogs, a pair of my designer friend Samantha's asymmetrical, arty earrings, and I was good to go.

On the way out the door, I grabbed my black leather jacket for good measure. Although it was February, and therefore normally sunny in the City, one never knew for sure. San Francisco's climate, like most everything about the place, was unique. The City was at its foggy coldest in the summer, and the local joke was that one could always spot the summer tourists because they were the only ones dressed in shorts and T-shirts. The ubiquitous sidewalk vendors made a killing selling sweatshirts emblazoned I LEFT MY ♥ IN SF AND GOT GOOSE BUMPS INSTEAD and THE COLDEST WINTER I EVER SPENT WAS THE SUMMER I SPENT IN SAN FRANCISCO—MARK TWAIN.

Pulling out of my apartment's parking lot, I glanced at the cheap digital clock I'd superglued to the dashboard and realized I still had time to pick up someone from the casual car pool, which ended at ten. When the 1989 Loma Prieta earthquake temporarily shut down the Bay Area's subway system and disrupted other commute options, perfect strangers were brought together by a mutual need to get into San Francisco, and the casual car pool was born. Those seeking transportation across the Bay Bridge waited on designated street corners, where they were picked up by drivers seeking passengers in order to qualify as a car pool. During rush hours, car pools zipped through the toll plaza, avoiding both the miles-long traffic snarl and the three-dollar toll.

Today I picked up a middle-aged Guatemalan woman and we enjoyed a speedy trip across the bridge. I had no idea who she was or where she was going, but that didn't matter. Casual carpooling etiquette did not encourage the exchange of personal information. Goodwill and mutual benefit were all that were necessary. I dropped her off at Harrison and Ninth and continued on my way.

Armed with the address Albert Mason had given me yesterday, I located Anton's place easily enough, but parking proved harder to find. There were two approaches to parking in San Francisco: the superstitious and the scientific. A lucky few had serious parking karma, but I was stuck with the scientific, grid approach. I circled the block twice, then broadened the search perimeter to a two-block radius. After circling for another fifteen minutes, I finally squeezed into a space at a green-curbed, twenty-minute loading zone, tossed my

CONSTRUCTION CREW PERMIT on the dash, and locked up. This was not strictly kosher, since I was supposed to use the coveted permit only when actually on a job site, but I was running out of time. I promised the universe I would not do it again, at least not anytime soon, and hiked up the block to Anton's studio.

It had been a very long time since I'd been here. The last time Anton and I had spoken, years ago, he told me I was wasting my talents by refusing to produce quality forgeries. He also insisted that I wasn't sufficiently devoted to my grandfather, which I thought was rather cheeky of him given their long-standing rift.

I let myself through the exterior gate in the tall redwood privacy fence. Inside was a courtyard formed by the fence at the front, the main house on the right, the neighbor's house on the left, and a sagging carriage-house-turned-garage at the rear. Anton's studio was above the garage. I crossed the weedy, neglected lawn and skirted a scummed-over birdbath. A broken flagstone terrace boasted a motley assortment of leggy potted plants, several of which looked suspiciously like marijuana. I climbed the steep, narrow exterior staircase on the right side of the garage and knocked on the workshop door, which Anton had long ago painted a bright red.

There was no response.

I knocked again and called out, "Anton! It's Annie. Georges' Annie."

Still no response.

I pressed my ear against the door.

Nothing.

Frustrated, I tried the doorknob, just in case, though I assumed a criminal would be more careful than to provide job opportunities for others of his ilk. To my surprise, the knob turned, and I pushed the door open.

"Anton?" I was whispering now, a response to the

decidedly creepy feeling caused by trespassing in some-one else's home. I might have executed a few forgeries in the past, but I was no burglar, and I usually respected other people's privacy.

I prowled around as best I could, hindered by the junk that was piled everywhere. The studio was one big, airy room that held a double bed, a hot plate and mini-fridge, a sink and a curtained-off toilet, in addition to the heaps of paintings, drawings, canvases, easels, art supplies, and frames. I did notice one unexpected item—a computer. I guess even old guard art forgers were giving in to tech-nology.

I spied some brushes standing in a jar of dirty turpen-tine, picked them up, and studied their ruined bristles. Pigment had settled to the bottom of the glass jar and formed a sludge, which meant the solvent was at least a few days old. These were good—read: expensive—brushes, made of sable and badger hair. No working artist would spoil fine brushes like these unless he was in a very big hurry.

What now? Look for an appointment book? Surely Anton was too experienced a felon to write down any-thing incriminating. Or not. I stumbled over to a large desk and riffled halfheartedly through a few piles. Hon-estly, Anton was even worse than I was when it came to organization. Looking through a couple of drawers jammed with odds and ends, the assorted detritus of a messy life, I noticed a dog-eared brochure for an upcom-ing "Fabulous Fakes" art show in Chicago. Idly I won-dered if there was a purse offered for the best in show and whether I had a shot. It might be an easier way to make the rent than my current line of work.

Nothing provided any insight into Anton's where-abouts, so I sat in the desk chair and waited for inspira-tion.

Aha! A portfolio perched on a worktable across the room looked suspiciously similar to the one Anthony Brazil had carried yesterday. I'd noticed it at the time because it was not the standard-issue black portfolio sold in most art stores. This one was marbleized, like the endplates found in expensive leather-bound books, and had a European-style gold crest in one corner and a gilt border along the top edge. I went over to the table and opened it.

As a former Old Master drawings forger myself, I immediately recognized what I'd found. Inside were numerous drawings, in the same league as the ones Brazil had shown me. Criminal mastermind that Anton was, he had left these forgeries lying right out in the open. The possibilities of what this meant were flooding my mind when a voice split the silence.

Chapter 5

Richard Parkes Bonington died at the age of twenty-six, yet since 1850, more than three thousand paintings have been attributed to him. Either Bonington produced a painting a day for ten straight years—or there is rampant fraud afoot.

—*Georges LeFleur, "Fakes and Forgers," unfinished manuscript,* Reflections of a World-Class Art Forger

"I take it you're an art lover?"

I jumped about three feet, dropped the drawings, and knocked over a half-empty cup of tea, splashing its contents on the cluttered worktable.

A figure was silhouetted in the doorway, leaning against a shelf crammed with art supplies. I could barely make out his face, but it was clear that this was not Anton. On the positive side, he appeared to have a neck and he was not holding a weapon trained on me.

"I was just . . . uh . . . looking for Anton," I stammered, surreptitiously shoving the incriminating drawings under a pile of painting rags before grabbing the rag on top and mopping up the tea.

"And you thought he might be under those drawings?"

the stranger asked, not budging from his post at the studio's only exit.

"Certainly not," I snapped, adrenaline coursing through my body in response to the fight-or-flight instinct. Not presently being criminally inclined and never, under any circumstance, cool under fire, my preference was to flee. However, since the stranger did not appear to be ready to move, and shimmying down the rickety lattice outside the second-story window seemed ill advised, I tried my best to adopt a menacing stance. At five feet three inches, it was a stretch. "Who the hell are you?" I demanded.

"Michael Johnson, at your service," the stranger said, bowing his head and stepping into the studio. He was wearing a dark brown leather bomber jacket, pressed khaki pants, and a snowy white shirt, open at the collar. A slightly lopsided smile showed straight white teeth and made endearing little wrinkles around sea green eyes. Not that I noticed.

"Unghh," I said suavely. "What are you doing here?"

"I was about to ask you the same thing."

"Well, I, uh . . . I have good reason to be here. Anton's practically my uncle."

Michael Johnson studied me for a long moment, the smile not leaving his face. Even though he didn't give off a police vibe, that was the thing about the cops. Sometimes they were devious. Sometimes they were smart. Sometimes they were undercover. I felt my heart speed up, swallowed hard, and tried to remember what the innocent folk do.

"I'm not a cop," Johnson said, apparently reading my mind. "Calm down, sweetheart."

"I'm not your sweetheart," I snarled. In my experience, men who called women they didn't know "sweetheart" could not be trusted.

"Then what should I call you?" Johnson encouraged me patiently, as if I were somewhat slow.

"Annie," I said and stuck out my hand, unsure of the social conventions that applied during an unlawful breaking and entering. He enfolded it in his much larger one. Maybe my imagination was running amok, but I could have sworn his thumb was gently caressing the back of my hand.

"Annie. What a lovely name. So, you're Anton's niece, Annie?"

"Mm," I murmured, a bit flustered by the hand-caressing thing.

"Would you happen to know where he is?"

"If I did I wouldn't tell *you*."

"Why not?"

"I don't know who you are."

"I told you. I'm Michael Johnson."

"So what are you doing here?"

"You mean in a metaphysical sense?"

"What?" I was starting to get confused, which pissed me off. Why couldn't the man answer a simple question?

"I'm a private investigator. I'm working on a case." He pulled a business card from his jacket pocket and handed it to me. Good card stock, I noticed.

MICHAEL X. JOHNSON
DISCREET INVESTIGATIONS
LICENSED, BONDED, AND INSURED

"What's the *X* stand for?" I asked.

"Xerxes."

Well, of course. So I asked the obvious question. "How come that's not spelled with a *Z*?"

"I don't know," he said, a genuinely amused smile re-placing the condescending one. "That's just the way it's spelled."

"Fine, then," I said brusquely, as if I'd made my point. I slipped his card into my jeans pocket. "What kind of case?"

He hesitated. "Does the name Harlan Coombs mean anything to you?"

At last my brain engaged, and it dawned on me that we were having an odd discussion in an odd location. Plus, if he was after the drawings, too, we were working at cross-purposes. "What does his name mean to *you*?" I shot back.

"Did you know he was involved with Ernst Pettigrew?"

"What? How?"

"So you do know Harlan, then?"

Oops. Looked like the X-man was better at this game than I was. No surprise there; my strengths were visual, not verbal. I pursed my lips to keep from saying anything incriminating.

The smarmy smile returned, and he rocked back on his heels before speaking. "I think we may be looking for the same man. Why don't we—"

He stopped suddenly, glanced toward the door, and put his fingers to his lips in the international shushing sign. In the silence I heard footsteps clacking on the stairs outside. Johnson nodded toward a large unfinished canvas leaning against the wall in a dark corner, which we crawled behind and hunkered down.

"Annn-tooon," a woman's voice cooed. "Anton? Are you here, darling?"

Johnson and I looked at each other in our shadowy hidey-hole, then peeked cautiously around one side of the painting. The new arrival's willowy frame was wrapped in a gauzy flowered dress more appropriate to summer picnics than to February in San Francisco. Her ash blond hair was pulled back tightly from a lovely, delicate face and coiled upon her head in a sleek modern style. I held my breath as she crossed straight to the portfolio and tucked it confidently under one arm, then paused to write a note that she left on top of the clutter on the desk. Her heels clattered as she went down the stairs.

Johnson looked at me and raised his eyebrows. "Well, well. The old dog Anton still has a few tricks up his sleeve, eh?"

"What's that supposed to mean?" I snapped. I hated mixed metaphors.

"Well, you have to admit, she's pretty attractive. And Anton's what, mid-sixties?"

I rolled my eyes. I was lurking behind a painting with a pig. A good-looking pig, but still a pig. On top of that, my knees were starting to ache. I did not squat well.

"Let me up."

"First tell me what you were looking for," he said.

"I will not," I said. "You're the one who's trespassing."

"And you're not?" Johnson scoffed.

"I told you. Anton's a courtesy uncle." I was lying through my teeth. Anton was more a marked-lack-of-courtesy uncle.

"Is that why you're hiding here with me, rather than greeting Anton's guests in his absence?"

The good-looking pig was displaying quite a flair for the snide comment, and a part of me rather admired him for it. I tried to keep focused, but those eyes were even greener up close, and in such tight quarters I noticed how nice he smelled. I caught myself sniffing. How embarrassing. My nonexistent love life was obscuring my logic.

"If you will kindly move aside, I'll do just that," I said, adding, "Xerxes" for good measure.

He leaned against the wall, but otherwise did not budge. "Tell me what you know about Harlan Coombs."

"First let me up."

"First tell me what you know."

"Are you saying you won't let me up?"

Before he could answer, a cell phone trilled and Johnson and I patted ourselves down. It was mine, and the number on the caller ID was extremely long, indicating an international call. Grandfather. Despite the circumstances, I had to answer.

"*Allô oui?*" I spoke in French, hoping to throw ol' Xerxes off the track.

"Annie my darling! How wonderful to hear from you!" My grandfather's voice echoed and the line was full of static, but his charmingly accented English was unmistakable. Georges François LeFleur had been born and raised in Brooklyn but insisted he was to the Eiffel Tower born.

"Georges—I need to speak with you, but this isn't a good time," I said, continuing in French.

"Annie? What is wrong? Why do you speak such horrible French?" Grandfather exclaimed.

So it had been a few years. I was struggling to dredge up the French equivalent for "Work with me, please, will you?" when Johnson interjected.

"*Ça m'est égal,*" he said with a shrug, in perfect Parisian-accented French.

In my experience American men who spoke French were of a certain type. This man was not that type. It didn't seem fair, somehow. I glared at Monsieur Big Ears, who smiled sweetly. I had no idea who Michael X. Johnson really was or what he really wanted, but I was pretty sure he was not who he said he was and that what he wanted was probably not on the up-and-up. In short, I didn't trust him. I didn't trust my grandfather to call me back, either, but I was going to have to take that chance.

"*Quel dommage!* I don't know when I'll have ze

chance to call again, *ma cherie,* you know how it is," Grandfather said blithely.

I knew how *he* was. I glanced at Johnson, who was examining his fingernails and humming Edith Piaf's "Je Ne Regrette Rien" slightly off-key. With *le chat* out of the bag, I switched back to English and tucked my head into my jacket, trying for a semblance of privacy. "Grandfather, please, just tell me if you know where Anton is."

"Anton? Anton Woznikowicz?" Grandfather shouted in reply. "Why do you want to speak with him?"

"Because I do, Grandfather," I replied, grinding my teeth. "He's not at his studio. Where else would he be?"

"Darling! Don't tell me you are resuming your true calling? *Mais ça, c'est super!* Forget Anton! *Viens!* Come to Paris! Your old grandpapa will tutor you as before! Come today!"

"I don't want to go to Paris, I want to talk to Anton about something he's involved with. Something bad. I'm worried about him."

"Ask him about Coombs," Johnson broke in.

I glared at him over my jacket collar.

"Just ask," he urged.

What the hell. "Georges, what do you know about Harlan Coombs?"

"*Quoi?* Annie, I cannot hear you. It must be a solar flare."

Solar flare my ass. Grandfather didn't want to answer the question.

"Harlan Coombs," I shouted. Johnson winced.

"Bernard Sahagun?"

"No, Grandfather, Harlan *Coombs.*"

"Sahagun? Never heard of him, darling."

I tried to make sense of that, even though I suspected my dear old grandpapa was fibbing again. "Is Bernard

Sahagun a friend of Coombs? Is that what you're trying to tell me?"

"Ah, my darling girl, I must go now. *Je t'aime,* bye-bye!" Grandfather disconnected.

"Who the hell is Bernard Sahagun?" I muttered, tucking my phone into my jacket pocket.

"Sixteenth-century Spanish priest. Converted the Aztecs to Catholicism," Johnson said.

Now I was really confused. What did Aztecs and Spanish priests have to do with a Polish art forger? "Was he an artist?" I asked, hoping for clarity.

"No."

"Was he an art dealer?"

"Don't think so."

"So what does he have to do with Harlan Coombs?"

"Nothing."

"Then why should I care?"

"I didn't say you should. Your grandfather did."

"No he didn't. He misunderstood what I was saying."

"Why is this my fault?"

"I didn't say it was your fault. How do you know about Bernard Sahagun, anyway?"

"The Jesuits. They teach stuff like that."

"Oh."

We had yet another staring contest. True to form, I blinked first. "Well, listen, Michael Xerxes Johnson, or whatever your name really is." I glared at him. He smirked at me. "It's been a whole heck of a lot of fun, but I have *got* to go."

Literally. My bladder was infamously small. Plus, my knees had just announced that if I didn't stop squatting immediately they would not be held responsible for the consequences.

Johnson rose gracefully and sauntered toward the door. I rose stiffly and lurched across the room, trying to work the kinks out. I hadn't been called Kinky Kincaid in college because of the hair alone. Then I remembered the note the mystery woman had left. Johnson intercepted my gaze and beat me to it.

"Hmmm," he said portentously.

"What? What's it say?"

"Oh, not much." He folded the note and nonchalantly slipped it into his pocket.

"Hold on there, Mr. Private Eye," I ordered. "You have no right to that note. Hand it over."

"Oh, I think not," he replied.

"Oh, I think so," I mimicked nastily. "Because if you don't, I'm calling the cops."

He snorted.

"I'm not kidding."

He snorted again.

"Okay, how about this?" I said. "You show me the note and then I'll tell you something about Coombs."

"You tell me something about Coombs, then I'll show you the note."

"We'll do an exchange on the count of three, okay?" He nodded. "Okay. One, two, three . . ."

I held out my hand for the note. "Coombs has a hide-out in Chinatown, where some scary people are waiting for him," I said as Johnson gave me the piece of paper.

"We need to talk," it said. "I'm at Q's. Important!!! Joanne."

We spoke at the same time.

"Who is Joanne?" I asked him.

"What scary people?" he wanted to know.

We shrugged in unison. I was beginning to feel as if I were back in middle school.

"You go first," I said.

"You didn't tell me anything I didn't already know," he

grumbled. "Harlan's operated out of that Chinatown place for years. And 'scary people' is pretty broad."

"Yeah, well, 'I'm at Q's' is pretty broad, too, so I'd say we're even. Who's Joanne?"

Johnson shrugged again. Frustrated, I dropped the note on the desk and headed for the door. "Don't you want the drawings?" he called after me.

Apparently my hiding place left something to be desired. Pulling the drawings out from beneath the rags, he placed them on the worktable and studied them. He looked up and held my gaze. "They're fake, aren't they?"

I had the distinct impression that he was reading me, not the drawings.

"Maybe."

"Here." He handed them to me.

"How did you know?" I asked.

"You don't have much of a poker face, honey."

"Don't call me honey."

He smiled and escorted me to the door.

"How do I get in touch with you?" he asked smoothly.

"Don't call me. I'll call you."

I waved his business card over my shoulder as I descended the outside staircase, slammed the redwood gate behind me, stashed the fake drawings behind the driver's seat of my truck, and took off.

I drove back to the studio, mulling over what had just transpired. I was no closer to finding Anton than I had been this morning, and now I suspected he had decamped. Judging from the stack of fake drawings stashed behind my seat, there were probably a number of disgruntled art dealers and clients looking for Anton, which would have driven him underground even if he had not been worried about the Caravaggio affair. And who was Joanne? She had zeroed in on the portfolio quickly enough, though she hadn't bothered to check if the drawings were actually inside. Had she commissioned the forged sketches? Was she working with Harlan Coombs? Who was the "Q" she referred to in her note? Most important: where were the original—and extremely valuable—sketches?

Michael X. Johnson was a new puzzle. The name sounded phony—Xerxes fell out of favor shortly after the Persian Wars in the fifth century B.C.—and I did not buy his PI routine for a second. As for the business card, it proved nothing. Once, for a sociology class assignment, I had gone to a crafts fair and handed out cards proclaiming me to be a licensed acupuncturist in order to see how many people were prepared to let me stick them with needles on the basis of nothing more substantial than a business card. The number was frighteningly large.

It was apparent that Johnson was also after the drawings, but why? Had one of Coombs' victims hired him to find them, or was he somehow connected to the forgery of *The Magi*? Johnson had suggested a link between Ernst Pettigrew and Harlan Coombs, though to be fair I had to remember that for years Coombs was a legitimate art dealer. He and Ernst would likely have met through the Brock's Acquisitions department.

But first things first. My bladder was informing me that I had five minutes tops before I disgraced myself and ruined my truck's already sad upholstery. Four minutes later I zipped into my building's parking lot and thundered up the stairs. I got as far as the first landing when a door downstairs banged open and somebody called my name.

Rats. It was my new landlord.

"Yes, Mr. DeBenton?" After yesterday's fiasco I thought it behooved me to be polite, but he had better make it quick or we would both regret it.

"May I have a word with you?"

"No problem, but I'm in a bit of a hurry at the moment," I said, emphasizing my haste by moving up another step. "Can I call you?"

"I wish you would. I've left several messages already this morning on your office phone. I don't expect a lot from my artist tenants. But I do expect common courtesy."

That stopped me. "I haven't been in my office yet this morning. And what have you got against artists?" I inquired, my nose so far out of joint I could smell my shampoo.

"Let me see." He shrugged. "Artists are unpredictable. They don't pay their rent regularly. They make huge messes and don't clean them up. They make noise at odd hours. They are dramatic and they cause scenes."

"I'm afraid I must disagree," I replied, trying to be civil. "First off, I'm very predictable." This was not strictly true. "Second off, I always pay my rent, and I pay it on time." Kind of. So far, anyway. "Third, I always clean up after myself." This was not even remotely true. "I don't make much noise at any time, I am *not* dramatic, and *I do not cause scenes.*"

Fender Bender was watching me with what appeared to be a ghost of a smile. I imagined he was trying to decide whether to call 911 to have me arrested or his lawyer to have me evicted.

"Now, if you will excuse me, I have some pressing business to attend to." I pivoted and charged up the stairs, sprinted down the hallway, and darted into the women's room.

Back in the studio I found Mary and her good friend Sherri sitting on the red velvet couch talking to three leather-clad young men sporting a variety of piercings and multicolored hair, who lay draped over cushions on the floor. Since I wasn't able to pay Mary enough for her to rent a decent apartment in San Francisco—heck, *I* couldn't afford a decent place in the City—I let her use the studio as a de facto living room, and it was not unusual for unnaturally pale musicians to clutter up the place. I nodded at them and went to the desk to check for messages.

"What's up, toots? Something wrong?" Mary asked, joining me at the desk.

"I don't think Fender Bender likes me," I said, deflated.

"Yeah, I met him today. He stopped me when I passed his office and asked what my business was here. Sexy, though," Mary declared. "Too bad he's gay."

"Gay?" I was surprised. "Are you sure? My gaydar didn't go off." True, there had been no wedding ring. In these parts, that was rare for a good-looking straight man with two nickels to rub together.

"With those spiffy suits and that slicked-back hair? *Totally* gay," Sherri declared from the sitting area. Sherri and Mary were from the same small town in Indiana. After devoting their adolescence to scoring illegal cigarettes and dyeing their hair with Kool-Aid powder, the two had hitchhiked to San Francisco. Here they found hordes of young people who shared their passion for smoking, black clothes, and Goofy Grape–colored hair. Despite her diminutive stature and baby-doll voice, Sherri worked alongside her leather-clad husband, Tom, as a process server.

The young men sprawled at Sherri's feet nodded in agreement.

"You've *all* met the man who owns the building?" I asked. No wonder Fender Bender was annoyed. Five sets of heavy motorcycle boots trodding the old wooden floorboards outside his office must have sounded like a contingent of Nazi storm troopers. I had to smile.

"I don't know," I continued, unconvinced. "He's too stuffy to be gay."

"C'mon, Annie. Have you *ever* seen a straight man in the City who dressed that well?" Mary insisted.

"True enough," I conceded. "But remember, he's not from here. There are men in other parts of the world who dress like gay men do here. The French, for instance. Stand in a room full of Frenchmen and you'd swear they were all gay, but they're just stylish."

"Huh. Maybe so," Mary said thoughtfully. "Guess we'll have to check it out."

"How do you propose to do that?" I said, suddenly wary.

Mary and Sherri smiled. "Don't worry—we'll come up with something."

"Hey, do not, I repeat, do *not* get me in any more hot water with the landlord, okay? I'm serious, guys." I was going for severe, but feared I'd hit only plaintive. The phone rang, and I answered it while shooting stern looks at my assistant. "True/Faux Studios."

"Ms. Kincaid."

Speak of the devil.

"Mr. DeBenton!" I cooed. "How nice to hear from you. And so soon!"

"Indeed. I thought I should inform you that two inspectors from the San Francisco Police Department are on their way up to see you," he said.

Two SFPD inspectors were *here*? To see *me*? I considered slipping out the back door but decided against it, seeing as there was no back door. And I figured that vaulting out the window and climbing down the fire escape might give the cops the wrong impression. It then occurred to me that this was the second time today I had considered escaping through a second-story window and I hadn't even had lunch yet.

"So," DeBenton continued, "would this be the part about not causing trouble?"

"Yeah, well . . ." Anxiety had jammed my brain's circuitry. "Anyway, I don't see how this is pertinent to . . . Oh, Lord, they're here." I slammed down the phone. My youthful interactions with the authorities had been unsettling, to say the least, and I harbored a sneaking suspicion that, as my grandfather always insisted, larceny ran in my blood. For whatever reason, I always assumed I was guilty until proven innocent. And in this case I *was* guilty, at least of not approaching the police earlier to tell them about the events at the Brock.

"May I help you, Inspectors?" I asked, using my best Citizen of the Year voice and trying not to hyperventilate. Filling the doorway were one pale, skinny, white man who reminded me a little of Ichabod Crane and one solidly built African Princess. Both flashed badges. Neither smiled.

"Anna Kincaid? We'd like to ask you some questions, please," the Princess said in a deep, authoritative voice.

None of Mary's friends had budged. I tried to imagine the scene through the inspectors' eyes and saw instead tomorrow's headline in the *Chronicle*: MUSEUM MURDER SUSPECT RUNS DRUGGIE DEN FOR YOUNG MUSICIANS.

"Guys, why don't you all run over to the park or something? Get some fresh air and sunshine?" I said to Mary's crowd, as if they were eight years old.

"We might need to speak with them," Ichabod intervened. "Do you know how to get in touch with all of them?"

"Certainly," I lied.

The group got languidly to their feet and clomped out, avoiding the official eyes. Grandfather's voice whispered, unbidden, in my ear: "It is important, my darling, when entertaining members of the constabulary, to act like a lady. It will mislead them."

Accordingly, I gestured to the now vacant sofa. "May I get you anything?"

"No, thank you. I am Inspector Crawford," the

Princess said, her voice terse, "and this is Inspector Wilson." Ichabod nodded and his Adam's apple bobbed. "We have reason to believe you met with Ernst Pettigrew two nights ago."

"Oh?" I tried to project interest without commitment.

"We found your name in his diary," Inspector Crawford continued, eyeing me.

"His *diary*?" I protested. "I hardly knew the man!"

I kept a diary when I was eleven. I found it last year, when my mother sent me an old box marked ANNIE'S STUFF—STAY OUT! The diary would have been hilarious if it were not so pathetic, since it was mainly a catalogue of how "barfy" I thought some of my schoolmates were. I didn't think grown men kept diaries. What had Ernst written about me? Was I barfy?

"It wasn't that kind of diary, Ms. Kincaid," Inspector Crawford said, her mouth twitching in an unwilling smile. Ichabod remained stone-faced. "It was his desk calendar. It indicated he had an appointment with you yesterday."

"Oh."

"And did he?"

A woman of few words, the inspector. What to say, what to say? Although I had fully intended to approach the police voluntarily, my reflex was to lie, and I had to remind myself that I had nothing to do with Ernst's disappearance or Dupont's murder.

"Yes, he did," I said, deciding that, notwithstanding my grandfather's example, sometimes honesty really was the best policy.

The inspectors scribbled something in their notebooks. To me, it didn't look like "Witness said yes." To me, it looked like "Suspect admitted meeting missing curator. This will crack the case! She'll rue the day she tried to fool SFPD's finest! Bwahahahaha!"

"—was that?" Inspector Crawford was asking.

"Pardon?"

"What. Time. Was. That," she repeated slowly.

Note to self: maybe if I acted really dim-witted, it would allay their suspicions.

"Um, around midnight," I said, realizing that sounding dim-witted was one thing, but sounding guilty was another.

"Isn't that a little late for a business meeting?" Inspector Crawford asked.

"Yes. But Ernst Pettigrew said he didn't want anyone to know." That sounded worse. "You see, it's . . . well, it's complicated. Ernst was worried that an important painting acquired by the Brock was not, um, genuine."

"Not genuine? You mean a forgery?" Inspector Crawford cut to the chase.

"Mm-hmm."

"Don't museums check these things out before buying artwork?" she asked.

"Of course." I decided to be up-front and share my professional expertise. "At least, they try. The painting underwent the usual tests and was authenticated by the Brock Museum's appraiser, Dr. Sebastian Pitts. Ernst was still not convinced, but he didn't want to cause an uproar without first getting a second opinion."

"Why would it have caused an uproar? Because of the money involved?"

"Yes, but it's more than that. The Brock got burned a few years ago when a British art historian proved that a Roman statue the museum had paid nine million dollars for was a modern fake. And a rather poorly done fake at that. It made the Brock's staff look like a bunch of amateurs, and in the art world reputation is everything. The Brock family has spent the past several years trying to put the incident behind them. The last thing they'd want is another well-publicized forgery."

The two inspectors seemed to be taking it all in. There was no more scribbling in their notebooks, which I hoped was a good sign. All they had wanted was a little cooperation.

"And did you see the painting?" Inspector Crawford inquired.

"Yes. Ernst showed it to me."

"Where?"

"In the vault."

"So you were in the vault?"

I hesitated. Was that bad? Probably. Had I left fingerprints? Assuredly. Might as well 'fess up. "Yes."

"By yourself?"

"No, with Ernst."

"And your assessment?"

Despite Inspector Crawford's formidable air, her steady brown eyes were reassuring, so I took a deep breath and went for it. "It was a fake."

Two sets of eyebrows shot skyward.

"How could you tell?" Inspector Crawford inquired.

"It's hard to explain. Contrary to what most people think, it's really not that difficult to fake a masterpiece, provided you know what you're doing, you have the talent, and you use the proper materials. Scientific tests can determine the age and place of origin of a canvas, as well as detect pigments or media that were unavailable before a certain date. But barring an obvious problem, appraisers have to go on gut instinct. And my instinct said this was not a genuine Caravaggio."

"How sure are you?"

"Very."

"Did you tell that to Pettigrew?"

"Of course."

"What did he say?" Inspector Crawford probed gently but firmly.

"He was pretty upset. I think he'd been hoping he was wrong. But Ernst would no more permit a forgery to hang in his museum than he would streak through the museum naked on a Sunday afternoon. By which I mean he wouldn't. Either of those."

"So are you suggesting, Ms. Kincaid, that Ernst Pettigrew would have made the news of the forgery public?"

"I don't see how it could have been avoided. The Brock has made a huge to-do over acquiring *The Magi*. In fact, there's a celebratory gala coming up soon."

"Then it seems to me he might have wanted to keep the news quiet," Inspector Wilson chimed in. "Do you know where Pettigrew is?"

"No. I haven't a clue."

"If you hear from him, please let us know. We'd like to ask him a few questions," Inspector Crawford said. "What can you tell us about Stan Dupont?"

"I scarcely knew the man. I didn't even know his first name was Stan."

"When and where did you last see the victim?"

I winced at the thought of someone I knew, however superficially, being reduced to "the victim." "In the museum's employee parking lot, after midnight on Saturday night. He unlocked the door for me after my meeting with Ernst. That's it. That's all I know."

"Do you have any idea why someone would want to murder him?"

"None at all."

"Perhaps because Dupont knew the painting was a fake?"

"I don't see how he would have known that, unless he overheard us that night," I protested. "Plus both Ernst and I would have been more logical targets."

"Have you told anyone about your meeting with Pettigrew?" Crawford continued.

"No," I lied. I had told my friend Samantha, a jewelry designer whose studio was down the hall from mine, but I figured she'd be safer if I kept my yap shut now.

The inspector watched me carefully. "You do realize that you may be in danger?"

Danger? Me? Why would anyone want to kill me? I was a mild-mannered faux finisher.

"Of course, the killer might not know about you," she continued. "With Dupont dead and Pettigrew missing, the killer may think there's no one left to cause problems."

"Do you have any idea what happened to Ernst?" I asked. "You don't suspect him of anything, do you?"

The inspectors ignored me. I guess I wasn't supposed to be the one asking the questions.

"What time did you leave the museum, Ms. Kincaid?" the Inspector asked.

"Twelve thirty."

"On the dot?"

"Pretty much. I noticed the time because I had agreed to meet Ernst at Grounds for Suspicion to talk things over."

The inspectors wrote furiously in their notebooks again. I wished they would stop that.

"So you saw him there?" Inspector Crawford asked.

"No. He never showed up." Sounded bad for Ernst, I realized. It cast suspicion upon him . . . or suggested he might be the victim of foul play. On the other hand, maybe Ernst simply hightailed it back to Austria to drown his sorrows in a barrel of peppermint schnapps.

"Could anyone verify you were at the café?"

"The barrista. And a weird guy in striped pajamas with a dog." It had never occurred to me that I would need an alibi. "And some students. I ordered a nonfat latte. And a big cookie. With M&M's instead of chocolate chips."

"Skinny latte, big cookie, M&M's," Inspector Crawford repeated as she jotted more notes. She kept a straight face, so I couldn't tell whether or not she was making fun of me. "The Grounds on Fillmore?"

I nodded, anxious for this interview to be over. I didn't like the implications of what had just been said, not one bit, and I needed to think. A hot bath and a big glass of wine wouldn't hurt, either.

"Did you see anyone else at the museum?" It was clear that Inspector Crawford wasn't going to leave just to suit me. I supposed homicide inspectors were like that.

"Nobody in the flesh. There were a couple of cars in the employee parking lot, which I guess belonged to the Housekeeping and Security staff. I didn't see or hear anyone else."

"You've been very helpful, Ms. Kincaid," Inspector Crawford said, while Ichabod squinted. "We do appreciate it."

I wasn't fooled. Former encounters with the police had not left me entirely clueless. She was setting me up for something.

"One last question. Why did Ernst Pettigrew ask to meet with you? I see you are a faux finisher, but are you an art appraiser, too?"

Here was the sticky wicket. No, I was not an art appraiser, and I was sure the inspector already knew that. It was simple enough to check a person's graduate training, institutional affiliation, and professional credentials— none of which I had. And what I did have—a felon of a grandfather and a "sealed" juvenile rap sheet in Paris—I preferred the inspector didn't learn about.

"In a manner of speaking," I said. "The art world is very small. Ernst Pettigrew and I had crossed paths professionally on a few occasions, and we'd developed a mutual respect for each other's eye for authenticity. An artistic eye is like perfect musical pitch—either you have it or you don't. I have it, and Ernst knows it. And, unlike most appraisers, I have no personal stake in whether a painting is real or forged. I also know how to keep my mouth shut." Boy, did I ever. "I think that's why Ernst felt he could come to me."

"Plus the fact that he's your ex-lover," Inspector Crawford said, cocking an eyebrow.

Damn. I was willing to bet the rent money Naomi had told them that.

"Ernst is a former boyfriend," I said, the very picture of cooperation. "But we broke up years ago. It's all water under the bridge now."

At an unseen signal, the two stood simultaneously, and Inspector Crawford handed me her business card.

"Thank you for speaking with us, Ms. Kincaid," she said as she opened the door. "If you think of anything else, please give me a call. I want you to know that in the interests of guarding your safety, we will not release the information that you met with Mr. Pettigrew. However, until this whole thing is sorted out, I encourage you to take basic precautions for your own safety. We'll probably need to ask some additional questions as we learn more. We'll be in touch."

I bolted the door behind them and slumped against it. I glanced at the business card Inspector Crawford had given me, then pulled Michael X. Johnson's business card from my jeans pocket.

Too bad I didn't still keep that diary. Today's entry would have been a doozy.

Chapter 6

Until the eighteenth century, blue pigment was made by grinding semiprecious stones, and was so expensive that owning a painting made with the color was considered a status symbol among Dutch merchants.

—Georges LeFleur, "Experts & Other Lower
Life Forms," *unfinished manuscript,*
Reflections of a World-Class Art Forger

I had few truly useful friends, probably because most of them were either artists or sociologists. My friends were perfect when I wanted to discuss politics, go out dancing, cry on a shoulder, or paint a brilliant forgery. They also threw terrific little dinner parties. But they were not much help when it came to the more practical aspects of life.

I had noticed that fictional heroines always had friends who were doctors, lawyers, and police detectives, people they could call on in the dead of night to perform kitchen-table bullet extractions, defend them from specious homicide accusations, and/or look up the license plates of suspected rapists and other miscreants.

My friends, however, would be able to deliver a moving eulogy over my grave, organize a rousing street demonstration to protest my being hauled off to the state penitentiary, and convince the legislature to pass an anti-stalking law, thereafter to be known as Annie's Law, in my memory.

None of which would do *me* any good.

The only exception to this friendship rule was Pedro Schumacher, whom I'd met a few years ago when our banners became entangled at the annual Save the People's Park rally in Berkeley. Having been burned by his recent foray with a computer start-up company, Pedro was now looking to make a quick buck in the lucrative world of computer consulting. A couple of years younger than I, he was handsome in a squat sort of way, with the dramatic coloring of his Mexican mother, his German father having contributed the last name and little else of substance. Pedro had a longtime workaholic girlfriend, lived in a modest apartment in West Oakland, and reveled in Mickey Spillane novels.

Once my new buddies at the SFPD had left me in peace, I started pondering the enigma that was Michael X. Johnson. It occurred to me that private eyes nowadays probably did a lot of their snooping on the Internet, so I decided to give my useful friend Pedro a call. We chatted for a few minutes to catch up on each other's life, then got down to business.

"Listen, Pedro, is there any way to track down information on somebody who claims to be a private eye?" I asked.

"Sure. What's his name?"

"Michael Johnson."

"You're kiddin' me, right?" Pedro snorted. "Jesus, Annie, don't you realize that 'Johnson' is the most common last name in the U.S.?"

"I thought that was 'Smith' or 'Jones.'"

"Nah—Johnson. How come you know so little about your people?"

Pedro insisted that I was the prototypical American, while I pointed out that since he'd been born in El Paso, whereas I'd been born in Paris, he was technically more American than I. Sometimes I called him "Peter Shoemaker" to drive home the idea.

"They're your people, too, Pedro," I reminded him.

"Yeah, yeah. So this is all you've got on the guy? I'm gonna get maybe a hundred thousand hits."

I had only a vague idea what that meant, but it sounded ominous. "That's bad, huh?"

"Not for me. I get paid by the hour."

I smiled. Pedro refused to allow me to pay him for his expertise, claiming it would be a violation of Article 3, Section 7, Subsection 32 of the "Pedro and Annie Friendship Agreement."

"How about this?" I offered. "His middle initial is X."

"As in *Mexico*?" Pedro asked.

"As in *Xerxes*."

"That's a weird name. Is that with two *X*'s?" he asked, and I spelled it for him. "Okay, what else can you tell me about him? The more details you can give me, the easier it will be to narrow things down."

"Well, let me see," I said slowly, conjuring up Michael Johnson's image. "He's well spoken and well educated, possibly at a Jesuit school. Knows fine art and art forgery. He's stylish and well mannered, so he's probably not a recluse. Dresses casually but expensively, kind of like a cross between L.L. Bean and Ralph Lauren. No wedding ring, earrings, or other jewelry. He's in his mid- to late thirties. Dark brown hair, green eyes, about six feet tall. Nice build, trim and muscular, but not *too* big."

A wistful tone had crept into my voice, and I wondered if Pedro had noticed it. I heard his computer keyboard clicking in the background, so maybe he hadn't been paying attention. Or perhaps he was signing me up for an online dating service.

"You got a little thing for this guy?" Pedro asked.

"Very funny. Is there some kind of state registry for PIs?"

"Dunno. If he's legit, he'll have a license to carry concealed. I could try that."

That was news to me. I was scared of guns. Had I been hunkering with a gun-toting stranger? Those sample boards were looking better all the time.

"Annie?" Pedro broke into my reverie. "Why don't I call you when I have something? Tomorrow, probably."

I thanked him, then put down the phone and leaned back in my desk chair. The African Princess and Ichabod had suggested that I take some precautions, which probably didn't include getting chased through Chinatown and meeting clandestinely with strangers in empty artists' lofts. But finding Anton and figuring out how he was involved with *The Magi* and if he knew where the missing drawings were seemed more important than ever. In addition to the reward money issue, I was really beginning to fear for Anton's safety, not to mention Ernst's.

The problem was, I still wasn't sure how to find him.

As I sat there thinking, however, realization dawned on me.

The first time I'd met Anton had been at a famous old North Beach bar called Vesuvio's, where he and Grandfather liked to spend sunny afternoons sipping espresso, smoking unfiltered French cigarettes, and gossiping. I was ten years old and proud to the point of bursting that my grandfather was introducing me to his world. The bartenders hailed him and Anton by name when we walked in, which at the time had impressed me no end. It had been many years since that meeting, but Albert Mason had mentioned spotting Anton at Vesuvio's not so long ago.

So here was the plan: I would do some actual work for the rest of the afternoon, and then head to North Beach. If nothing else, it would do me good to get out on a Friday night once in a while.

I spent a few hours organizing client files, researching images of ritzy European locales for an exterior mural I was designing for a Porsche dealership, and attending to my quarterly taxes. By eight thirty I was feeling positively virtuous and ready for a drink at Vesuvio's. Unfortunately, Mary had gone AWOL and my friend Samantha the jewelry designer already had plans for the evening, so I was on my own.

If parking in most of the City was nearly impossible, parking on Columbus Avenue on a Friday night was unthinkable. I took a halfhearted drive down the main strip to see if by chance the karma situation had changed. It hadn't, so I kept going. I didn't bother looking in neighboring Chinatown. I wasn't up to the public ridicule one courted when trying to squeeze a truck into a spot next to cages of live chickens.

Originally settled by Italian immigrants, North Beach stretched along the length of Columbus Avenue, from the downtown financial district almost to the Cannery building at Fisherman's Wharf. To the east it bordered Chinatown, while bumping up against the historic Jackson Street "Barbary Coast" on the west. At the intersection of Broadway and Columbus were a multitude of seedy strip joints and sex shops, and so within a few blocks' walk of North Beach one could find world-class Italian and Chinese restaurants, rare-book stores, soaring corporate skyscrapers, steaming loaves of sourdough, fabulous jazz, and a wide selection of dildos. Truly something for everyone.

I was nearing the end of Columbus, up by the Wharf,

before I found a space, but I figured the long walk would do me good. Fifteen minutes later I crossed Broadway, ignoring the strip show hawkers trying to lure me inside to see what the "girls" had to offer. I had the same reaction to those shows that I had to the lottery: my odds of profiting from the experience seemed astronomical.

The bar I was looking for was on the next block, at the corner of an alley named after Jack Kerouac. Vesuvio's was two stories high, but the second floor was mostly a balcony, so the downstairs was open to the gaze of those above. Pushing my way through a throng of beatnik wannabes, I headed toward the bar. A crowd two- and three-deep was vying for drinks, but with a bit of good-natured jostling I managed to elbow my way to the front. On the whole, San Franciscans were a civilized breed, prone to rebuff a shove but yield to a smile. New Yorkers had a hard time adjusting.

"Get for ya?" a young female bartender asked, her voice scarcely audible above the jazz music.

"I'm looking for a regular, a man named Anton Woznikowicz," I shouted.

"You want a WHAT?" she shouted back.

"Anton. Anton Woznikowicz," I repeated, louder this time.

"Never heard of an Anti-Whachahoochi. We got Anchor Steam on draft."

It took a few minutes before she understood what it was I wanted, and when she finally did, she shrugged and went on to the next customer. She was too young to have been working here long anyway, so I made my way down the bar searching for another source of information.

Bartender Bud—according to his name tag—was in his late fifties, with the bulbous nose and pronounced paunch of a habitual drinker. I thought I saw a flicker of recognition when I asked about Anton.

"Yeah, I know him," he said, as he mixed a local favorite, a wicked combination of espresso, grappa, Kahlua, and half-and-half guaranteed to keep you wide awake and drunk all night. "Haven't seen him for a while. Who wants to know?"

I said I was an old friend, gave Bud my business card, and asked him to call me if Anton showed up. He took it, though I had little faith that he would do anything but drop it in the trash.

I scanned the bar area halfheartedly just on the off chance that Anton had happened to walk in while my attention was focused on Bud. No such luck. Coming to the bar had been a long shot anyway. But seeing as how I was already parked—usually the most painful part of a night on the town—it seemed a shame not to take advantage of it. Maybe a handsome computer bazillionaire would ask to share my table, fall madly in love with me, and I would no longer be dateless. Or poor. Or lacking health insurance.

Bud mixed me a vodka martini. I left a large tip to help him remember me and climbed the cramped staircase at the back of the room to the second-floor balcony, where I paused at the top of the stairs, searching for a table. I spotted a heavyset woman who was either wrestling with a bear or struggling to pull on a fake-fur coat, and scooted over. I might not have parking karma, but I was no slouch when it came to restaurant and bar seating.

After about twenty minutes of sitting there, watching the ebb and flow of the crowd below, I felt someone approach.

"I understand you are looking for Anton, madam. Yes?"

He wasn't a computer bazillionaire, that was for sure. Nor was he handsome. In fact, he looked a lot like he'd been hit in the face with a truck at an impressionable age. And he reeked of cologne.

"Why, yes. Yes, I am. Would you care to sit down?" I asked politely.

"Thank you, madam," the Stranger replied as he settled his considerable girth into the chair across from me.

"By chance, sir, would you happen to know where Anton might be found?" I didn't usually talk this way, but I had an odd and generally unconscious talent for mimicry. Plop me down in the middle of a Texas barbecue and within minutes I would be twanging with the best of them.

"May I inquire as to the nature of your relationship with Anton?" the Stranger asked.

I was beginning to wonder about those rumors that Anton ran with the Polish Mafia, because this guy certainly looked the part. White hair, a deeply lined face, and a piercing gaze set him apart from the bar's youthful, hip crowd.

"He is an old friend of my grandfather's," I said. "Perhaps you've heard of my grandfather? Georges LeFleur?"

Among those who knew it, Grandfather's name elicited strong emotions. Lately I had become so conventional that I had nearly forgotten how much respect it commanded in certain not-so-mainstream circles. The Stranger's cold blue eyes warmed slightly.

"LeFleur, you say?" he repeated, his tone verging on the reverential.

"Just so." I was getting into this oh-so-Continental way of speaking.

"I hear he is writing a new book on his . . . profession."

I winced. "Yes. Yes, he is."

The Stranger smiled. "May I presume you have visited Anton's atelier?"

I assumed he meant Anton's sagging garage-top studio.

"Without luck, I'm afraid."

"I believe he recently sold some work to a dealer in the Napa Valley," the Stranger volunteered. "Yountville, to be precise. The Dusty Attic, or some such thing."

"Ah?" That didn't sound like Anton. "What kind of shop might that be?"

He shrugged eloquently. "An antiques shop, I've heard, just off the main highway."

"Why would Anton sell something to an antiques shop?"

He looked at me disdainfully. "My dear madam, who is to say? Perhaps he enjoys collecting those dreary silver teaspoons." And with that the Stranger rose and walked away.

"Ta!" I called out as he was swallowed up by the crowd.

Well, that was weird. Selling art forgeries to an antiques dealer was about the dumbest idea around. True, it was nigh unto impossible to get caught this way. Few antiques dealers knew much about forged art, and once the deal was transacted the forger simply drove off into the sunset. But an antiques dealer was unlikely to pay very much for artwork, and what was the point of being a forger if not to make money?

And why Yountville? San Francisco had all the hungry collectors, the greedy gallery owners, and the corrupt customs officials that an art forger needed to make a decent living. The Napa Valley, in contrast, had delightful small towns, whimsical Victorian houses, world-famous wineries, charming bed-and-breakfasts, plus expensive boutiques and "junque" shops catering to yuppies.

Definitely weird.

Finishing my martini, I surrendered my table to a boisterous group hovering near the stairs and hit the sidewalk. I got all the way to the sex shops on Broadway before I realized that I had left my purse hanging on the back of the chair at Vesuvio's. Rats. I hated it when I did that, and

I did it more frequently than I liked to admit. I turned on my heel and hurried back to the bar.

As I approached Vesuvio's crowded entrance a woman emerged, glanced down the street, tucked her head into her collar, and walked quickly in the opposite direction. She was tall and thin, and before she looked away I caught sight of two piercing feline eyes. I had seen those eyes before. In Harlan's apartment, in Chinatown, on an evening I would rather forget.

I entered the bar cautiously, keeping an eye out for the woman's less attractive sidekick, No Neck. The place was still bursting with yuppies, tourists, and pseudo-beatniks, but no one who looked as if he wanted to kill me. I slipped upstairs and found my purse right where I had left it, hanging on the back of the chair, which was now inhabited by a redheaded man with dreadlocks. He passed the bag to me and I checked for my wallet. It was there, with eight dollars and sixty-six cents, my two credit cards, and my driver's license.

The dreadlocked guy winked. Who said people couldn't be trusted?

Pushing my way downstairs, I trudged the twenty minutes back to my truck and stopped cold. The passenger-side window had been smashed, and beads of tempered glass covered the interior.

I looked behind the bench seat. The drawings were gone.

Shit. It was stupid of me to leave them in the truck.

I brushed the glass off the driver's seat, climbed in, and drummed my fingers on the steering wheel. Michael X. Johnson, perhaps? It didn't seem his style, but he was the only one who knew I had the drawings. Maybe some two-bit local crook happened upon the stash and found himself moved by a desire for culture. Or had it been someone with more sinister intentions? Maybe I should get the hell out of here.

I fired up the truck's engine and took off. I was wide awake and a little jumpy. Sleep was out of the question, so I decided to head to my studio. Seemed like a good time to work on the portrait I was painting of John Steubing.

In another era John would have been a celebrated patron of the arts along the lines of Lorenzo de Medici of Florence, who was known to his contemporaries as Lorenzo the Magnificent. In tribute, I called my patron John the Magnificent, though never to his face, since although John Steubing had a generous soul, he was also a gruff, no-nonsense entrepreneur uncomfortable with emotions like gratitude. John was well known around town for his political work as well as for his bank account, and painting his portrait was a great opportunity. But unlike much of my mural and faux-finish work, I needed peace and solitude when painting portraits, which I hadn't had much of lately.

I pulled into my studio's parking area and saw my landlord's fleet of armored cars lined up at the rear of the lot, like a miniature panzer division poised to invade some unsuspecting country. DeBenton's gleaming Jaguar rested in what was now, apparently, my former parking spot. A light shone in his office. The man worked even longer hours than I did.

I would never have admitted it to old Fender Bender, but it was nice knowing someone else was in the building. As much as I liked working at the studio late at night, at times it was undeniably creepy. Especially considering the SFPD's earlier warning. And the smashed truck window.

I hurried up the stairs and down the hall, footsteps echoing on the wooden flooring. Flipping on my studio's lights, I felt the usual proprietary satisfaction. It was peaceful here late at night, the red brick walls glowing warmly against the dark night framed by the huge windows, and I relaxed as I brewed coffee. I sat on the worn velvet sofa, sipped strong espresso, and reflected upon my conversation with the Stranger at Vesuvio's.

I still didn't know where Anton was, but at least I had a place to look for him: the Dusty Attic antiques shop in Yountville. I pondered the forged drawings I had taken from Anton's studio and that someone else had stolen from me. Had I merely been a victim of one of the hundreds of random break-ins that occurred daily in any urban center, or had someone been intent on getting those drawings back?

One thing I knew was that the cat-eyed woman from Harlan's Chinatown apartment didn't strike me as the type to be out carousing at Vesuvio's on a Friday night. I wondered if, like me, she had been following a trail to Anton, or whether she had been following me.

Frustrated, I refocused. John Steubing's portrait rested on its easel, awaiting my ministrations. It needed a lot of work. In terms of classical oil portraiture that meant a lot of time. I'd been trained in the traditional Italian method, in which the subject was first sketched in a single color— usually raw umber—so that problems of composition and the relative values of light and shadow could be worked out before the pigment was applied. This "underpainting" would not be perceptible in the finished piece, but it was as crucial to the portrait as a strong foundation was to a building.

Steubing's portrait was still in the underpainting phase, which meant that his face, although recognizable, was gray and muddy, the background shadows were too highly contrasting, and the sofa upon which he sat was indistinct and fuzzy. This was the stage I always thought of as a painting's awkward adolescence. And just as with that excruciating stage of life, there was nowhere to go but through it. I girded my loins and began squeezing pigment onto my palette.

A loud knock sounded on the door, causing me to jump and squirt a blob of raw umber paint on my apron. I bit off a curse.

It was nearly midnight. Given the crowd I ran with, it could be just about anybody. I tried to remember if I had locked the door. Surely I had. Only a fool would leave the door unlocked in a nearly abandoned building in the middle of the night.

I dropped my voice an octave to sound more formidable. "Yes?"

"Ms. Kincaid? It's Frank DeBenton."

I hesitated. What if it wasn't Frank? What if it was some psycho who was smart enough to read the names on the downstairs directory board and use that information to lure me into opening the stout wooden door that was keeping me safe? There would be nothing to stop him from doing all manner of hideous things to me, things too awful to even contemplate, things that would make an open-casket funeral impossible.

Not that I wanted one. A funeral, that is. Much less an open-casket funeral. How gruesome. When my time came, I wanted to be cremated. Had I ever told anyone that?

"Ms. Kincaid?" the voice called again.

My heart raced as the knob turned and the door slowly swung open. I held my paintbrush up high, prepared to poke some eyes out if I had to.

Frank DeBenton stood in the doorway, dressed in pressed khakis, a starched white oxford shirt, a gray wool cardigan, and buffed Weejuns. His dark hair was slicked back, his face was closely shaved, he smelled faintly of soap, and his hands appeared to have been recently manicured. It was midnight on a Friday, and my landlord looked as if he had just stepped out of the pages of *Gentlemen's Quarterly*.

I dabbed ineffectually at the paint smear on my apron, wondered what my hair looked like, and feared that I knew.

"Everything all right up here?" he asked politely.

"Sure," I replied nonchalantly, hoping my pulse returned to normal sometime soon. "Why do you ask?"

"I noticed your truck window was broken," he said. "You know, you really should keep the studio door locked when you're working late at night."

"Right you are," I said casually. "Life in the Big City." An awkward silence descended.

"I could smell the coffee all the way downstairs," he said. "Smells good."

Could he be any more obvious? I wondered. Still, here was my chance to curry favor with my landlord. "Would you like a cup?"

"If you're offering," he said with a smile.

I waved him toward the sofa while I went into the kitchen area and prepared another cup of espresso. "I used up the last of the milk, I'm afraid, but there's sugar if you'd like."

"No, thank you. Black's just fine."

How manly. I handed him a demitasse of rich espresso and joined him on the sofa. We sipped in silence as DeBenton took in the many painted canvases. His eyes came to rest on Steubing's still-adolescent portrait.

"Isn't that John Steubing?" he asked, surprising me with his discernment.

"Yes, it is," I replied, pleased. "Do you know him?"

"We have a number of associates in common. You're painting his portrait?"

What did he think, that I had it done at the local poster shop?

The look on my face must have given me away, because he added quickly, "I thought you just did faux finishes."

"I love painting portraits," I said with a shrug. "There just isn't any money in it. People spend thousands of dollars on a faux finish for their living room, but balk at paying more than a few hundred for a painting that lasts forever and takes months to complete."

"Americans have a strange relationship to art," DeBenton murmured.

Aha! A common bond.

"Which is not surprising," he continued, "considering that artists in this country are a rather spoiled lot."

The bond unraveled.

"What do you mean by that?" I hated the stereotype of artists as selfish, lazy, and irresponsible, even if it was sometimes true.

"Just that there's no such thing as a free lunch," he said pompously. "You're a businesswoman, Ms. Kincaid. You understand the value of a dollar."

"Yes, I do," I replied indignantly. "I'm also an artist who works twelve hours a day, six days a week. I have a tiny apartment in Oakland, an old truck I pray doesn't break down since I can't afford to replace it, no benefits, and a studio that, thanks to a recent rent increase, I can no longer afford. So remind me, please: how, exactly, am I spoiled?"

"I didn't mean—" DeBenton began.

"*I'm* not the one who drives a Jaguar and jacks the rents up on loyal tenants," I continued, cutting him off. "What's more, all the artists *I* know are decent, kindhearted people who work extremely hard just to get by and don't expect handouts."

The part about my artist friends being decent, kind-hearted, and hardworking was true. The part about their not expecting handouts was not. All artists dreamed of a patron who would allow us to focus only on our art. But I would be damned if I'd admit that to him now.

DeBenton stood and shoved his hands in his pockets. "I think I should go," he said quietly.

"Wait," I said, belatedly remembering that I was supposed to be getting on his *good* side. "I'm sorry if I overreacted. I guess it's a sore subject for me. So . . ." I paused. "I don't suppose this would be the best time to negotiate a break in my rent?"

I meant that last bit as a joke to lighten the mood. It didn't work.

"I suppose not," DeBenton said. "Thank you for the coffee." He left, closing the door softly behind him. I heard his footsteps echo down the hallway, and then the outside door slammed shut.

Good going, Annie, I jeered as I locked the door and returned to the portrait. Maybe I was in the wrong line of work. I should give up on painting and launch a new literary craze: the self-defeatist book. *How to Alienate and Lose All Influence with People within Mere Days of Making Their Acquaintance,* by Annie Kincaid.

I got home at two in the morning and woke up at nine, groggy but eager to pursue my new lead on Anton. Fortified with a steaming cup of Peet's coffee, I sat at my kitchen table and called Directory Assistance in Yountville for the number of the antiques store the Stranger had told me about last night. When I dialed the Dusty Attic's number, an answering machine picked up. The recorded voice of the shop's owner, one Joanne Nash, thanked me effusively for calling, told me the Dusty Attic would open at 10:00 A.M.—sharp!—and insisted that she just couldn't *wait* to meet me.

Joanne Nash, eh? Was she by any chance the Joanne I saw at Anton's studio yesterday? I started to leave a message, but changed my mind. For what I wanted to know I needed the face-to-face advantage. A trip to Yountville would be today's first order of business.

The stutter dial tone on my phone informed me that I had six new messages in my voice mailbox. Well, wasn't I the popular gal? Three were from my new buddies at the SFPD, Inspectors Crawford and Wilson, who wanted to talk to me at my earliest convenience, blah blah blah. Anthony Brazil had called, asking in his oh-so-refined way if I had made any progress on the drawings. *I'll be gettin' back to ya, Tony,* I thought as I erased the message. A gallery owner from London had called to urge me to "use my influence" to put a halt to the writing of Georges' memoirs. Fat chance. Grandfather had not called, surprise surprise. There was also a message from Mary saying she was taking off for a concert in Mendocino. Rats. I had hoped to drag her with me to Napa, since at the moment I was feeling frustrated and needed a dose of her cheery derring-do. Mary's call did remind me, though, that I still had to finish the sample boards and deliver them to my clients. I was supposed to be running a business, after all.

Having the new landlord breathing down my neck wasn't helping my mood. Since my campaign to win DeBenton over to my way of thinking wasn't going too well, it looked like I had a month to come up with some way to persuade him not to raise the rent. Or to figure out how to pay the exorbitant increase. Or to find a new studio. None of which, at the moment, seemed even remotely possible.

I needed that reward money from Anthony Brazil.

Picking up the phone again, I dialed the SFPD. Did homicide inspectors work on Saturdays?

"Homicide. Inspector Crawford."

They did.

"Annie Kincaid returning your call." I loved it when I sounded professional. It happened so rarely.

"Thank you for calling, Ms. Kincaid," she said crisply. "My partner and I are meeting with the board of directors of the Brock Museum this morning at eleven thirty. May I assume you will join us?"

According to the rules of grammar, the inspector had just asked me a question. Funny how much it had sounded like a command.

"Um, well, I've been awfully busy recently, Inspector," I replied. "And I'm afraid I've already made some plans for later this morning. I'm going to Nap—"

I caught myself at midsentence. I didn't know how much Inspector Crawford had figured out, but it seemed foolish to risk leading her to Anton.

While I was thinking this through, there was silence on the other end of the line. Then the inspector said, "Perhaps you could take your nap after the meeting, Ms. Kincaid."

Reluctantly, I agreed to be at the Brock at eleven thirty—I couldn't think of a way out of it—and hung up. It would take about two hours to drive to Yountville, so even if I left around one o'clock I should have plenty of time to get there before the antiques shop closed.

I considered going to the studio and getting some work done beforehand. After all, it had been all of five minutes since I'd been worrying about my finances. The problem was, by the time I showered, dressed, and drove into the City, I would have only about an hour until I had to leave again, which meant that I wouldn't be able to get into anything good and messy, like sample boards.

Finally I decided to take a walk to clear my head and shake the nervousness that had been plaguing me lately. If Stan Dupont had been killed because he stumbled across the truth about *The Magi,* and Ernst Pettigrew had disappeared because he knew the painting was a fake, then, as Inspector Crawford suggested yesterday, it stood to reason that anyone else who knew about the forgery was also in danger. Not that I was overly concerned about myself, since no one except Ernst and the SFPD could connect me to *The Magi.*

My apartment was only a few blocks from Lake Merritt, a tidal lake connected to the bay that was about three miles in circumference and encircled by a meandering pathway. There were several fountains, a couple of boathouses, a playground, and scores of squabbling ducks and geese. After half a mile I felt a surge of energy, and the leisurely stroll morphed into a power walk. It felt good to put the excess of adrenaline somewhere, and I vowed to exercise regularly. By the time I returned to my apartment and dragged myself up three flights of stairs I had, predictably enough, reconsidered.

I showered, blew my hair dry, and applied a touch of mascara, eyeliner, and lipstick before heading into the bedroom to dress for the meeting at the Brock. I was unsure what sort of image I wanted to present to this group of art mavens who had so thoroughly trashed my world. I wondered, in particular, whether Dr. Sebastian Pitts would be there.

Years ago, when Pitts had been a curator for Britain's elite Remington Museum, he had unwittingly trumpeted the authenticity of a number of my teenage forgeries. Art authentication is an inexact science, and all art authenticators make mistakes, but few made as many, and for such appalling reasons, as the oleaginous Pitts. When my grandfather decided to write an exposé of art authentica-

tors for the *London Times*—anonymously, of course—
Sebastian Pitts was a target too delicious to ignore, and
the ensuing scandal forced Pitts to resign from the Remington.

Unfortunately, he eventually resurfaced in San Francisco, where his academic credentials and snotty British
accent made him a darling of the art scene in a city where
only a gratifying few had so much as a nodding acquaintance with the *London Times*. I had been working for the
Brock for nearly a year, blissfully applying my talents to
legitimate restoration work, when Pitts recognized me.
One minute I was touching up a tiny Giotto religious
panel with egg tempera and twenty-four-karat gold leaf,
and the next I was banished from the Brock's hallowed
marble halls. Within a week, no reputable museum or
gallery in the City would return my calls.

Perhaps today was a chance for me to redeem myself,
if only a little. So: how best to dress for what was likely
to be a remarkably awkward meeting? Creative and
artsy? No, the line between artsy and tacky was a thin
one, and I didn't trust myself not to cross it. Buttoned-
down and businesslike? To the Brocks, success was
spelled *d-u-l-l*. Yes, that would work.

I almost never wore pantyhose and heels, which I was
convinced some demon had invented with the sole intent
of impoverishing and disabling intelligent women. But
sometimes one had to stoop to conquer, I reminded myself as I struggled into the pair of sheer black hose that I
saved for just such occasions. From the limited offerings
in my closet, I selected the conservative black wool
A-line skirt and matching waist-length jacket that my
mother had given me for my birthday last year. Since it
looked vaguely funereal, I decided to wear a red silk shell
under it. Red for power! Then I thought that might be pa-
thetically obvious, so I exchanged it for a coral-colored

shell that, I told myself hopefully, set off the auburn high-lights in my hair.

I slipped on my black leather pumps, the ones with the rubber soles and sensible two-inch block heels that I had bought because an advertisement on TV claimed they were comfortable enough to play basketball in. Which had turned out to be a big fat lie. But as heels went they weren't too bad, and they were reassuringly proper.

My sole concession to artiness was my jewelry. Around my neck I wore an exquisite hammered-silver chain with lines of garnet beads hanging down in strands beside a small antique key, which my friend Samantha had made me for my thirtieth birthday. She said it symbolized good fortune, and today I needed all the support—real and symbolic—that I could get.

I stood back and looked at myself in the nearly full-length mirror leaning against the wall in a corner of my bedroom. I looked businesslike. Respectable. Boring.

Perfect.

I was nearly out the door when I remembered the afternoon's itinerary. No way was I going to spend the afternoon in Napa in a wool suit, hose, and heels. Ducking into the bedroom, I grabbed the blue canvas tote I had received during a pledge drive at KQED, and shoved in a pair of jeans, a T-shirt, running shoes, socks, and a dark blue sweater. Now I was ready.

I felt pretty good about everything until I got to my truck and remembered I had yet to repair the broken window. By the time I crossed the Bay Bridge I would be my usual disheveled self. So much for respectability. My mood was not improved when I remembered that there were no casual carpools on Saturdays so I'd have to wait in line at the bridge and fork over the toll. I wondered if I could get the city to reimburse me, since I was on offi-

cial business. What was Inspector Crawford up to, anyway, and why were we meeting with the board?

I supposed the inspector wanted to go over my meeting with Ernst again, and thought that being at the
museum might jog my memory. Or maybe she wanted
me to take another look at *The Magi* with museum officials in attendance. I wondered if the board knew I was
coming, and whether they now realized that I had been
there that night. Perhaps I wasn't as anonymous as I
thought. On top of everything else, I could only assume
that Sebastian Pitts and Agnes Brock had wasted no time
in informing the police of my checkered past.

Arriving at the museum, I began the perennial search
for parking. Round and round I went, the added frustration doing nothing to calm me down. As I finally walked
up the broad granite steps to the entrance, ten minutes
late, I spied my SFPD escort waiting for me. Ichabod
nodded and the African Princess thanked me for coming.

The Brock was, as always, quiet. Too quiet. And not
because of the acoustics, either. The marble floor, walls,
and vaulted ceilings should have magnified sound, not
minimized it. I could only surmise that the Brock family's money had managed to corrupt even the laws of
physics. We passed through a set of heavily carved mahogany double doors into the administration wing and,
halfway down the hallway, turned into the Founders'
Conference Room.

Awaiting us was what promised to be the Meeting
from Hell. Grouped along one side of the absurdly large
and highly polished burled wood conference table was
everybody who had ever taken a dislike to me during my
brief tenure at the museum, and then some. The first un-
friendly face I saw belonged to Sebastian Pitts, who
curled his lip. Then came the Brocks: Agnes, the matriarch, who had signed the letter welcoming me into the

Brock Arts Internship Program seven years ago and personally ripped it up a year later; next to her was her only son and his wife, the boring Richard and the elegant Phoebe, both of whom I had met for all of twenty seconds at a Brock Employee Holiday Bash. There were also assorted lesser Brocks, each of whom had inherited the family's distinctive jutting brow ridge and protruding nose. The only non-Brock on the board was the sixty-year-old heiress Camilla Culpepper, a good friend of Mrs. Brock's. I knew Mrs. Culpepper only by her picture in the administrative lobby, but I remembered hearing that Camilla was so myopic she had once mistaken a Manet for a Monet. Thick, diamond-studded glasses hung unused from a filigree chain around her skeletal neck as she squinted at the attractive young man next to her. At least she was too distracted to glower at me as the rest were doing with what appeared to be varying degrees of ill will.

Never one to put off a confrontation she could enjoy immediately, Agnes Hilary Cuthbert Brock raised her plucked eyebrows, stared down her hawkish nose, and spoke. "My Caravaggio is most certainly *not* a forgery, young woman."

"Um . . ."

"The suggestion is supremely preposterous." Mrs. Brock's exquisite hauteur was marred just a smidgen by the fact that she spat a little getting out the *p*'s. Pitts surreptitiously wiped his glasses with a monogrammed handkerchief.

"The temerity! To challenge the word of Dr. Sebastian Pitts, the world's foremost expert on Caravaggio!"

I rolled my eyes. Pitts was no greater an authority on Caravaggio than he was on Cézanne, or, for that matter, on global warming. He was, however, a world-class sycophant.

"Um . . ." I tried again.

"I do not care to hear another word from you, young lady," Mrs. Brock informed me. "*The Magi* is exquisite, the jewel in the crown of the Brock collection. Unless you cease your outrageous slander this instant, I shall sue you for defamation."

Spit or no spit, Agnes was on a roll.

"Well? What have you to say for yourself?" she demanded, apparently forgetting that she had just ordered me to remain mute.

"Grandmother, for heaven's sake, let the poor woman speak."

I turned toward the unexpected source of support and saw a man sitting on my right who I assumed was Edward Brock, Richard and Phoebe's youngest son. He was about my age, give or take a few years, very tucked-in and preppy, with the look of an up-and-coming attorney or stockbroker.

"Yes, dahling," Camilla Culpepper said to Agnes. "Your handsome grandson is right. Let the woman speak."

All eyes slewed back to me.

"*Well?*" the dragon lady demanded shrilly.

I said nothing, trying to keep my temper in check. It wasn't my fault that her stupid painting was a fake, and I had had enough of her abuse. I didn't work for the family anymore, and I didn't have to take this crap.

"Speak! Speak!"

That did it.

"Woof!" I barked.

A collective gasp issued from the Brocks, though I could have sworn I heard a snort of laughter. It didn't come from Agnes Brock, that was for sure. The old woman made a choking sound, her face turned bright red, and for a horrible moment I thought she might collapse.

Taking advantage of the shocked silence, I spoke again, more reasonably this time.

"I realize this is an awkward situation," I told them. "Please bear in mind that the world's finest museums and galleries have bought and displayed fakes, and that those paintings had also been authenticated by experts—"

I thought my little speech was rather gracious under the circumstances, but apparently I was alone in this opinion, for at this point all hell broke loose. Sebastian Pitts and Agnes Brock leapt to their feet and started spewing invective, Edward Brock countered with a few tentative words in my defense, Camilla Culpepper seconded them, Richard and Phoebe Brock turned hotly on Edward and Camilla, the Brock cousins chimed in, and soon an all-out family shouting match was under way.

Inspector Crawford cleared her throat and a hush fell over the room. How does she *do* that? I wondered. When Pitts and old lady Brock took their seats, the inspector nodded at me.

"As I was saying," I continued, "I'm not trying to stir up trouble. But Ernst Pettigrew had his doubts about *The Magi,* despite the authentication." Note to self: avoid Sebastian Pitts' eyes, which were doing their best to turn me into a pillar of salt. "That's why he called me in. Whatever you may think of my personal history—indeed, for that very reason—if you are honest you will admit that I know forgeries when I see them. And there are several problems with the Caravaggio."

The conference room was now so quiet that I could hear the ticking of the ancient grandfather clock that Mrs. Brock's family had shipped all the way from Boston to California in 1852.

"First, the brushstrokes are off," I explained. "Not all of them, but in the background—"

"It was common in the sixteenth century for lesser

artists, or for artists-in-training, to fill in the backgrounds for the master artists," Sebastian Pitts interrupted. "Background work required minimal skill, and delegating it to assistants saved the masters a great deal of time, allowing them to create other masterpieces."

"True enough, but as I am sure you will recall, Dr. Pitts, Caravaggio was vilified by his peers because of his scalawag lifestyle, and cast out of society altogether when he was accused of killing a man over a tennis match," I responded. "He was a solo act. As I was saying, Caravaggio didn't use his brush that way, nor did he work in a studio with those who did.

"Second, until the eighteenth century blue oil paint was made from semiprecious stones, like lapis lazuli and azurite. It was extremely expensive, and used primarily by artists with rich patrons. Caravaggio could rarely afford it, yet in this painting the Christ child's blanket is lapis blue. The unusual use of color is another red flag that *The Magi* might be a fake.

"And finally, the lighting on Balthazar's face is off ever so slightly, and as you all know, Caravaggio's chiaroscuro, or dramatic use of light and shadow, was his trademark. The lighting here isn't wildly wrong, but it's not as strong as I would expect to see in a Caravaggio."

I stopped there. These problems alone were sufficient to cast grave doubts upon the painting's authenticity. But there were other, far more damning ones that I decided not to share with the Brocks and the inspectors. Thanks to my grandfather's tutelage, I had recognized that the apparent flaw in the lighting was not a mistake. It was an inside joke—a sure tip-off that the painting was a fraud.

One of the biggest problems an art forger faces is his or her own ego. It takes years of training and remarkable talent for an artist to create a copy worthy of being acclaimed as a true masterpiece, and in the end the forger does not have the satisfaction of claiming credit for the work. However, I knew that few forgers could resist secretly "signing" their best pieces. One of the keys to unmasking fakes by known forgers, therefore, was to know what signature to look for.

The trick with the lighting and the addition of a touch of lapis blue were Anton's signature. Grandfather's was the tiniest little hatch marks in the mottled background color. My signature, when I was forging Old Master drawings, had been the slight smile I gave to one of the subjects in the scene. Before the twentieth century, drawings or paintings rarely portrayed their subject smiling, and thus those that did were much more valuable. Unfortunately, my signature proved to be my downfall when I raised suspicions by flooding the market with too many smiles.

I said none of this to the group assembled. I wasn't about to rat out Anton. Or Grandfather. Or myself.

Predictably, Pitts was unconvinced and launched into a long and inventive tirade during which he condemned me, my grandfather, and pretty much all those of artistic temperament. When he finally wound down, he demanded we view *The Magi* so he could put the issue to rest, once and for all. Striding dramatically across the conference room to the covered painting on an easel in the corner just behind me, Pitts yanked off the cloth with a flourish and revealed *The Magi*.

The brush marks were consistent with Caravaggio's style, the Christ child's blanket was a classic Venetian red, the lighting on Balthazar's face was perfect.

I started to sweat. My face grew flushed, and the muscles at the base of my skull began to cramp. My wool suit was itchy and stifling. It was hard to breathe.

I walked over to the painting and peered at the background. There they were, plain as day: tiny, exquisite hatch marks. Georges François LeFleur, art forger extraordinaire, had struck again.

I looked up dully. Pitts' round face was split with a smile, relishing the prospect of my imminent humiliation. I caught Inspector Crawford's eye.

"May I speak with you for a moment, Ms. Kincaid?" she asked. I could have kissed her.

"Certainly, Inspector," I said, already halfway out the door. Ichabod followed us into the mahogany-lined hallway, shutting the door behind us.

"What just happened in there?" Crawford asked. "What did you see?"

"It's a fake."

"Yes, you've already said that."

"No, it's a *different* fake."

"*What?*" For the first time since we'd met, Inspector Crawford's face registered surprise. "Are you sure?"

"Quite."

"Why would anyone paint two fakes?" Ichabod piped up.

"They're two different fakes. Painted by two different forgers."

The inspectors stared at me. I shrugged. Well, *I* didn't do it.

"Do you recognize the artists?" Inspector Crawford asked.

"Why ask me?" I demanded disingenuously. "It's not as though I'm in the forgery business."

In politics, this was called the non-denial denial.

"Sebastian Pitts and Agnes Brock have suggested otherwise," Ichabod replied.

I shrugged again, in a "What can you expect from such people?" kind of way.

"You haven't answered my question," said the suddenly perceptive Ichabod, leaving me to recall his former silences with fondness.

"All I know is that the painting in that room is *not* the same painting Ernst Pettigrew showed me the other night, nor is it a genuine Caravaggio."

I was going to *kill* my grandfather.

"Okay, you two, that's enough," Inspector Crawford interjected. "This isn't getting us anywhere. Wilson, please see Ms. Kincaid to her car. I need to speak to the board."

Once again the Brock Museum had been the scene of my professional humiliation, and I hurried outside, Ichabod a silent escort. A few minutes later Crawford caught up with us as we started down the front steps. She looked royally pissed, but I wasn't sure at whom.

"How well do you know the Brock family?" she asked abruptly.

"Not very. I met Agnes Brock when I worked here, because for all intents and purposes it's her museum, but mostly I dealt with her secretary. The others I know only by reputation."

"What kind of reputation?"

"Richard Brock and his wife, Phoebe, are socialites, and they crop up in the society columns," I said as we reached the sidewalk and paused in the shade of a thirty-foot-tall palm tree. "I met them at a Christmas party, but I doubt they'd remember me. The interns used to call them Dull Dick and Fabulous Phoebe because he's so boring and she's such a clotheshorse. I never met their children. Rumor had it that Cousin Frederick wanted to bump off Mrs. Brock and take over, but that was probably just gossip."

"Any of the others?"

"Only by sight, and then only because of the Brock brow ridge, which you must have noticed. Mrs. Culpepper would show up for events and board meetings, but I never really met her. I heard she had an eye for young men, but rumors are always swirling in a place like this. It's just the nature of the institutional beast."

"Did you know anything about security when you worked here?"

"Just procedure."

"Who would have access to the vault?"

"Besides Mrs. Brock? Well, the head curators, of course. Probably Sebastian Pitts. But that wasn't the sort of thing that concerned interns, and we weren't allowed near the vault."

"What about the rest of the family?"

"As far as I knew, they showed up for parties but weren't involved in the museum's day-to-day business. It's been a while, though, so that might have changed. Agnes Brock always wanted the museum to remain in the family's control."

"Mm-hmm," she murmured, flipping through her notes. "What about the janitor?"

"You mean Stan Dupont? I don't think so. I never saw any Housekeeping staff in the vault, but then I wasn't there myself. The current staff would be able to tell you more, surely." I glanced at my watch. Quarter after twelve. "If it's all the same to you, I'd like to get going now."

The ten-minute walk to my truck helped clear my mind, but I still sighed with relief when I climbed behind the wheel and headed for the Golden Gate Bridge and points north.

Two fakes, two forgers, and one murder were adding up to one big boatload of trouble.

Chapter 7

Those who are not skilled artisans should never attempt to forge Old Masters. Instead, they should use their lack of talent to forge twentieth-century art, for which a dearth of artistic ability is routine. Even advantageous.

—Georges LeFleur, "Modern Masters?" unfinished
manuscript, Reflections of a World-Class Art Forger

My cell phone chirped and I snatched it up, hoping it was Grandfather. I stabbed blindly at the ON button, afraid to take my eyes off the busy approach to the Golden Gate Bridge. "*Allô oui?*"

"Wee wee yourself, Annie." It was Pedro. "What's with the fran-SAY?"

"Well, you know me"—I slammed on the brakes to avoid a collision with a faded blue Volkswagen Beetle that was covered with bumper stickers proclaiming its owner's outré political beliefs—"I hate to miss a chance to sound Frenchified."

"Listen, nothing checks out on your Michael Johnson as a PI, with or without an *X*. Oh, and I overestimated. I only got eighty-two thousand hits on the name."

"Uh-huh," I grunted.

"There's a Mike Johnson, but he's sixty-four years old and lives in Eureka, so I'm thinkin' he's not your guy. There are sixteen other licensed private eyes named Johnson, but no other Mikes."

Just as I suspected. "Okay, thanks for trying," I said, focusing on keeping my non-power-steering-equipped truck in its lane as I wheeled through the twists and turns of the wooded Presidio and headed for the Golden Gate. "What do I owe you?"

"Dinner. A cheap one. It took me all of thirty minutes. You should learn to do this yourself, toots."

"Naw, you know I like having you on call, snookums. Oh, and Pedro, one more thing. Actually, two things. I need Ernst Pettigrew's address."

"The Brock Museum dude who disappeared? Have you checked the phone book?"

"Uh, nope. Good idea. Okay, second item: I need background information on a friend of his, Quiana something. Q-u-i-a-n-a. I don't have a last name, but she's Ernst's girlfriend. Maybe a live-in."

"What's this guy to you, Annie?" Pedro asked. "You're not involved in this Brock thing, are you?"

As far as I knew, Pedro did not know about my less-than-completely-lawful past. So why did my friends always assume I would slip off the straight and narrow at the drop of a paintbrush?

"No, I'm not 'involved.' Just say no if I'm asking too much."

"Don't get snippy, *m'ija*. I was just curious. I'll check her out. You be careful."

"Thanks, Pedro. You're a pal."

I zipped around a lumbering tourist bus and onto the bridge. This maneuver required concentration. The graceful Golden Gate carried six lanes of traffic, two lanes headed north, two lanes headed south, and two lanes in the middle that changed directions during commute hours. Nothing separated you from the oncoming traffic except itty-bitty plastic rectangles stuck in the asphalt. To make things still more interesting, the cars were usually buffeted by gusting ocean crosswinds. However, the view from the bridge was spectacular, and I probably would have appreciated it had I not been so intent on maintaining my death grip on the steering wheel.

Safely aground on the other side, I entered Marin County, passing the quaint town of Sausalito on my right. Steadily expanding development had been rapidly chewing up former grasslands and spitting out high-tech companies, chain restaurants, and those god-awful McMansions so beloved by nouveau riche computerites.

This time when my cell phone rang, I risked a glance at the caller ID. It was an international number. "You are in very deep doo-doo, old man," I told my grandfather.

"*Cherie!*" Grandfather's resonant voice sang through the static.

"I'm serious, Georges," I said, using his Christian name, as I often did when I was angry with him. "You have *got* to tell me what's going on. *Now.*"

"Going on? Zis I do not understand. Whatever are you talking about, my darling girl?"

I took a deep breath and counted to ten. "*The Magi,* Grandpére." The old reprobate got all warm and fuzzy when I called him Grandpére. Worth a shot. "Ring a bell?"

"*Mais non! Ce n'est pas possible!* Who in ze world would be audacious enough to forge ze great Caravaggio's lost painting?" Grandfather's French accent was getting thicker by the second, a sure sign he was lying through his expensive false teeth. So much for warm and fuzzy.

"Who said anything about a forgery, Grandfather? All I mentioned was the name of the painting. Don't tell me you're losing your edge. Listen, old man, I saw the painting with my own two eyes, and it's yours right down to the hatch marks in the background and the perfect lighting. Don't even try to deny it. This is serious stuff. One person's already been murdered over it."

Silence followed. Georges delighted in fooling rich people and stealing their money, but he abhorred violence. "Murdered? Who?"

The minute his accent slipped, I knew I had his attention.

"Stan Dupont, a janitor at the Brock Museum and a very nice man," I said, stretching the truth a bit. "On top of that, the head curator, Ernst Pettigrew, is missing and I can't seem to find Anton."

"What does Anton have to do with this?"

"You tell me."

"Ah, *cherie,* I don't see how you can tie your dear old grandpapa into this. I may have executed a charming copy for a distinguished client, but zat is all," he replied, sounding more relaxed.

"Who, Georges? Who commissioned the forgery? And when?"

"I can't hear you, darling! *Allô? Allô?* Ah, *ma petite,* I am zo zorry, we air lozing ze connection . . . Annie, we air lozing ze connection . . ."

"Georges! Don't you dare hang up! Grandfather!"

Dead air. I stabbed the OFF button savagely, wishing I could throw the phone at my grandfather's elegant gray head. "We air lozing ze connection" my ass. With only one eye on the road, I switched the phone on and poked the tiny button that would automatically return Grandfather's call.

A woman answered. "*Allô oui?*"

"Georges LeFleur, *s'il vous plaît, madam,*" I said.

"*Comment?*" she replied, using the polite version of "huh?"

"Monsieur Georges LeFleur, *s'il vous plaît,*" I repeated more slowly.

"*Quoi?*"

"*Georges LeFleur!* Don't give me that crap, madam! I know he's there!" I was shouting now, having given up on both politeness and fran-SAY. I could have sworn I heard Grandfather chortling in the background, delighted with his clever ruse.

"*Bof!*" The woman hung up.

Shit! Shit shit shit! Georges was in this up to his fake French neck. And he would not tell me anything until he was good and ready.

Why would anyone commission two forgeries of the same painting? One could be used to replace a stolen original, but two? For that matter, why bother to replace the original with a forgery? Why not just steal the damn thing and be gone, like a good thief should?

I mulled this over as the truck steadily ate up the miles to Yountville. Soon small towns began to dot the landscape. In the summer the two-lane Route 29 was bumper to bumper as refugees from the city hurried to relax in the mud baths and natural hot springs of Calistoga, and to indulge themselves at the many picturesque wineries and top-notch restaurants. Today, in midwinter, the traffic slowed to a crawl only once or twice, so I arrived at my destination before three o'clock.

Yountville was a small collection of fine homes, adorable shops, and exquisite restaurants, all surrounded by vineyards. I was eager to check out the Dusty Attic, but was hot and sticky in my suit and a little woozy from a lack of food. Yountville was the kind of town where even mom-and-pop stores sold cappuccino, fresh pasta salads, and sandwiches made of sun-dried tomatoes, portobello mushrooms, and locally produced goat cheese served on freshly baked, grilled panini. I ordered one of each, and while the proprietor whipped up my lunch, I changed my clothes in the restroom. At home again in my jeans, T-shirt, and running shoes, I took my food to a picnic table at the edge of a vineyard.

As I sat gazing out at the gently rolling hills covered in bare grapevines, enjoying the sunny February day, I pondered what I might find at the Dusty Attic, or what I even wanted to find. Other than Anton or the stolen drawings, that is. There was nothing to connect Anton to the shop except the word of the Stranger in Vesuvio's, which was not exactly an unimpeachable source.

The fact of the matter was that, although the need for money and the obligations of friendship drove me to find the drawings and Anton, the whole thing was starting to get a little scary, especially now that the Brock family knew that I knew about *The Magi,* which meant that the whole damn art world would soon know that I knew. Including the murderer.

Then again, now that the forgery of *The Magi* was out of the bag, I was not in danger from anyone who may have killed Dupont to keep that knowledge a secret. Assuming, of course, that was the reason he had been killed.

But what I could not figure out was why *The Magi* had been forged twice. The most common use for a forgery was to hide the fact that the original had been stolen or sold. But if this was the case, it seemed unlikely that the Dusty Attic had anything to do with that particular painting. It would be like trying to sell Elvis Presley's Rolls-Royce at Smilin' Sam's Used Car Lot—it was going to stick out amid the banged-up Fords and Chevys.

So the *Magi* forgeries must have been commissioned to disguise the fact that the original had been stolen from the Brock. If so, who was likely to be involved?

Ernst Pettigrew? Maybe he had switched the paintings—after all, he had access to the vault where the painting was stored—and had brought me in as part of the cover-up. Ernst knew my background. Had he been setting me up? A famous painting goes missing, a shocked curator discovers the fraud, and voilà! a former forger is on hand to take the fall.

But if this were true, why would Ernst have disappeared? I was starting to fear that he was gone for good. I hated to even imagine it. Then again, it was almost as unthinkable to believe that Ernst had taken part in anything criminal.

On top of everything else, I had gotten so caught up in *The Magi* imbroglio that I had forgotten the real moneymaker in this mess: the missing drawings. They were far more easily bought and sold than a masterpiece painting and could be stashed in a small antiques store if they became too hot to handle. Where better to hide them than out in the open, among far less valuable sketches and paintings? Perhaps Anton had dumped the drawings at the Dusty Attic until things cooled off, or asked Joanne to sell the sketches, no questions asked.

Or maybe she was a friend whom he visited for a weekend, who had nothing whatsoever to do with anything. Except—she had taken that portfolio from his studio as if she knew what was in it—or what *should* have been in it.

So many questions, and only one way to get some answers.

I gathered up my crumpled napkins and empty coffee cup, tossed them in the trash can on my way to the truck, revved the engine, and drove off toward the Dusty Attic.

I felt a surge of hopefulness. Joanne and I might hit it off. We would commiserate over rascally old art forgers and the ways they could better apply their talents. She would lean back, reach under the counter, and bring out a portfolio of genuine Old Master drawings worth tens of thousands of dollars. "Here you go, Annie," she would say to me. "I want them to be well taken care of, and I know you're the woman for the job." Hmm.

I had a *Thomas Guide* for Napa County, so I found Landacre Street easily enough and pulled up in front of the Dusty Attic. It was a cute bungalow, one of several on the street that had been turned into boutiques and curio shoppes. Dormer windows indicated a second story, and I wondered if Joanne Nash, like many small-business owners, lived above her shop.

I climbed out of my truck and crunched up the gravel path to the front door. I would have thought that a warm, sunny weekend afternoon would bring out a few customers, but there were no signs of life. On the front door hung a cheerful buttercup-yellow wooden sign, decorated with hand-painted blue pansies, that announced the shop's hours were WED. THRU SUN., 10 TO 5. It was now three thirty on Saturday.

I pounded loudly on the periwinkle-blue door, in case someone was in a back room, and waited, but got no response. I tried calling Joanne's number on my cell phone, but the machine picked up once again. Finally, I followed a neat brick pathway around the side of the house. A white picket fence surrounded the small garden, which was filled with carefully tended flower beds of irises and daffodils, outlined by box hedges. At the rear of the yard, under a mulberry tree, sat a white wicker chaise longue. It was serene and inviting, the neighboring yards scarcely visible through the leafy foliage.

Knocking on the back door, I called out for Joanne, but once again there was no answer. Frustrated, I returned to the front of the house and peeked in the window to the left of the door, trying to see around the pink chintz café curtains. But what with the bright sun outside, the shadowy gloom inside, and Joanne's apparent disinterest in window washing, I could not see much of anything.

I pressed my nose against the glass and cupped my hands around my face to block out the light. As my eyes adjusted I began to make out a great jumble of stuff, but it was clear that the mess within was not the usual antiques shop potpourri. Bits and pieces were tossed everywhere: books lay on their backs, pages fanning the air; furniture was overturned and the stuffing ripped out; shards of smashed china and pottery littered the wood floor. Either Joanne Nash was the world's worst antiques dealer, or something out of the ordinary had happened in there.

Intent as I was on surveying the damage, I forgot to worry about a lurking murderer.

Until I felt a puff of breath on the back of my neck.

I yelped and whirled around, leaping several feet in the air. Despite my frenzy of activity, I accomplished nothing that would have helped in terms of self-defense. The moment I landed on earth again a large hand covered my mouth and I was backed up against the dirty window. Luckily—I supposed—the body pressing into mine was a particularly nice-smelling one.

The X-man was back.

"Shut the hell up," he growled.

I looked over his shoulder to the parking lot, chagrined to see that not only had he walked up behind me while I was peering in the window, but he had driven a red Jeep into the gravel lot and parked without my noticing. Maybe this was not the best time for self-reflection, but I thought I might want to reconsider the whole cloak-and-dagger thing. I did not seem to have much aptitude for it.

Just then, a car came down the street toward us, slowing as it approached. Michael leaned into me and ducked his head, his lips gently brushing my cheek, as if we were indulging in a lovers' sweet embrace right there in the doorway of the Dusty Attic. Well, this *was* a town for honeymooners. The car rolled on past.

We shared a look as Michael reached around me to try the front door. Locked. Pivoting neatly on his heel, he walked along the front of the building and around the corner.

I hustled along behind him. "What are you doing here?" I demanded

"I was about to ask you the same thing," he snarled in return.

"You scared the hell out of me."

"You didn't exactly soothe my nerves either, screaming like that," he retorted as we reached the rear of the house.

Michael tried the door handle and then the windows, but they were all locked. He pulled up the doormat.

"Like she'd leave a key under the mat," I jeered.

"You'd be surprised."

I spied a bronze elf with an evil grin in a flower bed to the left of the back door. Seemed promising. I knocked it over with my foot. Nothing.

Michael looked under some potted plants, a coiled garden hose, a few plastic lawn chairs. No luck. Finally, he banged on the back door and demanded that someone open up. No one did.

So he picked up the heavy elf and smashed a pane in one of the windows next to the door.

I screamed. Just a little. More like a screech, really. Faux finishers don't normally do a lot of breaking and entering.

Michael glared. "*Will* you shut up already?"

I bit my tongue. Literally. I think I was a little pumped on adrenaline.

The X-man reached through the broken windowpane, flipped the latch, and slid the double-hung window up. Then, taking off his padded windbreaker, he wrapped it around his hand, brushed the glass shards away, and spread the jacket on the sill before effortlessly hoisting himself onto the four-foot-high ledge, swinging his long legs around to the inside, and dropping out of sight.

"Michael? Hello?"

I had a sneaking suspicion that if I was waiting for a hand up I was going to wait a very long time. Grumbling to myself, I walked over to the window, put my hands on the jacket-covered ledge, and hoisted away.

I managed to get about six inches off the ground. I tried to "walk the wall" the way Ms. Ortone had shown us in eleventh-grade gym class, but since that maneuver didn't work any better now than it had then, all I accomplished was a lot of straining and huffing and banging on the siding with my shoes. I let go and dropped back down to the flower bed.

Grumbling aloud now, I dragged a blue garden chair over and positioned it beneath the window. I stepped cautiously onto the frame of the seat as it rocked from side to side. Fortunately, a lifetime of foolishness had inured me to public humiliation. I did not mind looking stupid so long as the odds of success were reasonable.

Using my rib cage as leverage, I managed to get my upper body past the windowsill, and ended up hanging facedown inside the house. Unfortunately, my hips were still stuck on the ledge. I was trying to wriggle free when I looked up to find Michael's face about six inches from mine.

He had crouched down and was contemplating me as I hung there, head down and butt in the air like Pooh stuck in Rabbit's hole. A smile spread slowly across his face, making his green eyes go ever so slightly crinkly.

"I opened the door for you," he said simply.

"Ah," I said, wondering whether it would be less foolish to go forward or backward. Either option pretty much sucked. Retreat seemed to endanger the fewest body parts, so I went for it, but my feet could not find the chair. I tossed them around a bit, but to no avail, so I tried to scoot backward. This was an unfortunate decision, because the windowsill was pressing hard into my diaphragm, which meant that each time I kicked or scooted, air was forced out of my lungs and I grunted like a pig.

"What in the world are you doing?" Michael asked in wonder.

The only way the situation could possibly have been more embarrassing would have been if I'd had a sudden attack of uncontrollable flatulence. Given the way this day was going, the odds were not in my favor.

Michael sighed, went outside, grabbed me by the hips, and guided me backward.

"Thanks," I said, wiping my hands on my jeans nonchalantly.

"Any time," he said, handing me a pair of latex surgical gloves. "Put these on."

"Why?"

"Because, although you and I know we're not criminally inclined, the fact is we have no right to be here," he said. "I think it would be best if we didn't leave our fingerprints all over everything."

While I struggled with my gloves, he snapped his on with brisk efficiency, then wiped the windowsill and door with a blue-striped handkerchief. Clearly, this was not his first breaking-and-entering. Michael gestured "after you" with his latexed hand, and I preceded him through the back door.

"Wow," I exclaimed as we surveyed the damage. "This is terrible. What do you think they were looking for?"

"Same thing you are," he replied.

"Did you know Johnson is the most common last name in the U.S.?"

"What?"

"You heard me."

"Yes, I did. It just seems an odd thing to bring up."

"Not really. Who did you say you worked for?"

"Excuse me?"

"Oh, right. Pardon my grammar. For whom do you work?"

Finally, he smiled. "Raymond Ozeki," he told me.

"Raymond Ozeki? What kind of name is Ozeki?"

"What is it with you and names? I didn't christen the guy, I just work for him."

"No you don't."

"Yes I do."

"No you don't."

"Yes I do."

"*No* you *don't*." I could keep this up all day. I had been a bratty younger sister once. The X-man was out of his league.

"I don't?"

"No you don't, because you're not a PI!"

"Yes I am."

Hmm. He was better at this than I had thought. Maybe he had been a bratty younger brother once.

"No you're not. There's no use denying it."

"Then what am I?"

"You're trespassing, that's what."

"And you're not trespassing because, what, Joanne Nash is practically your aunt?"

I glared at him. He smirked at me. The trashed antiques shop came back into focus.

"What a mess," I said. Michael was standing next to a long counter near the rear wall that Joanne Nash appeared to have used as a desk.

"Check behind the counter," I said. "I had a visual of her keeping the drawings there."

"You had a vision? What are you, a Psychic Friend?"

"Not a *vision,* moron, a *visual.*"

Michael's temper seemed to get shorter the longer he was around me. I was having that effect on a lot of people lately.

"Just look," I said.

"I'm looking, I'm looking," he groused. "It's not as though I'm the first. If there was anything obvious to be found, it's been found already."

Nonetheless, we sifted through the bric-a-brac and combed the scattered contents of upside-down drawers. I found a bunch of old drawings and started sorting through them, in case the precious sketches had been hidden "in plain sight" among less valuable ones. Time passed slowly. It was dusty, tedious work—never my strong suit.

Next I began searching Joanne's many canvas paintings, in case the drawings had been tucked into the frames or between layers of canvas. It was an old smugglers' trick to disguise great art behind wretched art.

"So," I said, for conversation's sake, as I abandoned the canvas search and pawed halfheartedly through a hatbox overflowing with old lace, most of which was stained, ripped, or moth-eaten. "What brings you to Napa?"

"You," he answered without hesitation.

I looked over to where he stood flipping through a stack of picture frames, and felt a smile tug at the corners of my mouth.

"Really?" I asked, pushing aside a Tiffany-style lamp and opening an old tooled-leather trunk with brass fittings.

"Really," he said, moving on to a battered file cabinet covered with orange and pink flowered stickers circa 1972. "You mean you didn't notice a bright red Jeep following you all the way from the Brock Museum? It's amazing you've survived this long, you know that?"

"I don't believe you," I protested. "I would've noticed a bright red Jeep. I hate Jeeps. They're always owned by people who live in the city and have no use for four-wheel drive."

"Whether you hate Jeeps or not is immaterial. The fact remains that I followed you here."

"So what were you doing at the Brock Museum, anyway?" I demanded, climbing over the trunk to get at a carved walnut sideboard that had been overturned.

"Appreciating art, of course. I am a great admirer of beauty." He tossed a leer in my direction.

I wasn't buying it. My grandfather had taught me the many uses of flattery to distract a listener.

"Uh-huh. Then why'd you decide to leave the museum and follow me?"

"Oh, just curious. Besides, I had nothing better to do."

I glared at him as he stood hunched over an open file drawer. I had covered half my self-selected search quadrant, while Super Sleuth was stuck with his head in the file cabinet. "What's taking you so long over there?"

"I like to be thorough," he replied softly.

I spent the next few moments examining a Victorian fainting couch and wondering whether he did everything as thoroughly. Probably.

I noticed some silver frames on a mahogany end table, most of which held sepia-toned prints. However, what stopped me in my tracks were the glamour shots of the elegant woman with catlike eyes whom I had last seen leaving Vesuvio's in North Beach.

I was about to say something when tires crunched in the gravel parking lot out front. For a long moment we gaped at each other, cartoon fashion, then Michael stepped from behind the counter, grabbed my arm, and pulled me into a shallow alcove beneath the stairs.

"This seems strangely familiar," he whispered, his breath tickling my ear as we crouched behind a dusty purple velvet curtain.

We fell silent when the new arrival knocked on the front door and tried the knob. More gravel crunched as footsteps circled the house, approaching the back door.

The door slowly swung open, flooding the room with the pinkish-orange glow of twilight. I held my breath. For several minutes we listened to a general banging around and shuffling of papers that suggested a search was being conducted. I had a sinking feeling that we might be stuck here a while if the newcomer decided to examine the same stuff we had been riffling through for the last hour and a half.

I was beginning to regret squatting instead of sitting when I heard footsteps on the treads just above us. Our heads swiveled in unison as we followed the sounds of the intruder moving about upstairs. I heard a door open and then the creaking of the floorboards stopped abruptly, only to begin again, faster this time, as the intruder flew down the stairs and out the back door. An engine roared and I heard gravel spurting as the vehicle sped away.

Michael and I stared at each other. Had the intruder found what he or she had been searching for—whatever that might be? Had I let the drawings slip through my fingers?

"Maybe we should have looked upstairs," I suggested.

"You think?"

Hiding seemed to bring out the X-man's rude side.

My knees protested as we stood up.

"What is *that*?" I asked, my nose wrinkling, as we approached the stairs.

"What?" Michael asked, looking around.

"That smell. Gack." I was nearly gagging, afraid I knew what it was. About a year ago, a rat had died under the eaves of my apartment house. The smell got pretty funky and I had had to sleep with all the windows open for days. The closer we got to the stairs, the more something up there smelled like that dead rat. And then some. Opening the windows was not going to solve the problem this time.

I indicated that Michael should feel free to go first.

The stairs led to a short hallway with three doors opening off it. It was hot and stuffy up here, and the smell was much stronger.

Michael started down the hall and I followed, glancing over my shoulder somewhat compulsively. I bumped into him when he stopped to open a door.

"Sorry." I started to giggle nervously. Michael gave me a look. Grasping the door handle, he jerked it open to expose a small linen closet, which revealed nothing more sinister than Joanne's fetish for embroidered sheets.

We proceeded down the hall.

Behind the next door was a bedroom decorated in a pretty, feminine style. Empty.

We turned back to the hall.

The last door, partly open, led to what appeared to be a study. Michael took a step into the room before his arm shot out to keep me from following him. Later I would think of this as a patronizing but endearing gesture. At the time, my response was to bat his arm aside and blunder in.

I drew a sharp breath preparatory to a scream but ended up with a mouthful of cotton shirt when Michael grabbed me and pressed my face into his chest. I got a grip on myself and pushed him away.

I had never seen a dead body that was not dressed up and surrounded by flowers, so I was uncertain what corpses looked like before the funeral home makeover. If this was it, it was not good.

On the floor of the study was the woman we had seen at Anton's studio yesterday. Poor Joanne lay on her side, her arms flung out as if in surrender. Dried blood matted her ash blond hair and formed a red halo around her head.

I always thought that our last mortal act was to close our eyes. Joanne's, on the contrary, stared at us unblinkingly. I recalled how attractive she had been yesterday—how vibrantly alive—and felt a wave of sadness at the death of a stranger.

"I swear to God, I don't know what the art world is coming to," Michael said, then looked at me. "Let's get the hell out of here."

"Wait." My voice was tinny and sounded far away. "There's something underneath her."

"What?"

"Something. Underneath her."

Poking out from under Joanne's back were some drawings. From this distance, in the dim light, I could not tell if they were the originals or the forgeries. Michael swore softly, took a deep breath, stepped over to the body, and eased one of the drawings out from under an arm.

It was one of the sketches stolen from my truck last night, now partially soaked in blood. Anton's work. Michael held up a second drawing, but I had seen enough. "They're Anton's forgeries. Leave them."

Michael nodded. "Let's get the hell out of here," he said again.

We hurried out of the room and started down the stairs, but as we neared the bottom we heard a scraping at the front door. The early winter evening was now upon us, and we saw a flashlight beam glinting through the transom.

"Shit," we whispered simultaneously.

Flying back up the stairs, past the linen closet and the bedroom, we turned into the study and nipped behind the door. My heart was racing, my breath was labored, and I was trying, without success, to remember why I'd thought chasing forgers to Napa was a good idea.

We stood there listening to someone rummaging around below. Time seemed to have stalled, and I could have sworn an hour passed. Then we heard whoever it was climb the stairs and come down the hall toward us. Magically, time sped up.

Through the crack near the door hinges I stared at the shadow this new intruder cast on the wall. He looked even bigger than my old pal No Neck. The absurdly broad shoulders and square head were reminiscent of the Incredible Hulk, except I did not think the Incredible Hulk carried a gun. The shadow revealed that this hulk was clutching a really big one.

Michael grabbed a Chinese porcelain vase from a bookshelf and held it high over his head.

It all happened so fast. Just as the Hulk entered the room, Michael stepped out from behind the door and slammed the fragile porcelain onto the back of his head, shattering the vase into a thousand pieces. He followed up with what looked like a karate chop to the neck, a chop that the Hulk blocked with his gun hand while punching Michael in the gut with his other.

Michael grabbed the gun and they wrestled for control, walking in a strange embrace backward into the hallway, before falling to the ground and rolling toward the stairs. Michael was putting up one hell of a fight, but the Hulk outweighed him by at least fifty pounds.

I could not tell what, if anything, Michael's plan was, but I knew I was being no help at all. I grabbed a large, sharp piece of the broken vase with the idea of stabbing the Hulk with it, but the hallway was so narrow, and the two men were flinging themselves about with such energy, that it was impossible to be sure of landing a good jab without inadvertently wounding Michael. Just as I spied an opening and was moving in for the kill, the men started tumbling down the stairs.

I squeezed my eyes shut for a moment and tried to discern whose grunts were whose. When I opened them again I saw that the men had landed at the bottom, where they continued their deadly duel, thrashing about amid the broken furniture and shattered pottery of the shop. I half ran, half slid down the stairs and looked about frantically for something better than a broken vase with which to attack the Hulk. A big leather book? A tacky watercolor? An evil elf?

The elf statuette lay on the floor near the back window, where Michael had dropped it after smashing the windowpane in what now seemed like far more innocent times.

The elf was bronze. It was heavy. It should work.

I snatched it up and started circling the struggling fighters, trying to time their movements and work up my courage. Finally I took a deep breath and rushed in, swinging the heavy elf around and down somewhat at random.

I might have screamed. I don't remember.

The evil elf glanced off Michael's brow on its way to smacking firmly against the Hulk's crown. Both men went down.

The Hulk stayed down.

Michael crouched on the ground, his rear in the air, groaning and swearing like a drunken sailor. After a moment he rocked back on his knees, pressed the heel of his right hand to an area just above his right eyebrow, and glared at me.

"Jesus Christ, Annie! You *hit* me!"

"I didn't mean to. Besides, I hit *him* harder," I said, pointing to the Hulk, who lay unconscious and bleeding on the floor. "Let's try to see the big picture, shall we?"

Michael did not answer. He also did not look so hot.

"Maybe we should get you to a doctor," I said uncertainly.

"I don't need a *doctor*," he spat. "I need a *drink*. Badly."

I looked over at the Hulk, who was still motionless, and bit my lower lip anxiously.

"Do you think I killed him?"

The Hulk groaned as if on cue.

"I think that's a 'No,'" Michael replied. "Let's go before he comes around."

We sprinted out the back door into the cool evening air, down a dirt alley to the road beyond, and around the corner. I started toward my truck and skidded to a halt.

It was not there.

Michael gestured toward his Jeep.

"I moved it."

"You did *what*?"

"I moved your truck. I'll explain later. Get in the Jeep, Annie."

"Where is it?" I was furious at his high-handedness. I needed my truck.

"*Get in the goddamn Jeep!*" Michael shouted.

Since we were fleeing a crime scene containing one dead body and one very angry Hulk, my fear overrode my fury, and I decided to worry about the truck later.

"You drive. I'm a mess," Michael said, tossing me the keys.

We hopped in. My hands were shaking. I tossed the evil elf, which I was still holding, into the backseat.

"What the hell is that?" Michael demanded.

I ignored him until I got the engine started and the lights turned on. "What does it look like? I kind of forgot I was holding it. Besides, it's evidence. It may have some of the Hulk's blood, maybe some of your hair and skin and stuff, too."

"Blech," he said.

I slammed the Jeep into gear and peeled out, spewing gravel behind us. I heard some sputtering from the passenger seat and looked over to see Michael laughing weakly. The pain from his head wound was probably preventing more energetic guffaws.

"You've spent the last how many days looking for fabulously valuable artwork, and you wind up stealing an ugly bronze *elf*?"

"You focus on the strangest things, Johnson," I responded as we bounced along. Jeeps were not famous for their smooth ride.

I spared Michael a glance. He had stopped laughing and he looked awful. He had an egg-sized bump on his forehead, abrasions on his cheek and chin, and his upper lip was beginning to swell. I, on the other hand, did not have a scratch on me, and I felt a surge of gratitude toward him. Whatever else Michael was, he was not a coward.

I pulled up to the stoplight at the highway and signaled a left turn. I could hardly wait to get home to Oakland, shut the blinds, and crawl under the covers with a heavy tire iron, a shot glass, and a cold bottle of Absolut.

"Take a right," Michael directed, pushing in the Jeep's cigarette lighter and pulling a package of wet wipes out of the glove compartment.

"A right? Why? Where are we going? And this is no time to smoke."

"We'll go into town, find a place to wash up, and get a drink," he said quietly. "There's still the small matter of a dead body. We have to call the cops. Give me your gloves."

I ground my teeth. I hated it when others were nobler than I. Fine. We would do the right thing. Anyway, there were worse ways to spend a weekend than visiting Napa. Especially when being chased by scary men. I turned right and we headed toward the town of St. Helena.

Once we were under way, Michael helped me to strip off the gloves, then held the red-hot cigarette lighter to the fingertips, filling the Jeep with the toxic stench of burning latex.

"What are you doing?" I yelled, and cranked my window open, blasting us both with the cold evening air.

"Destroying evidence. Fingerprints can be lifted from latex gloves. This should take care of it." He did the same to his, after which he took out a penknife, ripped the remnants of the gloves into pieces, and threw the shredded bits out the window.

Frankly, his criminal expertise was starting to worry me. Whoever Michael X. Johnson was, he was suspiciously competent when it came to breaking and entering, finding dead bodies, and fleeing from threatening strangers.

"How do you know all this?" I asked him. "And do you always have wet wipes in your glove compartment?"

"I read a lot. And I used to have a slobbery dog. He lives with my sister in Fremont now," Michael said, then closed his eyes and leaned his head against the back of the seat.

"I need a drink," he said after a minute.

"You already said that."

"It's still true."

"I need food," I said.

"Again?"

"What do you mean, 'again'? I haven't eaten since lunch," I said self-righteously. "You should probably eat something too. As my grandfather says, 'Starve a cold, feed a flesh wound.'"

"Your grandfather sounds fascinating," he commented dryly.

"You have no idea."

Chapter 8

When smuggling art objects across international borders, play upon the tourist's fondness for cheap souvenirs. Dip your genuine artifacts in plastic, paint them a gaudy black, and mix them in with worthless reproductions. The border guards will hold you in disdain and you will hold on to your artifacts.

—Georges LeFleur, "How to Market
Your Forgery," unfinished manuscript,
Reflections of a World-Class Art Forger

Twenty minutes later we were sliding into a padded orange vinyl booth at Tiepolo's Tavern, a dimly lit hangout favored by the unyuppie set. The X-man was a sorry sight, though I supposed I didn't look so hot myself. Tripping over dead bodies and beaning Hulks with evil elves had kind of taken the spring out of my step.

Michael winced and sighed as he relaxed into the booth. A young blond waitress in hip-hugger jeans and a cropped T-shirt brought us water and complained about the rude customers. Michael nodded sympathetically as he surveyed the Grand Tetons inside her push-up bra.

She took our order for two vodka martinis, a jumbo serving of extra-hot buffalo wings, and two Tiepolo's cheeseburgers with fries. The drinks arrived quickly, and disappeared just as fast. We ordered another round.

There was little conversation as Michael and I lost ourselves in our thoughts. When the food arrived I savored the spicy heat of the buffalo wings followed by bites of crisp, cool celery dipped in tart blue cheese dressing. The burgers were served in red plastic baskets, piled high with glistening hot French fries. As if we had done it for years, Michael and I moved with choreographed precision, he seizing the ketchup and squirting, I grabbing the salt and sprinkling. Then we dove in. For several minutes we ate and drank in companionable silence. Michael emptied his basket first and started eyeing mine, but he was plumb out of luck, as I finished every scrap.

I sat back and sighed, feeling more human. Since the second round of martinis had gone down so well, we put in another order. After all, we both needed what my mother used to call "Dutch courage," which seemed rather unfair to the Dutch, since they were not the only ones who drank to work up their nerve.

"We have to call the cops, remember?" I said. "Just how do we go about this? You seem to be the resident expert."

"We phone in an anonymous tip."

"Give me your cell phone," I said, holding my hand out. My battery was almost out of juice.

"It's in the Jeep. Use the pay phone."

"What if the cops trace the call?"

"That kind of thing only happens on television," he said loftily. "You really should spend more time reading."

I thought that was rude, even if it was true. I tried again. "Don't the cops have caller ID on their phones?"

"How should I know?"

"You claim to know they don't trace calls."

"Even if they do have caller ID, what difference would

it make? It's a public phone, and we'll be leaving soon anyway."

"Should I call it in?" I figured it was high time I started acting like a woman and taking the initiative, even though I could think of a few things I would rather do than call the cops to report a dead body.

Be Agnes Brock's love slave, for one.

Michael smiled. "Why don't you just let me take care of it?"

My first reaction was relief. My second was annoyance. Did he have to sound so bloody condescending?

"No, really. *I'll* do it." I inched my way out of the booth. "Give me some quarters."

Michael raised an eyebrow but reached into his pocket and handed me several coins.

I marched across the bar and down a short hallway to the restrooms, where a pay phone hung on the wall between two swinging doors marked COWBUDS and LIL' FILLIES.

I stared at the phone. Whom should I call? 911? I knew from watching TV that the emergency lines *were* recorded, and I did not want my voice captured on tape for possible criminal prosecution. Plus, it was not an emergency in the strictest sense. Poor Joanne would not be going anywhere, and even though I might go to hell for thinking it, I didn't care if the Hulk recovered or not.

Fortunately, the number of the non-emergency police line was written in large red letters on the front of the phone, along with the fire department and rescue squad phone numbers.

But exactly what should I say? "Hello, you don't know me, but I'd like to report a suspicious murder." Short and sweet. I dropped the quarters in, panicked, and depressed the lever. The coins jingled back out.

A suspicious murder? Was there any other kind? Something that stupid would raise eyebrows on its own, prompting the cops to begin a trace, so they could come and arrest me, even though I was mostly innocent.

I decided to go to the bathroom, because otherwise I might blurt out something incriminating under the pressure to pee. I hurried into the LIL' FILLIES room, did my business, looked in the mirror, raised my chin, squared my shoulders, and emerged, ready to beard the dragon.

Michael was on the phone. "Good evening, Officer. I should like to report a crime," he said in an upper-crust British accent.

Now why hadn't I thought of that? Hadn't I brought down the house as Eliza Doolittle in the John F. Kennedy Jr. High School production of *My Fair Lady*?

"Officer," he continued in a voice that sounded as if his mouth was full of mush. "I just saw a man break into the Dusty Attic on Landacre Street. Big chap. Rather ugly. Square head."

He hung up and smirked. "Got tired of waiting. Now was that so hard?"

I trailed along as he strutted back to our booth. *Big jerk,* I thought resentfully. *What I wouldn't give to show him a thing or two.*

Then I remembered.

When we walked into the tavern, I had spotted an air hockey table in the rear, near the pool tables. Air hockey was the one and only game I excelled at. I was so good, in fact, that when I was in college the occasional weekend tournament had kept me in pocket change.

I tugged on Michael's shirt and nodded toward the table. He followed my gaze and raised his eyebrows in a silent challenge.

Grabbing my drink, I sauntered over to the table, Michael hot on my heels. I parked my glass on a ledge behind me and took up my post at one end of the table, Michael facing me on the other end.

Reaching into my jeans pocket, I pulled out the two quarters I hadn't needed for the phone. I plunked them into the slot; a flat plastic hockey puck popped out and the rectangular table started to hum as the air jets kicked in.

We grasped our paddles and the game was on.

I began by slamming the puck directly at Michael, who stood at his end with his drink in one hand. The puck smashed into the goal and dropped down the slot.

Score!

"Too much for ya, big guy?"

"It'll be a cold day in hell before you're too much for me to handle, lassie," he replied, setting down his drink and preparing to serve.

I hunched over, ready to rumble. The puck shot toward me, I parried and banked it off the side at a perfect forty-five-degree angle. The puck slammed into Michael's goal and rattled down the slot. Score! 2–0.

I yawned. "Boy, am I bushed. Had enough?"

Michael ordered another round of drinks.

A handful of the bar patrons had started to gather, watching in delight as the air between Michael and me crackled with tension. I inspected my nails. "Care to make it interesting?" I asked him. "Because, frankly, so far there hasn't been much action."

"How interesting?"

"Loser drinks straight vodka shots."

"Go, *dude*! Show her what you can do!" The good ol' boys rallied around, urging Michael to defend the honor of Cowbuds everywhere, while a group of Lil' Fillies, led by a buxom redhead, gathered around me and shouted a riposte.

The air hockey battle of the sexes was on.

Michael tossed another puck on the table. I parried. He challenged. I feinted. He made his move. The puck rocketed toward me, but I blocked the shot and quickly returned it, slamming the puck into his goal. Score!

The good ol' boys groaned while the good ol' girls roared. Money changed hands as the dudes were forced to make good on their bets. The redhead asked my name and started chanting, "Annie! Annie! Annie!" and the other women picked it up. Encouraged, she got more creative, chanting "Two, four, six, eight. Annie's hot. She's just great!"

As poetry went it kind of sucked, but I liked it.

"Loser pays!" the women shouted, forming an *L* with their fingers and holding it to their foreheads to signal just what they thought of Michael's gamesmanship. Michael bowed, ordered a round of vodka shots for the crowd, chugged his, and slammed the empty glass down on the table.

He wiped his mouth with his sleeve and smiled, but his green eyes were furious as he stared at me across the expanse of the tournament-sized table. As if in slow motion, I watched him drop more quarters in the slot, toss another puck on the table, and send it hurtling in my direction. It was nowhere near the goal, and with a flick of my wrist I sent it spinning, hitting a three-point shot off the sides before zipping back to me. As soon as it crossed the centerline, I tried to hammer it into the goal, but he beat me to it, scoring on me fair and square.

I drank my obligatory shot of vodka, and after that, the rest of the evening was a bit of a blur.

I remembered the bartender mixing up a commemorative drink that I christened the Anti-Whachahoochi. I remembered leading the house in a dance of the same name, set to the tune of "The Hokey Pokey." I remembered green eyes throughout.

What I did not remember was how I ended up at the motel. The bad news was that I awoke in a strange bed.

The good news was that I was wearing the jeans and T-shirt I had put on yesterday afternoon. At least I presumed it was yesterday, because a grayish light came in through the window curtains, and I was pretty sure it had been dark when we were at the bar. I was feeling fuzzy on the details, but it seemed to me that traditionally meant that it was now the next morning. I registered the throbbing headache, the dry mouth, and the general listlessness that indicated I'd had *way* too much fun the night before. Bleary eyes took in the green glow of digital numbers on the bedside clock. 10:23 A.M.

I lifted my head carefully and looked around: a standard-issue king-sized motel bed, a dresser, a desk and a chair. I was alone not only in the bed but also in the room.

I buried my nose in the rumpled pillow beside me. He had been here. I could smell the man.

"Michael?" I croaked.

Silence.

I tried again, a little louder. "Hello?"

No answer. No manly sounds of showering or shaving. I sat up, took a minute to adjust to my spinning head, and noticed there were no clothes strewn anywhere.

I got up on shaky legs and stumbled over to the bathroom. No manly naked man, no manly toothbrush. I splashed water on my face, rinsed my mouth, drank a lot of water, and used the toilet. Feeling more human now, I started to think. I crossed the room and peeked through vinyl-backed, brown plaid curtains. There was no red Jeep in the parking lot.

Maybe he had gone out for coffee and bagels. Maybe it was time to give the guy the benefit of the doubt. He had been pretty helpful with the Hulk, after all. And darned if I could remember, but it seemed to me we might have shared a little kissing and snuggling last night.

Or not.

But still. He wouldn't abandon me here, not after all we had been through.

Would he?

I didn't even know where my truck was.

The important thing was not to panic. First things first. Item Number One: a shower. I stripped off my rumpled clothes and stood under the hot water for a half an hour, using the diminutive bottle of shampoo and minuscule sliver of soap provided by the motel. Refreshed, I dried myself with the baby towels that were neatly folded on top of a metal contraption screwed to the wall. As I brewed really bad coffee in the wee, tiny Mr. Coffee machine I wondered if there was any chance that the owners of budget motels thought they catered exclusively to Lilliputians.

I was forced to dress in the same jeans and shirt, but at least I felt more like a real person now. I emerged from the steamy bathroom nurturing a tiny flame of hope that Michael would be sitting at the desk, cups of Peet's coffee and plates of Noah's bagels spread out before him.

As I took in the empty room, the flame fizzled, and I started to get really, really pissed. Sitting on the edge of the bed, I began to assess the situation. My purse was in my truck. My truck was somewhere in Yountville, several miles south of here. My credit cards and bank card were in my purse, along with my identification. All I had with me were my keys, a dead cell phone, and two dollar bills in my jeans pocket. I had no friends within two hours' drive of here.

So all I had to do was find a taxi driver to take me to Yountville and cart me around town until I found my truck, all the while avoiding the cops who would no doubt be swarming around Joanne's shop. How hard could that be?

The room's phone had no dial tone, so I went to the

motel office to use the pay phone. As soon as I walked in, the desk clerk informed me that the motel room had not been paid for and would I kindly take care of it.

"Well, you see, here's the thing—"

I got no further. Apparently the desk clerk had a pretty good idea what the thing was and called in the manager, an extremely polite, middle-aged Pakistani named Rafi who patently did not believe a word of my story. I flashed on a visual of days spent scrubbing motel toilets and nights spent listening to drunks at the local pokey, and almost lost it.

Maybe it was the genuinely stricken look on my face that convinced Rafi I was telling the truth. Or maybe he calculated that indulging me was his best shot at getting his money. Or maybe he was simply a kind man. Whatever the reason, he ushered me into his office, asked me to sit down, fixed a cup of the most delicious tea I had ever had, and made a phone call that, he said, would take care of things for me.

We spent the next twenty minutes chatting companionably. Rafi showed me pictures of his family and regaled me with stories of his uncle Farhad in Karachi, who was a great fan of Humphrey Bogart and ran an illegal but highly lucrative nightclub called the Casablanca. I countered with the tale of how my uncle Alfred got drunk one night, decided to castrate his Brahma bull Sweetmeat with a twist tie, and nearly lost an ear in the process.

Ah, memories. By the time Rafi's teenaged nephew Suresh pulled up in a beat-up silver Toyota Corolla, Rafi and I were chums.

Suresh drove me around Yountville for nearly an hour searching for my beloved truck, which I finally spied tucked behind a closed service station. I got in, retrieved my wallet, and rode with Suresh to an ATM, where I withdrew enough cash to pay for the motel room, the drive to Yountville, the time it took to find the truck, the tip I felt I owed Rafi for his understanding, and the jar of curry and package of naan that Rafi said was the best I would ever taste. Back at my truck, Suresh drove off with a wave.

I settled into the driver's seat, but when I turned the key in the ignition I heard a whining, straining sound that was nothing like its usual rumble. The CHECK ENGINE light came on, so I climbed out of the cab, lifted the hood, and checked the engine. I was going to need a whole lot more instruction from the truck if this was going to work.

I slammed my fist on the fender. That did not help.

Looking around, I realized that Yountville was a forlornly sleepy little town on a wintry Sunday. The brilliant sunshine and puffy white clouds of yesterday had given way to dismal overcast skies and rapidly cooling air.

My dead cell phone being of no use, I hiked, resigned, toward the highway, where I found Ernie of Ernie's Gas Station open for business and delighted to charge me seventy-five dollars to tow my truck less than half a mile. At the garage, Ernie popped the hood, inspected the engine, and presented me with a laundry list of problems that might or might not be the cause of my current misfortune. It would be at least an hour before he would be able to get to it, though I saw no evidence that ol' Ern was doing anything else.

I kept these thoughts to myself. The last thing I needed at the moment was to offend the one person who could remove the final obstacle between me and the road home.

After spending a few minutes flipping through the tattered magazines in Ernie's unheated and grimy waiting room, I trudged over to a coffee shop a few blocks away, only to find they did not accept credit cards. I spent my remaining two dollars on a watery cup of coffee, and glumly nursed my persistent headache. Last night's meal of buffalo wings, cheeseburger, fries, vodka martinis, and Anti-Whachahoochis was not sitting well. I must have looked as miserable as I felt, because a sympathetic waitress slipped me some dry wheat toast when I explained that I had no more money.

An hour later I trudged back to the service station, where Ernie, grinning dementedly, said he had been able to fix my problem for the low, low cost of two hundred forty dollars. Plus, he fixed my broken window for only another hundred fifty. Unlike the coffee shop, Ernie was more than happy to run my credit card up to its spending limit.

As for the X-man, he was dead meat. I would hunt him down to my dying day and when I found him I would kill him with my bare hands.

Or with the evil elf—now *that* would be an appropriate use of creepy garden statuary.

Chapter 9

The paint color known as Indian yellow was de-
rived from the urine of cows fed an exclusive diet of
mango leaves. The use of this acid yellow will date
a work of art to before 1900, the year the pigment
was banned.

—*Georges LeFleur, "Tools of the Trade," unfinished*
manuscript, Reflections of a World-Class Art Forger

Around five that evening, I limped into Oakland. It had been a very slow trip home. Halfway there, the gray skies that followed me from Yountville turned into a drizzle, always a dangerous thing in these parts since, although many Bay Area drivers hailed from less temperate climes, most were now incapable of driving in any conditions other than bright, arid sunshine. I fought my way through the snarled traffic, parked behind my building, and plodded up the stairs to my apartment, bone-tired. All I wanted in life at this moment was a long, hot soak in the bathtub, something bland to eat, and an early bedtime. It had been quite a weekend.

The phone started ringing as I was fiddling with the dead-bolt lock, so I wrenched the door open, dumped my things on a chair, and snatched up the receiver. As I fielded a call about which candidate I should elect to the school board, I noticed something was amiss.

I was not known for my spic-and-span housekeeping. I liked a clean living space as much as the next person, but tidying up was not high on my list of priorities. And even if it had been, after a long day in the studio or on a job site, the last thing I was in the mood for was vacuuming. As a result, my apartment often gave the impression of having been ransacked on a daily basis. Some people, my mother most famously, would have been astonished that I could tell that anybody had been here. But I knew immediately that my apartment, although not torn apart like the Dusty Attic, had been gone through carefully.

I said something to get rid of the campaign worker—something subtle like "Comrade, I only vote for the Communist Party"—and hung up.

I looked around my living room, unsure of how to proceed. Was the intruder still here? I snuck into the kitchen and peered around. No one there. That left two rooms. I grabbed a cast-iron skillet from the top of the stove and tiptoed grimly down the short hall to my bedroom.

One might think that my recent encounter with the Hulk would have encouraged me to be more circumspect than to blunder about armed only with a skillet. But the truth was, I was exhausted, hungry, hungover, out a whole lot of cash, and not in the mood to be reasonable.

I approached the partly closed bedroom door and threw it open. It made a satisfying crashing noise as it bounced against the wall before swinging back and slamming shut in my face.

Damn.

I turned the knob and pushed the door open again, more slowly this time.

Nothing. No one.

I poked around, holding my breath while checking in the closet and under the bed. I was not sure why I thought a lack of oxygen would improve the situation. The bedroom was empty.

Tiptoeing back down the hall, I spent five seconds searching the tiny bathroom. A clear plastic shower curtain surrounded the tub, and the only scum in there was the soapy kind. Nothing larger than a small cat could conceal itself behind the toilet.

Satisfied there was no one in the apartment but me, I checked to see if my valuables were still there. The TV and the stereo were in the living room. That pretty much exhausted the list.

I was starting to think that this had not been a burglary. Petty crime was a problem in my neighborhood, but I had never been bothered. The other tenants were also professional women, and we were scrupulous about keeping our sturdy front doors dead-bolted and our eyes peeled for each other's safety. My apartment's third-floor location would also discourage the average junkie or junior high school kid. A professional thief could manage it, but why would a professional thief bother? Nothing I owned was worth anything. In fact, it was entirely possible that my meager belongings would inspire pity from a criminal.

Okay, I sighed. The bogeyman was no longer here and had not taken anything. So what had he, she, or it been looking for? I sat at my desk in a corner of the living room and tried to think. Could it have been one of the intruders from Joanne Nash's place? If so, how had anyone connected me to her? And even if someone had made that connection, how had they known where I lived?

That stumped me, so I tried another approach. I was looking into two separate art forgeries: the drawings, which involved Harlan Coombs and Anton; and *The*

Magi, which involved the Brock Museum, Ernst Petti-grew, and Anton. The only links between them were me and Anton, and I had nothing to do with forging them. I started feeling anxious again. I had only a few more days to find Brazil's drawings and claim my reward money, and so far two people had been killed and Ernst was still missing. I needed to find Anton fast.

I vowed to try harder. I just was not sure how to do that.

Frustrated, I picked up the phone. Fourteen messages. Two of the morning calls were hang-ups, and one was from Inspector Crawford, asking to speak with me. There was a message from my father telling me, in his clipped, scholarly way, that he was disappointed to learn that I was charging Anthony Brazil for my services. What, did he think I was going to get involved with characters like the Hulk for old times' sake? I could feel my blood pressure spike. I took a deep breath, deleted his message, and went on.

The next three calls were from what sounded like a very old woman trying to reach Thomas Surgical Supply on Fifty-First and Broadway. She seemed confused, but did not leave her number. I felt bad for her. I deleted those messages, too.

Mary had called to say she would be staying a few more days in Mendocino. Rats. I could use a dose of her cheeriness right about now.

The next message was from Grandfather, maddening as always, saying he hoped everything was working out and that he was certain Anton was safe. Oh? Care to elab-orate, old man? Apparently not.

Two more hang-ups followed, and then a garbled mes-sage from Pete, who lost his English when he became excited. He had called at noon today. He said something about the studio, and unless I was mistaken there were sirens in the background. I felt my stomach clench. The last time I'd heard that many sirens, somebody had died.

Finally, there were two messages from Frank. He had called shortly after noon to say there was some trouble at the studio, but did not explain. He called again at two, to tell me to get my butt down there ASAP.

I tried to remain calm, but the truth was I would much rather that my apartment burn to the ground than anything happen to my studio. I could replace the contents of my home with a check from the insurance company and a trip to Target, but the contents of my studio—paintings and paints, business files, drawings and books and reference works, pencils and pastels and brushes—were uninsurable and would take years to replace. And oh my God!—John Steubing's portrait!

I looked at the clock on the mantel over the closed-off fireplace and saw that it was five thirty. I snatched up the phone and called Pete, but there was no answer at the warehouse. Mr. Fat Cat Landlord had not left his number, nor did I have it committed to memory. There was nothing for it but to go to the studio. I still had my jacket on and my wallet and keys were in my pocket, so I hustled out the door.

A second later I hustled back in and grabbed a box of Triscuits to munch on the way to the City. Whatever was going on probably should not be faced on an empty stomach.

It was then that I saw it, propped in a corner of the kitchen: the ugly bronze elf.

The X-man had been here.

Abandoning me many miles from home, penniless and truckless, was not bad enough—he had to break into my apartment and go through my things? Why? What had he been looking for? That clinched it. The X-man must die.

No time for that now, I thought, as I scrambled down the stairs, Triscuits under one arm, and raced to my truck.

Sunday evening traffic into San Francisco was awful, the freeway jammed with urbanites in SUVs returning from ski weekends in Tahoe, sunburned, grumpy, and aggressive. As I queued up to cross the Bay Bridge, tapping my toes, munching my crackers, and trying not to panic, I realized that I still had not charged the battery on my cell phone. Idiotic technology. Promised you would be in touch any time, all the time, and then did not deliver.

As I inched nearer the tollbooth I realized something worse. I had no money. None. I frantically checked the glove box, the ashtray, and the door pockets, then under and behind the seats. I came up with thirty-seven cents, nowhere near the three dollars the nice woman at the tollbooth would be expecting in a few minutes. So what happened if a driver had no money? There had to be some kind of procedure, right?

There was. They gave out tickets. *Expensive* tickets.

Twenty minutes later, newly ticketed and totally frazzled, I finally crossed the bridge, skirted the bay to China Basin, and approached my studio. I pulled in next to my landlord's Jaguar and had not even planted both feet on terra firma before DeBenton was in my face, eyes blazing, hands on his hips, ready to eat nails.

"Where the *hell* have you been?"

"Just tell me what's going on."

"There was a fire. Possibly arson." His voice was cold and accusing.

My eyes flew to the second story. "Arson! My studio?" I was so scared I was whispering.

"Yes, your studio. Fortunately, the smoke detector tripped the sprinkler system and automatically dialed the fire department," DeBenton snapped, crossing his arms over his chest. "You've been my tenant for less than a week and you've already been visited by the police, your truck's been broken into, and now your studio has been set on fire. What *is* it with you?"

"With me? What is it with *me*?" I replied, my voice scaling upward. My studio had just gone up in smoke, everything I had spent the last few years working like a dog for may have just been destroyed, I couldn't pay the rent, much less the rent increase—and this man thought it was somehow *my* fault?

As my grandfather always said, the best defense is a good offense.

"What about putting in a decent security system, Mr. 'Secure Transport'?" I snapped. "Maybe if you stopped staring at the bottom line for a moment, you'd see that people's lives and art are more important than your bank balance!"

As soon as I said the words, I regretted them. True, I was tired and stressed and scared spitless. But it wasn't my landlord's fault that catastrophe had sought me out once again. I had started to apologize when a large Bosnian jogged up and scooped me into a bear hug.

"Thank the heavens, my Annie. The police, they have come and gone. But they say you must go at your earliest convenience to make the further report."

I came up for air. "Thanks, Pete," I mumbled.

"I'll need to speak with you when you're free," DeBenton said stiffly and stalked off to his office.

Pete supported me as I began the long climb to my studio, petrified about what I might find. The exterior door to the second-floor hallway stuck again, and I nearly lost it then and there. Pete spoke soothingly and yanked the door open with brute force. "I will lead," he offered.

"No, let me go first," I said. I had to see the place for myself. My mind was numb, processing the facts slowly, but already pondering where I would go from here. Did this mean the end of my business? Had I lost everything?

As I walked down the hallway I took in the extent of the damage. Everything was soaked—the walls, the floor, the bulletin board in the common area, everything. The firefighters had wrenched open the door to my studio, splintering the wood around the handle and separating the doorframe from the wall. My TRUE/FAUX STUDIOS sign, happily enough, was well varnished and so had not sustained serious injury. I pushed the door open slowly, stomach clenched and dread in every pore.

"This is abominable," Pete murmured as we looked upon a scene of utter chaos.

The cushions from the sofa and the two chairs had been tossed onto the worn Oriental rug, and papers and canvases littered the floor. Pigments were scattered liberally over every horizontal surface. Powders, several kinds of paint, pastels, and artist's crayons had been ground underfoot, whether by the intruder or by the firefighters, it was hard to tell. The loose powders and pastels had mixed with the water from the sprinklers and the fire hoses to create bizarre watercolors on the wide wooden floorboards. *Modern art,* I thought dully.

It was hard to take it all in. It was hard to take.

My attention wandered to a far corner, near the pathetic ficus tree, where there were discernible scorch marks. Picking my way through the debris, I saw that someone had tossed a cigarette butt near an overturned can of turpentine. A good way to start a blaze, though I supposed it could have been accidental. I imagined that criminal types who break in and destroy places weren't the sharpest tools in the shed.

My eyes searched for John Steubing's portrait. It had been knocked off the easel and lay facedown on the heavy tarpaulin that protected it when I wasn't working on it. I approached cautiously and slowly turned the canvas over, then sighed and relaxed a fraction. Oil-based paint did not absorb water, and the tarp had minimized the damage to the canvas. The portrait could be restored. A lucky break.

Maybe the only one.

"Who does such a thing?" Pete wondered, as if reading my thoughts.

I shook my head. As much as I would have liked to blame Michael for everything that was going wrong with my life at the moment, I was willing to bet that arson wasn't his style. "I don't know, Pete," I responded listlessly.

Were they looking for the drawings, or *The Magi*? Had whoever tossed Joanne's shop been responsible for this as well?

I tried to figure out how long it would take to dig myself out of this mess. I could hire some of Mary's chronically unemployed musician friends to help clean up, and Mary and I would salvage what we could. Apart from John's portrait, the only thing with any market value was my computer, which contained all my financial records. I made a mental note to call my insurance agent in the morning. I prayed I was up to date on my premiums.

"Come to the warehouse, Annie," Pete said, startling me. "Wanna cuppa coffee?"

I smiled despite myself. Pete had learned English and American cultural ways by watching the daytime soaps. "Wanna cuppa coffee?" had been Pete's first English sentence. "Is Shane the father of Britney's baby?" was his second.

"Tomorrow you will call the insurance. Come," Pete said, steering me gently toward the door. "Tonight you must rest."

The numbness was wearing off now, and I was starting

to feel afraid. What if Mary and I had been here when whoever had done this arrived? I glanced up at Pete, grateful for his concern. It was reassuring to have six feet six inches of solid muscle by my side. We closed the shattered door as best we could, walked down the hall, and descended the wooden stairs.

As we passed DeBenton's office, I thought of going in to apologize for my earlier rudeness, but decided I didn't have the strength. I peered through his window and offered him a wan smile, but he was mopping up the mess caused by the runoff from the indoor rainstorm upstairs and didn't see me.

Pete and I crossed the parking lot to the stained-glass warehouse, a vast room with row upon row of brightly colored glass in sheets, each about three feet wide and four feet high. The glass was made in Germany, Japan, and Eastern Europe, as well as in Washington and Oregon. Since it was Sunday, the warehouse was empty of the workers who usually milled about, carefully shifting fragile crates and sorting through the colorful wares. The dusty corner office was similarly deserted. Tomorrow the phone would be ringing off the hook and Pete's employees would be hunched over computer terminals, tracking shipments of special-order glass and filling large architectural orders.

The last of the sun's rays sifted in gently through a few gorgeously swirled panels that Pete had hung in the old multipaned windows near the loading dock. He decided coffee was too much for my nerves and instead brewed me a pot of chamomile tea. It was an endearing Old World gesture, although I must admit I would have preferred an endearing New World gesture like a shot of bourbon. Too edgy to sit, I wandered the warehouse aisles, looking at the magnificent glass and taking pleasure in an art form about which I knew almost nothing.

Pete brought me a steaming mug of tea, kissed me lightly on the forehead, and returned to his office to finish up the paperwork for an order that was being shipped out first thing in the morning. I sipped the tea, which really did make me feel better, and became lost in the sheer translucent beauty of a sheet of ruby red glass, swirled with tints of yellow, orange, and purple.

A deafening crash came from the direction of the office. I dropped the mug on the nearest crate and sprinted toward the noise.

"Pete!" There was no answer. "Pete?"

As I rounded the corner into the office, I saw shards of cobalt blue glass everywhere.

"Pete!" I called, but still there was no reply. I started toward his desk and spied a pair of size thirteen work boots sticking out from behind a table. "Pete?"

Someone grabbed me from behind and clamped a beefy hand over my mouth. Twisting and kicking, I was lifted off the ground. I wrenched my teeth open and bit down, hard. A pained grunt was the only response before a gun was shoved against my temple.

I was half carried, half dragged down the ramp of the open loading dock to a shiny black Lincoln Town Car, where I was dumped, facedown, on the leather seats; then the car pulled away with a screech of tires.

Scared but furious, I flipped over and sat up to find my old pal the Hulk, with a large bandage on his head, aiming a gun right between my eyes. The driver, who sported a ducktail like the Fonzie character on the old TV show, stomped on the gas as we vroomed out of the parking lot and sped toward the docks. We careened into an alley behind two large, seemingly abandoned factories and jerked to a halt. Grabbing my arm in a bruising grip, the Hulk dragged me from the car. Seagulls squawked overhead, and I smelled a whiff of the bay. There was not a soul in sight.

The Fonz yanked open an unmarked door in a building made of cinder blocks and corrugated tin, and the Hulk hustled me roughly through a small front office and down a scuffed, narrow hallway. The place smelled musty, as though it hadn't been inhabited in years. I was shoved into a room that held nothing but a single chair in the center of a pool of light.

Either I was in very big trouble or I had stumbled onto the set of a B movie.

"Ms. Kincaid," a man said in a deep, cultured voice.

Maybe it really *was* a B movie.

He moved toward me out of the shadows. He was fifty-ish, medium height, with a clipped salt-and-pepper mustache and expensively styled gray hair. He wore beautifully tailored wool slacks, leather loafers, and a V-neck burgundy cashmere sweater over a white oxford shirt. Apparently he and DeBenton shopped at the same stores.

"Have a seat, won't you?" he said.

I started to decline, but a meaty paw on my shoulder pressed me down. The Fonz materialized with a nylon rope and tied my wrists tightly to the arms of the chair, and my ankles to the legs.

"Who are you?" I was pleased that I kept most of the fear out of my voice.

"Why don't you allow me to ask the questions, Ms. Kincaid," he replied suavely.

"All right, Mister, um, but please, call nine-one-one for the man back at the warehouse. He's injured. He had nothing to do with any of this. You can call anonymously." The thought of Pete lying on the warehouse floor, unconscious and bleeding to death, was horrifying.

Mr. Suave dismissed my plea with a flick of his manicured hand. "Why don't you tell me what I want to know, then you can go back to the warehouse and help your friend yourself."

I stared at him. *Annie,* I lectured myself sternly, *whatever else you do, cooperate. Swear to God you will cooperate, and maybe, just maybe, you'll get out of this.*

"What do you want?" I asked, the very picture of cooperativeness.

"The Caravaggio."

"And you think *I've* got it? Are you nuts?" My vow didn't seem to be taking hold.

"I assure you, I am not." He didn't seem offended by my remark. Maybe he heard it a lot. "If you don't have *The Magi,* then where is it?"

Who was this guy and why did he want *The Magi*? More to the point, what made him think *I* knew where it was?

"I don't know," I said. "I've been looking for it myself."

"Ah? And why are you looking for it?"

I forced myself to stay focused, knowing that if I didn't pull myself together and get out of here, Pete was in trouble. I sat up straighter. "Well, actually, I'm not. I'm really looking for the man who painted a, um, a temporary replacement for it," I finished lamely.

"Indeed? Well, well, it seems we have a great deal in common, Ms. Kincaid."

I somehow doubted that.

"You see," he continued, "I purchased a—what was the charming phrase you used? Ah, yes—a 'temporary replacement' myself. Unfortunately, I had been led to believe that it was the original."

Yikes. No wonder he was upset. "Yeah, well, there's a lot of that going around," I said.

The hand on my shoulder squeezed. Hard.

"Ow!" I said. "That *hurts*."

The Hulk yanked my head back by my hair. It was not a pleasant sensation. Note to self: when being held hostage by menacing thugs, adjust the attitude.

My host chuckled. "Thomas here becomes impatient easily, don't you, Thomas?" His voice turned cold. "Now where's Anton Woznikowicz?"

"I wish I knew," I said in a strangled voice. My scalp was *killing* me.

"Where's Harlan Coombs?"

"I wish I knew that as well," I said. "I truly do."

"Ms. Kincaid, you are trying my patience."

"I'm sorry, but I don't know where they are!"

"Where's Colin Brooks?"

Who the hell was Colin Brooks? Feverishly I flipped through my mental Rolodex. Pete's life might depend on my giving the right answer, but I could not recall having met anyone by that name. "Never heard of him."

The Hulk released my hair and slapped me. I tasted blood in my mouth, my ears rang, and my vision blurred as tears flooded my eyes.

"Stop that!" I shouted.

"Let me refresh your memory, Ms. Kincaid," Mr. Suave said in a voice oily enough to lube my truck. "You went to Napa with him."

Well, duh. Wasn't I the one who had been so sure that Michael X. Johnson was an alias?

"Oh," I said. "I didn't know that was his name. I don't know where he is."

Mr. Suave raised his eyebrows. "You expect me to believe that you don't know where your lover is?"

"He's not my lover."

He sighed, in a "kids today" kind of way. "Fine. Your boyfriend, then. Come, come, Ms. Kincaid. I'm not your father, I don't care about your morals. I know you spent the night with him."

"He is *not* my boyfriend," I repeated emphatically, wondering how Michael was involved in all this. "I don't know who he is, and maybe we did sleep together, but I don't remember. I was drunk. I got drunk and spent the night in a motel with a man whose name I don't know. I don't remember anything about it, and in the morning he was gone. As far as I'm concerned he's just another good-looking scumbag. Old story. Okay?"

The Hulk lifted his hand.

"Don't hit me again!" I yelled.

Mr. Suave looked pained and squeezed the bridge of his nose with his thumb and forefinger. "Ms. Kincaid. I imagine you've never done this before, so perhaps I should explain the procedure to you. You are here because we desire information. In order to convince you to give us that information, we hurt you. That is how it is done. Please don't interfere with the process."

My mind reeled at the notion that these goons were sticklers for procedural details.

"So, who *is* this Colin Brooks, anyway?" I asked, hoping to calm things down. "I know you're supposed to be asking the questions here, but I'm curious. I mean, technically I did sleep with the guy, even if I don't remember it."

"He is a *thief*," Mr. Suave said, his voice ringing with disapproval. His contempt struck me as ludicrous under the circumstances, but I kept that thought to myself. He continued. "Brooks was working with Harlan to steal the Caravaggio and replace it with the forgery. What I need to know is, what happened to the original? Is it back at the Brock?"

"No." Was that the right answer? Should I have said

yes? Which answer would convince him to let me go help Pete? "Maybe," I added for good measure.

"If it is not there, then where is it?"

"I don't know."

"Where *is* it?" he hissed, his face inches from mine.

"I—don't—know."

"What about the key?" the man with the ducktail asked. "Eddie was goin' on about a key that night, remember?"

"Good point. I knew I paid you for something." Garnet beads flew as Mr. Suave reached out and ripped off my necklace.

"What are you—?!" I began.

The Hulk yanked my head back again and pressed a knife against my throat for good measure. The sharp blade pricked my skin and I felt a drop of what I presumed was my life's blood trickle down my neck. It did not hurt, but it scared me witless.

A thud sounded from one of the outer rooms, and Mr. Suave jerked his chin toward the ducktailed Fonz, who hurried out. Seconds later we heard a second thud, followed by a third.

And then silence.

"Hanks!" Mr. Suave called out.

There was no response.

"Hanks!"

Still nothing.

"Come on," my captor told the Hulk. "Let's check it out. Are the ropes secure?"

They left me alone and I immediately leaned forward, gnawing on the rope to free my hands.

"I thought you said you never caused trouble," a voice murmured.

"Frank!" I lifted my head so fast I nearly clocked him

in the chin as he crouched down in front of me. "Is Pete all right? How did you find me?"

"Don't move," he commanded, sawing vigorously at the rope. He looked kind of rumpled. For Frank. His pinstriped oxford shirt was open at the collar, and he wasn't wearing a tie.

"Where are the bad guys?" I asked.

"They're outside," he told me. "I locked them out."

I felt sure there was a story in there somewhere, but Frank didn't elaborate.

"The lock probably won't hold for long, but I'm hoping the police will arrive soon," he said as the ropes fell away. "Don't worry; Pete's taken care of. For now I suggest we focus on saving ourselves. This is my only weapon."

He held up a tiny Swiss army knife. It had been sufficient to saw through nylon rope and could probably clean fingernails pretty well. But unless Mr. Suave had a pathological fear of needles I doubted he would run in horror.

"This way," Frank said, leading me out the room's single door and heading down the dimly lit hall, deeper into the building.

"Shouldn't we . . ."

"Trust me."

Since Frank had done so well thus far—certainly better than I had—I followed him until the hallway opened onto a shop floor, where we skittered to a halt. I was hoping Frank had a better sense of what we were looking for than I did, since I was clueless. Sure enough, he seemed to spot something, because he was suddenly galvanized.

"Up there," he said, pointing to a loft high above the shop floor.

"There?" I squeaked.

"There."

"You sure?"

"Trust me."

Again with the trust. He was really pushing it.

We rushed up a rickety staircase that hugged one wall of the large room. The loft offered a panoramic view of the factory, with the exception of the front offices, from which we'd just come. The metal door at the top of the staircase was locked, but Frank whipped out his handy knife, pulled out a screwdriver attachment, and removed the small screws that held the lock in place. The door swung open and we entered an office furnished only with a dented metal desk and three ugly beige plastic chairs. The air was stale, as if the door had been shut for a long time.

I looked around, dismayed. I had secretly hoped to find a SWAT team, but Frank seemed pleased. Crossing to the far wall, where there was a large ventilation grate, he knelt down, and, again using his tiny knife, unscrewed the four corners, lifted off the grate, and lay on his stomach to peer into the hole. Then, pulling a tiny flashlight out of his pocket, he shone the light down the vent. When he looked up at me, I had the uncomfortable feeling he was taking my measurements, assessing what my mother referred to as my "womanly" figure. To me, this had always translated into "big hips."

"It'll do in a pinch," he murmured to himself.

I was offended until I realized he was talking about the grate.

"We're going in *there*?" I had a touch of claustrophobia, which was magnified when I was being chased by goons with guns in abandoned factories. I knew what Frank was proposing was wise—in the fourth grade I had listened attentively as Officer Friendly had told us that in case of danger we should "hide and wait for the police"— but I was beginning to wish I had taken my chances and run like hell.

"Don't worry, it's only a last resort," he reassured me.

Frank fiddled with something at the control panel above the desk, and floodlights suddenly illuminated the factory, the glare accentuated when he turned off the lights in our little room. It was dark, but I could make out Frank's face in the reflected glow. He sat down on the floor, legs stretched in front of him, back against the wall. Unable to think of anything else to do, I slid down next to him and tried to appear as calm as he did, even though my mind was whirling. Was Pete okay? Who were these men, and how had they connected me to the fake *Magi*? And what in the world was Michael's connection to it all?

"San Francisco's finest," Frank said quietly when, at long last, we heard far-off sirens. "Took long enough."

I was relieved, but a tad annoyed, by Frank's obvious competence. "How did you know what happened?" I asked.

"I'd just left the office—everything was so damned wet and I wasn't accomplishing much except getting myself steamed—and was sitting in my car listening to my cell phone messages when I saw a Lincoln Town Car pull up and some really big guy go into the warehouse. I know Pete's not open for business on Sundays, so I was curious. Next thing I knew, this guy was shoving you into the car, and it seemed pretty clear you weren't happy about it. I figured Pete must have been badly hurt because otherwise he would never have let them take you. So I called nine-one-one on the cell phone. Then I followed you here."

He spoke casually, but I was stunned.

"And what about the goons? How'd you take them down?"

"I didn't exactly 'take them down,'" Frank said. "I knocked the first one out with the help of an abandoned muffler, then made some noise to coax the others out of the building. I hid inside and managed to lock the two men out of the building when they went to investigate."

I gaped at him.

"Don't let the three-piece suit fool you," he added. "I did a stint in the military."

I leaned my head back against the wall. Pete and I owed Frank our lives.

Kind of put that rent hike in perspective.

"Frank?"

"Yes, Annie?"

"Thank you." That didn't seem to cover it, but I didn't know what else to say.

"No problem."

We sat in silence for a few minutes.

"I really am sorry for going off on you earlier. When I'm scared I say the first thing that comes to mind. I've been told it's not my best quality," I said.

"No problem."

We were silent for a few more minutes, and I strained to listen for either the cops or the bad guys.

"Annie?"

"Yes, Frank?"

"I'm sorry, too. I was pretty rough on you today. I guess you weren't the only one who was scared."

"No problem."

The sirens were getting closer, but we were far from out of danger. To distract myself I searched for a topic of conversation and noticed he was still holding the knife and the pocket flashlight. "So, you came prepared, huh? Just like a Boy Scout."

As conversation went, it wasn't first-rate. But it was a start, and I figured Frank would follow up.

"Yep. I've even got a condom in my wallet."

Well, I sure hadn't expected *that*. Mr. Uptight had made a joke. A risqué joke, too.

"I thought you were gay," I blurted out.

Frank looked amused, his brown eyes black in the dim light. "What, gay men don't carry condoms?"

"Well, now that you mention it, I guess maybe they do. I mean, they should, shouldn't they? I mean if they want to be . . . prepared. Safe. You know." I was kind of wishing I'd kept my mouth shut. Conversation was severely overrated. At least, mine was. "So, where are the cops?"

"Relax. They're on their way. Just because I didn't respond to the overtures from your assistant and her friend doesn't mean I'm gay, Annie."

Uh-oh. "What did they do?" I asked, not really wanting to know.

Frank's lips twitched. "I'll spare you the details. Suffice it to say they made a valiant effort."

"Not your type, huh?"

Frank raised his eyebrows. "Just because I'm not gay doesn't mean I want to sleep with girls young enough to be my daughters. I prefer women, Annie. Grown women."

Well, what did you know. I hated to admit it—I *really* hated to admit it—but it looked like I had misjudged ol' Fender Bender here. Not only had he displayed bravery and ingenuity above and beyond the call of a landlord's duty, but he might just have good taste as well.

"So how do you feel about supermodels?"

"Too skinny."

"*Playboy* centerfolds?"

"Too fake."

"Actresses?"

"Too vapid."

"Artists?"

He gave me a slow smile. "Too unpredictable."

Chapter 10

How fickle is the world of art! For decades the works of Vermeer were sold under the name of Pieter de Hooch, a far more popular artist throughout the nineteenth century. Now those holding de Hooch's works scrape off the signature, hoping to find Vermeer's name beneath!

— Georges LeFleur, "Art and Artifact," unfinished
manuscript, Reflections of a World-Class Forger

"SFPD! Freeze! Down on the ground! Down on the ground!"

We heard a commotion in the factory below, doors banging, voices yelling, footsteps pounding. Sounded like the good guys had arrived.

"We're up here!" Frank shouted. He turned to me. "Get up slowly, Annie, and raise your hands over your head. They'll be a little jumpy until they sort everything out."

I shot my hands high over my head, and we stood there, waiting. My arms started getting tired and wavered a little. When the cops arrived they would think we either were law-abiding citizens or had just been moved by the Holy Spirit.

While we waited to be rescued, I glanced at Frank. His hair was mussed, his clothes were rumpled, and he had a smudge on one cheek. Some people, like me, cleaned up well. After an hour or so in the bathroom, I was reasonably presentable. On the right day I even turned a head or two. Mr. Slick here, though, was the kind of guy who messed up real good.

Interesting.

The door to the shop floor flew open, and in poured a dozen cops dressed in bulletproof vests and headgear and pointing some serious hardware at us. They ordered us out of the room and down the stairs, where we were searched and hustled off separately for questioning. I was interrogated by a series of officers, checked over by paramedics, and taken outside to a waiting squad car.

A handsome young officer named Chris listened to my concerns about Pete and kindly agreed to make a few calls. He returned with the news that Pete had been admitted to UCSF Medical Center in serious but stable condition. He had sustained a concussion and several lacerations that required stitches, but the doctors expected him to make a complete recovery. Visitors would be allowed at ten o'clock tomorrow morning.

I sagged with relief. Chris-the-Cop handed me a Styrofoam cup of coffee poured from his private thermos and settled me in the back of the squad car, a blanket around my shoulders, my legs and feet dangling out the open door. I inhaled the rich aroma, thinking that with good coffee all things were possible. That was when I saw the African Princess walking toward me, her shoulders back and head held high, looking impressive, as always, in a starched white shirt and burgundy wool pants suit. Strangely enough, I suddenly felt safe.

"Annie Kincaid," she said with a warm smile.

"Inspector Crawford," I replied.

"Call me Annette," she told me. "I'm getting the feeling that I've missed something here. Got time to answer a few questions?"

"Yeah," I replied wearily. "Listen, could we do this at my place? I'd really like to go home."

Annette agreed, so I tracked down Frank, who was chatting with the lieutenant, and gave him the update on Pete's condition. He nodded and flashed me a brief but beautiful smile.

Twenty minutes later I waved Annette into a chair at the pine kitchen table in my apartment, pulled a cheap bottle of Cabernet from my meager wine rack, and arranged smoked Gouda, salami, and a sourdough baguette on a wooden cutting board.

"Hey, where's Ichabod tonight?" I asked.

"Who?"

"Icha—Sorry. Inspector Wilson."

"What did you call him?"

"Um, Ichabod? No offense intended."

"As in Ichabod Crane, from the *Legend of Sleepy Hollow*?"

"That'd be the one."

Annette laughed and accepted a glass of the ruby red wine. "You know, he's always reminded me of someone, but I couldn't quite put my finger on it. I think you may have nailed it."

"So how'd you know what happened?" I asked as I settled down at the table.

"I was passing by your studio earlier and saw the patrol cars," she said, cutting a wedge of the Gouda. "I've been a little worried about you. The patrol officer told me about the call and where you could be found."

"You were worried about me? Why?" I asked as I sawed off pieces of the sourdough baguette. Nothing like being kidnapped and held at knifepoint to pique a woman's appetite.

Annette's eyes shone with amusement. "Let's just call it policewoman's intuition. Seems like I was right, huh?"

"Yeah, I guess things have been a little exciting lately. It's not my fault, though, honest."

I chewed my dry-salami-and-smoked-Gouda-on-baguette sandwich, took a sip of the Cabernet, and decided to come clean. It didn't look like I was going to get Brazil's reward for recovering the drawings anyway, and I was *not* willing to go up against any more murderous goons. I was occasionally heedless, but I wasn't stupid. So I told Annette an abridged version of my search for the drawings that Harlan Coombs had taken and how I thought Coombs might be connected to the *Magi* forgeries. I did not tell her about Anton, although I did mention Michael X. Johnson, figuring the X-man could take care of himself.

"Michael X. Johnson?" Annette repeated.

"You know him?"

"I've heard the name." Her cop face was back. "Listen, Annie, you ought to get some rest. Thanks for the wine and conversation."

"Wait a minute!" I protested. "Who's Michael X. Johnson?"

"I've got to go," she said firmly. "I promise I'll get in touch just as soon as I can. Go to bed." And with that, she was gone.

Why did a homicide inspector know Michael X. Johnson? Why did the well-dressed goon know Michael X. Johnson? Why did *I* know Michael X. Johnson? I tried to sort it all out, but my mind seemed to be shutting down now that it had been wined and dined. I managed to put the food away, brush my teeth, and kick off my shoes before falling into bed with my clothes on.

*   *   *

Ten hours later I awoke, my mind clearer, my body aching. I had studiously avoided the mirror last night, figuring the odds of my having nightmares were bad enough as it was, but this morning I girded my loins and sneaked a peek. Hmm. Could have been worse. I had some light bruises on my cheek and lower jaw, a cut at the corner of my mouth, and a scab on my neck from where the Hulk's knife had pricked my skin. My muscles were sore, but whether it was from being tied up or from the unaccustomed running around, I wasn't sure. As for the rest of me, my hair was snarled and frizzy, and I smelled pretty funky. Day Three in the same set of clothes.

I stripped and tried to brush out my hair. Usually I was ruthless with it, but today my scalp ached so much from the Hulk's manhandling that I tried to be gentle. Unfortunately, gentle was not effective, so I decided to leave the worst of the snarls until my scalp was less tender. I shampooed and stood under the hot spray until the water ran tepid, and did my best with the conditioner, but it was going to be a really bad hair day no matter what I did.

Wrapping my newly clean self in a mint green terry-cloth robe, I wandered down the hall into the kitchen. I rooted around in the refrigerator until I found a container of leftover hot-and-sour soup that appeared to still be edible. I ate at the kitchen table, staring out the window and thinking about yesterday. My humdrum life had become rather more interesting lately, and I wasn't at all sure that was a good thing. My friend had been attacked, my studio was trashed, and I had been kidnapped and threatened by goons. Worst of all, since I wasn't sure why, I had no idea how to make it stop. On the plus side, I'd have some ripping good yarns to tell at the old folks' home—if I lived that long.

Rinsing my bowl and spoon in the kitchen sink, I scuffed back into the bedroom, changed into an Indian wrap skirt and a black T-shirt, slipped on my Birken-stocks, snagged my leather jacket, and hurried down-stairs. I was anxious to get back to my studio, assess the damage, and track down my insurance agent. But first things first. I headed to the UCSF Medical Center to visit my Bosnian hero.

Pete looked awful. His usual hale and hearty self had a number of tubes stuck in it, his skin had a grayish pal-lor, a large white bandage swathed his head, and his face was swollen. My heart sank into my shoes. A pretty nurse caught my stricken look and assured me he was on the mend. I wanted to believe her, but he sure didn't look like it.

"Pete?" I said gently.

His eyes flickered open, then focused. "Annie, thank the goodness you're all right. But what happened to your face?"

That was Pete for you, more concerned with my safety than his own. I felt tears start in my eyes and my throat constricted. "I'm fine, just a few scratches. How are *you*?"

"I am itching where they make the stitches. But I am not too aggrieved."

"Oh, Pete, I'm so sor—"

"Annie. Please." He reached a large hand out, and I grabbed it. His touch was as warm and comforting as ever.

"But Pete—"

"Annie. No sorrows. Please. We are friends, yes?"

"Yes, yes. Good friends."

"Good friends," he echoed, with a smile. "So, no more."

I smiled, a bit unsteadily, trying to get my emotions under control. "What happened?" I asked him.

"They hit me with a sheet of beautiful glass. Cobalt

blue. Can you believe? Thank God she was not the hand-made."

Pete was well known for pinching a penny, but I thought being grateful for being coshed on the head by the cheap glass instead of the expensive stuff was taking thriftiness too far.

"I can't believe you're worried about cost at a time like this," I told him.

Pete's heavy eyebrows arched. "The machine-made, she is thinner than the handmade. With the thicker glass, I might have had deeper cuts and bleeded more."

Oh.

"Can I call your mother or anything?" I offered.

Pete's extended family lived in Hayward, just south of Oakland. I'd never met them, but I knew from Pete's stories that they were a boisterous, loving bunch.

He winced. "Please, Annie, no. My mama, she worry. She would make me go home with her. This would be bad. The doctors say I will be fine soon. So no mama. I will tell her when I am stronger."

The sight of big, tough Pete shrinking from a confrontation with his mother made me smile. We chatted and I told him the rest of the story, downplaying the more dangerous aspects so as not to upset him. Then for the heck of it I asked, "Have you ever heard of a Colin Brooks?"

"He was watching for you yesterday."

I sat up straight. "What? Where? What did you tell him?"

"He was at your studio when I went to make coffee. I told him to watch for you at your apartment."

"Did you tell him where my apartment was, Pete?" I said, trying to keep the outrage at Michael's effrontery out of my voice.

"He said he knew. He is Egyptologist at the Brock. He

told me he is dating your friend . . . Nancy? No . . .
Naomi!"

"An Egyptologist? An *Egyptologist*?"

Pete's bloodshot eyes widened. "What is wrong?"

Immediately, I felt contrite. *Get a grip, Annie,* I scolded
myself. *This man is in the hospital because of you.*

"I'm just surprised, that's all," I told him. "You go
back to sleep and get well *soon*, okay? Maybe there's a
nurse around here you could marry. I just saw one who
seems awfully nice. Probably just waiting for a chance to
talk with you alone." I gave him a kiss and headed out the
door.

Since I had, once again, neglected to recharge my cell
phone battery, I stopped at the bank of pay phones in the
lobby, dug through my leather fanny pack, and finally unearthed two slightly fuzzy quarters. As I dialed the Brock
Museum I felt assaulted by the hospital's medicinal
sounds and smells and broadsided by what I'd learned
about Colin Brooks.

"Naomi Chadwick Gregorian."

I wondered if she practiced sounding so snooty or
whether it came naturally. I suspected it was a bit of both.

"Naomi," I said. "It's Annie."

There was a pause. When she spoke again, the cheery
tone rang false. "Annie, how nice to hear from you. What
can I do for you?"

"I need information. Do you know someone named
Colin Brooks?" No use beating around the bush. It had
been my experience that social amenities were wasted on
Nancy Fancy Pants.

"Of course. He's the new Egyptologist here at the
Brock."

As if I didn't know what the "here" referred to. Naomi
loved reminding me that she worked at "the Brock"—and
I didn't.

"Really? Do you know him well?"

"Actually . . . I've been seeing Colin socially. Annie, he's sooo cute!"

"So, where did this Brooks fellow come from? You've never mentioned him," I said, keeping my tone light. As if Naomi and I had ever traded girlish secrets. Even when we were girls we never traded girlish secrets.

Naomi giggled. I gagged.

"Edward Brock—do you know him? Dull Dick and Fabulous Phoebe's son? Well, he's started to take a real interest in the museum, and old lady Brock couldn't be more pleased. So anyway, Edward started studying Egyptology, and he met Colin on a buying trip last fall. And since the Brock didn't have much representation in the Egyptian field, Edward convinced his grandmother to hire Colin."

"So Edward has the museum board's ear, does he?"

"I'll say. He's next in line to the Throne of Power."

During my ill-fated internship at the Brock, I'd taken to calling Agnes Brock's antique burgundy-and-brass-studded leather desk chair, which had been her husband's and his father's before him, the Throne of Power, and the name had stuck. Agnes revered the Throne with a love that was surely unholy, and one of Housekeeping's jobs was to wipe it down with saddle soap and oil the springs once a week. The year I was there, Carlos Jimenez had finally succeeded in convincing the museum to hire his son, Juan, as a housekeeper trainee. On his first day on the job Juan had been so eager to please the Brocks and his father that he'd polished the marble foyer within an inch of its life, but, unfortunately, he forgot to bathe the Throne. The next day Agnes called Juan into her office and fired him on the spot. Carlos had been devastated.

That night I had snuck into the Throne Room and slid a whoopee cushion behind Agnes's lumbar pillow. As a result, the next morning, when Agnes sat down to meet with the mayor, the Throne of Power emitted a very loud and extremely vulgar noise. We'd heard the repercussions all the way down in the basement, and Carlos had smiled for a week.

"Edward's got the big corner office," Naomi continued, "the mahogany-lined one with the great windows, remember? God, what I wouldn't give to have an office like that. I had to smile when Mrs. Brock took away access to the vault from everyone but herself—including her family. I thought Edward would have an apoplectic fit when she announced it. Anyway, if they want to keep the Throne in the family, who else is there?"

"Hmm. Listen, Naomi. Funny thing. It's just such a coincidence. I have a few things I need to discuss with an Egyptologist. Is this Colin guy around today? Where's his office?"

"He's out of town." Naomi sounded suspicious. "At a conference in New York."

Did she think I would make a play for her lying, cheating, conniving fake of a boyfriend? Better check those airline ticket stubs, Naomi, I thought, and got off the phone before I said something I might have to apologize for one day.

Egyptologist, my ass. Not a bad cover, though. Not even the other curators would have asked detailed questions. Everybody in the business thought ancient Egyptian art was fascinating, but nobody except the specialists knew squat about it, and certainly nobody at the Brock, which had a very small Egyptian collection and, up until now, no specialist curator. The position would give Michael access to just about everything at the museum. Except the vault. He was too new to have been given access to that. Agnes Brock was a mean old cuss, but she wasn't stupid.

So Edward Brock had recommended hiring the X-man, had he? Kind of made a person pause and think. Given the facts that Harlan was missing, and Anton was missing, and I had no idea where to find Michael, maybe I should see if I could track down the one person who might have a clue as to what was going on: the estimable Mr. Edward Brock.

I searched my fanny pack for more quarters, but only came up with a bunch of pennies and a couple of nickels. Damn that cell phone. When somebody finally designed a model that recharged itself, I would be the first in line. I checked the clock at the nurses' station. It was a little before eleven. I had to get back to my studio and do some damage control.

First, though, I wanted to see if I could find out anything else about Edward. What I needed was someone who was in the City's art gossip loop. I pointed the truck toward the Mission District, a part of San Francisco that used to be labeled "affordable," which meant it was crime-ridden, drug-ridden, and the only place that would rent to poor immigrants. On the other hand, it was full of the sense of community that develops when thousands of people from Latin America live, work, and raise their children in the same area. Along Valencia, bands played loudly until all hours, tacos were served twenty-four hours a day, and funky used-book stores stayed open until midnight. As in so much of the City, the Mission's affordability had dissolved in the past few years as more and more yuppies and dot-com well-to-dos had moved in.

It was still a lively area, though, edgy, artsy, and young. I squeezed into a hard-won parking space and walked over to a small doorway sandwiched between a sushi bar and a Laundromat. I rang the bell before using the low-tech way to gain entry to the apartment building's quirky front door without a key: by holding the ring in the back, pulling it forward, and pushing the door in at the same time.

I started climbing the cramped staircase and spotted Bryan Boissevain coming down, a buff, handsome black man dressed as if heading off to the beach, in a tight T-shirt and cutoff jeans. My dear friend Bryan worked as a freelance architect in the top-floor apartment he shared with his partner, Ron. The two were big boosters of the City's culture, and Bryan was a huge gossip. If there were dirt on anyone at the Brock, he would know about it.

"Annie!" he exclaimed. "To what do I owe this pleasure? And what in the world happened to your face, girl?"

"You should see the other guy," I said with a smile. Visiting Bryan was always a mood-booster. He flung an arm around my shoulder and escorted me up to his place, talking the whole time.

Bryan and Ron had a wonderful apartment that they had stripped to the bare bones and painstakingly redone, salvaging most of the original intricate molding that rimmed the twelve-foot-high ceilings. Colored light beamed in through a large stained-glass window on one wall of their living room. Bryan started showing me their latest project, a full-scale arboretum on the rooftop deck, but I interrupted to say I was in a huge hurry and then got to the point.

"Edward Brock?" he exclaimed when I had finished. "Oh, my God, *yes*, baby doll. I can't believe you haven't heard. I mean, even you must hear *something* once in a while, no?" Bryan seated me on a Lucite barstool at the granite kitchen counter and started opening cupboards and taking out glasses.

"I've been kind of busy recently, Bryan," I apologized. Somehow, when I was with Bryan, I felt completely out of touch, yet also totally at home.

"Oh, honey," he said as he began to fix me a glass of

fresh lemonade, over my halfhearted objections. The scent of lemon oil filled the sunny kitchen as he enthusiastically squeezed the fruit halves by hand. "Let me tell you. He's got the taste for blow, in a big way," he said as he set a frosty glass in front of me, leaning on his elbows over the counter.

"Cocaine?" I said, sipping the sweet, tangy drink. "So you're saying he's hooked?"

"Oh, yes, baby doll. A big-time clubber, too, although he's a little old for it, in my book. Straight people should stop clubbing when they turn thirty."

"Is this from the book of rules for straight people as written by a gay guy?" I teased him.

"You bet your booty it is," Bryan asserted. "The problem with straight people is that they don't pay enough attention to things like etiquette."

"I take your point," I replied dryly. "So, do you know if Edward has any steady girlfriends?"

"There's that Q girl."

I practically spit my lemonade out through my nose. "Q?"

"Quiana Nash. Goes by Q. A bit of a skank, in my book. *Great* eyes, though."

"Tall, blond, skinny?"

"Like every other model out there."

"I thought Quiana was seeing someone else."

"Who isn't she with? Supposedly she's been living with some other fellow from the Brock—you never see him out in the scene, though. And there are others, believe you me."

I mulled that one over. "So, what would you think if I told you Edward Brock had developed a sudden interest in Egyptology?"

Bryan let out a snort. "That boy is interested in fast cars, fast women, and easy drugs. End of story. If he went to Egypt, you better believe it was to score something illegal. Don't tell me you're interested in him, Annie. I know you're hard up, but you can do *so* much better."

"I am not hard up." *As if celibacy were something to be ashamed of,* I thought grumpily. *Or maybe it was only celibacy by choice that was admirable.* "I'll have you know I spent the night with a *very* attractive man last Saturday."

"He was gay, right?"

"Not every attractive man in this city is gay, Bryan. Most of them, but not all."

"Did you do the wild thing? C'mon, girl, dish!" The look on my face must have dished me out because he continued, "Oh, no, honey, that's even worse. You mean you spent the night with a cute guy and you didn't get any? And he wasn't gay? What am I going to do with you?"

"What about Harlan Coombs?" I asked in a blatant bid to change the subject. "Ever heard of him?"

"You mean that art dealer fellow? The one that disappeared? There were rumors that he was doin' the horizontal tango with a sixty-something femme fatale on the Brock's board of directors."

"Please tell me you're not talking about Agnes Brock," I said, feeling a bit queasy.

"No, the other one. Camilla Culpepper."

"You're kidding me."

"Camilla was a bit of swinger in her salad days. And she still has *quite* the eye for the young men."

"But isn't she married . . . ?"

Bryan sighed. "Oh, baby doll, wake up and smell the twenty-first century."

I glanced at the kitchen clock, which was inching toward noon. "I've got to go, Bryan. Thanks for the lemonade, and the information," I said.

"Baby doll, I *know* you aren't involved in what's going

on at the Brock, right? It sounds like something dangerous happening with that crowd. Did you hear about that
poor janitor who was killed the other night?"

I assured Bryan I would be careful, then hurried to my
truck and navigated the lunchtime traffic over to the
Brock, parked on a side street, and started rummaging
through the mishmash of junk behind my seat. Beneath a
layer of trash and miscellaneous art supplies, I unearthed
a clipboard with a number of invoices on it, some pink
reading glasses decorated with rhinestones that I'd
bought at the drugstore because I thought they looked
campy, and a large faux-tortoiseshell hair clip.

Piling my hair atop my head as best I could and fas-
tening it with the hair clip, I put on the glasses, applied
some lipstick I kept in the glove box for emergencies, and
buttoned my black coat over my Indian skirt. I was re-
gretting my casual dress, especially the Birkenstocks.
They were clunky and ugly, and a bit of a local joke, but
were also supremely comfortable if you were on your feet
a lot, as I was. Oh, well. Maybe no one would notice the
shoes.

Clutching the clipboard to my chest officiously, I
strode up to the museum entrance. "Good afternoon," I
said in my most professional voice. "I am here to see Mr.
Edward Brock."

An elderly docent with a pleasant smile hurriedly
stashed a crossword puzzle below the counter. "Do you
have an appointment?" she asked.

"Is that the *New York Times* Sunday crossword?" I
gushed in a conspiratorial whisper as I leaned closer. "I
am a *fiend* for the Sunday crossword."

She laughed. "Me too, but I'm not supposed to be
doing it while on duty."

I rolled my eyes in commiseration. "Great-aunt Agnes
has quite a hawk eye, hasn't she?"

"Ah—Great-aunt Agnes? Mrs. Brock is your aunt?" The docent looked at me with respect tinged with worry.

I rolled my eyes again and added a little shoulder hike, hoping I wasn't overdoing it. I was counting heavily on the widely shared dislike of the old bat to work in my favor. "Yeah, can you believe we're related?" I said. "Anyway, I promise I won't mention the crossword puzzle if you'll tell me what you got for thirty-two across."

"Meringue," she said, glancing down at the half-hidden puzzle. She waved me through with a hesitant smile, even offering to call ahead for me. I told her not to bother—I wanted to surprise dear Cousin Edward. I winked at her and she winked back.

I hurried down the Brock's lushly detailed hallway for the second time that week, keeping my head down in case I passed someone who might recognize me. The museum's offices didn't see a lot of Indian skirts and Birkenstocks.

While pondering the most effective means of attack, I searched for Edward's discreet brass doorplate and finally found it at the end of the hall that led to the conference room. I raised my hand to knock, then reconsidered. Maybe a frontal assault would make more sense. Pushing the door open, I was relieved to see that the outer office was devoid of a secretary.

"Edward?" I called, wading through the thick red pile carpet to the inner office door.

No response.

I felt a tingle on the back of my neck and spun around. Nothing. I needed to calm down. But what if Edward were in there, lying in a pool of blood like poor Joanne? What if the Hulk were lurking inside, waiting for me? What if . . .

Hearing Edward's voice from down the hall, I ducked into the inner office. Rats, he was with someone. Either

that, or he had gone off his meds and was talking agitatedly to himself. The surge of confidence I'd gained from
my interaction with the woman at the door had yielded to
the realization that I might be out of my league here.
Tricking a kindly docent was one thing; conning a con
man like Edward was quite another. I spied a carved
black lacquer chinoiserie screen in the far corner of the
office, gave in to cowardice, and hid behind it. I'd just
wait here for him to finish up his business, then slip out
and try to talk my way through the embarrassment if
caught. Anyway, it was too late now—Edward and his
guest were coming into the inner office.

"For God's sake, Edward, calm down," his companion
said.

Well, well. The X-man must have caught a fictional
red-eye from the fictional conference in New York. Now
we were getting somewhere.

"That's easy for you to say," Edward snapped. "She
just called Naomi to ask about me. And about you, in case
you've forgotten."

"She didn't ask about me, she asked about Colin
Brooks. She knows me by a different name entirely,"
Michael said in that calm, patronizing tone he so often
used with me. "Now, here's what we need to do—"

"I'm sick of you deciding what 'we' need to do," Edward told him. They were standing close to me now, just
on the other side of the screen. I held my breath. "I need
to find Harlan, that's what *I* need to do! He had you put
the wrong painting back in the vault, damn it! My ass is
hanging out in the wind and you tell me to calm down?!"

"Listen to me, Edward, and listen carefully," Michael
replied soothingly. "You need to get hold of yourself. All
you've done is borrow family property for a little while,
right? That's not a crime."

What a load of bullpucky. Yeah, Edward had "borrowed" *The Magi*—to have it replaced with a forgery. If Edward bought what Michael was selling, he was dumber than I thought.

"So here's what we need to do," Michael said again in that ever-so-reasonable voice. "You stay here and act like you're doing something useful. I'll find Harlan and the other painting. It stands to reason that if the one in the vault is a fake, and the one Harlan sold to the New Yorker is a fake, too, then the real painting is still out there. Harlan probably has it or sold it, so at the very least, I can steal it back. *If* you don't blow it for us in the meantime."

"I need the money, Colin, and I need it soon," Edward whined. "The people I owe are breathing down my neck. Plus, there are those goons from New York. I sent them to see that Kincaid chick, but they'll be back—"

"You sent them *where*?"

"I had to give them something. I told them she knew where Anton and Harlan were."

Hearing a muffled scuffling, a thud, and a gagging sound, I peeked around a corner of the screen and saw Michael was holding Edward by the collar, up against the wall.

"You sniveling little shit," Michael spat. "That woman is *my* concern, do you understand? They better not have hurt her, or I'll take it out of your worthless hide—you got me?"

Edward gagged and whimpered as Michael tossed him into the desk chair like a discarded doll.

"Try to act like you belong here, will you?" Michael said with angry disdain, turning on his heel and stalking out of the office.

I was ashamed to admit that I'd felt a little thrill when Michael had Edward by the throat. For a pacifist, I seemed to be responding rather readily to violence these days. And what was that about "That woman is *my* concern"? At the moment, though, more urgent worries took precedence.

Number One: I had to get out of my hiding place and follow Michael somehow. Number Two: I had to find a bathroom. The lemonade was making itself known in a big way.

I soon caught a break. Edward sat at his desk, no doubt licking his wounded pride and trying to figure out how to pin the blame on someone else. After a few moments, he picked up the phone and dialed.

"We have to talk. *Now*. No, in person. Meet me at the diner. Mm-hmm. Twenty minutes." Edward stood, smoothed his shirt, and left the office at a trot.

Priority Number Two moved into the Number One spot. But first I wanted to try something. I walked over to the desk and saw that Edward's phone had a tiny digital display screen. When I hit the REDIAL button a telephone number popped up on the display.

Just call me Super Sleuth, I bragged to myself as I wrote the number down and waited to see who answered. Although the phone rang and rang, no one picked up. No problem, I thought smugly. Now that I had a friend in the SFPD this would be simple. I'd give Annette the number and ask her to find out to whom it belonged. Pleased with myself, I turned to leave and find a bathroom.

Unfortunately, the man standing in the doorway seemed to have another plan in mind.

Chapter 11

I let out a little screech.

The X-man rolled his eyes.

Michael was standing in the doorway to the outer office, much as he had been when I first met him at
Anton's: shoulder against the doorframe, arms crossed
over his chest. He was wearing his brown leather bomber
jacket, a bright white T-shirt, and well-worn Levi's.

He did not look surprised to see me.

"If you're going to continue in this line of work,
Annie, you will have to learn to stifle your scream im-
pulse." He gave me a leisurely once-over. "Love the hair.
But what in the hell happened to your face?"

My hand darted up to soothe my wild curls. "*I* am not
in 'this line of work.' I am a legitimate small-business
owner who gets a little jumpy around you criminal
types."

"That so? What about those stunts you and your dear grandpapa pulled off in your younger days?"

Maybe I could bluff. "I don't know what you're talking about."

Michael snorted.

Maybe not.

"Who told you?"

Crossing over to Edward's desk, he began searching for something, cool as a cucumber. "Well, let's see," he said. "There was Ernst Pettigrew. And Anton. And Harlan Coombs. Plus Joanne Nash. And let's not forget Naomi. She mentioned it several times, I believe. Then there was Agnes Brock. And Sebastian Pitts. No love lost there, eh? Oh, and your grandfather, of course. He's very proud of you, you know."

My grandfather? He'd spoken with my *grandfather*? I couldn't get Georges to return my calls, but he was happy to chat with Michael the art thief?

"I think maybe your Slovak friend said something about it as well," he added.

"Bosnian." I sighed. "He's Bosnian."

Seems the whole world was in on my little secret. I could move to Chicago, I thought. I liked Chicago. Except for the weather. Sometimes I wondered why I was working so hard to be a legitimate artist.

Michael paused in his methodical search and looked at me. "You seem a little jumpy today, Annie."

"Two people have been killed, Michael—Colin—whatever your name is. *Two.* And Ernst is still unaccounted for. Not to mention that someone torched my studio, put my friend in the hospital, and kidnapped me. And for all I know, the man responsible is standing across the room from me. On top of everything else, I have to pee like nobody's business."

"Oh, *please.* You don't really think I had anything to

do with the murders, do you? I'm a thief, Annie. A *non-violent* thief. I swear, though, this is the last time I do a group job." Michael spoke in the melancholy tone normally reserved for those lamenting the decline of morals in our modern society.

"So—you admit you're a thief!" I said, feeling triumphant.

Michael looked at me disdainfully. "Usually I'm a solo act," he said, "but I thought it would be good for me to work with people. Annie, please stop twitching like that—there's a bathroom over there." He nodded toward an intricately carved door next to the black-lacquer screen. Well, what do you know.

I used the facilities and afterward was able to think more clearly. I had no reason to believe Michael, but I did. He had been as shocked as I to find Joanne's body, and, so far at least, he had been violent only in self-defense. Plus, he owed me money, so I thought I would give him the benefit of the doubt.

"So what's the deal with Edward?" I asked as I emerged from the bathroom.

Michael was engrossed in opening a wall safe.

"Don't you need a stethoscope or something to hear the tumblers fall?" I whispered, drawing upon my vast knowledge of *Mission: Impossible.*

"Not if you find the combination in the Rolodex."

"You're kidding. Edward filed the combination in his *Rolodex?*"

Michael looked at me. "Does Edward seem like he could keep a long series of numbers in his head? I found it under 'C' for 'Combination.' He'd also programmed Harlan's and Anton's numbers into his speed dial until I pointed out the error of his ways. What a moron."

So much for the brotherhood of thieves.

"Why did you get involved with him if he's such a moron?"

"Anton's an old friend," Michael answered while riffling through the safe's contents. "Harlan Coombs got Anton into this Internet trading thing. When tech stocks crashed last year, they lost most of their money, but Harlan convinced our dear naïve Anton to invest more, thinking the market would turn around."

"But Anton doesn't know squat about anything except art," I said.

"Which may be why he lost almost all his life savings. He'd been wanting to buy a condo in Boca and retire, and Harlan assured him he'd make a bundle, fast. Anyway, Harlan started borrowing against drawings that didn't belong to him and had Anton make forgeries. The plan was for Harlan to sell the originals and he and Anton would share the proceeds. But Harlan put most of the money back into Internet trading, leaving Anton high and dry. Now Harlan owes big bucks to some real bad guys—loan sharks as well as the art dealers he and Anton were duping. Some of those dealers are mean SOBs, too. Don't let the bow ties fool you."

"But where does *The Magi* fit in? And Edward?"

"*The Magi* was the magic bullet that would solve their problems. I owed Anton a favor from an incident in Ireland a few years ago. He introduced me to Harlan, who said he had a private New York buyer lined up."

"So Harlan had Anton paint a fake *Magi* . . ."

". . . and I switched it with the Brock's real one. The idea was a simple trade and sale, the forgery for the original. I would be paid a hefty fee, Anton could rebuild his nest egg, Harlan would get the loan sharks off his back, and that would be the end of the story. Unfortunately, Harlan brought in Edward as our inside man." Michael wiped a large hand over his face and sighed. "As you may have noticed, Edward is not exactly a criminal mastermind."

"Hmm," I murmured, unable to offer the X-man the sympathy he so obviously felt he deserved.

"I made the switch easily enough, but then Edward panicked," he continued, leafing through a pile of documents he'd pulled from the safe. "It seems Ernst Pettigrew was raising questions about *The Magi*'s authenticity. That was bad enough, but then you showed up and confirmed that it was a fake. Then Dupont was killed, Ernst disappeared, and Edward was petrified that our scheme would be uncovered. So he insisted Harlan return the original *Magi,* and I made the switch again—at no small risk to my own neck, I might add. Then you came along, *again,* and told everyone that one was a fake, too."

He looked at me as though this were somehow my fault.

"It *is* a fake."

"Yeah, well, I'd like to know what happened to the original. Because the one Harlan sold the guy in New York was a fake, too. I'm assuming that Harlan was double-crossing us all and that he sold the original *Magi* to yet another buyer, or has it hidden in a safe place. But there's a part of me that's starting to wonder if there ever *was* an original."

Now that caught my attention. The reappearance of the long-lost Caravaggio had been little short of miraculous. Had it been a fake all along?

"Who authenticated *The Magi* in the first place?" I asked.

Michael frowned. "It hardly matters now. What's important is that Harlan skipped town without paying me or Anton."

"It matters a lot," I insisted. "If there's no genuine Caravaggio, then two lives have been lost and a lot of people have been hurt over forgeries. Whoever originally 'authenticated' the painting from Anton might have been in on this whole thing."

"Aha!" he said, ignoring me and holding up a piece of yellow paper. "A bill of sale to a Camilla Culpepper, of Belvedere and the Cayman Islands. Maybe *she's* got the damned original." He shoved the paper into his jacket pocket and glanced at his watch. "Time to vamoose. Edward's secretary will be back any second. The woman's as regular as a machine."

"Hold on. Why would a criminal issue a bill of sale?"

Michael shooed me out of the inner office, closing the door behind us. "We can talk more in the car, Annie. Right now we have to move. If I'm not mistaken, you ratted me out to the SFPD."

"Ratted you *out*?" I now recalled why I'd been so angry with the X-man: the motel bill, the abandonment, the lies. " 'Ratting you out' implies that we are working together, which we most certainly are *not,* and that I owe you some kind of loyalty, which I most certainly do *not.* I—"

"Yeah, whatever," Michael said as he opened the door to the hallway. "Yell at me later, Annie. Right now let's *go.*"

"I'll leave after you," I said, deciding that the less time spent with Michael, the better. I had more pressing items on my agenda today, such as getting back to my studio and salvaging what I could from yesterday's arson disaster.

"I think you should come with me," he said. "We need to talk."

"No. I want nothing to do with you, or your thieving friends. I—"

Someone was coming toward us.

Michael stepped into the hallway, saying, ". . . catch

up with him later. Oh, good. It's Sylvia. Sylvia, would you tell Edward I was looking for him? I wanted to introduce him to my cousin, who's visiting from Wisconsin and just loves art! Sylvia, this is my cousin Susie. Susie-Q, say hi to Sylvia."

Susie-Q choked out a garbled greeting.

In her sixties, gray-haired, plump, with pronounced frown lines, Sylvia looked as if she played bridge with "the girls" every Saturday, brought tuna noodle casseroles topped with crushed potato chips to church functions every Sunday, and spent the rest of the week making life hell for everyone else. In short, she looked like she was born to work at the Brock. I could only imagine what she thought of Edward, Michael, and Michael's cousin from Wisconsin, Susie-Q. Sylvia glared suspiciously at Michael, who stood his ground, smiling brightly. She said she would give Edward the message. She did not sound pleased about it.

Michael steered me out the door and into the hallway, his hand gripping my upper arm. I tried pulling away, but he held on tighter and muttered through clenched teeth, "Just keep quiet until we get outside. Then we'll discuss this."

Dragging me down the hall, Michael used a key to open a door marked MAINTENANCE. Behind it was a passageway lined with archival drawers as well as the large pipes and air ducts required for an operation the size of the Brock. I remembered getting lost in these corridors after the whoopee cushion incident. Michael hustled us through the twists and turns without hesitation, finally taking a sharp right in order to tap a code into the keypad next to a fire exit. He opened it cautiously, peering about to see if the coast was clear.

We left the building and I blinked in the late-morning sunshine. The fresh air felt wonderful after the stuffiness

of the museum, but I wished Michael would slow down—
I needed to get in better shape if I was going to run
around like this. He continued in a half jog over a land-
scaped hillock and out onto the street, where he broke
into a full run, dragging me behind him the length of a
city block, then ducking into an alleyway where the red
Jeep was hidden behind a Dumpster. Michael unlocked
the doors and we jumped in, winded. Well, *I* was winded;
he was just breathing a little fast. I wanted to yell at him
but my brain had ordered all available oxygen to report to
my lungs, *stat*. Michael fired up the engine and we took
off, away from the Brock and toward the Golden Gate
Bridge.

"Where-are-we-going?" I puffed.

He glanced at me. "You all right?"

"Just-peachy-keen. So, is this another—" I gasped.
"—kidnapping?"

"What are you talking about?"

"What I *mean* is—" Breathe, Annie, breathe. I was
starting to find my rhythm. "—You're taking me away
from the Brock and out of the city against my will."

Michael snorted. "Don't be so melodramatic. It's not
against your will."

"Yes it is."

"Do you see a gun anywhere? Did you call for help
when we were in the museum or on the street? Have I
threatened you in any way?"

"Just stop the damned Jeep," I commanded.

So he did. Right in the middle of a four-lane thorough-
fare.

"Not here!"

Michael shook his head. "I really don't know what you
want from me sometimes," he said, gunning the engine.

"What I *want* is my money back, you big jerk. You

abandoned me in Napa and then stuck me with the cost of the motel room."

"Ah, so *that's* what this is all about. What's that saying about a woman scorned? 'Hell hath no fu—' *Oomph!*"

I hit him. In the gut. Now he was the one with the breathing problem.

"That's not the reaction of a woman scorned, asshole," I snarled. "That's the reaction of a woman stranded hours from home, with no ID, no cash, no idea where her truck is, and a huge motel bill. Plus a hangover."

I was beginning to regret not having called the cops down on his admittedly handsome head when I had the chance. I ignored a stunning view of the Golden Gate Bridge in favor of glaring at him.

His lips twitched. "The hangover wasn't *my* fault, Annie. So, how'd you talk your way out of it?"

"None of your beeswax." Funny how, when one acted like a child, one spoke like one, too. "But it cost me more than four hundred dollars to get back home. You *owe* me."

The Jeep had started to wind through the Marin hills as Michael looked at me in astonishment. "Four hundred dollars! For what? What did you do, switch to the penthouse suite after I left?"

"The motel room was forty-five. It cost me sixty for the ride to Yountville, the search for the truck, and the understanding of the motel manager."

"I hope he was very understanding, at that rate."

"Plus another ten for the curry and the naan."

"Curry and what?"

"Naan. And seventy-five for the tow to the service station, then two hundred forty for the repair."

He looked shocked. "What tow? What repair?"

I sighed. "Once I finally found the truck, it wouldn't start. I had to have it towed, and the garage replaced the distributor cap, or spark plugs, or something. It cost two hundred and forty dollars."

"Jesus, Annie, don't you know anything about cars? The distributor cap was sitting just to the side of the heads. All you had to do was snap it back on."

I experienced a moment of horrifying clarity. "You mean *you* disabled my truck? You are the lowest-down, lyingest piece of—" Furious, I fished around in my fanny pack and pulled out my cell phone, determined to call a certain friend of mine in the SFPD. Then I remembered that its battery was dead.

Michael, not knowing that, leaned over and snatched it out of my hand. "Calm down, Annie," he said in that infuriatingly even voice before tossing the phone out the window.

"I don't believe you did that!" I said, outraged, as I watched the phone bounce on the pavement and be smashed under the tires of the car behind us.

Michael snorted again.

I slumped in my seat and crossed my arms over my chest. "I want my four hundred dollars. Plus a new cell phone."

"Look," Michael said, his tone utterly sincere, "let's make a deal. First, no hitting."

"That goes both ways, you know."

"I have *never* hit you," Michael said, clearly appalled.

"No arm grabbing, then."

"Deal. Second, you help me figure this out, and I'll pay you much more than four hundred dollars plus a cell phone. I have an idea where *The Magi* might be. Possibly even the real one this time. And that might well lead us to Harlan, and the stolen sketches."

I mulled that over. I figured there had to be a catch somewhere, but I just didn't see it. The money was enticing, but it was more than that. Two people had been killed because of *The Magi*, Anton and Ernst had disappeared, and I wanted some answers. Besides, who was I kidding? I wasn't about to bring the cops down on Michael's head. He reminded me too much of my grandfather.

"If I help you out," I said, "then you pay me the money and make sure Anton's okay. I'm worried about him."

"I think he already left town. He got wind of things going south long before I did."

"What about Ernst?" I asked.

"I don't know," he said quietly, with a shake of his head. "I have no idea what went down that night at the Brock. As far as I knew, Ernst had nothing to do with any of this."

I pondered that for a minute.

"So where are we headed now? You're saying Edward issued a bill of sale for a stolen painting?" To hell with the ethics of keeping company with thieves. I was looking for answers, and at least Michael had some suggestions.

"Not for the stolen painting, but for something referred to as an 'anonymous sixteenth-century Italian oil painting.' And it wasn't from Edward. It was from Harlan, and written out to Robert and Camilla Culpepper. It was with a bunch of other receipts, but dated the day after Harlan disappeared. It's the timing that makes me suspicious. Plus, Harlan mentioned Culpepper a few times. The name rings a bell."

"Mrs. Culpepper is on the Brock's board of directors," I said, glad to be able to contribute to the puzzle. "And rumor has it that she was having an affair with Harlan Coombs."

"You're kidding me," Michael said, glancing at me out of the corner of his eye. "She's twenty years his senior. Then again, if she has enough money to buy stray Caravaggios . . ." He shrugged.

"One thing I don't understand," I said. "Why would Coombs bother writing receipts for stolen merchandise?"

"I can think of two reasons. The Culpeppers need a paper trail in case questions arise about their ownership of the painting. With a receipt, they can claim they bought from a reputable dealer—which Harlan used to be—and were the victims of fraud."

"And the other reason?"

"Harlan might be hoping to return to the legitimate world one day. He might be able to talk his way out of this mess—he's really quite charming. In that case, he would have to claim his income for tax purposes."

"Like he's going to claim income from selling a stolen painting!"

Michael looked at me. "Don't you know what most drug kingpins are taken down for? Tax fraud. Just like the Mafia guys. Here's the kicker: if a drug dealer or a Mafioso claims his ill-gotten gains on his income tax return, the IRS isn't allowed to turn him in."

"You have got to be kidding."

"Look it up. To the IRS, the only crime is hiding income. Harlan's lifestyle is too extravagant to pretend he's not well paid. He needs invoices for everything."

"That Chinatown dump didn't seem particularly posh."

"Honestly, Annie, are you that naïve? That wasn't his home. It was more like an office. He dealt in forgery there. He didn't want his 'associates' to be hanging around his home in Presidio Heights. Which, by the way, is worth a small fortune."

"Dang," I said. Something else occurred to me. "But if Harlan wrote the receipt, why did Edward have it?"

"Edward didn't know he had it. I've been looking everywhere for some trace of Harlan, or at least some paperwork that would give me a lead on the real *Magi*—"

"Including my place?" I interrupted angrily, recalling a certain evil elf grinning up at me from my kitchen corner.

"Hmm. Maybe I should apologize for that."

"You think?"

"Annie, listen. I had no way of knowing where you fit in. Things were falling apart and there you were, casting doubts on a painting I thought was real and showing up in places you had no business being. I thought you were involved. I didn't realize until recently just how clueless you really were."

"Well, gee, thank you very much."

"I meant that in the most positive way imaginable." He grinned at me. I scowled at him. "Anyway, it finally dawned on me that if I were Harlan and wanted to disappear, but wasn't ready to destroy all my records, where better to hide them than among Edward's stuff? Edward doesn't do any actual work, so he would never find them. Plus, the likelihood that anyone would search Edward's office was minimal, because of the museum's security and because so far as anyone knew he wasn't involved in the theft."

"What exactly was Edward's role in all of this?"

"All he was supposed to do was to shut off the motion detectors and get the combination so I could access the vault. He couldn't even manage that."

"Then how *did* you get in?"

"Naomi."

"Naomi!"

"She had access and she was gullible. Useful qualities in a dupe."

I recalled Naomi carrying on about the divine Colin Brooks, and felt sorry for her.

It passed.

"So who killed Dupont and Joanne Nash?" I asked. "Harlan Coombs?"

"I don't know. I wouldn't have thought Harlan capable of such a thing, but then I also thought I could rely on him in this deal, and clearly I was wrong about that." He shook his head. "It could have been someone else. Maybe those goons from New York, or someone else Harlan double-crossed. I just don't know."

"Was Dupont in on the deal? Do you think that Dupont's murder was related to my identifying *The Magi* as a fake?"

"I hope you're not thinking that was your fault, Annie," Michael said. "Things got a little crazy, that's all."

I knew he was right, but I couldn't help thinking that if I hadn't confirmed Ernst's suspicions about *The Magi* that night, Stan Dupont and Joanne Nash might still be alive. The esoteric knowledge my grandfather had so lovingly taught me may have led to two murders. It was a sobering thought.

I'd been so engrossed in our conversation that I hadn't been paying attention to the passing scenery. We had left the freeway and were speeding down a two-lane highway that led past the chichi town of Tiburon on the way to the exclusive island of Belvedere, which boasted multi-million-dollar views of San Francisco, the Golden Gate Bridge, the Bay Bridge, Oakland, and the entire East Bay up to Richmond. You couldn't touch a place on this island for less than several million dollars.

"So, you never told me where we're going," I said.

"We need to make a house call," Michael said enigmatically. He stopped once to consult his Thomas Guide, then drove along a narrow, twisty lane lined with lovely estates. He checked an address on the piece of paper in his hand as we passed an Italianate brick-and-cream palace on our left. Driving well past it, he made a U-turn, and we slowly rolled by it again. Then he kept driving.

"I thought we were making a house call," I said.

"We are. First we need to prepare, though." Michael pulled the Jeep over to the side of the road and brought out his cell phone. There was no question in my mind that *he* remembered to charge his batteries. He punched in a number and waited while it connected. When he spoke, it was with a lilting Irish accent.

"Angela? 'Tis Patrick. How are you, darlin'?" He listened for a minute, laughing softly. "Me too. It was brilliant. Listen, I need a full personal on a Camilla Culpepper, 12 Oakmoor, Belvedere." He spelled the first and last names, as well as those of the street and town. "Uh-huh. An hour, you say? Brilliant. Ta, luv."

I was stunned at his lack of self-consciousness.

"*Patrick?*" I asked scathingly. "*Ta, luv?* Tell me something, *Mr. Johnson,* do you ever get your names or personas mixed up?"

"Rule Number One, Annie: never forget who you are."

"Or who you're not?"

"Precisely."

"You're very scary, you know that?"

"Hungry?" Michael asked.

"Sure." I was easily distracted by food, something Michael seemed to have noticed. "You're buying, though."

"But of course, Annie, me darlin'," he said suavely as he steered the Jeep confidently around the island's hairpin turns. "I know just the place."

Ten minutes later we pulled up in front of a restaurant called Guaymas, on the water in Tiburon. A couple of years ago I'd had the worst date of my life here, a setup with a nuclear physicist named Bradley whose best friend was married to my sister Bonnie's best friend. Bradley spent the entire evening detailing the wacky hijinks he and the other nuclear fizz majors had perpetrated at Cal Tech and explaining why time travel was a practical impossibility. Not that I'd asked. Soon enough, though, I was willing to volunteer as a time-travel guinea pig, if it meant being far, far away from Bradley.

Despite the company, Guaymas was possibly the best Mexican restaurant I had ever been to, serving such specialties as duck in pumpkinseed mole, and enchiladas made of *huitlacoche,* a mushroomlike fungus that grew on ears of corn. I was willing to bet that my lunch with Michael the Thief would be an improvement over my dinner with Bradley the Boring.

When we were seated in a private corner of the dining room, I stopped salivating long enough to order the duck, and had just started stuffing my mouth with tortilla chips and salsa when I heard Michael order two margaritas on the rocks, with salt. That seemed unwise. The last time I had spent an evening with good old Patrick, I had drunk so much I'd lost my truck.

"Iced tea for me, thanks," I said.

"Oh, bring her a margarita anyway," Michael said gaily. The waitress beamed at him and scurried off.

"It's bad form for a grown man to manipulate young women."

"I'm not manipulating anyone. And you're not that young."

"You know what I mean." I leaned back and studied him. Michael was the kind of man who had a woman at every computer terminal. So why would someone so intelligent and attractive do what he did for a living?

"Doesn't your line of work ever bother you?" I asked.

"No."

"How could it not?" I persisted.

The waitress simpered over with the margaritas in

glasses big enough to dunk your face in. She smiled at Michael, caught my scowl, and left.

Michael lifted his glass in a toast. "To us."

"You've got to be kidding."

He looked wounded, the big fake. "All right, then, to success."

We clinked glasses and drank. The mixture of tart lime, rock salt, and cold tequila made me feel like relaxing on the beach for a week. Or ten.

"It's like this," he told me. "I take only from the very wealthy, and I rarely go after museums. It's not as though I damage the art. I simply make it possible for it to be embraced by a new audience."

I interrupted this self-serving claptrap with a noise commonly referred to as a raspberry. Juvenile, but apropos.

Michael ignored me.

"And in the case of this job," he continued, "the idea was to replace *The Magi* with a forgery everyone would believe to be genuine. The Brock Museum would have an 'original,' and the buyer would have *the* original. Everybody would be happy. I'm just spreading the wealth around."

I raspberried again. Michael looked somewhat distressed, so probably I had misgauged the saliva content.

"You sound like my grandfather," I said, "and everyone knows he's full of—"

"Georges LeFleur is a brilliant man."

"Oh, that's right, you know him. Well, pull up a four-leaf clover, Paddy my boy, and I'll tell you what my grandfather is: he's a crook, you hear me? *That's* what he is."

The thread of a first-rate dressing-down was lost in favor of the succulent food laid before us. My duck was to die for. Michael's lunch was shrimp in a cilantro and tomatillo sauce, with a side of mushrooms in chipotle, and we shared bites. The flavors were sublime. Even the intrigue of art theft and murder could sometimes take a backseat to really good food and drink.

By the time we left an hour later I was sober, sated, and mellow. I waited in the car while Michael called Angela again. He stood by the Jeep, using the hood as a desk as he jotted down notes. His side of the conversation consisted mostly of "uh-huh's" and chortles that made me roll my eyes. I did catch something about some unfortunate soul named "Pookie" and an appointment. Another "Ta, luv," and the X-man got into the driver's seat.

I'd strapped myself in and was ready to go when I realized that Michael was not starting the car. Instead, he was staring at his notes. After several long moments he took out his cell phone and turned to me.

"Okay, here's the deal," he said. "I want you to get on the phone and say that you are Emily Caulfield, Camilla Culpepper's assistant, and that Mrs. Culpepper has to cancel her appointment for today. If the massage therapist is already on her way, she is to be recalled *immediately*. That is very important. Mrs. Culpepper is not to be disturbed under any circumstances. Got that?"

I nodded. As my grandfather always said, "If a job's worth doing, it's worth doing well enough not to get caught."

Michael dialed and handed me the phone.

The part of me that had always wanted to be a star of stage and screen surged to the forefront, and I repeated Michael's words in a slightly nasal voice. The woman replied that she would call Pookie on her cell phone immediately, and assured me that Mrs. Culpepper would not be disturbed. I thanked her, hit the OFF button, and turned to Michael, who was looking at me with the approval that my grandfather had shown when I sold my first forgery.

"You know, Annie, you might have a real career ahead of you," he said.

"I already *have* a real career, thank you very much," I replied snippily. "One that does not involve running from law enforcement."

While we drove toward Belvedere, I used Michael's phone to check my voice mail. Linda Fairbanks had called to inquire, pleasantly but firmly, where the hell her samples were, Irene Foster wanted me to confirm that I was still "on track" with her harlequin and wood-grain samples for her home in the Richmond District, and the phone company computer told the phone company voice mail that my account was delinquent.

These reminders that I had a business to run, Mary and myself to support, a scorched and waterlogged studio to clean up, outstanding bills to pay, and a rent hike to talk my way out of produced a tightening in my gut. I had no business having lunch with an art thief and conning my way into a rich woman's home. The contentment of the meal and the margarita ebbed away as I stared reality in the face.

I looked over at Michael, who seemed to be lost in thought.

"Listen, I really need to take care of some things at my studio," I said. "Any idea how long this will take? Do I wait here, do I drive the getaway car, do I fall down and sprain an ankle to distract the guards?" I was toying with the thought of stealing the Jeep while he was inside the Culpepper place. See how *he* liked being stranded.

"Why, you're the star attraction," he replied. "I need you to find the painting and tell me if it's real."

"*I'm* the star attraction? What if Camilla recognizes me?"

"You know her?" Michael asked.

"Not really," I admitted. "I saw her at a board meeting

just a few days ago, but she seemed pretty distracted. Plus, she wasn't wearing her glasses, so I doubt she would recognize me. Still, I'm not what you'd call cool under fire. I tend to scream, in case you've forgotten."

"How could I? Look, Annie, it's simple. I'll keep Camilla busy while you nose around. You'd be amazed how many people keep something like this out in the open, on the dining room wall for all to see. I'll case the joint and find a way to get back in and steal it. But I hate to go to all that bother if it's not what we're after."

"Michael—"

"Annie, Camilla Culpepper bought a stolen masterpiece. At least she intended to. Just think about that for a moment. You don't owe her anything. Not even common courtesy."

He had a point. If Camilla Culpepper had the real *Magi,* I would be helping to return it to its rightful owner. After all, we weren't breaking any laws. We were just taking a quick look around, right?

Michael pulled over in the same spot as before, circled to the rear of the Jeep, opened the back, and began digging through a green athletic bag. As I joined him, curious, he took off his leather jacket, pulled on a sweatshirt emblazoned with the Nike swoosh, kicked off his boots, put on running shoes, and hung a clean white towel around his neck.

"Stand still," he snapped, whipping an Indian-style scarf out of the same bag and tying it around my head like a turban. When he finished, I looked at myself in the Jeep's side mirror. The effect wasn't half bad, if you ignored the faint bruises and scratches on my face. I looked kind of exotic, with wisps of curls sneaking out from under the beautiful fabric. Rummaging in his bag once more, Michael brought out a large, chunky necklace of lapis lazuli and fastened it around my neck. "We'll go for ethnic, instead of athletic," he announced. "Suits you better."

I was afraid to ask what that meant.

Ten minutes later we were driving up the circular driveway. As Michael and I got out, he grabbed a few more towels. Gargoyles leered at us from either side of the two-story front door, and I was ready to hightail it out of there. Michael only looked bored.

The bell was answered by a young woman who I assumed was the real Emily Caulfield, Mrs. Culpepper's assistant. She was about my age, but slender and buttoned-down, her pretty blue eyes hidden behind severe tortoise-shell glasses. Michael turned on the charm, and within minutes they were pals, commiserating over poor Pookie, whose car had been stolen an hour ago, and discussing the hands-on training I was getting by accompanying Bruno here on his rounds. Bruno complained loudly that Pookie's massage table had been in the stolen car, and he did hope Mrs. Culpepper had her own.

Emily led us down a flight of stairs to a ground-floor exercise room, where a professional massage table was set up. She asked if we needed anything, told us Mrs. Culpepper would be with us shortly, and left.

By the time Camilla Culpepper arrived by elevator a few minutes later, Michael had already scoped out the ground floor. It consisted of utilitarian rooms like laundry and storage and a computer room. Not a Caravaggio in sight.

"Oh, Mrs. *Cul*pepper," Michael gushed at the woman with the brittle, pulled-tight look of the undernourished and overexercised. It was a look I saw a lot in my line of work. Clearly Camilla Culpepper had been pampered within an inch of her life. "We've had *such* excitement this morning, have you heard? Poor Pookie had her car stolen!"

Camilla Culpepper smiled carefully as Michael nattered on and on, not allowing her a chance to get a word in edgewise. By the time he whipped off his sweatshirt and slowly rolled up the sleeves of his white T-shirt to better show off his muscular biceps, she was practically eating out of his hand. Within five minutes Camilla was facedown on the massage table, eyes closed and naked except for a towel across her hips. Michael began rubbing her back with lavender-scented oil.

"So I said to Sir Elton, I don't care what anyone says, 'Candle in the Wind' is the best song, like, *ever*—" He looked at me and jerked his head toward the door.

I hesitated, loath to skulk around the cavernous house, not knowing who or what I might run into. But Michael's pantomime took on a frantic quality, so I decided to go for it. Plus my sanity was at stake, since Bruno had launched into an analysis of the fashions worn at the recent Grammy Awards—"Did you *see* what Babs was wearing? She was a *goddess*. I've said it before and I'll say it again, a woman doesn't reach true beauty until her sixties . . ."

I crept back up the small staircase to the front hallway, at one end of which was the kitchen. I headed the other way. Even the most casual collector wouldn't hang a masterpiece in the kitchen, especially if, as seemed to be the case with Camilla, she never ate.

I found myself in the dining room and hoped Michael's earlier words were prophetic. They weren't. There were several expensive oil paintings by third-rate artists, but no recently stolen *Magi*.

A door on the opposite wall led to a broad corridor with various doors and halls leading off it. For a moment, I despaired of being able to find my way back to the exercise room, much less find an oil painting that measured only two feet by three and a half feet. Footsteps from the vicinity of the kitchen spurred me on.

Sneaking down the corridor, I peered in the first open doorway, which led to a lovely, sunny sitting room with lots of windows, a couple of watercolors, and no oil paintings.

The next door was shut, so I listened for a moment before gently pushing it open. It was a shadowy room that looked a lot like a study. I closed the door behind me, and groped in the dark for a light switch, finally locating one on the wall to the left. The light revealed that it was, indeed, a study, with built-in bookshelves, a huge walnut desk, and leather club chairs. There were no paintings on the paneled walls, other than the one over the fireplace, which portrayed an English hunting scene. Oh, puh-leeze. The lack of imagination among those who could best afford to be imaginative never failed to both surprise and depress me.

I turned to leave, then stopped. What would Michael do? Maybe take a gander at the papers in the desk?

The desk, like the English hunting scene, turned out to have been chosen by the decorator as a stage prop. There was nothing on it but an embossed leather desk set that appeared never to have been used. I tested the top drawer, which slid open smoothly. The drawers were empty.

Switching off the light, I slipped back into the hallway. Other than some muffled clangs and bangs emanating from the direction of the kitchen, the house was eerily quiet. I wondered what it would be like to call such a beautiful mausoleum home and decided that, all things considered, I preferred my humble apartment.

Proceeding down the corridor, I checked out an overdecorated living room, a self-consciously "country casual" family room, a second sitting room—people sat a lot in this house—a guest bedroom with a pastoral motif so over the top that it looked as if a florist's shop had detonated in there, and a rather nice orangerie.

But no *Magi*.

I decided to head upstairs. I wasn't sure if my search qualified as thorough, but I was getting antsy and, wanting to get the hell out of there, I scurried down the corridor toward the entry hall, which I remembered opened onto a sweeping staircase. I poked my turbaned head out and glanced around to see if I was alone, then scampered up the plushly carpeted stairs.

I relaxed a bit in the upstairs corridor when I realized the thick carpeting must muffle the sound of my footsteps, until I realized that it would do the same for anyone else. I strained my ears listening for housemaids, footmen, butlers, governesses, chauffeurs, or even family members. Nothing. Taking a deep breath, I decided to start my upstairs search with whatever was behind the large set of double doors at the end of the hallway. I didn't care what Michael said—if I had a stolen masterpiece, I would hang it in my bedroom. I pressed my ear to the door, heard nothing, and eased it open.

My heart leapt in my chest when I was attacked by an animatronic mop that turned out to be a small dog, one of those cosseted pets whose hair care products alone would more than cover my rent. There was something deeply disquieting about an animal whose personal hygiene received more attention than my own.

Small, white, and very fluffy, with an upturned tail that fanned the air vigorously, it stared at me with bright eyes while wheezing through its smooshed nose. It bounced around, delighted to make my acquaintance. It wasn't much of a watchdog, but I supposed I wasn't in a position to complain about that. A set of dog tags on the jeweled collar—I had a sneaking suspicion those were real diamonds, too—indicated it was up to date on its shots and was named Miss Mopsy. How original of the Culpeppers.

I had always found dogs hard to resist, and gave Miss Mopsy a quick belly rub before resuming my search. The pooch wouldn't leave me in peace, though, and tried to instigate a game of tug-of-war with a Hermès scarf she dragged out from under the bed.

The Culpeppers' bedroom was large, about twenty-five by thirty feet. At its center was a hideous four-poster festooned with exquisitely embroidered brocade draperies. If I'd known anything about sewing—and I did not—I would have guessed that the drapes had been handmade in a French convent by nuns who had clearly had a lot to repent. The bed itself was covered in acres of melting pink satin and about forty froufrou pillows in hues of pink, beige, and cream. The whole thing looked like the sort of altar to lovemaking that would be more at home in a Poconos honeymoon resort than in uptight, old-money Belvedere. I craned my neck upward. Nope, no mirrored ceiling. I had caught a glimpse of Mr. Culpepper in the family photos downstairs, and it was disconcerting to imagine him and the desiccated missus getting down and dirty behind the delicate brocade.

There were a few paintings on the walls, but not the one I wanted. I was about to leave when Miss Mopsy trotted down a passageway that led off the bedroom. I followed.

The hall opened onto a second large room, apparently Camilla Culpepper's office or private sitting room, which was decorated with English rose wallpaper. A green-and-cream striped loveseat sat under a bank of windows, and in the far corner was an untidy walnut desk. In terms of sheer messiness it was not in the same league as my desk at home, but it did indicate that, unlike the one I'd seen downstairs, this desk was actually used.

And hanging above the fireplace was one recently stolen Caravaggio.

I peered closely. Correction: one recently stolen ersatz Caravaggio. Damned if Anton hadn't painted this one, too. If my artistic memory served—and it almost always did—this was not the forgery Ernst had shown me in the vault. The small chest of frankincense in King Melchior's arms, which had been wide open in that painting, was nearly shut in this one. I dragged a chair over to the hearth and climbed on it to double-check, but there was no doubt in my mind.

Maybe Michael was right and there was no original *Magi*.

The good news was I could call off the search. The bad news was I had to find my way back to the exercise room without being spotted. I climbed off the chair while Miss Mopsy danced about at my feet, as if this were all some elaborate game for her entertainment. Just as I was re-placing the chair, I heard someone enter the bedroom. I froze. This time there were no large canvases, no velvet curtains, no lacquer screens to hide behind. It was just me and Miss Mopsy, right out there in the open.

I looked at the dog, she looked at me, and I did the only thing that occurred to me: I crawled into the knee-hole of the desk and curled into a ball. Miss Mopsy joined me. I hoped that whoever it was did not come in here, sit down, and get to work, because talking my way out of this one would be tricky.

There was a rustle of clothing as someone entered the room. I squeezed my eyes shut, although I was not sure why I kept thinking that depriving myself of one of my five senses would help me out of these situations. It must have worked, though, because the desk creaked and I re-alized that the intruder was sitting on it, probably doing that hip-on-the-desk, foot-on-the-floor sit-stand that I did all the time, even though it made my thighs look huge. I heard the telephone being dialed.

"It's Emily," a woman said. "I know, but we need to talk. Yes, *now.* Yes, well, the only reason I agreed to any of this was that I was to be paid a percentage, remember? Having a massage. Well, there *is* some risk to me, there's always a risk."

There was silence for a few minutes.

"I don't like it, Harlan, I don't like it one single bit. Uh-huh. No. Where? When? Are you crazy? Why did you put them there?" Emily sighed. "All right, *fine.* Yes, I said I'd be there. I've got to go. 'Bye."

Harlan? With Emily? I could hardly wait to tell Michael. Not only had I found the painting but I had a lead on Harlan. I cocked my head at Miss Mopsy and she cocked hers at me. Damn, I was good! I was a natural for this sleuthing thing! I was—

"What are you *doing* here?"

Miss Mopsy barked. Or sneezed. It was hard to tell the difference.

I looked up to see Emily crouched down, staring at me as I sat curled under the desk. "Well, I, um . . ."

So maybe I had a bit to learn before getting my detective wings.

Emily stepped back, and Miss Mopsy and I unfolded ourselves from our hidey-hole. By the time I was upright Emily was fretting, big time.

"What did you hear?" she demanded.

Like, duh, Emily. As if I could have missed anything you said. I was all of two feet away. However, I decided not to point this out. Emily, for her part, began pacing and wringing her hands, something I had always assumed was purely a convention of bad community theater.

"I knew something like this would happen. I knew it," she muttered. "I knew I shouldn't get involved." She stopped pacing and shot me a look chock-full of disdain. "I knew you weren't a *massage therapist.*"

"Why'd you let me in, then?" I said belligerently. I wasn't the one betraying my boss, after all. Emily lived in an interesting moral universe.

"Who are you? What do you want?" she demanded.

I decided to come clean. Sort of.

I shrugged in a you're-not-going-to-*believe*-how-silly-this-is kind of way. "Emily, you're right," I said, my face perfectly straight. "I'm not a massage therapist. I'm a special agent for the California Fine Arts Commission. I don't want to get you or anybody else into trouble, but we received an anonymous tip last week and I am duty-bound to investigate. I'm afraid the commission has reason to believe that Mrs. Culpepper might have been sold a fake Caravaggio."

A long time ago Grandfather told me that if you were going to lie, make it a whopper. For some reason, he said, people were more likely to believe a lie if it was so outrageous that it had to be true. And Grandfather should know.

"The California Fine Arts . . ." Emily repeated. "What are you *talking* about? There's no such thing." Apparently she was the exception to Grandfather's little rule.

Miss Mopsy, bored, barked to get my attention, whereupon Emily scowled and kicked her. Yelping, Miss Mopsy dashed back under the desk.

Now I was pissed. If I lived to be a thousand I would never understand what made some people pick on defenseless creatures. I'd learned a few things in the past couple of days about how to intimidate people, and without thinking I put that knowledge to good use. I grabbed Emily hard by the upper arm, slammed her against the wall, and leaned in close. "Don't you ever, *ever* hurt that little dog again, you understand me?"

Emily was turning an unattractive shade of green, which I assumed meant she was not used to this sort of treatment. She nodded.

Letting her go, I stepped back, rearranged my disheveled clothing, and continued the conversation as if nothing had happened. "I can see now that this painting is not the original. That's fine. I'm not about to tell anybody. What I *do* need is information."

"What kind of information?" she asked weakly, rubbing her arm.

"Where's Harlan Coombs?"

Emily shook her expensively coiffed head. "I can't help you."

"Protecting him, are you? You do realize, Emily, that the last woman who tried to protect poor Harlan wound up dead?" So I stretched the facts a bit. Something about this woman got me in touch with my inner bitch. "Plus, a janitor who got in the way ended up dead, too," I added. "And a curator disappeared that same night."

"You're wrong," Emily said shakily. "The curator shot the janitor."

"Who told you that? Harlan? Oh, yeah, he's to be trusted. You need to get a better class of friends, Emily. Because on top of everything else, no one on this job, *no one,* has gotten any money from dear old Harlan for those fakes he's been peddling." I pictured myself in an old *Perry Mason* episode. Just what did the defendant have to say about *that,* ladies and gentlemen? "Oh, and by the way," I said, "did you know about Harlan's affair with Quiana?"

Emily reached out a trembling hand to grab the arm of an upholstered chair and eased herself into it. She was even worse at this cloak-and-dagger stuff than I was.

On the other hand, *she* hadn't screamed when she'd found me.

"He's not with Quiana!" she gasped.

"Are you sure?" I asked her. "Because that's not what I hear. She's about ready to spill everything, too. I've already met with her. Twice."

I decided the bad cop had done her job. Maybe it was time for the good cop to come out and play. Hitching my right hip on the desk, I planted my left foot on the floor and leaned forward to project sincerity. "Look, you're not in too deep yet, Emily," I said soothingly. "The Culpeppers don't know that their painting isn't genuine, and as far as I'm concerned there's no reason for them to find out." Why should I care if people willing to buy stolen masterpieces were ripped off? Served them right.

"Harlan has put a lot of people in danger and stolen a lot of money," I continued, assuming an air of confidentiality. "He might very well be a murderer. Believe me, you don't want to be associated with him. Tell me how I can find Harlan, Emily, and then you can step out of this mess entirely."

I wasn't sure what Emily was focusing on, but it wasn't me. Suddenly, she drew herself up, looked me in the eye, and snapped, "I don't know where he is. All I have is a phone number that he e-mailed me. It's probably a pay phone or something."

"Give it to me anyway," I said, handing her a pad of paper and a pen. "You say he e-mails you? Better add his e-mail address. Now, tell me this: weren't you supposed to meet him somewhere to get your money?"

The greenish hue washed over her again as she handed me the notepad. "I was just supposed to arrange to switch the Culpeppers' Caravaggio for a fake. But—"

"You think they once had the real one? Harlan made a change?"

"That Polish guy came and switched it. He's been

working with Harlan. But now Harlan needs help, because he left some drawings at the Brock."

I stared at her. "Why would he have left them there? How's he going to get them back?"

"They're having some big event on Saturday and he's going to be there. He wants me there, too."

"That's crazy," I replied without thinking.

"That's what I said," she whined. First Edward, now Emily. I had to wonder about Harlan's taste in coconspirators. "He said he had a disguise and that with the party and all, everyone would be distracted and he'd be able to retrieve them. He wanted to make sure I'd be there with Mrs. Culpepper, although I'm not sure why."

I wasn't sure why either, unless he needed someone to fall apart under pressure and start spewing her guts.

And speaking of guts, it would take a lot of them for Harlan to return to the Brock, disguise or no, and mingle with the best and the brightest of the City's art scene, a significant percentage of whom he had recently ripped off.

"So what happened to the real Carav—" I began.

"Emily?"

I recognized Camilla Culpepper's voice. Emily and I froze.

For once I was ready. "Oh, Mrs. *Cul*pepper! You know, I simply *adore* dogs," I gushed as she appeared. I scooped Miss Mopsy up and gave her a squeeze. She burped. "And my poor Snookie went to live with the puppy angels just last month, boo-hoo. I got to talking about him with Emily here and I started to cry, I felt so sad. Then Emily said, did I want to see the cutest dog alive, and I said, did I *ever,* so we came up here and I have to say that Mopsy Wopsy is just *adorable*! I mean, could you just *die*?"

Camilla didn't look convinced, so I continued.

"And then I wanted to show Emily some acupressure

points as a way of saying thank you, so I did, but I forgot to check for medical conditions first—I'm still learning, you know—and it turns out that the poor girl is prone to migraines, so the last thing I should have tried was the ching-li zone, because that could bring up bad chi, and then she began to feel a little faint."

I ended.

Camilla looked at Miss Mopsy, who was staring up at me adoringly, and at Emily, who was still rather green, and must have decided that at least part of my ridiculous saga was true, because she laid a hand on Emily's forehead and said, "Yes, dear, you do look terrible. Perhaps you should lie down for a few minutes. And you," she said, turning her beady, makeup-encrusted eyes on me and reaching for her dog, "should not practice until you're fully trained. I'm sure Bruno will be quite upset when he hears about this. And widdle Miss Mopsy Popsy Poo here would not wike it if her Emiwee was feewing sickle wickie, would she, Mopsy Popsy mumsy's widdle wuzzie?"

Emily looked nauseated, and even I was given pause. I was as quick to indulge in doggie talk as the next fatuous dog lover, but I usually made sure there weren't any witnesses.

Time to go.

Muttering something about seeing myself out, I hurried down two flights of stairs—and found the ground-floor exercise room empty. "Michael?" I called. "I mean, Bruno?"

For one terrible moment I thought he had stranded me again. Then I reminded myself that he needed to know if I had found the Caravaggio.

"Bruno!"

"Dahling, do keep it down," Camilla called from the top of the stairs. "Poor Emily is trying to rest. Bruno came up to the study earlier to tell you that he was leaving and that you should catch a ride with someone named Angela. Didn't he see you?"

Michael had come up to the study? Had he, by any chance, overheard my little chat with Emily?

He had done it. He had gone and done it. He had stranded me.

Again.

I was going to murder the X-man the very next time I saw him.

Swear to God.

Chapter 12

The painter Ingres once said that he had no scruples when it came to copying Old Masters, and that he would look with pride upon being copied himself. More recently, Pablo Picasso declared that he would happily sign any fake shown to be worthy of his talent.

> —Georges LeFleur, *"What's in a Name?" unfinished manuscript,* Reflections of a World-Class Art Forger

An hour and a half later I stood on the deck of the Larkspur ferry, watching the island of Belvedere slide by. The ocean wind blew still more knots into my already snarled hair, which seemed a fitting metaphor for the day.

When I realized that the despicable Michael-Colin-Paddy-Bruno had stranded me yet again, I used the Culpeppers' phone to call my friend Elizabeth. A writer and a former client, Elizabeth lived with her attorney husband, two adorable kids, and a sweet golden retriever in nearby Larkspur Landing. A small town on a finger of the bay, it had fabulous views, a ferry landing, and San Quentin Prison, an imposing structure that housed some of California's worst felons on some of California's best real estate.

Elizabeth picked me up in her gold Volvo station wagon, no questions asked, genuinely apologetic that she couldn't drive me all the way into the city because Jason had a Little League game and Sarah had to eat by six in order to get to her violin recital on time. Not for the first time, I wondered what it would be like to live such a normal existence. It didn't seem to be in the cards for me anytime soon.

From Larkspur Landing it was a straight shot across San Francisco Bay to Pier 41, from which I could catch a bus to the Brock, retrieve my truck, and head back to my ruined studio. With luck, I'd be there in an hour.

It was a gorgeous afternoon, sunny and mild, so I bought a cup of coffee at the canteen and climbed up to the forward deck, taking a seat on a bench. During commute hours the ferry was always packed, but at the moment it was just me and a few tourists murmuring among themselves as they gazed at the sights of San Francisco, Oakland and the East Bay hills, Marin, and Alcatraz. I used the time to reflect and to decompress.

What exactly had I thought I was doing, poking about a stranger's home? Not to mention hiding under her desk with her dog and intimidating her secretary? *The Magi* wasn't even my concern—I was supposed to be looking for Anthony Brazil's and Albert Mason's stolen drawings. I didn't know what on earth had come over me. I seemed to make such lousy choices whenever Michael was around.

What I should be doing was salvaging what I could from my studio, assuming I still had a business to go back to. I had spent the past three years working my fingers to the bone trying to get True/Faux Studios off the ground, and just when I seemed to be on solid footing what did I do? I ignored it for days on end in favor of galloping around with an admitted art thief, breaking and entering,

snooping, hitting a Hulk, being stranded, getting kidnapped, being hit by a Hulk, and having my studio
torched. It would be the ultimate irony if I lost my business and had to fall back on a life of crime after all.

The thought made me want to cry.

I fought the urge, breathing in great gulps of fresh sea
air, and watching the seagulls dive and dance in our wake.
I wasn't sure if they were looking for fish churned up by
the ferry or if they just liked to play in the breeze. Seagulls were obnoxious birds, in a beak-and-beak tie with
pigeons for the title "rats with wings," but I had a soft
spot for them. Their distinctive *caw* reminded me that I
was near the ocean, which always seemed like a good
thing. If life got too tough on the mainland, I could build
myself a raft and sail off into the sunset for a grand ad-
venture. Or certain death. One of the two.

By the time the ferry docked at Pier 41 and disgorged
its passengers, I had made a few resolutions. First, I
would stop worrying about *The Magi*. It wasn't my concern. Second, I would take my grandfather's word for it
that Anton was safe, since he wasn't my problem either.
Third, I would clean up my studio, get back to work, and
make some money, like a grown-up. While I was running
around playing junior detective, people were getting
killed. This was a job for the police, not a faux finisher.

I straightened my shoulders, held my head high, and
marched down the gangway.

And I would do it all first thing tomorrow morning. All
I wanted to do tonight was to hole up in my apartment.

After reclaiming my truck from where I'd left it near
the Brock—I hadn't even gotten a parking ticket, which I
took to mean that fate was smiling on my new resolutions—I drove back to Oakland, where I swung by An-
dronico's for some gourmet deli takeout, splurged on a
twelve-dollar California Merlot, and stopped by my local

video store for a couple of trashy movies. Parking behind my house, I hurried upstairs, turned off the phone, and made a beeline for my bedroom, where I changed into a pair of ratty old shorts and a torn T-shirt. Then I pulled my hair back with an elastic hair band and proceeded to scrub the apartment from floor to ceiling until every surface glowed.

By the time night fell, I was exhausted but content with my home-sweet-and-clean-home. I'd take this place over a Belvedere mausoleum any day. I curled up on my living room futon sofa with a plate of takeout and a glass of the smooth Merlot. I thought about Michael, wondered what he was doing now, and wished him ill.

"C'mon, Naomi. Be a pal. Surely with all *your* influence you could get me an invitation to the gala on Saturday?"

Notwithstanding last night's resolutions to concentrate more on work and less on criminals, I had awakened this morning with a plan for laying my hands on the drawings. According to Emily, Harlan was going to retrieve the drawings on the night of the Brock gala. So that was where I needed to be, as well.

I'd been on the phone with Naomi Gregorian for twenty minutes trying to wangle an invitation, firing every weapon in my arsenal. I appealed to her professionalism (a long shot), to our many years of friendship (a real wild card), and, finally, to her ego (much better odds). But for once Naomi was adamant.

"No, Ann. Absolutely not. The Brock is devoted to keeping its Diamond Circle exclusive. Besides, you wouldn't feel comfortable with these people."

What the hell was a "Diamond Circle" anyway? I grumbled to myself. Sounded like a cattle brand.

I sighed. Appeals to Naomi's better nature having

failed to produce the desired invitation, she'd left me no choice. It was time to drop the Bomb.

"Listen, Naomi," I said, choosing my words carefully, "I didn't want to bring this up, but out of respect for our friendship, I feel I must tell you something."

Naomi fell silent, but I could sense her tension reverberating through the phone wire. The day I called to give her career a boost would be the day we both rolled over in our graves.

"Are you aware that the new Egyptologist you're so gaga about is wanted for questioning by the police?" I continued. "I'd hate to think what it could mean for you if Agnes Brock ever heard about it."

I felt kind of dirty putting the screws to Naomi like this. But, I rationalized, had she been more reasonable, I wouldn't have had to resort to this type of thing.

I could practically hear her teeth grinding. What was her worst nightmare? To have me spill the beans about her new art thief boyfriend? Or to be publicly associated with someone who might show up at the Diamond Circle gala in an Indian wrap skirt and Birkenstocks?

"I'll see what I can do," she snapped. "Don't call me."

I put down the phone, satisfied for the moment. It was two o'clock on Tuesday, and I was sitting at the desk in my studio. The usually cluttered desktop was devoid of papers, since everything that had been there was now either laid out under the heat lamps or had been tossed into one of the many black plastic garbage bags that dotted the room like so many bulbous alien life-forms.

Mary had returned from Mendocino the night before. First thing this morning we had visited Pete at the hospital and made arrangements to bring him home tomorrow. Then we returned to the studio to tackle the mess. I put a Carlos Santana CD on the player I'd brought from home,

threw the windows open wide, ripped into a box of
garbage bags, and got to work.

Around noon reinforcements arrived. Sherri, her husband, Tom, and five of Mary's band mates showed up
with soda, pizza, and still more garbage bags. Thus fortified, we made the cleanup move along nicely. Nine pairs
of hands could accomplish amazing things in a short
amount of time. Together we lugged the upholstered furniture and the rug onto the first-floor roof, where they
would sit in the sun and, with luck, dry out enough to he
salvageable. My standards weren't especially high, but
the fact that I had let everything sit in water for a day dramatically lessened its chances of recovery. For the hun-
dredth time, I cursed myself for being so stupid as to
traipse around with the X-man when I had important
things to take care of here.

The irredeemable items were sketches, art papers, and
assorted business records, many of which, fortunately,
were duplicates or should have been shredded long ago
anyway. The espresso machine and the mini-fridge had
survived unscathed, but the microwave made scary pop-
ping and hissing sounds when we turned it on, so I decided to toss it. Most of the paint supplies and sundry
brushes and applicators were either protected in cupboards, or would be no worse for the wear once they'd
dried out. I lost a book of genuine gold leaf, which hurt,
but in a moment of absentminded tidiness I had stowed
several others in a plastic bin under the counter, and these
were untouched.

The saddest losses, for me, were a number of reference
books and several of my old paintings that had once
graced the walls. We decided to set them out to dry as
best they could and assess their integrity later. Fortunately, the special heat lamps and light tables so impor-

tant to a faux finisher were still functioning, and we put them to work drying out whatever items we could.

After the microwave incident I was afraid to touch the computer, so I called Pedro and threw myself on his mercy. He agreed to come the next day to look at it, assuring me that even if the computer no longer worked he could probably retrieve my data from the hard drive, download it onto floppies, and upload it later. I wasn't sure what all that involved, but what did I care so long as Pedro was on the case?

While I had him on the line, I asked if it was possible to track someone down through an e-mail address. He said it depended, took down the information Emily had given me on Harlan Coombs, and promised to let me know if he found anything.

While the others scrubbed and dried the floors, walls, and ceiling, washing away the soot from the fire and the assorted flotsam from the flood, I worked the phone. First I called Linda Fairbanks and Irene Foster to apologize profusely for the delay on their projects, at the same time giving them an abridged version of the recent disaster, and after a moment of initial frostiness each woman tsk-tsk'd sympathetically. Their samples, though slightly warped, were ready and I would deliver them tomorrow.

There followed a series of other necessary yet stressful calls to those I owed money to, including the phone company, during which I assured all and sundry that they would be paid as soon as my checks dried out. I didn't know whether I sounded especially desperate, or whether they were just being humane, but all were remarkably understanding.

The day's biggest frustration was dealing with the one person I paid to be helpful: my insurance agent. After cheerfully collecting my premiums every month for the past three years, my agent became a fountain of ignorance the one time I needed him, claiming to have no idea whether or not I was covered for such damage. When I suggested that perhaps he should look it up, he became particularly obtuse. Seething with indignation, I made another call, letting his supervisor know just what I thought of the company and its so-called professional agents. However, considering the fact that I was trying to get them to send me a check for a rather large amount, I wasn't sure how effective my threat to take my business elsewhere was. The turning point came when I started making vague references to "my lawyer." That lawyer didn't exist, but the supervisor didn't know that. He said he'd call me back.

My last call was to Anthony Brazil, who was not exactly overjoyed at the prospect of being my escort to the gala and claimed he already had a date. Before signing off, however, he agreed to give me an extension on our original one-week deal, so long as the drawings were in his hands by Sunday morning.

One thing was indisputable: I needed an infusion of cash and I needed it soon. Since ol' Frankie downstairs had acted so heroically when Pete and I were in danger, I was less committed to complicating his life by fighting the eviction notice I was sure to receive if I didn't sign a new lease at double my current rent. I was scraping the bottom of my checking account, and that Napa stunt hadn't helped matters.

I was flirting with a full-fledged bout of self-pity when Mary called my name. The gang beamed proudly as they showed me what they'd accomplished. The studio looked a million times better, and although a lot of repairs were still needed, everything was more or less ready for me to get back to work.

Reality check. All these people had just knocked themselves out for my benefit. I might not have much money, but I was abundantly blessed with friends.

We continued working into the early-evening hours before collapsing with a well-deserved sense of accomplishment. We uncorked two bottles of cheap Chilean Merlot that had survived the deluge and sprawled on the floor, chatting about Pete, the concert in Mendocino, whether to have Thai or Vietnamese food for dinner, and the situation in the Middle East. I avoided sharing the details of Sunday's abduction.

There was a knock on the partially open door. Despite the wine, the company, and my prone position, I jumped. After all the drama lately, I was a nervous wreck.

It was Frank DeBenton, whom I hadn't seen since the excitement Sunday night. He looked nonplussed at the sight of us lounging among the wine bottles. I noted with regret that Mr. Slick had returned: Frank was once again buttoned down.

"Hey there, Frankie baby," Mary sang, making the situation even more awkward.

"Yo, Frankie!" Sherri echoed.

Poor Frank looked as if he wanted to flee. Given our very special bonding experience at the factory, I felt compelled to rush to his rescue. I hauled myself up from the floor, noting as I did several new sore muscles. "Hi, Frank. Good to see you. What's up?"

"Could I speak with you for a moment, please?" he asked in a low voice. "In private."

"Sure," I said, and followed him out the door.

We stood in the hallway, which I noticed had been mopped until it shone. It looked better than it had in months. Maybe somebody should set the sprinklers off regularly. Maybe I should suggest it to Frank. I glanced at him.

Maybe not.

"Listen," I began. "I'm really sorry—"

He stopped me with an economical shake of his perfectly groomed head. "Where were you yesterday?" he demanded. He wouldn't look me in the eye.

"Well, I . . ." Why was Frank asking? Was he worried about me? Seemed unlikely. Was he upset because I wasn't here bright and early yesterday to clean up? Probably. Was that really any of his business? Nah. "I had some things to take care of."

"Something more important than this?" he snapped.

Now that he was looking at me, I kind of wished he weren't.

"Well . . ." I could hardly tell Frank what I had been up to yesterday. Not only did it now seem irresponsible, it also seemed exceptionally dangerous and downright stupid. After all, Frank had risked his own safety to save me from a close encounter with a bad guy's knife.

He looked me in the eye for a long moment, and I thought he was going to say something. Instead he turned on his heel and stalked down the hall, his back ramrod straight, probably because of that stick up his—

"Annie!"

Samantha emerged from her studio at the end of the hall. "Hey, Sam," I said, glad to see a friendly face.

"What you doin', girl? Why you don't call me to come and help you?" she chided in her lilting English, before enveloping me in a patchouli-scented hug. "I was worried about you. Where you been all yesterday?"

"It's kind of a long story," I said. "And I would have called you, but I had plenty of help today. Come say hi to everybody."

She did, and we chatted for a while until, one by one, the crew departed. As dusk fell, Samantha and I were alone in the darkening studio, sitting on the floor with our backs against the brick wall and our legs sticking out in

front of us. Through the studio's huge windows we
watched as the sky changed from a brilliant blue to a soft
pink to a blazing orange-red. I poured her the remains of
one of the bottles of Merlot and we held our glasses up in
a toast.

"To more relaxing days ahead," Sam said.

"I'll drink to that," I replied. "So, what do you think of
our new landlord?"

She shrugged gracefully. "Dunno. A bit stuffy, isn't
he? But what can you expect from a landlord?"

I laughed. Samantha and her husband, Reggie, had recently bought a duplex in the Castro, one of several in
their small but growing stable of rental properties.

"What about the rent hike?" I asked. "Has he said anything about that?"

She shook her head. "No, but I have three more years
on my lease."

Apparently I was the lone idiot in the building with a
year-to-year lease. I gulped some wine.

"Still, he's not bad-looking," Sam continued. "Plus,
he's pretty well connected to the whole art scene here.
You could do worse."

"I'm not interested in Frank that way," I assured her. "I
was just wondering about him as a landlord. Mostly because I can't make the rent hike."

"How much of a rent hike?"

I realized it had been a while since we'd talked. "Double."

"You're shitting me!"

"I shit you not."

She shook her head. "Capitalists," she said with disdain.

I smiled again. Sam and Reggie, a social worker for
the city, were natural entrepreneurs who were always
starting or selling one business or another. They had an

almost magical ability to wring money from any enterprise they touched, which was why Sam could afford to pursue her jewelry design business and still send their eighteen-year-old daughter to Stanford and their twenty-year-old son to Brown. Sam pointed out that the family lived in a modest Chinatown apartment—albeit in a building they owned—but I knew she loved the neighborhood, one of the city's oldest ethnic enclaves. I had a sneaking suspicion that Sam also enjoyed her clients' reactions when they learned that their Jamaican jewelry designer lived above the best dim sum restaurant in Chinatown.

"Anyway," I went on, "I'm not sure what I'm going to do now. Maybe I'll move the studio to Oakland."

"Nah, you can't leave us. Say what you will about this area, it's becoming known as an arts district. Why do you think I stay here instead of working out of one of my apartments? Besides, Frank's no ogre. There must be some reasoning with the man."

"I don't think he liked me much to begin with, and the fire didn't help. He doesn't like drama. I have a feeling he would be happy to personally escort me to Oakland."

By now the sun had set and the studio was dark, and I was enjoying not having to look at the confusion that remained. The day's labors had accomplished wonders, but the studio was still not completely back together. I admitted to myself that Frank had a right to be upset. I had, after all, threatened his investment and pulled him into a dangerous situation. Frank's stuffiness just seemed to bring out the worst in me. It reminded me of my relationship with my father.

Great. Michael made me think of my grandfather, and now Frank put me in mind of my father. Maybe I needed therapy.

"What did you mean about Frank being well connected in the art world?" I asked Sam.

"Don't you know?" she said. "Frank has real estate investments, like this building, but his main business is art security. All those armored cars downstairs? He transports art all over the world."

Oh, wasn't *that* just peachy? I had noticed Frank's trucks, but assumed he used them to pick up bags of cash from supermarkets or fill ATMs or something. It was just my luck that he specialized in *art* transportation. Could he have heard rumors about my grandfather, the art forger extraordinaire, or about Michael, the international art thief who was my new best friend? Could the huge rent increase and Frank's undisguised desire to see me gone have anything to do with my past?

Of all the landlords in all the buildings in all the world . . .

Or maybe I was getting paranoid. I leaned my head back, closed my eyes, and let out an exasperated breath. Sam must not have noticed, because she was still talking.

". . . asked him yesterday if he'd seen you, and I stayed to help a bit with his cleanup."

She wasn't going to get a massive rent hike, now was she? Maybe I should take a few lessons from Samantha on how to handle people, since my current strategy of outright antagonism toward Frank didn't seem to be working too well.

". . . gala invitation. It was water-damaged, but you could tell because of the gold edge and that stupid Brock crest. Ooo, now that is one gala even I wouldn't mind going to, if only for the people-watching. You still know folks over there?"

Once again I was reminded of how little we had talked recently and how quickly everything had happened. I brought her up to date, starting from the meeting with

Anthony Brazil and ending with my jaunt with Michael to Belvedere.

Samantha was not amused.

"So you're telling me you're going to try to get into the Brock gala and hunt down this Coombs fellow?" she asked, incredulous. "Weren't those men the other night scary enough for you? Have you had your head examined lately?"

I made a mental note to look into therapy when all this was over.

"What I *need,* Sam, is to find those drawings, collect the reward money, and get Frank to lay the hell off." I was feeling a little touchy.

"Girl, you know I speak my mind," she said. "There's no one but a fool who would go after this kind of thing after all you've been through. Let me talk to Frank. Maybe if a few of us tenants band together we can work something out. You don't need the money bad enough to get yourself killed, my friend."

Fine. If Sam wanted to be reasonable, then let her be. I, however, was tired, and cranky, and one way or another I was going to get invited to that damned gala. Contrarily, the more that people tried to talk me out of it, the more determined I was to see this thing through to its conclusion.

Maybe I could get Frank to take me as his date! We could spend quality time together *and* I would get to go to the ball. Okay, it was a long shot, but it would be the perfect solution.

I didn't know whether Sam took my silence for acquiescence, or whether she decided she'd said her piece, but she gave me a hug, told me to be careful, and went home to fix dinner. Ten minutes later, after a little puttering around, I walked down the stairs and saw a light in

Frank's office. What the hell. I took a deep breath, opened his door, and stuck my head in.

"Heya, Frank," I said as cheerfully as though we had parted friends. "How 'bout some dinner? My treat." I plopped down in an armchair. "Or *you* could take *me* to dinner. I wouldn't want to step on any old-fashioned toes."

Maybe the perky approach would work. It often did with these older guys.

His somber brown eyes took in my T-shirt and paint-spattered overalls.

It didn't seem like perky would cut it.

"I'm flattered." He didn't sound it. "But I'm involved with someone."

"I wasn't asking you to sleep with me, Frank," I assured him. "I was inviting you to dinner."

"Uh-huh," he murmured. He seemed engrossed in a stack of official-looking papers on his desk.

This was not going well. I decided to try contrition. "Listen," I said, "I'm really sorry about all the drama. And especially about the water damage. I hope you'll let me make it up to you."

Frank did not reply.

"Sooo," I said, trying to sound casual. "Are you going to take her to the Brock gala?"

"Who?"

"The woman you're seeing. Remember?"

"No," he said stiffly. "She's out of town."

I decided to press on. "Funny thing, Frank. I had an invitation, too, but it was destroyed in the recent catastrophe. I think one of the guys probably threw it out. They're sticklers at the Brock for official invitations at events like this. I used to work there—did you know that?"

"Then perhaps you could have them send you another," he suggested.

Rats. Busted.

"Um, yes, well, perhaps I could, couldn't I? But you see, I was thinking, since you don't have an escort and I don't have an escort—"

"Is that what this whole thing has been about?" Frank clasped his hands on the top of the desk. If he'd been wearing a clerical collar he would have been a dead ringer for someone who was ready to hear my confession. "You want me to take you to the Brock gala, and rather than just ask me straight out you've put us both through this labyrinthine babble?"

I thought "labyrinthine babble" was a bit harsh. Granted, I had not been as forthright as I might have been, but still. However, under the circumstances I decided to let it go.

"I was shy," I suggested.

Frank snorted.

"So will you take me to the Brock gala?"

"No."

"Do you already have a date?"

"No."

"Then why not?"

He looked at me, a pained look on his face. "For one thing, you scare the hell out of me."

"You're scared of *me*?" I was genuinely shocked.

"You show very poor judgment, Annie. You leave this little trail of bad things behind you, like Gretel and her bread crumbs. I don't want to get stuck having to follow the bread crumbs back to the biggest disaster of all."

I pondered that for a minute.

"You kind of lost me with the whole bread crumb thing, Frank."

He sighed. "Then let me make it simpler. The answer is *no,* Annie. Regretfully, respectfully, no. Now, if you don't mind, I need to finish up a few things."

I'd just been dismissed. I rose with as much dignity as my scruffy overalls allowed, and stalked out.

Driving home across the Bay Bridge, I was pissed off and discouraged. As the traffic stopped and started, I entertained myself by inventing snappy comebacks to the little Frank had said to me until I'd worked myself into quite a state. Low blood sugar was not helping the situation, so I stopped at a Vietnamese restaurant in Oakland's Chinatown and ordered eggplant in garlic sauce, garlic rice, and shrimp rolls to go. All the way home, the savory aromas wafting from the pink plastic bag tormented me. By the time I had pulled into the parking lot of my house and climbed the three flights of stairs to my apartment, I was nearly faint from hunger. I never would have lasted on that *Survivor* show. One missed meal and I would have skewered one of my juicier tribe mates with a *punji* stick, which I'm pretty sure would have gotten me voted off the island.

I was brushing my teeth and getting ready for bed when the phone rang. It was nearly midnight. Lord, please don't let it be bad news, I prayed as I leapt across the bed and snatched up the receiver.

"Annie, *ma petite*! How are you?"

Not bad news, but definitely trouble.

"Grandfather," I cried. "What is going on? Did you paint that copy of *The Magi* for Harlan Coombs?"

"Ah, but you have always been so intelligent, so discerning, *ma cherie*! Yes, yes, I did. It is very fine, no?"

"Grandfather—"

"I have only one minute on ze phone, my darling girl," he interrupted. "I wanted to tell you zat I have found Anton, so you must not worry."

"Anton? Where is he?"

"Chicago, *cherie*."

"What's he doing in Chicago?"

"Why, ze same zing I am doing, *cherie.* We are going to ze Fantastic Fakes exhibition."

"You're going with Anton? I thought you hated Anton."

"Ah, all zat is in ze past. You should see what he has done! He has liberated my exquisite copy, and entered it in ze Fantastic Fakes competition! Is zat not marvelous?"

"Yeah, great," I said, distracted. "No, wait—what do you mean, liberated it? Georges? Liberated it from whom?"

"From Coombs' *petite amie,* I forget her name. *Bof!* Zis I do not care. Ze fact remains zat Anton brought it here and has entered it for me. We are renewing our friendship, and zis is a marvelous zing. *Cherie*! Why don't you join us?"

"Georges, how many copies did you paint?"

"Only one, *ma cherie.* Only such a fool as Anton would paint two! Did you hear? He painted an extra to replace ze one I painted, so zat he could bring mine here. Now zis is true friendship. I must go now, bye-bye!"

"Grandfather, don't hang up! Listen to me. Your painting is in the Brock—or at least it was last time I looked. I think the museum has your painting, not the original. Grandfather? Georges, do you hear me?"

There was no answer. I slammed the phone down in frustration, switched off the light, and slid under the covers, but my mind was whirling.

What did all this mean? If the Culpeppers had one of Anton's Caravaggio forgeries, and presumably the New Yorker I called Mr. Suave did as well, but the Caravaggio at the Brock had been painted by Grandfather, then—

Then what? It was Colonel Mustard in the kitchen with a candlestick?

I needed to sleep, but I lay awake for a long time, thinking. It was now Tuesday. Could I, should I, go to

Chicago? No, I could not, should not, because I was after Brazil's missing drawings, not *The Magi,* not to mention that I had no money and no room left on my credit card. *Remember that, Annie,* I scolded. I could give the information to the authorities, but they wouldn't know how to tell if a painting was a fake or not. What to do, what to do . . .

I had just drifted off when the phone rang again.

"Hullo?" I rasped.

It was Samantha. "Annie, I'm sorry to call so late."

"Sam, what is it? Is something wrong?" I asked, awake now.

"I just heard on the radio that Ernst Pettigrew has been found."

"Ernst? Where is he? Is he okay?"

"He's dead, Annie. His body was found in the bay. A presumed suicide off the Oakland Bay Bridge."

Chapter 13

Ink can be mixed with tap water and left to evaporate to its former strength. It will then be somewhat impure, and when it is viewed under a microscope, a powdery residue will be apparent, instantly "aging" the ink.

—*Georges LeFleur, "Tools of the Trade," unfinished manuscript,* Reflections of a World-Class Art Forger

I was stunned. Even though I had suspected, deep down, that something bad had happened to Ernst—the disappearing act simply wasn't in character for him—the confirmation of his death still came as a shock. I had cared for him once, and although our breakup had been too painful for me to harbor any lingering romantic feelings for him, I did still respect him as a top-notch curator.

Something else Samantha said bothered me.

"You mean he jumped off the Golden Gate," I said.

"No, the radio said the Oakland Bay Bridge."

"That makes no sense," I replied, confused. "The Bay Bridge has no pedestrian access. Somebody would have had to see him jump. Was his car found on the bridge?"

"What difference does it make?" Sam said gently.

"I'm not sure . . ."

"Are you all right?" Sam asked, sounding worried. "Why don't I come over?"

"No thanks, Sam. I'm fine. Really." I paused. "Ernst didn't kill himself, you know. Someone did it for him."

"How can you be so sure?"

"Because Ernst was too arrogant to commit suicide. Besides, he was a fighter. He didn't run away from his problems."

"Annie, promise me you'll be careful," Sam responded. "And if you need me, for anything, just call."

I put the receiver down with care. The body count was now up to three. And I still hadn't a clue what the hell was going on.

I was going to figure this out if I had to stay up all night.

The next thing I knew, my alarm was blaring and it was seven in the morning. With a jolt, I recalled the conversation with Sam. Ernst's death rendered moot my resolution not to get involved with *The Magi*. Not only had Ernst been my friend, but since all three victims had known something about the forgeries it now seemed apparent that I might be Number Four on some homicidal maniac's list of "The People I Most Want to Kill."

It was more important than ever that I find a way to get invited to the Brock gala on Saturday. Then I might be able to find Harlan Coombs and wring an explanation out of him. Plus, Emily told me he had stashed the drawings at the Brock. And just to prove that slothfulness was occasionally virtuous, I had worked a few things out in my sleep.

I bounced out of bed, energized. I now had a Plan to get myself invited to the Brock gala. Granted, it wasn't a very complicated Plan, but therein lay its genius. This morning I would Dress to Kill.

One of my better features was my long legs, so after coffee and a shower I chose a short, plum-colored silk skirt and a low-cut, snug camel-colored sweater. I slid my feet, sans stockings, into a pair of strappy, heeled sandals made of faux leopard skin. I piled my hair on my head, allowing a few tendrils to escape, took extra care with my makeup, applying mascara and a little eye shadow, and even putting on some blush. Luckily my bruises and cuts were hardly noticeable anymore. I selected gold-and-tortoiseshell earrings that picked up the leopard theme of the shoes and, after some consideration, added a small, tinkling anklet. Spritzing on the tiniest whiff of my favorite Ralph Lauren perfume—my gift to myself on my last birthday—I headed out the door.

This time my casual carpooler was a young financial type from Piedmont whose Beemer was in the shop and who violated carpool etiquette twenty seconds after he got a gander at my leopard outfit. Ben the Banker practiced his pickup lines all the way into the City, desperate to impress me. Thinking he'd lose interest, I played at being Amber the Airhead on her way to her job as a cocktail waitress. Instead, he handed me his business card and offered to set me up with a low-fee personal retirement account. Hey, the guy was working with what he had. I promised to call to set up a Roth IRA, dropped him off on Front Street, and roared off in a cloud of exhaust fumes.

I tossed his business card onto the pile of flotsam behind my seat. Although it seemed kind of premature to worry about retirement when I barely had a functioning business, who knew? Maybe I'd find those drawings, maybe I'd win the lottery, maybe a long-lost relative would turn toes up and leave me stinking rich, and I'd actually end up having some money to invest.

Swinging into the building's parking lot, I was pleased

to see Frank's Jaguar in its usual spot. I sashayed to his office and pushed open the door.

"Morning, Frank," I crooned. "I'll need you to sign off on some insurance forms. Will you be around later?"

Frank's eyes swept over me and he stared for a long moment, not speaking. The Plan was In Play.

"Uh, sure. Be happy to."

For some reason Frank seemed nervous. "Thank you so much. See you later, then?"

"Um, yeah."

And with that the masked faux finisher was off. It wasn't an invitation to the gala, but the wheels were in motion.

I climbed the stairs, fought for a moment with the sticky outer door, and clacked down the hall to my studio, opening the damaged door to find the place dark and silent. A wave of nostalgia washed over me. I missed my old life. I missed Pete's happy demeanor over espresso first thing in the morning. I missed seeing him blush at Mary's jokes. I missed the way things used to be before some idiot came and trashed my studio.

The euphoria of yesterday's progress ebbed with the realization of all that remained to be done. I'd forgotten that I needed to move the furniture back inside, and I could hardly do that in my girlie clothes. I needed to replace some supplies. I needed to harass my insurance agent.

I needed to kick somebody's ass.

"Knock, knock," came a voice from the doorway, and in walked Pedro, loaded down with black canvas bags, presumably his computer equipment. "Not bad," he said, looking around. "I've seen worse after some of our parties."

"Yeah, but we didn't get invited to this one." I gave him a hug.

"Wow, look at you," he said, holding me at arm's length. "You got a hot date? You smell good, too."

"Thanks, sweetie. Maybe I got dressed up for you," I teased. "Ever think of that?"

"Naw, Elena would kill you. Besides, you know I love you just as you are."

I started getting misty. Man, I really was a basket case. "Thanks for coming, Pedro. You're a lifesaver."

Pedro stretched his arms out in front of him and wiggled his fingers. "Just leave it to the maestro, kiddo," he said, sitting down at the computer and switching on the CPU. "Oh, you know that e-mail you asked me about? Piece of cake. The sender didn't encode or anything. It was sent from a hotel up in St. Helena. The Gray Goose. Here, I wrote it down. And I wrote down that Ernst guy's address, too."

He handed me a folded piece of yellow legal paper. So Harlan Coombs had been in Napa at the same time Michael and I were there? Quite a coincidence.

"And that Quiana chick?" Pedro continued as his fingers flashed across the keyboard. "Last name's Nash. Doesn't really go with 'Quiana,' does it? She does the occasional bikini photo shoot, strictly small-time catalogue stuff. Gets mentioned a lot in the papers, so maybe she's a debutante. There's money somewhere, 'cause she's got a place in Mendocino and drives a Lexus. Easy on the eyes, I'll give her that."

He handed me a photo he'd downloaded from the Internet. Those feline eyes were hard to forget. I remembered Joanne lying among blood-soaked, forged drawings. I wondered whether Quiana had been involved with Joanne's death but then dismissed the thought. They were sisters, after all. But how exactly was Quiana linked to Harlan?

That thought reminded me that I still hadn't heard from

Inspector Crawford about the phone numbers I'd asked her to trace. I tried calling her office and was informed that she was out, presumably pursuing bad guys—hopefully no one I knew. I settled for leaving a message insinuating that I had some information about the upcoming Brock unveiling.

Pedro informed me that the computer was history but he could retrieve the data. I watched, fascinated, as he took a screwdriver, opened the outer shell, and unscrewed something he said was the hard drive, a revelation to me, since I hadn't realized that a hard drive was an actual *thing* that could be removed and reattached elsewhere. I thought computer stuff existed in a theoretical cyberspace.

And that reminded me to call my insurance agent, who also seemed to exist only in the theoretical sense. He was remarkably more helpful today. It probably cheered him up to inform me that my policy had a substantial deductible.

At about eleven Mary trudged in, dressed in faded jeans and a torn concert T-shirt touting a group called Three Boring Ladies and One Pompous Ass. Unkempt and half asleep, she still looked cute. I stifled the urge to ask her whether or not she had slept last night, reminding myself that I was not her mother, and we set off to pick up Pete from the hospital, leaving Pedro to continue working his magic.

"Do you mind if we make a quick stop?" I asked as we headed across town. I wanted to scope out Ernst's place, and there was plenty of time before Pete was scheduled to be released.

"We're not going back to that Chinatown place, are we?" Mary asked. "'Cause you're not gonna be able to run in those shoes."

"No—it's not that place. And," I added hopefully, "there won't be any running involved. I learned yesterday that an old friend of mine from the Brock—Ernst Petti-grew—was found dead. The cops say it was suicide, but I don't believe it. I don't know what I'm looking for, I just want to go by his place in the Marina District. It's not far from the hospital."

It was in fact quite a ways from the hospital, but for a bike rider like Mary, distance was relative.

Twenty minutes later, we pulled up in front of Ernst's condo, in a white stucco fourplex with a beautiful view of the bay and easy access to what passed for a beach in this part of the City. The building's entry, which was filled with lush exotic plants and a tasteful koi pond, had two doors leading to the first-floor units, and a stairway lead-ing to the upstairs units, both of which were fronted by balconies. Access from the street was cut off by the kind of barred security gate that always reminded me of a prison.

I double-parked, flicked on the emergency blinkers, and we climbed out, peering through the bars into the courtyard. Since units A and B were visible on the ground floor, I was betting Ernst's condo, C, was upstairs.

Mary pressed the doorbell next to PETTIGREW on the entry panel.

"He's not home, Mary," I said impatiently. "Remem-ber? He's dead."

"So maybe someone else is home."

"Yeah, well, the last time that happened things didn't turn out so well. I can't run in these shoes, you said so yourself."

"So why are we here?"

She had me there.

"You know, I'll bet we could climb up to that balcony," Mary mused.

"Are you insane?" I said.

"*You're* the one who drove clear 'cross town to stand in

front of a dead guy's condo," Mary pointed out with a shrug.

She was right. Ernst was dead, and there wasn't a thing I could do about it. "I'm sorry, Mare," I said. "I just don't know what's going on."

"I'm starved. How about we grab some food and sit on the beach for a few?" Mary suggested, throwing a long arm around my shoulders and turning me away from Ernst's place. "That way we can live up to the world's stereotype of Californians having picnics by the ocean in February."

When in Doubt, Eat was a motto that had served generations of Kincaids and LeFleurs well, so who was I to argue? I moved the truck into a newly vacated space near the corner, then we grabbed sandwiches and sodas from the Safeway, crossed the boulevard, and sat on a faded wooden bench at Marina Green Park, the Golden Gate Bridge to our left and Alcatraz off to our right.

"It blows that your friend died," Mary said, her voice soft.

Mouth full, I nodded. It did indeed blow. It was hard to avoid the thought that I was somehow connected to his death. His and Dupont's and Joanne's. And I didn't know how. There was something missing, but I didn't know what.

"Hey, s'up? Spare change?"

A skinny, sandy-haired adolescent approached, wearing an oversized Oakland Warriors sweatshirt and torn jeans so low on his hips that we were invited to inspect his red boxer shorts.

"Go away, kid," Mary said curtly. "How come you're not in school?"

"School sucks."

"So does your vocabulary," Mary replied. "Scram."

"Give me some green and I go away."

"Go away or I kick your butt," Mary said flatly. When she'd first arrived in San Francisco, penniless and jobless, Mary had lived on the streets for a few weeks. The experience had left its mark.

"Okay, okay. Chill," the little delinquent said, holding up his hands but standing his ground. "How 'bout if I tell you something, you give me some money. Straight trippin'."

I had to give him points for persistence.

"Maybe. If it's good." Mary took a swig of her soda, her eyes never leaving the kid.

"They found a dead body over there yesterday," he said, pointing to the beach.

I looked at my pastrami-on-rye distastefully. Talk of corpses just killed my appetite.

"Sick," Mary said, taking a big bite of her marinated tofu on whole wheat.

"Yup. They said he prob'ly jumped off the Bay Bridge and drifted this way with the current. Trippin'. All white and bloated and shit."

"That's *really* gross," Mary said. She took another bite.

"Then this crazy bitch? She comes runnin' from over there"—the kid pointed at Ernst's condominium—"says she knows the homey, and starts looking through his pockets."

"No way," Mary interjected.

"Straight up," the kid insisted. "The cops had to drag her off, said she had to come to the station for his belongings and shit if she was a relative. That was one weird chick. I mean, the dude was covered in flies and . . ."

I tuned him out. Was that Ernst he was talking about? My heart started pounding, and my lunch sat like a lump in my stomach.

"Well, it's been great chatting," I said, wrapping up my mostly uneaten sandwich. "But we have to run."

"What about my money?"

I pulled a crumpled dollar out of my purse and handed it to him.

"That's it?" he sneered.

"See ya, kid," Mary said menacingly, and he wandered down the beach, probably on the prowl for tourists to harass. I tossed the remnants of my lunch in the nearest trash can, and we hurried back to the truck.

"Whaddaya make of that?" Mary asked as we belted ourselves in. "Do you think he was talking about your friend?"

"It seems like it," I conceded. "San Francisco isn't the Barbary Coast anymore—it's not like bodies are fished out of the bay every day."

But if it was Ernst, I thought to myself, *then who had been looking through his pockets, and why? How long had he been dead?* The kid said the body was white and bloated and crawling with flies . . . My artistic imagination generated a visual, and I fought to push it aside.

"So, listen, about Pete," Mary said, and I was glad to be distracted. As we drove to the hospital we worked out the Pete-sitting arrangements. The doctor had said Pete would be back on his feet in a few days. Until then Mary would stay with him, and I would spell her in the evening if she had a gig.

Pete was delighted to see us. A little high from the painkillers, he insisted on lustily singing Bosnian folk songs all the way home. What he lacked in vocal skill he made up for in volume, a musical style that Mary could appreciate. Although to my certain knowledge she did not speak Bosnian, the two of them sang several rousing choruses of something that sounded like "Bucket Me Want Cracker Die."

It was a *long* trip.

After Mary and I maneuvered Pete up to his apartment,

I ran to the grocery store for food and to the pharmacy for his medications. When we left an hour later, he was happily settled in with painkillers, videos, and lots of food and drink.

After a couple of hours of paperwork back at the studio, I ran the samples over to Linda's office on Polk Street—saving that business contact was paramount—then took the harlequin and woodgrain sample boards to Irene Foster's house in the Richmond District. Cross those two items off my To Do list.

Driving back to the studio, I tried to keep my mind off of Ernst's death by thinking about Grandfather's phone call. It was now late Wednesday afternoon and I had a million things to do before Saturday, including wangling the invitation to the Brock gala. It was madness to think I could fit in a trip to Chicago. I didn't have the time, and I definitely didn't have the money.

I pulled into the studio parking lot at five thirty. Frank was just getting into his Jaguar but stopped when he saw me, and waited as I climbed out of the truck.

"Is that for my benefit?" he said without preamble.

"Is what for your benefit?" I asked, mincing toward him.

He made a sweeping gesture with his hand. "The getup."

"It's not a 'getup,' Frank," I said, striking a subtle pose. "For your information, sometimes I dress for messy work, and sometimes I dress for clean work."

"Hmm," he responded ambiguously.

"What does 'hmm' mean?"

"What do you think?"

What the hell, I thought, *go for broke.* "I think it means you'll take me to the Brock gala on Saturday."

"I knew it was for my benefit," he said with an enigmatic smile. "Keep it up. I like it."

And with that he eased into his shiny car and took off.

"'Keep it up, I like it,'" I mimicked as I climbed the stairs. That did it. The warm feelings prompted by Frank's heroics the other day were gone. He was officially back in the scumbag category.

Why was I fixating on the man, anyway? I'd call Bryan. If anyone would know how to crash an elegant party, it would be my friend Bryan Boissevain.

"Sorry, baby doll, but from what I hear, the Brocks are more uptight than an alligator at midnight," he said. Bryan had grown up in a swamp in Louisiana, and although he cultivated his big-city persona, the bayou seeped out from time to time. "You couldn't beat one of those invitations out of them with a stick. You know that better than I. Although you could hang around the employee entrance and try to sneak in."

"I have to get in like everyone else," I persisted. "Otherwise I'll be challenged, which will cause a scene and defeat the whole purpose. Are you *sure* you can't think of anyone to take me?"

"Honey pie, the gala's in *two days*. Everyone who's going has a date by now, believe you me. And think about this—" Bryan continued with a gasp. "If you *do* snag an invite, you won't have anything to wear!"

Working in San Francisco as I did, I knew a lot of gay people, both socially and professionally. Most were pretty much like straight people. Bryan's partner, Ron, for example, was about as straight as men came, a total corporate yuppie in his pin-striped suit and shiny shoes. Bryan was not like that. Bryan was the type of gay man who loved show tunes, Barbra Streisand, redecorating and cooking and fretting about having only two days to find the right evening gown.

"Tell you what, baby doll," Bryan offered. "You get an

invitation, and I'll take care of the rest. I have this friend
Paul who has absolutely the best salon for trannies."

"But I'm not a transvestite, Bryan," I said, surprised
that I needed to remind him. Maybe I *should* pay more attention to my wardrobe and makeup.

"Honey pie, I know that, but the gala's going to be a
transvestite's wet dream."

Point taken. I had no idea how to dress for a gala. I
didn't own a formal gown and didn't fancy the idea of
storming the mall on Friday night, trying on prom dresses
elbow to elbow with seventeen-year-old high school sen-
iors. I would doubtless purchase some kind of pastel chif-
fon concoction, overcompensate with dramatic hair and
makeup, and wind up looking like a really sad, badly
dressed transvestite.

"Deal," I said. "If I manage to scrounge up an invitation, we'll go shopping."

I hung up and tried a few gallery owners I knew
slightly, most of whom responded to my plea to be my escort with shocked silence. After the umpteenth call, my
ego couldn't take anymore. This was pathetic.

Pedro had taken a fresh-air break and was back working on the computer. He looked up, concern in his eyes.
"How about your friend the cop? Couldn't she get you
in?"

Well, duh. What good was having a new buddy on the
police force if I couldn't exploit the hell out of the relationship? I tried Annette again. She answered on the third
ring.

"Inspector Crawford."

"Annette, it's Annie."

"Annie, hi. Got your message. What have you got for
me?"

"I'll tell you in a second. First, though, and we're just

speaking theoretically here, if you wanted to get a person into the gala at the Brock, could you do it?"

"Yes."

"Okay. So, and I'm not being at all theoretical here, will you get me in?"

"No."

"Why not?"

"Because this is a police matter, Annie. You have no business being there."

"Yeah, but . . ." I trailed off. What was I going to say? That I wanted her to use her influence to help me set up a possibly illegal business transaction?

"What information do you have for me?" she asked.

Maybe I'll just keep that to myself, Inspector By-the-Book, I thought crankily. Then I reconsidered. Annette was just being responsible. Maybe I should try it some-time. "I think Harlan Coombs will be there."

"Oh?" Now I had her attention. "How do you know that?" she asked.

Oops. Hadn't seen that one coming. What was I going to tell her? That I overheard it when an international art thief and I had fraudulently gained access to a rich woman's home and I was stashed in the kneehole of her desk?

"I just heard it. You know. Around. And I think Coombs is behind the whole *Magi* thing."

"You heard it 'around,' huh? Okay, Annie. But just as a point of clarification, I want you to know I'm not buying that for a second. Anything else?"

"Did you get those numbers I left on your voice mail?"

"Yes."

"Will you tell me what you found out?"

"No."

I thought about that. "Will you tell me if I tell you something else?"

There was a long pause.

"Annie, this isn't how our relationship works."

"Please?"

There was a shorter pause. "The first call was to the residence of a Mr. and Mrs. Robert Culpepper in Belvedere," she said. "The second was to the Gray Goose Inn in St. Helena."

"Oh?" I said. I knew about the Gray Goose, but the other was news. Camilla Culpepper was working with Edward as well as with Harlan Coombs? Interesting. I thanked Annette and prepared to say my good-byes.

But Annette wasn't the type to miss a trick.

"I thought you had some more information for me," she said.

"Uh, yeah, right," I stalled, wondering which of my many new acquaintances I should rat out. Ooo, how about Emily? Anyone who would kick a dog deserved a nice, long talk with my pals Homicide Inspectors Crawford and Wilson.

"I thought you might want to know that Emily Caulfield, Camilla Culpepper's personal assistant, is linked to Harlan Coombs in some way," I said. "She'll be at the gala, too, with Camilla. You know, the gala I should be going to as well."

"Uh-huh," Annette replied, clearly unimpressed by this last-ditch attempt. "Okay, thanks."

"Wait!" I said. "Have you heard anything about who killed Ernst Pettigrew?"

"The preliminary findings suggest suicide, but it's still under investigation. Tell me anything you know."

"I know it wasn't a suicide—Ernst wasn't the type. Was there anything in his pockets when he was found?"

"In his pockets?"

"Yes."

"Why are you interested in the contents of Ernst Pettigrew's pockets?"

I didn't even try to answer that one. "What about Stan Dupont? Was there anything in his personal effects, like a combination or a key?"

"The man was a janitor. He had a million keys."

"But no special little key in his pocket, or something?"

"I think you should tell me what you're after, Annie."

"I was just thinking that, you know, maybe one of them had something that someone was after. Something that had to do with why they were killed, with the fakes or something. Maybe a safe-deposit key? I don't know. It's just a hunch."

"I'll check," she said tersely and hung up.

That evening I took Pedro to dinner at Fiori d'Italia in North Beach as a thank-you. He had managed to download several years' worth of data from my hard drive to install on my new computer—when and if I got the insurance money. I vowed that one day, when I made it big, I'd surprise him with whatever it was that computer geeks coveted. Maybe more memory. I wish I could buy myself more memory. That would be cool.

I didn't sleep well that night, awakening at seven on Thursday morning with the remnants of a vivid dream involving a dwarf, a donkey, and the Miami Dolphins football team composed in part by Michael, Frank, Edward, Mr. Suave, the Hulk—and me as the quarterback.

I spent the day continuing to organize the studio. Sam helped me move the furniture back, but the finer cleanup took several more hours of sorting and organizing. Afterward, I returned a few query calls, set up a meeting with a prospective client, and returned the call of a contractor prepping the wall for my mural in the St. Francis Wood neighborhood. Finally, Mary and I went to OfficeMax, where we filled a cart with supplies and a few essential non-essentials like coffee filters and M&M's, then to the art wholesale outlet, where we stocked up on items that had been ruined, such as sketch paper, two rolls of canvas, and specialty paints. I was living on credit at this point and could only hope to have some way to pay the bills next month.

That evening Samantha and Reggie prepared a huge dinner of Jamaican jerk chicken, red beans, and rice in honor of Pete's recovery, and we took it over to his apartment, where we spent the evening eating our fill and celebrating our friendship. Pete had recovered sufficiently to be bored with his convalescence. With all his stitches, he looked like a grumpy Bosnian Frankenstein.

The following day was Friday, and since I had to swing by a new interior designer's office first thing in the morning to show her my portfolio, I didn't get to the studio until nearly eleven. As I started for the stairs I saw Frank in his office, hunched over some blueprints. By now I was desperate.

I opened his door and said, "You don't have a date, do you?"

"Nope." He didn't bother looking up from his desk.

"You can't go alone, you know."

"Yes I can."

"No you can't. Not to the Brock."

He took the bait. "Why not?"

"Because although this may be San Francisco, the Brock is very Old World. *Everyone* has to have an escort."

I was lying through my teeth, but I was counting on the fact that Frank didn't know me well enough to realize it. He hunched his shoulders.

"Aw, c'mon, Frank," I said impatiently. "I need a date. You need a date. We're the perfect couple."

"Why do you want to go so badly, Annie?" he asked,

finally looking up. "I would've thought you'd hate this kind of thing."

Frank didn't know about my connection to the Brock, eh? That was good. So what kind of answer would Frank respect? One that involved money, I'd bet.

"You're right," I said. "A fancy ball is not my cup of tea. Normally. But everyone who's anyone in the art world will be there. Lots of rich folks. It's important that I be seen there and make those kinds of connections."

Frank seemed to be thinking this over. "Give me one good reason why I should take you."

"Because we're friends."

"No, we're not. I'm your landlord. Keep going."

"I'm a lot of fun to be with."

"You do shake things up. But perhaps I'd prefer a more relaxing evening."

"It would be a nice thing to do."

"What—rescuing you once already this week doesn't earn me nice-guy status?"

"Because . . . because your mother would approve."

Frank looked me up and down. "Oh, I doubt that."

I was stumped. "The only reason you wouldn't is if you were being mean and ornery."

He turned back to the blueprints. "Mmphht."

"What was that?"

"I said, all right. You win."

"We both win, Frank," I said solemnly.

He fiddled with the pen in his hands and gestured to my overalls. "Just, please—promise me you'll wear something . . . appropriate."

Elated, I blew him a kiss. "Don't you worry, Frank," I said. "You'll see. I look *great* in sequins. And I have a feather boa to match."

Frank grinned.

"I'll just bet you do," he said.

Chapter 14

There's no one like a successful transvestite to teach a woman how to dress. Especially if the woman needs a little help. And I certainly did.

Bryan and Ron picked me up at my studio on Saturday morning at eleven and ferried me over to their friend Paul's salon in the Castro, which catered mostly to the alternative crowd. Not being a salon type, I'd never been there. But on this day, escorted as I was by Bryan and Ron, my predicament was taken as a professional challenge, and I was given special treatment.

Seven hours later I emerged, sloughed, waxed, descaled, highlighted, styled, and starved. Armed with an industrial-strength straightening iron and an impressive assortment of chemicals, Paul had expertly beaten my hair into submission. The usual riot of frizzy curls was now swept up into a sleek French twist that managed to look both regal and alluring. However, even with Bryan's last-minute alterations, I could barely fit into the floor-length, embroidered crimson gown that Paul had selected from his cramped closet. The low-cut, form-fitting silk hugged my body like a too-tight glove, cinching at the waist and following the line of my hips and legs, interrupted only by the thigh-high slit up the left side. A line of black pearls edged the low neckline, highlighting the impressive display of my bare chest. When I bent over to adjust the strap on my scarlet stiletto heels, a slight ripping sound issued from somewhere behind me, so I was forbidden lunch. By evening I was ravenous, nervous, and afraid to sit down.

But I had to admit that I looked fabulous. I didn't look much like myself, but I did look fabulous. Bryan presented me with a pair of beautiful black pearl chandelier earrings to top it all off and smiled proudly at me.

I had arranged for Frank to pick me up at Paul's at a quarter to eight. Although the boys wouldn't let me eat, they did allow me one martini to take the edge off. It hit pretty hard on an empty stomach, and by the time Frank pulled up in front, I'd been regaling the gang with Frankie stories for an hour. I watched from the back room as Frank ran the gauntlet and endured my friends' flamboyant teasing with good humor. In his elegant traditional tuxedo, my landlord looked more handsome than ever.

Interesting.

As I made my grand entrance, I noted with satisfaction that Frank's eyes widened, taking in my décolletage and the length of leg revealed by the skirt's slit. Offering nary a clever or biting remark, he held out his arm.

"Have you ever *seen* such a handsome couple?" a misty-eyed Bryan demanded, draping a black lace shawl around my shoulders while Ron and Paul beamed their approval.

Frank navigated the crowded streets of the Castro with ease as we headed across town to the Brock. The Jaguar smelled of buttery leather upholstery, the temperature control kept the air circulating at a perfect seventy-two degrees, and the heated bucket seat tenderly embraced me. I caressed the inlaid wood on the door. A person could get used to this.

Frank spoke his first words as we crossed Fell Street. "You look very nice."

"Thank you, Frank," I replied. "You do, too. But then, you always do. That's why we're always teasing you." One martini made me honest. Two martinis made me stupid. Fortunately, I'd stopped at one.

"Is *that* why?" He looked at me, eyebrows arched.

Time for a change of subject. I wondered why our conversations always became so tense, and vowed that this evening would be a new beginning. After all, Frank was doing me a favor.

"So, what's your girlfriend's name?" I asked.

"Ingrid."

"*Ingrid?*" I caught myself. "I mean, my, what a pretty name. Is she Swedish?"

"She was born in San Francisco but her family's originally from Sweden."

It seemed to pain him to answer.

"Ah. So where are *you* from, Frank?"

"What makes you think I'm not from here?"

I had to laugh. This was not a good move, for my breasts swelled up and nearly spilled over the red silk dam. Frank almost steered us into the back of a Volkswagen microbus that was double-parked in front of a head shop.

We both settled down.

"Let me count the ways," I finally answered him. "First, you dress too well. Second, there's not a single soda can or crumpled piece of paper in your car. Third, you're a tad on the formal side. Fourth—"

He interrupted. "What do you mean, 'on the formal side'?"

"What I said. It's a polite word for stuffy. You know. Stuck up. Tight-assed—"

"Got it. Go on."

"What did you mean the other day in your office when you said you were scared of me?" I asked.

"Just that. You're scary."

"Am not."

He looked at me, puzzled again. I sighed. Looked like ol' Frankie and I were going to have to work on our communication skills.

Now was not the time, however. We'd arrived at the Brock.

The museum was lit up like a Christmas tree, and throngs of over-waxed, over-dyed, and over-medicated beautiful people were emerging from their BMWs and Mercedeses and Lexuses—or was that Lexi?—and sauntering up the front steps. When we pulled up, a nattily dressed young man hustled over to take Frank's keys to the Jaguar. A second valet opened my door and held out his hand to assist me. I stepped gracefully out of the car, tripped over my skirt, used my hands to hold up my bodice, and fell into the valet's arms.

Frank kept a good hold on me as we walked up the wide granite steps. He handed his gilt-edged invitation to the doorman, who was wearing a white wig and dressed in eighteenth-century splendor, the Brock crest stitched in gold on his crimson vest. I was perversely pleased to see someone tonight who looked even more uncomfortable than I.

I had to hand it to the Brocks, though. They didn't do anything halfway.

The museum's main hall, with its Carrera marble floors and soaring domed ceiling, had been transformed into a grand ballroom. A twenty-piece string orchestra played softly in one corner. I caught a glimpse of linen-draped buffet tables hugging the rear walls, piled high with delicacies. A glittering crowd filled the room with lively chatter, the men in black tuxedos, the women arrayed in brilliant silks and satins, their jewels winking in the subdued lighting.

Waiters dressed in red boleros, white shirts, and black ties discreetly roamed the room, some offering crystal glasses of wine, others carrying silver platters of enticing appetizers displayed on ornate doilies. There was an open bar in one corner, where two bartenders were frantically pouring drinks. Little twinkle lights were everywhere, along with huge bouquets of flowers in urns the size of my kitchen table, and in the center of the room, a fountain with a frolicking cupid at its center spouted champagne.

We were savoring our very dry, very fine champagne when I spied Anthony Brazil in the crowd, his signature bow tie replaced by a glorious sapphire and gold silk ascot. On his arm was a woman old enough to be his mother, clad in what looked to be a pearl-and-diamond breastplate. Apparently realizing he'd been spotted, he and his escort sidled over, and he acknowledged me with a slight nod.

"Anthony. How nice to see you this evening," I said properly. Earlier today Bryan and I had pondered how I should behave tonight, and we decided I should pattern myself after Queen Elizabeth. The second, well-mannered one, not the first, decidedly bawdy one. "May I present my escort, Mr. J. Frank DeBenton? Frank, this is Mr. Anthony Brazil."

Frank ruined the effect of my royal graciousness by staring at me as if I'd lost my mind, and Anthony introduced his companion as Catherine Marvin, whom I now recognized as one of the wealthiest women in the city. Her late husband, Melvin, had made a fortune importing cheap footwear from Southeast Asia. Rumor had it that Melvin's real money hadn't come from rubber flip-flops, but high-grade heroin. I figured with a name like Melvin Marvin the guy was destined to go bad. Two years ago Melvin had dropped dead of a heart attack in the arms of his longtime mistress. According to the word on the street, after the funeral the new widow's first act was to send the mistress back to Topeka with a comfortable pension and a warning that the checks would cease if she ever opened her mouth about Melvin. Catherine's second act was to burn all known photographs of Melvin, as well as all his personal belongings. She was now spending what was left of her merry widowhood redecorating her Victorian Gothic mansion and making the Marvin money respectable by becoming a patron of the arts. For a social-climbing art dealer like Anthony Brazil, she was quite a catch.

Anthony glanced at me, looking rather nervous. "Why, I hardly recognized you, my dear. You look very . . . nice."

"Thank you, Anthony," I purred. "You also look very . . . nice." Two could play the snotty game.

"Perhaps you would be good enough to call me in the morning about that business we were discussing last week?"

"Certainly," I replied, grinning as he rushed to lose himself and his upper-crust date in the crowd.

"What was all that about?" Frank asked.

I tried for offhand. "Oh, some drawings he wants my opinion on."

He wasn't buying it. "Uh-huh. Your talents seem to be . . . much in demand these days."

I was saved from answering by a waiter who just then

offered up a silver platter of exquisite shrimp puff pastry. I bit into one and nearly fainted from joy.

As we chatted, I began to relax. Maybe it was the champagne kicking in, maybe it was the music and the party atmosphere, but Frank seemed to be loosening up, too, discreetly pointing to the other guests and telling amusing anecdotes about them, some of which he swore were true.

A waiter hurried by, carrying a tray of Chinese steamed dumplings. I loved those things and gestured to him, but he was looking elsewhere, and Frank had to tap him on the shoulder to get his attention. The waiter jumped, sending two of the dumplings skidding onto the marble floor. Mumbling his apologies, he handed the tray to Frank, then began cleaning up the mess with cocktail napkins. Frank looked around, clearly not comfortable holding the tray.

I had to laugh. "I take it you've never been a waiter?"

"It never was a goal of mine," he admitted. Still, although Frank's collar was as white as snow, there was something about him that suggested he was no stranger to physical labor.

"I waited tables for four long, hot summers when I was in college," I reminisced. "At a truck stop in the Central Valley, off Interstate 5, no less. You haven't lived unless you've schlepped steak and eggs for exhausted truckers at three in the morning. The work was awful, but the truckers were good tippers. And if they weren't, I usually managed to spill coffee in their laps."

Frank grinned. I could get used to that smile.

The waiter stood and reclaimed his tray, mumbled more apologies, and hurried away. Something about him nagged at me. "Did that waiter look familiar to you?"

"First valets, now waiters," Frank teased. "I take it you have a thing for working stiffs?"

"Tell you what, Frank. I need to eat something, or I'm going to get drunk on this champagne and make fools of us both. My friends at the salon wouldn't let me eat today. They were afraid I'd burst out of this dress."

Frank peered over the edge of his champagne flute and gazed at my cleavage as if to assess the danger of that happening. I felt a jolt of electricity and my face grew warm, so I turned away, ostensibly to survey the buffet offerings. And then, hearing a rustle of fabric and a rattle of jewelry behind me, I froze.

"Why, *Frank*," gushed Agnes Hilary Cuthbert Brock. "I'm *so* glad you could come. Isn't everything simply *divine*? Couldn't you simply *die* to see my Caravaggio? No peeking, now. The unveiling will be at nine o'clock sharp, and not one minute earlier! Do tell me, Frank, where is that *charming* Ingrid creature?"

Since my back was to them, I thought it might be best to just keep on going and disappear into the crowd. Unfortunately, Frank had other plans. I felt his warm hand on my bare shoulder and heard him begin to introduce me.

Agnes's watery blue eyes bulged and her face turned a bright red. "You!" she squawked. "How ever did *you* get in here?"

Couples standing nearby ceased their conversation and looked over to see what all the excitement was about.

"Hello, Mrs. Brock. I—"

"Get out of my museum this minute, you—you—dubious person!" she spat, and with a grand sweep of her arm she pointed dramatically to the front entrance.

I was impressed, both with the gesture and with the fact that of all the names she might have called me, she'd limited herself to "dubious person."

"Now, Mrs. Brock, you're causing a scene," I said in a low voice, hoping an appeal to decorum would help.

It did, a little. I didn't dare look at Frank.

Agnes took in the curious stares and regrouped. "I will not tolerate any further slander of my Caravaggio, young lady," she said, more quietly. "I—"

"Mrs. Brock, please. I'm not here for anything even remotely connected to the Caravaggio," I said, improvising as I went along. "Frank's charming Ingrid creature is out of town, and he was without an escort, that's all. Besides, I thought it might be a chance for me to make amends."

I hazarded a glance at Frank. He looked stunned. The best I could hope for, at the moment, was that he would hold his tongue.

"Very well, Ms. Kincaid. If I have your assurance that you will behave yourself, I will refrain from asking Security to escort you from the premises. But no more scenes." She swept off regally.

There was a very awkward, very long silence.

"Perhaps you'd like to tell me about the circumstances under which you left the Brock's employ?" Frank finally said through clenched teeth, anger and suspicion radiating off of him.

"It was a mutual decision," I replied curtly. This was the sort of thing that always seemed to happen when I played by the rules. Maybe Grandfather was right. Maybe I should bag the respectable life and go paint forgeries in Paris. At least I'd make some decent money. And they had really good coffee in France.

"In what sense was it mutual?" Clearly Frank was not ready to drop the subject.

Aw, screw it. "In the sense that if I hadn't left voluntarily, Agnes would have had me arrested," I said.

"Any particular reason?" A muscle in his jaw had begun to twitch.

"It was a long time ago, Frank. Let it go. It's really none of your business, anyway."

Why did I feel I owed everybody in the world an apology for my past? Did they offer me one for theirs?

"It *is* my business that you are not welcome here," he said heatedly. "It *is* my business that you finagled this date with me under false pretenses. You've made me look like an idiot in front of one of my most important clients."

Oh. Well, he had me there.

"Frank, I'm sorry," I said, chastened. "I didn't think—"

"Of course not. Have you ever thought about what *I* might be feeling, Annie? And for future reference, you might keep in mind that I detest being played for a fool."

"Played for a— Now wait a minute," I protested. "It was nothing like that."

"Wasn't it? Excuse me. I need some fresh air." He strode away stiffly.

That's just great, Annie, I muttered to myself as I made a beeline for the champagne fountain. *You have perfected the art of repelling men.* As I concentrated on filling my glass without splashing any liquid on Paul's red silk gown, I felt annoyed with Frank, but mostly with myself. I had been so focused on the gala that I hadn't given any thought to what it might mean for him to be escorting someone who had been banned from the Brock. Given his line of work, I should have realized that he would know Agnes. And it was stupid to have assumed I could manage to avoid Agnes all night.

These unpleasant thoughts were derailed, however, when I spied a familiar figure standing near a huge floral arrangement.

The X-man was back.

Wasn't he wanted by the police? How stupid could he be, to stand out there in the open like that, in a museum filled with the City's movers and shakers?

I scouted out the room and finally glimpsed Inspectors Crawford and Wilson hovering near an archway leading to the Early American collection, both dressed to the nines and trying to fit in. Just your average gorgeous black woman in a beautiful amethyst velvet gown, paired with an ugly, skinny white guy pulling at the collar of his ill-fitting tux.

Views were sporadic through the shifting black-and-white tuxedo forest, but I headed in the direction of the last X-man sighting, filled with grim determination to get the truth from him, once and for all. I tippy-tapped around on my little Cinderella high heels, but try as I might I lost him. Damn.

I had just about given up when I practically bumped into my old pal, the goon I called Mr. Suave, aka the New Yorker, whom I had last seen when he was threatening me in a vacant factory. And unless I was mistaken, standing next to him was none other than the lovely cat-eyed Quiana, blond and statuesque in an ice-blue satin sheath. I swallowed, hard, and frantically looked around for Annette. No luck.

"Why, Ms. Kincaid. I thought that was you," Mr. Suave said, grasping my arm in a bruising grip. "What a delightful coincidence, running into you tonight. I know so few people in town."

"Is that right?" I said, trying to pull free. "Why, we'll just have to remedy that, won't we? I have this friend, Annette, whom I could hook you up with. I feel sure you two would have a great deal to talk about. She's right over—"

"Oh, but Ms. Kincaid, I'm perfectly content being with you. And the lovely Miss Nash, of course. I believe you two have met?"

"Cut the crap, asshole," Quiana said. Such ugly words from such a pretty mouth. Her catlike eyes fixed on me feverishly. "Where is it?"

"Not here," Mr. Suave said. "Let's take a little walk, shall we?" he whispered as he propelled me toward a side door.

"Thanks, but I'm fine right here," I said as I minced along unwillingly. I was trying to drag my feet, an exercise that my spike heels made almost impossible. In response to this ineffectual show of resistance, Mr. Suave flashed me a glimpse of the gun in his coat pocket.

That did it. No way was I going anywhere with this character. I was dropping a dime on Coombs.

"Listen," I said. "It's not me you're after. It's Harlan Coombs."

"Where is he?" Quiana demanded.

The gun in Mr. Suave's jacket scared me, but not nearly as much as the look in Quiana's eyes.

"He's here," I said. "At the gala."

"We know that, imbecile," Mr. Suave hissed. "That's why we're here. But *where* is he here?"

That was the question of the hour, wasn't it? I flashed on the clumsy waiter. He'd seemed a little old to not know what he was doing. And anyway, surely the caterer would have hired only professional waiters for a gig this important. It finally clicked. No one had ever seen Harlan Coombs without his beard. Shaving a beard could dramatically alter a man's appearance.

"He's in the kitchen," I said, trying to yank my arm away.

"I'll go," Quiana said.

"Let's all go, shall we?" Mr. Suave added, and started to hustle me toward the swinging door.

"Annie! How nice to see you."

I heard a welcome voice behind me. Mr. Suave turned reluctantly, pulling me around with him. Quiana adopted a simpering stance, eyes half-lidded and lips pouty, in what I could only assume was the "come hither" posture of the successful man-magnet.

It was wasted in this case. Michael looked neither at me nor at Quiana, but stared intently at Mr. Suave. "Let her go, Gordo," he said quietly.

Gordo? Mr. Suave's name was Gordo?

"Always a pleasure, David," Suave/Gordo replied. "Oh, that's right, you're going by Colin these days, aren't you?"

David? Michael/Paddy/Bruno/Colin was also known as David?

"I believe you've met my friend Ms. Kincaid?" Suave Gordo inquired politely.

"We're acquainted. She has nothing to do with this."

Gordo chuckled. "I beg to differ. She says she knows where Harlan is."

Michael lobbed a chuckle right back at him. "She doesn't know *anything*, Gordo. She's a third-rate painter who sticks her nose in other people's business and mucks things up."

Well, that was a little harsh. I glared at him.

"I want Harlan as much as you do, Gordo," Michael continued, unfazed. "Why don't we throw in together and figure out what's going on here?"

Gordo mulled it over. "What do we do with this one?"

"Oh, just let her go," suggested Michael. He still had not met my eyes, and I was starting to wonder about his intentions toward me. How far would he go to acquire the precious Caravaggio? Would he remain loyal to his criminal colleagues? Or had I thoroughly beguiled him with my womanly charms?

I was in trouble.

"She'll talk," Gordo said. "Or follow us."

He seemed to have a pretty good read of my character. Frankly, that didn't sit well.

Michael shrugged. "So we'll stash her somewhere. How about in Edward's office? That's out of the way."

And then I was dragged toward a door near the kitchen. I was about to yell to attract attention—this did not seem to be the time for demure silence—but Michael curled his arm around my shoulders and shoved my face into his tuxedoed chest. Thus effectively muffled, all I could do was smear lipstick all over his lapel.

Quiana stayed behind as Michael opened a door and Gordo shoved me forward into a maintenance corridor. The three of us followed it along to the left and through another unmarked door that opened onto the hallway leading to the museum's administrative offices. Simultaneously being pushed by Michael and pulled by Gordo was no joke. My feet were hurting, and now that the panic was subsiding, I was becoming angry.

I opened my mouth to scream, and this time a familiar hand came down on top of it. I heard Michael's voice in my ear and felt his warm breath on my cheek. "Shut the hell up, Annie," he muttered. "Gordo here is not playing around."

I shut up.

Michael used a master key to open the door to Edward's office and the three of us slipped in. The room was a shambles. The desk had been ripped apart, drawers flung to the floor, and papers strewn about. The wall safe Michael had riffled through the other day stood open and empty.

When I got over the shock, I turned to Michael. "Jackass!"

"Lovers' quarrel?" Gordo asked, leering at my cleavage.

"That goes for you, too," I snarled. "By the way, in my book you're no longer Mr. Suave. From now on, you're Gordo the Goon."

"Jesus, Annie," Michael sighed, shaking his head in exasperation.

Gordo reached out and slapped me across the face.

"Hey!" Michael said, stepping toward him, but Gordo pulled out his gun and pointed it at both of us.

Michael put his hands up. I did the same.

"Listen, Gordo," Michael said. "I can't stand to see a woman hit, you know how it is. Tell you what. We'll lock her in the closet and go find Harlan. Looks like he's already been through the office here."

"No, David," our friend with the gun replied. "I'll tell *you* what. I'll lock the both of you in the closet and take care of Harlan myself. Move it. Now."

Michael reluctantly surrendered the master key to Gordo, who opened the closet door, pushed us both inside, and shut and locked the door behind us. It soon became apparent that we weren't alone.

"Hiya, Edward, how's it going?" Michael asked in a jovial tone in the pitch-black darkness.

"How do you think it's going, jerk-off?" Edward spat. I wondered whether Agnes missed her favorite grandson at the gala, and what she would think if she knew he was locked in a closet with me, Annie Kincaid, forger's spawn. "You left me here for hours! What's going on, you son of a—"

"Tsk. Such language, Edward. There's a lady present."

"You mean Kincaid? Isn't she just another one of your whores like Qui—"

There was a scuffle and a choking sound.

"I thought we'd gone over this, Edward," Michael said almost pleasantly. "You keep your filthy mouth shut. I know it's tough, but if you say anything else about Annie, I am going to beat the crap out of you."

A low moan was his reply.

Michael switched on a small penlight, and used it to

find a bare lightbulb in the ceiling, attached to an old-fashioned string pull. He gave the string a tug, and the bulb's twenty watts glowed weakly.

"Take this," he said, handing the penlight to me. "Shine it on the door lock."

I hesitated for a second, loath to take orders from the X-man, especially after everything he'd put me through. But my common sense won out—there'd be plenty of time to kick his ass after we got out of the closet. I took the light.

Michael drew a Swiss army knife from his pants pocket and started picking the lock with a tiny screwdriver. I was going to have to get me one of those knives. They were clearly handy in cases of abduction.

After he fiddled for several minutes, the lock turned. Michael smiled and pushed on the door.

Nothing happened.

"Shit."

"What is it?" I asked.

"Gordo must have barricaded the door. Edward, get over here and help. We'll push together."

Edward shuffled forward, and we took up positions on either side of Michael.

"Okay, on my count. Ready? One. Two. Three."

We heaved. The door budged about an inch. We tried again, but it wouldn't move any further.

"Shit," we said in unison.

Edward returned to the rear of the closet, where he'd made himself a nest of coats. He had a flask with him and seemed to be getting drunk, mumbling something unintelligible about crooks and artists and their ilk.

Michael started checking out the contents of the closet, apparently looking for resources among the coats and office supplies. I joined the hunt and found a stapler, locked and loaded. I decided I could use it as a weapon if somebody got really, really close and held really, really still.

Michael ran his hand through his dark hair. "Shit."

"You're repeating yourself," I grumbled.

He sighed. "Annie, I'm sorry."

"Really? For what? There are so very many things you should apologize for, *David*."

"His name's not David. It's Colin," Edward threw in helpfully.

But we had lost Michael's attention. He was searching coat pockets.

"Even if you find a gun, I don't think you can blast us out of here," I said.

"You never know. It would be more use than that stapler you're wielding. And we can't just sit here and wait for Gordo to return."

He was interrupted by an electronic version of Beethoven's Fifth. A cell phone! Michael was right, the coats did provide a way to get us out of here! Now, we just had to find it. I started furiously patting them down.

"It's mine," Michael said sheepishly, pulling a phone from his tuxedo pocket. "Hello? Naomi! I need you, sweetheart. Yes, right now. Well, I can't explain at the moment, but I'm in Edward's office, locked in the closet. There's been a slight misunderstanding. Please hurry. Me, too. Listen, sweetheart, I need you to come now, and then you can tell me in person, okay? Great. Yes . . . Honey? Are you on your way?"

He snapped the phone shut and rolled his eyes.

"I wouldn't look a gift horse in the mouth if I were you, Super Thief," I said waspishly.

"I said I was sorry." Michael sounded annoyed.

"I don't believe you."

"Why not?"

"Because you're a liar and a thief."

"Oh, that."

"Your sister and your dog live in Fremont? Give me a break."

"What?"

"You said your sister and your dog live in Fremont. That was a big fat lie, wasn't it?"

Michael looked perplexed. "After everything we've been through, that's what you focus on?"

"If you'd lie about a sister and a dog, then you'd lie about anything." Made perfect sense to me.

"She's got a point, there, Colin," Edward piped up from the rear of the closet.

Michael sighed. "Annie, honey—you're a very unusual woman."

"You got that right, sport."

There was a noise on the other side of the door, and then we heard Naomi's distinctive nasal voice. "Colin? Colin, darling?"

"Naomi!" Michael called out. "We're in here."

" 'We'? Who's in there with you, darling?"

There were sounds of shifting furniture.

"Edward," Michael said.

"Oh no!" she cried.

"I'm here, too, Naomi!" I shouted.

All activity ceased.

"Ann? Ann *Kincaid*?"

Good going, Annie, I told myself. Edward and Michael glared at me.

"Hi, Naomi," I said, with false cheer.

"Why are you in there with Colin?"

"I'm not in here with Colin. I'm in here with Edward." This made no sense, of course, but Naomi tended to be easily confused.

"Honey?" Michael cooed. "Please hurry. It's difficult being locked in with . . . well, you can imagine."

"What the hell is that supposed to mean?" I whispered. "Or are you trying to give me a reason to use this stapler in my hand?"

There was more shuffling, a little grunting, and the closet door swung open.

Michael stepped out and swept Naomi into his arms. "Sweetheart! Whatever would I have done without you?"

Oh, puh-leeze, I thought, but Naomi seemed to lap it up. That is, until Michael pushed her and Edward into the closet, slammed the door, and shoved a heavy desk in front of it.

I grinned.

So did he.

And then he sprinted out of the office.

I followed as fast as my high heels would allow, but by the time I got to the door the corridor was empty. I considered my options. Finding Harlan seemed like a good place to start, so I hustled toward the kitchen. Gordo the Goon had no doubt already been there, but it was possible he wouldn't recognize Harlan without his beard. As an artist, I had been trained to perceive facial structure and even I had been fooled at first.

Three minutes later I burst through the kitchen's swinging door, nearly taking out some poor guy carrying a tray of caviar canapes. Chefs in white coats and waiters in red bolero jackets were scurrying about, but I snagged one of the youngest by the arm.

"Was there anyone you didn't recognize working here tonight?" I demanded. "A new guy?"

"You mean the man that just left?" he said, pointing to the back door.

But of course.

I edged my way across the kitchen, trying not to look too conspicuous, and nipped out the back door, which opened onto an empty hallway. I paused a moment to

ponder. It seemed clear that the drawings were not in Edward's office, which had been thoroughly tossed. But
now something occurred to me: why would Harlan risk
coming to the Brock during the gala? Why not wait for a
quiet Sunday evening when nobody was around? It was
true that the gala was chaotic and that no one would be
expecting to see him there. Still, it took a certain kind of
audacity to stage a crime in the middle of a crowded
affair such as this one, with potential witnesses everywhere. Especially since it would have been a whole lot
easier just to convince Edward to let him in after hours.
But Harlan hadn't done that. So that must mean there was
some advantage to being here during the gala.

The only thing I could think of that might have
brought him here tonight was the unveiling of *The Magi*.
But why would Harlan care about *The Magi* if he knew it
was a fake? Had Michael switched the paintings yet
again? That seemed overly complicated. Besides, Michael
was after Harlan, too, which meant that Harlan still owed
him money from the first switcheroo. Surely he wouldn't
have done it again without getting paid up front.

And what about Gordo the Goon, formerly known as
Mr. Suave? He was angry about having paid Harlan real
money for a fake painting. Maybe he wanted to kill Harlan for the sheer pleasure of it? He seemed the type. I
couldn't imagine Gordo trying to steal the Caravaggio
himself—he would pay someone else to do that kind of
work.

My head was beginning to spin. Bottom line: the key
to this whole mess was *The Magi*. I felt an urge to hurry,
and tried trotting toward the elevator, but after a few steps
my feet shrieked in protest. As we used to say in the
truck-stop trade, my dogs were barkin'. Frustrated, I
yanked the wretched high heels off, hoisted up my trail-
ing skirts, and ran along in my stocking feet. Bryan and

the gang would be horrified, but I was no longer willing to cripple myself for fashion.

I had almost reached the service elevator when a burly, middle-aged security guard turned into the hallway and started toward me. I stopped running and smiled, trying to pretend that there was nothing even slightly odd about my presence in a rear hallway, disheveled, in a red ball gown, with my shoes in my hands. Happened all the time at the Brock.

I was about to launch into the whole "Great-aunt Agnes" gambit when he spoke, cordial but guarded. "Ms. Anna Kincaid?"

It seems I was expected.

This couldn't be good.

No good ever came from the bowels of the Brock.

Chapter 15

A painter's autograph should be approached as a series of abstract lines and forms on the canvas, rather than as a series of letters. Never overlook the importance of these magic lines, for they tell the auctioneer where to start the bidding, the art lover whether to admire the work, and the art expert whether to hail the piece as worthy of merit.

—Georges LeFleur, "Experts & Other Lower Life Forms," unfinished manuscript, Reflections of a World-Class Art Forger

Think, Annie, think.

If I admitted that I was, indeed, Anna Kincaid, it seemed likely I would be booted from the Brock forthwith. Even I had to admit that I had no business cavorting around the museum's innards, shod or unshod. My fears were confirmed as I glanced over my shoulder and saw a big blond security guard approaching from the rear. Both men carried guns, as well as those nasty batons for hitting people. I, on the other hand, had only a pair of high heels, having dropped the stapler in Edward's office. Not exactly a fair fight.

"Um . . ." said I, always cool under fire.

"Come with us, please, Ms. Kincaid," the first guard said politely.

"Um . . ." I hesitated.

Big Blondie grabbed my arm. "You heard the man."

I was escorted none too gently along the hallway, around a couple of corners, down a flight of stairs, and into a small room. I didn't know what was going on, but part of me was starting to worry that I might shortly end my days here at the Brock, my bones entombed forever beneath the marble floor of the tacky "Modern Masters" exhibit. That would be Agnes Brock's ultimate revenge. The only thing that kept me from panicking was the sure knowledge that the old bat didn't possess anywhere near enough imagination to dream up such a fitting reprisal.

A door opened, Big Blondie pushed me forward, and the door slammed shut behind me. I was relieved to see neither Agnes Brock, Gordo the Goon, the Hulk, nor the Fonz, but my buddies from the police department, Inspectors Crawford and Wilson.

Strangely enough, they did not seem equally delighted to see me. In fact, they looked rather grim.

Annette told me to have a seat on a metal folding chair by a small worktable. Ichabod leaned against a filing cabinet, his skinny arms crossed over his chest. Annette walked over to me, arms crossed over *her* chest. I wasn't much into body language, but there was no mistaking that message.

"What in the *hell* are you doing here?" she demanded.

I could think of more positive directions for this discussion to take. "Um," I said.

"Spit it out, Annie. And cut the crap."

"I . . . actually, I was invited by a friend. I'm here legitimately, Annette. Really."

"Uh-huh. And were you 'legitimately' running around the back hallways barefoot?"

"Is *that* what this is about? Is there a law against bare feet in public?"

"Stow it, Annie. This is serious."

Chastened, I fell silent and chewed my lower lip. Annette sat down across from me, put her hands flat on the table, and looked me straight in the eye. "Tell me what's going on," she said firmly. "Tell me *now*, or you're out of here and I'm charging you with something."

"It's not illegal to go barefoot. Which I'm not, strictly speaking. I have stockings on." To prove it, I hoisted my skirt and stuck out one foot.

She was not impressed. "Oh, I'll think of something," she told me. "Trespassing. Interfering with a police investigation." She glanced at my chest and raised an eyebrow. "Indecent exposure."

I looked down and saw that my décolletage was in serious danger of revealing too much, doubtlessly as a result of being manhandled by Big Blondie. I hooked a finger in the neckline and hiked it up as best I could. So much for acting like the Queen Mum.

Ichabod politely looked away.

"Okay, Annette," I said. "Point taken. No more crap. I'm here because I think I know where the drawings are."

"You mean the drawings you were trying to find for the art dealers?" she asked. "Remind me what this has to do with the Brock Museum in general, and this gala in particular."

Might as well come clean. There were goons with guns on the loose. Where to start?

"Harlan Coombs ran into money problems and stole some valuable drawings from his clients," I began. "I think he hid them in the museum and that he's come here tonight to retrieve them. I also think I may know where they are."

"Why would he hide them here?" Annette demanded.

"And why would he risk coming back for them tonight of all nights?" She hadn't gotten her gold shield out of a cereal box.

"Can you think of a safer place to hide fragile old drawings than a museum?" I asked. "They're quite valuable, and are much easier to fence than a famous painting like *The Magi*."

Annette looked at me severely. "I'm not going to ask how you knew he hid them here. So I'll ask you this: where are the drawings now?"

That was the question, wasn't it? I wasn't positive, but I was willing to hazard a guess.

"With *The Magi*," I said. "Behind the canvas, in a false insert in the frame . . . I think. It's an old trick used for smuggling documents. That would explain why Coombs had to be here tonight, to get access to the painting. It's usually in the vault."

"Uh-huh. And why were you asking me about a key the last time we talked?"

"Just a wild guess. You know how in the movies people are always after a nondescript safety-deposit box key? And then just getting the key isn't enough—you have to know which bank to go to? I heard something about someone looking through someone else's pockets, and it occurred to me that one of the thousands of archival drawers lining the back rooms of this place would make an excellent hiding place."

"For the drawings?"

"Or for a lot of money. Seems to me that there's more than one fake Caravaggio floating around, and maybe a real one, too, and that somebody's gotten paid for those paintings by collectors, each thinking they're buying the real one."

"Uh-huh. Do you also think Harlan Coombs killed Stan Dupont?"

"I have no idea, but Harlan is here tonight. I saw him earlier. Maybe we should find him and ask. Plus, the guy who attacked Pete and kidnapped me is here tonight, too. He looks capable of murder, if you ask me."

Annette looked at me sternly. "I didn't ask you. And you are not going anywhere, Annie. *You* are going to wait here with Officers Campbell and Westmont." She rose and turned to go. Ichabod stood up straight.

"Annette, wait," I said, prepared to beg if I had to. "With all due respect, you're a cop, not an artist. You might find something and not even recognize it when you see it. You could even irreparably damage the drawings and the oil painting if you're not careful." I threw that last bit in for good measure, since most people handled expensive art the same way they did newborn babies—gingerly.

Annette looked at Ichabod, then back at me, and sighed. "All right," she relented. "But no more bullshit, you got me? We're dealing with murder here."

"I realize that," I said, trying to sound chastened. It wasn't too hard.

"Come along, then." She pulled a police radio out of her spangled evening bag and asked someone if the Caravaggio had been brought downstairs yet, only to be told that it was currently under guard in the Blue Room.

Annette led the way, bustling down the hall in her amethyst gown. I couldn't help but notice that her heels were easily two inches higher than mine had been, yet she could really move in them. I had to ask.

"Six months undercover, Vice," she told me, a note of pride in her voice. "You have any idea how high the average hooker's shoes are? That'll train you for these little bitty things. I could run a marathon in these babies."

That clinched it. When I grew up, I wanted to be as cool as Annette.

Annette, Ichabod, Officers Campbell and Westmont, and I took the elevator to the ballroom, where we had to wade through the jabbering crowd of partygoers to get to the Blue Room.

As I walked along with my armed police escort, I saw the one person I most wanted not to see—my date, Frank. He watched as we passed, his face grim. I couldn't help but notice the voluptuous brunette hanging on his arm, gazing up at him adoringly. Helga—or was it Ingrid?—had better get back from her trip pretty soon.

I scanned the crowd for Harlan, or Michael, or Gordo, or Quiana, but without luck until, as we neared the double doors that led into the Blue Room, I saw a man in a waiter's red bolero slip in through a side door. I nudged Annette, who radioed Security to be on alert for any uniformed waiters trying to get near the Caravaggio.

Officer Campbell opened the door and we walked into mayhem.

The room was full of thick smoke. I heard a muffled shout, and then a series of small explosions that, to my untrained ear, sounded like gunshots with a silencer. Annette immediately stepped in front of me, reached under her dress to her thigh holster, and drew her weapon. She and Ichabod peered around cautiously, then charged into the center of the mess, shouting their identity as police. Officers Campbell and Westmont guarded the door.

Since no one in the smoke-filled room seemed to be watching me, I edged around it, keeping low and hugging the wall. The first person I bumped into was Michael.

"Oh, for Christ's sake, Annie," he swore, then added something that was unintelligible above the noise of the shouts, before turning to run the other way, deeper into the smoke. Only then did I realize that he had something clutched under his arm.

Something large. And flat. And painted.

I took off after him, flinging myself through the dense smoke. I stumbled over not one but two bodies of uniformed police officers or security personnel, I couldn't tell which. Taking heart from the fact that I didn't see blood anywhere, and praying that they were just unconscious, I kept on going and bumped into a podium, which sent me spinning off in a new direction. I heard yells somewhere up ahead, but by now I had no idea where I was or what was going on, and was just starting to think it might be time to find an exit, when I tripped over a third body.

Michael.

As much as I'd threatened, at various points in our relationship, that I would see him dead one day, I hadn't really meant it. Despite the chaos all about us, I sat down and lifted his head onto my lap. "Michael? Michael, are you okay? Colin? Paddy? David? Somebody answer me." I started examining him for signs of a wound.

"You realize that in some cultures this means we're engaged?" Michael said groggily.

I took that to mean he wasn't dead, and was surprised by a surge of emotion as he gazed up at me with those piercing green eyes.

"For the love of God, Annie," he barked. "Stop fussing over me and go find that damn painting!"

Jackass. I dropped his head, and took off in search of *The Magi.*

Finally, in the midst of the shouts and the smoke, the scuffling feet and the yells, I reached a door and pushed through it, regaining my eyesight just in time to catch a glimpse of a waiter's red bolero jacket. Running after him, I found myself back in the grand ballroom, where people were milling about, chattering excitedly, and trying to figure out what on earth was happening.

I searched for my quarry. If I were Harlan, dashing

through this crowd with a stolen Caravaggio tucked under my arm, I would head for the nearest exit and take my chances outside. Using my elbows to shove the gawking glitterati aside, I finally reached the main doors, where several security guards stood, looking bored. Red Bolero obviously hadn't gone out this way, but I thought Annette and the crowd in the smoke-filled room might need some backup.

"Officer," I said panting and pointing behind me. "Trouble. The Blue Room."

The young Latino guard looked as if he didn't know whether to believe me.

"Smoke!" I cried.

That did it. Pausing long enough to bark orders into his shoulder mike, he plunged into the crowd. I followed suit, but veered off toward the maintenance corridors. Maybe Red Bolero would try the service exit.

Pushing my way through the crowd, I suddenly came face-to-face with Camilla Culpepper, who was wearing a black-and-gold-striped satin gown and an extravagantly feathered turban. There was no sign of a Mr. Culpepper, but Camilla had brought along her assistant, Emily Caulfield, who carried the charming Miss Mopsy in a brocade doggie carrier slung around her shoulders. I could only wonder how much the Culpeppers paid Emily to submit to this kind of humiliation. Since we had not parted on the best of terms, I was not particularly surprised when Emily turned and bolted, dog and all, in the opposite direction.

"Emily!" Camilla squealed.

I grabbed Emily by one arm and swung her around. Miss Mopsy started squirming, trying to lick me.

"Where's Harlan?" I hissed.

"Harlan?" Camilla echoed.

"Who?" squeaked Emily.

"Don't play coy, Emily. Now tell me. Where. Is. Harlan." I was not in the mood for more attitude from Miss Priss here.

"How would I know?"

"Yes, how would she know?" Camilla interjected. "You don't even know Harlan, do you, Emily?"

"She most certainly does," I said, then turned back to Emily. "You were supposed to meet him here tonight, remember, Emily?"

Wait a minute. Why *did* Harlan want Emily here tonight? For that matter, why did he want Camilla here tonight? Unless, perhaps, they were part of his plan to smuggle the drawings out?

The doggie sling! It was ridiculous to bring a dog to a ball, something Camilla surely knew. But what was the likelihood that a doggie sling would be carefully searched?

"Give me the dog," I told Emily.

"She won't!" cried Camilla.

"Go to hell!" spat Emily.

I grabbed the doggie sling, Miss Mopsy started to bark, and Emily took a swing at me and missed. The upshot of all of this was that the sling ripped, the dog flew, and a quick inspection revealed there were no drawings anywhere. Emily ducked past me, Camilla following her in hot pursuit, while Miss Mopsy landed nose-first in the truffled mousse paté and started mowing her way down the rest of the buffet table.

There were more screams and the clatter of breaking dishes, but still the orchestra played on. Turning to continue the hunt for Harlan, I came nose to nose with Agnes Brock. What luck. Beside her was Sebastian Pitts. Luckier still.

"What in the world is going on here, young lady?" she demanded, livid. "Did you just throw a *dog* in my paté?"

I didn't know how to answer a question like that, so I didn't even try, taking aim instead at an easier target. "You know, Sebastian," I said, "if I were you, I'd be worrying more about the fact that your precious Caravaggio has been stolen. Good thing it was a fake, huh?"

Leaving the two gaping in my wake, I spun around and ran smack into the elegant Quiana, who proved surprisingly strong as she grabbed me by my already bruised arm.

"Where is it?" she demanded.

"Back off!" I snarled, and to my surprise, she let go and disappeared into the crowd.

I turned toward the kitchen, still hoping to find Harlan before he managed to flee the building. However, moving across the great hall was now like swimming upstream against a surging torrent of tuxedos and silk. The smoke-bombed Blue Room was finally attracting the attention it deserved, and security and police officers started flooding the ballroom. Shrieking had begun in earnest, and I had a feeling that the loudest of all was Agnes Brock. Or maybe it was Sebastian Pitts.

At long last the waltz music ground to a halt, "Tales of the Vienna Woods" being replaced by the sounds of alarms and hundreds of frantic voices. A few of the hardier souls and leveler heads were shouting instructions for everybody to remain calm, in an attempt to direct the traffic toward the front doors. A mass exodus began, but with all those high heels and swelled heads it was slow going. Mostly people milled about aimlessly, and despite the general atmosphere of catastrophe I noticed that more than a few were still enjoying the buffet table and the open bar, indicating, as far as I was concerned, that there was no real consensus on what the appropriate course of action should be.

Until somebody pulled the fire alarm. Warning sirens

screamed, the overhead sprinklers went off, and a recorded message began repeating, over and over, "The fire alarm has sounded. Please do not panic. Proceed calmly toward the clearly marked exits. Please do not panic."

Immediately the crowd panicked, as water cascaded down like a tropical monsoon. My dress was now officially a disaster. If I got out of here alive, Bryan was going to kill me.

I made my way slowly through the throngs trying to exit, and finally reached the kitchen, where I asked the gaping serving staff if they'd seen a waiter rush through here with a painting in his arms. Surprisingly, three of them pointed to the back door, so I ran into the maintenance corridor once again. Trying to decide which way to go, I saw what appeared to be a hand peeking out from around a corner, and slowly eased toward it and around the turn.

Harlan Coombs lay motionless on the linoleum floor, a pair of strange-looking glasses askew on his face, his white shirt and red bolero jacket stained by a much deeper red. There were three small holes in his chest.

I swore and jumped back, looking around wildly. Which way, which way? If Gordo the Goon or his sidekick the Hulk had just plugged Harlan and grabbed the painting, wouldn't they head for the nearest exit?

I tore down the hallway until I heard voices coming from an open door about ten feet in front of me. Pressing myself against the wall, I held my breath, and listened. The voices were muffled, but I recognized Suave Gordo's velvety tones.

". . . and you weren't supposed to kill him until he told you which drawer the key fits." He sounded aggrieved. "Let's get out of here."

With dawning horror, I realized they were coming

straight toward me. What was wrong with these guys? They were supposed to go the other way! I looked around frantically, but there were no doors except the one I was standing next to, and it was locked. Deciding to run for it, I barreled back the way I had come, knowing I'd never reach the end of the hallway in time but hoping they would be so surprised to see me that they might pause. Or that, at least, they would have to slow down to shoot.

"What the—" Suave Gordo the Goon exclaimed. "Hanks! Thomas! Stop her!"

I bent forward and began swerving, hoping to make a harder target. At the same time, I heard a gun roar and the explosion echoed down the corridor, almost deafening me. My lungs were screaming in protest, and so were the muscles in my thighs, but the adrenaline carried me along. There was another shot, followed by another, this one originating much closer to me, and, unless my ears deceived me, traveling in the opposite direction. A glance over my shoulder confirmed that the Hulk had been hit. As I was looking back, I ran smack into a very solid mass that yanked me around the corner into the side corridor.

Michael.

"I thought you hated guns," I said, panting.

"I'm not the world's greatest shot," he confessed, hunkering down, "so I suggest you keep running. I don't know how long I can keep them pinned down."

I hunkered down beside him. "Did you see Harlan?"

"Yeah," he said grimly. "Get out of here, Annie. I mean it."

"I'm not going to leave you here like this."

"I'd leave you."

"No you wouldn't."

"I've already left you a couple of times, haven't I?"

"Not when somebody was shooting at me, you didn't. Give me your cell phone. I'll call for help."

"Lost it in the Blue Room."

"Yeah, what was all that about?"

Michael peered around the corner and fired another round. "The museum has a smoke security device that's supposed to blind thieves if they tamper with the artwork. Harlan set it off on purpose, then used a stun gun on the guards," he said. "He even had special thermal glasses to allow him to see through the smoke. Gutsy bastard." He paused and shot again. "Okay, here's the plan. I'll fire another shot or two, then we run like hell the other way. Got it?"

He fired and we took off.

I wish I could say that I easily kept up, but the truth was that Michael pulled me down the corridor at full throttle. Unfortunately, we were not fast enough. There was another volley of shots, Michael stumbled, I tripped over him, and we both landed on the linoleum with an audible splat. The gun skittered down the hallway, out of reach, and a red flower blossomed on Michael's left shoulder.

I looked up. The Hulk and the Fonz were upon us. Grinning ominously, the Hulk pointed a gun at my head.

"Not here, idiot!" Gordo intervened, clutching a painting protectively in his arms as he trotted up to us. "This place is going into lockdown soon, if it hasn't already. Take them into the supply room over there, and *then* shoot them. Get Harlan's body in there, too."

Michael's face had a grayish cast, but he struggled to his feet, with my help, one arm around my shoulder for support. I pressed my hand against his wound to stanch the bleeding and hoped this would be one of those times when the doctor would materialize and say, "Oh, it's just a flesh wound. You'll live." Assuming we survived the next few minutes.

Gordo used Michael's master key to unlock a door and

made an "after you" sweep with his hand. Since I figured this was the aforementioned Supply Room of Doom, I thought it best to stay out of it. Searching for some way to divert Gordo, I focused on the painting he was holding.

"How do you plan to get that out of here, Gordo?" I asked, nodding toward *The Magi*.

"Shut up, you stupid twit," he replied rudely.

"I may be a stupid twit, but at least I'm smart enough not to steal a fake."

Gordo glared at me. "It's not a fake."

"Bad news, pal. It's as fake as a three-dollar bill. I should know. My grandfather painted it."

Michael groaned.

"David here swore this was the original," Gordo announced.

Oops. How was I supposed to know? Anyway, whatever Michael—or "David"—had been trying to accomplish by telling Gordo the painting was real, we were about to be murdered by the bad guys, so his plan wasn't working.

"If it's not genuine, then where is the real one?" Gordo demanded, eyes narrowed speculatively.

"Release us and I'll tell you," I said, trying to buy us time.

"Tell me and I'll release you," he replied.

Hmm. We seemed to have a bit of a standoff here.

Suddenly, a woman screamed. "Harlan!"

Camilla Culpepper staggered around the corner, feather turban askew, tears coursing down her face and mixing with her heavy makeup to create a grotesque mask of grief. An ugly patch of crimson stained the front of her striped dress. More frightening still was the gun in her hand.

"Wh-which one of you murdered my darling, my Harlan?" she demanded in a broken voice.

Duh, Camilla!—how about the guys with the guns? What a dingbat. I started making surreptitious little head nods in the direction of Gordo, the Hulk, and the Fonz. Next to me, Michael was doing the same thing.

Camilla did not seem to notice. "Murderers!" she shrieked just before she started blasting away at random.

Gordo dropped *The Magi* and returned fire while Michael pushed me into the supply room, then grabbed the painting, jamming the doorknob from the inside and wrapping his arms around me and *The Magi*. I pressed my face into his chest, holding his large, warm body tightly and listening to the reassuring sound of his heart beating. True, it would have been more reassuring if his heart hadn't been beating quite so rapidly, but I wasn't about to quibble.

After what seemed like an eternity, the shooting and the screaming stopped. Neither Michael nor I moved a muscle for a long time, our breath coming fast and loud in the sudden silence. Finally, Michael relaxed a little.

"Are you badly hurt?" I whispered.

"No." He brushed a damp curl from my forehead. "You all right? You look like hell."

I was drenched from the sprinklers, my beautiful evening gown was torn and soaked, and my stockings were ripped and full of runs. My unruly hair had overthrown Paul's taming, and I was willing to bet that at the moment it was standing on end. I had no idea where my shoes were, I was sweaty, and my nose was running. I didn't think it was very nice of him to draw attention to my appearance at a time like this.

"Yeah, well, thanks," I said. "You look like hell, too." I lied. He looked good enough to nibble. I wondered if I'd ever get the chance.

"You're all right," he said again, as if reassuring himself. His hand fell from my disheveled hair to my cheek, which he stroked with the back of his hand. He took a deep breath. "You're a real pain in the ass," he said. "You know that?"

"I bet you say that to all the girls," I replied, batting my eyes. I felt a flutter in my stomach, but I didn't know whether to attribute it to the recent gunfire or to Michael's closeness. Just then a commotion in the hallway suggested that the authorities had arrived.

"We're in here!" Michael shouted through the door. "We're unarmed!" He turned to me. "Keep your hands up and move slowly. The police will have to sort out who's who."

Why was it that the last two men I'd spent quality time with both knew the best way to act in a police raid? Maybe I needed to give that one some thought.

"Do you think it's . . . ?" I started, but Michael had already opened the door.

I peeked over his shoulder. The Hulk and the Fonz lay motionless on the floor, covered with blood. Gordo was nowhere in sight, though large red drops left a gruesome trail down the hall. Camilla Culpepper was slumped on the floor, stunned and disheveled. That should be quite a story to share with the girls over gin and tonics at the Belvedere Country Club. Apparently she was quite a shot.

The Magi lay at our feet. A lot of people had been hurt because of this painting, I thought, so I should probably treat it carefully and not, say, put my foot through it, which was what I felt like doing. I tucked it behind some mops.

"So is it really a fake?" Michael whispered

"Not if you're in the market for a genuine Georges LeFleur," I said.

"Then where's the original?" he asked, frustrated.

I shrugged. As if I would tell him, even if I knew.

Michael and I emerged with our hands up. Annette the

Unconquerable looked, I was pleased to see, a little worse
for wear.

"What in the hell happened here?" she demanded.

Behind her, Camilla Culpepper was being cuffed and
read her rights while cops were swarming over the bodies of Harlan and the Hulk. The goon I called the Fonz
was moaning while two paramedics bandaged his arm.

Michael started talking, portraying himself as a poor
art curator caught up against his will in this web of lies
and deceit. Colin Brooks was the name. Egyptology was
his game.

Two officers led Gordo down the hallway, handcuffed
and bloodied, no longer Mr. Suave in any sense of the
word, while Camilla started to babble something that
made it sound as though she and Harlan had been in ca-
hoots. It seems they were very much in love and had
planned to elope with the proceeds from selling the drawings and the fake Caravaggio, but then that dreadful
Joanne woman and her sister, Quiana, had tried to steal
their money.

Harlan and Quiana, Harlan and Emily, Harlan and
Camilla. Evidently, this time at least, Harlan had been
playing a few too many hands.

Michael was still droning on, all innocence and cooperation. I began to wonder if he was delirious.

"He's shot in the shoulder," I told Annette.

"Get that man to the paramedics," she ordered a uniformed officer. "And stay with him."

She turned hard eyes back to me. "You all right?"

I nodded, suddenly overwhelmed. The adrenaline high
that had sustained me through the worst of the evening
was giving way to a major energy crash and I needed to
sit down—fast. I also felt a little nauseated. Without in-
tending to, I slid down the wall to sit on the floor.

There was a loud and distinct ripping of cloth. I didn't

want to know, couldn't bear to look, so I put my head on my knees. Someone draped a blanket across my shoulders.

The next thing I knew, a familiar tuxedoed figure was crouched beside me, speaking in soothing tones. I looked up to see Frank, his face inscrutable.

"What are you doing here?" I asked, always the lady.

"Are you all right?"

"I'm okay." I still felt shaky, but the nausea had passed. It couldn't have been the champagne. That was too long ago. Must have been the blood and the bullets that had taken the starch out of me.

"Let me help you up," Frank said, and I felt a strong arm around my waist. Without thinking, I pushed him away, but immediately regretted it as black dots danced before my eyes and the noise of the hallway suddenly sounded very far away. A pair of arms wrapped themselves around me. "Whoa, there, now." It was Frank again. "Why don't you let me help you, Annie?"

"My dress . . ." I said inanely, focusing on the least important aspect of this crisis.

"Your dress, like you, my dear, is somewhat bedraggled. The good news is that you'd do very well in a wet T-shirt contest," Frank joked softly.

I focused on him with effort. "What are you doing here? I thought you'd already left with the bimbo."

"What bimbo?"

"You know what bimbo."

"No I don't." Frank sounded honestly puzzled.

"The woman you were talking to—the one with no body fat but enormous hooters."

"Francesca?" Frank sounded shocked. "She's an old friend."

Oh, please. The name was as fake as the boobs.

"She's not old enough to be an 'old friend,' Frank. I

don't care who she is or what you do with her—though you should know that Frank and Francesca is too cute for words. I mean, come *on*—I just thought it was kind of inconsiderate of you, considering Hildegard."

Frank looked me over as if to determine if I'd sustained a brain injury. "Who's Hildegard?"

"Oh, right—I meant Helga."

"Helga?"

"Heidi?"

"You mean Ingrid, don't you?"

"It's about time you remembered her!" I nodded triumphantly.

Frank smiled. "There's an old saying, Annie. 'You leave the dance with the one who brought you'."

"I thought that was 'You dance with the one what brung ya,'" I replied.

"No, that's 'You smooch the one that brung ya,'" he said.

"No, it *isn't*. Besides, you hate your date," I said, with a little sniffle. It had been a very long evening.

"I don't hate my date," he said patiently. "I'm annoyed with my date, but that doesn't mean I intend to leave her stranded."

Whether Frank was here out of a strict adherence to dating protocol, or because he gave a damn about what happened to me, didn't much matter at the moment because his arms were strong, warm, and welcome.

Annette appeared again, an island of efficiency in a sea of chaos. "I need to speak with Annie," she said. "Mr. DeBenton, take her to the grand hall upstairs, would you, please? I'll be up as soon as I can."

The grand hall was empty now except for the uniformed officers and a few damp partygoers wrapped in blankets, like me. We looked like a bunch of *Titanic* survivors, the bejeweled ones from first class.

I saw Emily talking to a cop, but Miss Mopsy was nowhere in sight. The crackle of police radios and the murmur of official personnel filled the air. The area near the buffet table was a shambles, with slivers of paté and imported caviar spread across the floor. Forgotten scarves and dropped gloves and other debris were also strewn around.

Frank guided me to an armchair near the entrance. The double doors were propped wide open, and I gratefully gulped deep breaths of fresh night air. He took a seat in a chair beside me. I couldn't help but notice that, unlike me, he didn't look at all bedraggled.

"Kind of a fiasco, huh?" I ventured.

"Just a bit."

"So much for a relaxed evening. I'm sorry, Frank."

He shrugged.

A screech pierced the air.

I had heard it once before, during an incident involving a whoopee cushion and the Throne of Power.

"My Caravaggio! Where is my Caravaggio?"

Agnes Brock. Who else.

Chapter 16

*History will redeem the truly gifted art forger.
Guido Reni copied the Carracci brothers so bril-
liantly that his works were considered genuine for
many years. Although many are no longer so authenticated, Reni's fakes are now nearly as valuable as the genuine Carraccis.*

—*Georges LeFleur, "The Art of the Fake," unfinished
manuscript,* Reflections of a World-Class Art Forger

I had to hand it to Agnes. She sure knew how to make an
entrance.

"You!" she screeched, zeroing in on me despite my efforts to blend into the wallpaper. She pointed dramatically with a long, bony finger tipped with a bloodred nail
that looked as if it were sharpened regularly with a whet-
stone. "I knew you would be trouble the moment I spotted you! Frank! What is the meaning of this?"

"Mrs. Brock, please, try to remain calm," Frank said
soothingly as he positioned himself between us. "I'm
sure this will all be sorted out to your satisfaction in the
next day or two."

Fat chance of that, I thought.

"But, but . . ." Her shoulders slumped and all at once

she looked old and confused. I felt a spurt of sympathy. Even though it wasn't really my fault, I had had a hand in ruining her gala. Frank put an arm around her and escorted her to her office.

I tipped my head back against the wall and closed my eyes, too exhausted even to think. In fact, I may have snoozed briefly. I heard footsteps approach and cracked one eye open. It was Inspector Crawford. Her gown was also wrinkled and stained, though nowhere near as tattered as mine. I wondered if she had borrowed her dress from a transvestite, too, but didn't dare ask. Even in San Francisco few women could hear, "Did you borrow your dress from a transvestite?" without being at least mildly insulted.

"What a night," she said, sinking into a chair. "Well, Annie, in the immortal words of Ricky Ricardo, 'you've got some 'splainin' to do.'"

I nodded, though I wasn't taking any bets on how coherent my explanation would be.

"Any idea where your Egyptologist friend got to?"

"I thought he was with the paramedics," I said, surprised.

"So did I," Annette said wryly. "Apparently we were both wrong. I hope he didn't take off with the painting."

"He didn't."

"How do you know?"

"Because I've got it." I could tell from her expression that Annette wasn't convinced. Perhaps the fact that I wasn't clutching a large oil painting made her skeptical. "Or I think I do. It's in the supply room downstairs, where we were hiding. I took it from Harlan." I had actually taken it from Michael, but Harlan was in no position to rat me out. "Which reminds me," I added. "I have to check *The Magi* for the missing drawings."

"*Sit*, Annie. I'll check this out, and I'll be very careful. By the way, you were right about the key, we found one on Harlan Coombs. Security traced its serial number to an archival drawer, and we found records of overseas bank accounts, including one in Dupont's name."

"So Stan Dupont was in on the whole thing?"

"Seems like it. It's not quite clear yet. We're still looking for a common link among the players." She stood. "Don't you *dare* move a muscle, my friend."

I watched her stride toward the service door, nodding to Frank, who was carrying a Styrofoam cup of steaming coffee. He handed it to me, and I silently blessed his thoughtfulness.

"So, no dramatics, eh, Annie?"

"It was the situation that was dramatic, Frank, not me. Be fair."

Our eyes met for a moment, and for the life of me I couldn't tell what he was thinking. Was he angry? Disgusted? Did he think I was horribly embarrassing? Adorably sexy? What? I wouldn't blame him if he never wanted to see me again, considering I had dragged him into the middle of what was sure to become one of San Francisco's most talked-about galas ever. He probably wouldn't rent to me now, even if I could afford it. Looked like it was time to start collecting cardboard boxes for moving day.

"You do realize you could have been killed tonight," he said.

"I'm kind of getting that impression."

"Is that what this was about? Some missing drawings?"

I nodded glumly. "Well, it's mostly your fault, you know."

"Excuse me?"

"If I hadn't been so desperate to make money because you doubled my rent, Frank, I might have been more cautious. Anthony Brazil was going to pay me a lot of money for finding those drawings."

I thought my logic was impeccable, if a touch self-serving. Frank didn't seem to be buying it.

"What were you thinking, going after those guys?" he demanded. "What the hell kind of artist gets shot at, anyway?"

"I'm guessing you're angry here, Frank."

"Hell yes, I'm angry."

"Exactly how is my welfare any of your concern?"

"Look, I saved your life once—"

"Sure, throw that in my face! Of all the two-bit heroics—"

I was saved from my unruly tongue by Annette, who hurried over to us from the direction of the Blue Room. I immediately felt chagrined that my temper, once again, had gotten the best of me. After all, Frank was innocent of anything having to do with either the Caravaggio or the drawings, which was a good deal more than I could say for a lot of people right now.

Frank yielded his seat to Inspector Crawford and leaned against the wall, arms crossed over his chest, an unyielding expression on his face.

"Where's *The Magi*?" I asked Annette, avoiding Frank's eyes.

"With Dr. Pitts. He's looking it over for damage. What a piece of work that guy is."

"You don't know the half of it," I said wearily, running a shaky hand through my snarled, damp hair. "Did you find the drawings?"

"Yes, we did. You were right. They were behind a canvas insert, behind *The Magi*."

Well, whaddaya know. I basked in the glow of having done something right. "Great! Can I have the drawings now?"

"I'm afraid not. They're being held as evidence."

"But—"

"Annie, don't even waste your breath. The drawings will be released when they're no longer needed by the district attorney, and not a moment sooner. Understood?"

I scowled. "You know, Annette, when you get all high-handed like this you're not my pal anymore."

Annette started to smile. "I'm afraid I'll have to find a way to live with that, my friend," she said. "Now, who did you say was the rightful owner?"

"Anthony Brazil. He owns a gallery downtown. Oh, and also Albert Mason. He does, too. A gallery. Runs one, I mean. Probably there are others." Fatigue and the adrenaline crash were setting in. I took a big gulp of coffee.

She nodded and jotted down some notes. "They have proof of ownership?"

"Well, of course they—" I broke off. With the kind of company I'd been keeping lately, I couldn't be confident that anyone was who they said they were. "I would assume so," I amended.

"What do you think Harlan was doing here?" Annette asked, flipping through her notebook. It seemed unfair that I should be such a mess while she was as cool and confident as always.

"As far as I can tell, he was trying to get to the painting. He and Edward—" Oops. I'd forgotten about Edward. Oh, Lord, and Naomi, too. Maybe I should mention them. "You should know that Edward Brock is trapped in the closet in his office. With Naomi Gregorian. She's an art restorer here at the museum."

"Where are they?"

"In the closet."

"In the closet?"

"In his office."

"In his office?"

I was suddenly reminded of an old Danny Kaye routine about a vessel with the pestle and a brew that was true. I started humming.

"May I ask why?" Annette inquired.

"It's kind of hard to explain," I said.

Annette radioed another officer to check out Edward's office, paying special attention to the closet. "Now," she said firmly, "you were saying?"

"Right. From what I can tell, Edward and Harlan made some sort of deal to steal the Caravaggio from the Brock Museum. Edward would help Harlan switch the real *Magi* with a fake one, so nobody would know it had been stolen. Harlan would then fence the real painting and split the proceeds with Edward. Camilla Culpepper had a personal relationship with Harlan and was supposed to buy the original from him."

Annette nodded. I'd been hoping she would fill me in on what else Camilla may have said, but it looked like I'd have to read about it in the papers.

"Then Emily Caulfield, Camilla Culpepper's assistant, helped switch Camilla's painting for another fake. I believe that Gordo, the Hulk, and the Fonz, the three bad guys from New York who were shooting at everybody, were also duped by Harlan. Harlan sold them what he said was the genuine Caravaggio, but Gordo discovered his *Magi* was a fake, so he came to get the real one and didn't much care who he killed in the process. They're also the ones who assaulted Pete, kidnapped me, and torched my studio. That's about all I know."

Annette's expression suggested that I'd lost my mind.

"And this Naomi Gregorian?" she said grimly. "Where does she figure in?"

"She doesn't, she just works here. She happened by and opened the closet door. Somehow she ended up inside."

"Uh-huh," she said, not buying what I was selling. "Now what about this Colin Brooks character?"

"What about him?"

"He sort of happened to be a pretty good shot for an Egyptologist, didn't he? And just out of curiosity, tell me: do most art curators carry weapons?"

Despite my doubts about Michael, I liked him. Maybe too much. In any event, whatever scores I had to settle with him did not involve the police. I cast about for a plausible explanation of his role in the gunfight, decided there wasn't one, and said nothing.

Annette continued, "And does this Colin Brooks, our gun-toting Egyptologist, have anything to do with a man named Michael Johnson, art thief extraordinaire, currently wanted for questioning by Interpol?"

"Did you know Johnson is the most common last name in America?" I dodged.

She fixed me with a Master Interrogator stare and spoke slowly. "I'm going to ask you this once, and you damned well better tell me the truth. To the best of your knowledge, Annie, is Colin Brooks in league with Michael Johnson?"

I looked her straight in the eye and lied my head off. "To the best of my knowledge, Annette, Colin Brooks and Michael Johnson have never even met, much less worked together."

The evil eye did not let up, but she leaned back a bit. "Anything else you can think of that might be of help?"

Well, there was the bit about my grandfather. And Anton, of course.

"Nope," I said. "Can't think of a thing. Oh, wait! An antiques dealer named Joanne Nash was also associated with Harlan somehow. She had a shop up in Yountville and was, um, found murdered. Over the weekend."

"And I'm only hearing of it now?"

"I didn't kill her, Annette," I said waspishly.

"I never suggested you did," she replied. "Go on with your story."

"Anyway," I continued, "Joanne Nash's sister, Quiana, was *also* associated with Ernst, and Harlan, and Edward. Quiana would probably be a good person to talk to."

"I guess I'll be making a few calls to Yountville," Annette said, closing her notebook and recapping her pen. "Anything else you want to add? Anything at all?"

It took an effort just to shake my head.

"You can go for now," Annette said. "Don't leave town, though. I imagine I'll have a few more questions for you."

"Sure, you bet." At the moment I was willing to agree to just about anything if it meant I could go home.

"And Annie?"

"Yes?"

"Get some sleep," she said with a small smile. "That's an order."

"Aye, aye, Inspector."

Miracle of miracles, my black lace wrap was still in the coat-check room, so I retrieved it and waited on the museum's front steps while Frank brought the car around. The night was cold and crisp and beautiful, and I could hear foghorns blowing somewhere in the distance. The minute I hit the Jaguar's warm leather seats, I fell into a stupor.

The next thing I knew I was being gently shaken and told to wake up. I opened my eyes and saw I was in a parking garage.

"Where are we?" I croaked as I climbed out of the car.

"My place," Frank replied.

"Why?"

He headed toward a bank of elevators in the rear wall. I followed him like a tired puppy. "Because I'm going to ravish you," Frank said as he hit the button for the top floor. "Why else?"

"Unngh?" I replied. It appeared I was de-evolving.

"You're in no shape to drive, Annie. Believe it or not, I'm tired, too, and I don't feel like driving to Oakland and back."

When the elevator doors slid open, we stepped into a thickly carpeted hallway. I was so exhausted I could have happily curled up there.

Frank's apartment was sparsely but exquisitely furnished, but what caught my eye was the signed Casseri poster leaning against one wall. Works by the Art Deco master were extremely valuable, and I knew that a similar—but unsigned—lithograph had sold at Bloomberg's Auction House last year for just over thirty-five thousand dollars.

While I was gawking, Frank disappeared into another room and then returned with a pile of linens, which he tossed on the couch. "There's the bathroom," he said, "and there's the kitchen. Make yourself at home. Good night."

"What, no kiss?"

Frank cocked his head to one side, took a step toward me, and kissed me lightly on the forehead. His lips were warm and soft, and I leaned into him for a moment. *That Bratwurst is one lucky girl,* I thought idly.

"Good night, Annie." Frank went into his bedroom and closed the door.

I sank onto the couch, exhausted, but suddenly not a bit sleepy. I stared at the T-shirt on top of the pile of linens. Maybe I should get changed? But I had so much to think about . . . Man, the couch was soft. Down-filled? But of course, I thought, right before I fell asleep.

I awoke, disoriented, in a beautiful room flooded with sunshine. My eyes found the Casseri and I remembered: Frank's place. Sitting up, I shook my head to try to clear the cobwebs. It didn't work. I shuffled over to the window and looked out at a breathtaking view. It was one of those unbelievable San Francisco days, with an azure sky and puffy white clouds that looked exactly like skies and clouds always did in really bad watercolors. The air was crystal clear, and I could see across the bay to the Berkeley and Oakland hills. I glanced back at the elegant living room. Frank must be loaded, I thought.

I took stock of my own situation. I had expended a great deal of time and energy, had risked life and limb, and had succeeded only in giving just about everybody a reason to hate me. I ran down the list. Frank was being kind but probably thought I was stupid—and scary. Anthony Brazil would denounce me when I told him that his drawings were being held indefinitely, and indiscreetly, by the police, as would Albert Mason and any number of other dealers, I was sure. Paul and Bryan would not be pleased when they found out that I had ruined their fabulous dress. Michael was probably in jail and would hate me as soon as I was compelled to testify against him. Annette wasn't going to want to be my friend anymore once she discovered that I'd lied to her. The Brocks—well, nothing new there.

Let's see, who else? Naomi was no great loss, either, but her feelings for Michael did make me feel kind of sleazy. Mary would shortly be out of a job, and I would soon be out of a studio, since Brazil was not going to pay me for drawings I had found but couldn't give him. I sure hoped my grandfather didn't find a reason to spurn me, because I had a feeling I'd be needing to flop on the floor of his atelier for a while.

On top of everything else, I needed to pee and to eat something, in that order. And fast.

I tiptoed down the hall to the guest bathroom, used the toilet, washed my hands, and splashed water on my face but, in an all-too-rare act of self-preservation, did not look in the mirror. I was very much afraid that I wouldn't be able to handle it this morning.

One pressing need taken care of, I headed toward the kitchen in search of food and heard the muffled sound of a running shower.

In the refrigerator, I found two takeout Chinese food containers, picked one up, and opened it cautiously. I was always on guard when looking into closed containers in my fridge—as a friend of mine once said, if it fights back, it's time to throw it out. Frank's leftovers not only did not sport whiskers, they smelled fabulous and looked even better. Chicken and mushrooms in black bean sauce. Yum. I pulled open a drawer and found spatulas and wine openers and all manner of yuppie kitchen gizmos. I tried the next one and found chopsticks. Perfect.

Leaning against Frank's kitchen counter, I munched away and studiously avoided thinking about the mess I had made of my life.

"I never could get the hang of those things," Frank said from behind me.

I started at the sound of his voice and inadvertently squeezed the chopsticks, flipping chicken and black bean sauce into the air. It skittered down the front of my once-beautiful dress and landed with a splat on the white ceramic tiles of the kitchen floor.

I looked at Frank. He looked at me. "Jumpy?"

"A little, I guess," I mumbled, wanting to cry. "I've positively ruined this dress." As if on cue, a black pearl popped off the neckline, fell to the floor, and rolled under the fridge. I watched it, speechless.

"Well, it has seen better days, I suppose," Frank replied, handing me a paper towel. While I cleaned up the chicken, he turned to the stove and put some water on to boil. "I don't have coffee, I'm afraid. I drink tea at home. Can I fix you a cup?" Frank leaned against the counter, hands in the front pockets of a pair of jeans with creases so crisp they must have been pressed with an iron.

"Thanks, but I'll get coffee later. Do you iron your jeans?" I had to ask.

Frank looked at his pants. "No. They come this way."

"Mine don't."

"I mean they're like this when I get them back from the cleaners."

"You *dry-clean* your jeans?" Wait until the gang heard about this!

He looked puzzled. "I dry-clean everything. I don't have time to do the laundry."

"Everything? Including your, um, jockey shorts?"

Frank smiled. "I don't wear jockey shorts. So—I've got eggs, toast, and cereal if you're hungry."

"No, thanks," I answered, waving the carton I was holding. "I hope it's all right that I helped myself. This is perfect breakfast food, in my book."

Frank nodded, grabbing the whistling kettle and pouring himself a nice cup of tea.

"Beautiful place you've got here," I said. "That couch was mighty comfy."

"I like it," he replied, pleased. "I haven't quite finished moving in yet."

"How long have you lived here?"

"About a year." He smiled wryly. "It's been hard to find the time to settle in."

The phone rang. Frank picked up the kitchen extension and said, "DeBenton."

I would have rolled my eyes if I hadn't been preoccupied slurping up a lo mein noodle. Could Mr. Iron Jeans here take himself any more seriously?

"Yes, she is." He handed me the receiver.

It was Annette. "So, tell me," she said in a conspiratorial whisper, "how was he? Or did you fall asleep?"

"What?"

"Frank. He's obviously got a little thing for you."

"Inspector . . ."

"No luck? I suppose it was a long evening. Maybe next time, huh? When I couldn't get you at home, I thought I'd try Frank's."

"I'm kind of surprised at you, Annette."

"I'm a cop, Annie. I'm not dead."

"Oh. Good point."

"Anyway, I'm calling for a reason. I thought you'd be interested to learn that last night Edward Brock confessed to the murder of Stan Dupont."

"He didn't!"

Frank looked up. I mouthed, "Edward killed Dupont," and his eyebrows shot up.

"He did. Claims it was a tragic accident, although it's not quite clear how one 'accidentally' shoots someone four times at close range in a museum at midnight and fails to call an ambulance. It seems Dupont had discovered Edward's scheme to steal the Caravaggio and was blackmailing him. Edward also admitted to panicking and taking the security tapes, but he claims he left them in his office, where they disappeared. My guess is that they went up in smoke the next morning. His lawyer arrived and shut him up before he confessed to anything else, but he did finger Harlan for Joanne Nash's murder. Said Nash double-crossed them, sold a fake instead of the real painting to the New York contingent, and split the money with her sister, Quiana. I guess that's why the New Yorkers were gunning for Harlan. The Yountville police recovered some excellent fingerprints at her antiques shop, so we'll see."

I recalled Michael's insistence upon our wearing the latex gloves, and silently thanked him. If the Yountville police had found our fingerprints at Joanne's, we would have had trouble talking our way out of that one.

"The DA isn't buying Edward's self-defense story, by the way," Annette continued, "although between the Brock family's money and their political connections, who knows what will eventually happen. Edward also spilled the beans about the scheme to steal the original Caravaggio and replace it with a fake. How well did you say you knew Colin Brooks?"

"We met once or twice, that's all."

"Hm. He's still missing. You be sure to let me know if you hear from him, you understand?"

"No problem," I lied.

"We're also holding Camilla Culpepper for manslaughter in the death of the man whose body we found in the basement hallway—a big, ugly dude named Thomas. Hired muscle, most likely. And for the attempted murder of the other two guys we found down there. Looks like they'll both recover from their wounds eventually. We're holding them for the murder of Harlan Coombs. Kind of a war zone, wasn't it?"

"Yeah, you could say that." So the Hulk was dead. I tried to muster some sense of loss at the death of a fellow creature, but couldn't manage it. "What about Ernst Pettigrew?"

"As far as we can tell, he was killed the same night as Dupont, and his body dumped in the Bay a few days later, to make it look like a suicide. I think one of this cast of characters was looking for that drawer key, and didn't realize Coombs had it. And it turns out that Camilla Culpepper had an arrangement with Harlan, too. They were going to soak her husband for the cost of the original Caravaggio, but give him a fake they'd commissioned from some well-known forger."

"Is that right? What *is* the art world coming to?"

"Guess you're probably shocked to hear about such things, eh, Annie?"

"You have no idea, Annette. No idea."

"The Brocks, by the way, are overjoyed to have the Caravaggio back. I think that for Agnes Brock it almost balances out discovering that her grandson and heir apparent is a thief and a murderer. Incidentally, I told her that you're the one she should thank, not me."

"I'll bet she just loved hearing that," I muttered. It would be a cold day in hell before that woman expressed gratitude to me for anything.

"I also suggested she give you a reward. I figured you could use it."

"Yeah, well, I won't hold my breath. Listen, there's something I've been wondering about. What's going to happen to Camilla's dog?"

With Mr. Culpepper out of town and her mumsy wuzzums in jail, I figured it would take Emily all of ten minutes to drop the dog off at the pound before she fled town.

"Funny you should ask." Annette sounded sheepish. "Miss Mopsy's right here with me. She seems to be settling in pretty well, aren't you, my widdle biddy Bopsy Boo?"

I smiled. Another dog lover heard from. "She's a sweetheart, all right. Oh, Annette, one more thing: the other painting's a fake, too."

There was a pause.

"But if the Brock Museum has a fake, and the New Yorkers have a fake, and the Culpeppers have a fake, then where's the real one?"

"Chicago," I said without thinking.

"What? Why Chicago?"

"At the Fabulous Fakes Exhibit. It's a long story."

There was another pause. "Look, I'm just a cop, Annie. If the Brocks say their painting is real, it's not my business to tell them otherwise. Well, I've got to go. Miss Mopsy here needs her walk."

Frank gave me a lift back to the studio, where I'd left

my truck. I'd locked my wallet and house keys in the glove compartment yesterday, figuring the last thing I needed to worry about during the gala was keeping track of an evening bag. Considering I'd managed to lose even my shoes, that had been a good instinct. Frank had kept my truck key for me, and handed it to me now. I thanked him for everything and was about to close the Jaguar's door when he said, "Annie, hold it."

I held it.

Frank looked unaccountably uneasy. "Listen, I've been thinking," he said. "I might be able to hold off on that rent increase for a little while. I have something in mind that could use a good eye—it's nothing as exciting as what you're used to, but I would be willing to trade some rent for your expertise."

I was flummoxed. And to think, all it had taken for Frank to see things my way was one especially disastrous date.

"Plus, I was thinking about sprucing up the building a little. Maybe we could showcase some of your faux finishes in the hallways. You know, make the place more interesting and increase the property value. Then I could jack up the rent for the architects and computer designers. Come by my office tomorrow morning at nine, and we'll hammer out the details."

"I will," I said, nonplussed. "And Frank—thanks for not leaving without me last night."

"No problem," he said with a shrug.

I stared as the Jaguar drove off. I didn't have to worry about being thrown out of my studio! Relief washed over me. Ol' Fender Bender there was a hard one to figure out.

Firing up the truck, I pulled out of the parking lot. It was early on Sunday morning, and apart from a few joggers and assorted health nuts, most of San Francisco was still tucked in bed. Traffic on the Bay Bridge was light.

As usual, it was warmer in the East Bay than in the City, and I rolled down the window and enjoyed the balmy morning air as I drove to Fanny's Café on San Pablo Avenue for a latte to go. In my stocking feet and wrinkled ball gown I felt like a disreputable Cinderella, but I was beyond caring. Being sophisticated Berkeleyites and all, the café's other customers pretended to ignore me, and I caught only one or two surreptitious stares.

At last I headed home, parked in back of the house, let myself in the front door, and trudged up the three flights of stairs to my apartment, holding my skirt in one hand and the latte in the other. All I could think about was how delighted Grandfather would be to hear the news: his fake *Magi* was hanging in the Brock Museum, displayed as an original, while the real Caravaggio was hanging in the Fantastic Fakes exhibit in Chicago, displayed as a fake. Georges and his felonious cronies would be high on life for a week.

But what would happen to the real Caravaggio when the Chicago exhibition was over? The thought gave me pause. It needed to be taken care of, before some un-scrupulous lowlife caught wind of it and . . . and speaking of which, where had Michael gotten to? Had he figured it out, too?

Was the pope Catholic?

I entered my apartment and locked the door behind me. With a sigh I went into the bedroom, stripped off the ruined dress and filthy stockings, and slipped into a pair of shorts, a T-shirt, and my Birkenstocks. I wiggled my toes. Heaven.

I scuffed down the hall to the kitchen and flopped into a chair. As I reveled in the latte's rich flavor, my eyes were drawn to the evil elf, perched in a corner of the kitchen. It leered at me, a souvenir of better times—of an-other time, anyway.

What caught my attention, though, was the envelope in the elf's little hands.

The envelope that hadn't been there yesterday, and that had my name on it, written in a bold, unfamiliar script.

I set the latte down and approached the elf cautiously, as if it might, at any moment, spring to life and attack me. I snatched the envelope out of its hands. It was thick, but gave no clue to its contents. I tore it open.

Inside was a round-trip plane ticket to Chicago, departing Oakland International Airport tomorrow afternoon at 12:40. The enclosed note read:

> *Join me for a fantastic art show.*
> *Miss you already.*
> X

I sat at my kitchen table for a long time, thinking.

I could make the meeting with Frank tomorrow morning at nine to discuss the break in the rent and still have time to catch the plane. However . . .

Annette had specifically requested that I not leave town. I was supposed to give her a formal statement about what had happened last night at the Brock gala.

I had a good friend who was recuperating from injuries sustained in the course of trying to protect me.

I had several faux-finishing jobs that were due and John Steubing's portrait to finish.

I had bills to pay.

In short, I had a life and obligations here, and none of them included the X-man, or my grandfather, or Anton, for that matter.

I pondered some more. Then I picked up the phone.

"Mary? It's Annie. Could you watch over Pete and the studio for a few days? I'm on my way to Chicago."

Annie's Basic Old Master Glaze
(For faux finishing walls and furniture)

⅓ Mineral spirits
⅓ Artist's quality boiled linseed oil* or a commercial alkyd faux-finishing liquid (available at most paint retailers)
⅓ Alkyd tinted wall paint

*Linseed oil is the traditional painter's medium but it tends to be very shiny and slow-drying. It also may yellow over time, making blue finishes especially difficult to achieve. For a completely matte finish and shorter drying time, substitute a commercial alkyd faux-finishing liquid.

Before you paint.

Mixing Glaze: Mix all ingredients well before and during the project. If any pigment is not thoroughly mixed, it will show as a blotch on the wall. A large mayonnaise jar full of glaze is usually sufficient for an average living room, but it is always best to mix extra glaze. It is very hard to achieve exactly the same color in a different batch of glaze!

Basecoat: Remember that the wall base paint will show through the glaze coat. The base is typically lighter than the glaze, but the color choices and combinations are limited only by one's imagination. A typical parchment finish is a raw sienna glaze over a Navajo white base coat; burnt umber creates a mellow brown antique feel; burnt sienna gives an orangey-red earthy glow. Choose an eggshell latex paint for an even base coat surface that will not absorb too much of the glaze. While painting the wall with the base coat, paint a few big pieces of heavy cardboard or scrap lumber to test your glaze color intensity as well as to practice your technique. Allow the base coat to dry for forty-eight hours before faux-finishing.

Glaze Technique:

Glaze is a translucent film of pigment which alters but does not hide the base coat. The best way to learn how to achieve the finish you want is to experiment. Apply the glaze coat to a base-coated surface with a regular brush or sponge, then try any of the following:

To achieve an all-over "broken" finish: Use cheesecloth, wadded up paper, T-shirt rags, or even plastic bags. Press one or all of these into the wet glaze, lifting up in a dabbing motion. Each item leaves a different sort of imprint behind in the wet glaze. You can soften any of the textures in the glaze by *very* lightly brushing over them with an extremely soft, dry brush. If you're using cloths, change them frequently as they get saturated.

To achieve a "dragged" finish: Use a comb or dry paintbrush. Rather than dabbing, drag these through the glaze from top to bottom, or in a squiggle, or criss-cross, or any design that appeals to you. Be sure to wipe excess glaze from the tool frequently.

Glazing a wall is a fast, intense job usually best done with a helper. Starting in the uppermost left corner (for right-handers, the opposite for lefties), one person begins painting the glaze on the wall loosely with a brush. The second person follows, creating the desired texture, moving to the right and down the wall rapidly. Both of you should move back and forth quickly so that the "edge" of the glaze is never allowed to dry; if it does so, it will create a "hard edge" that is impossible to mask. Similarly, going back "into" glaze that is already drying usually creates a blotchy mess; it is better to leave light or missed areas alone and feather in fresh glaze afterward, when the surface is completely dry.

Nobody's Perfect: If you do happen to end up with a lot of blotches and hard edges, try over-glazing with another coat of glaze, either in the same color or a coordinating one. Or just go with the "old plaster" theme—paint in a few more "cracks" and "veins," and pretend you did it on purpose. If all else fails, you can start all over again, this time approaching the wall as an experienced faux-finisher. Just remember: it's only paint!

Hailey Lind is the pseudonym of two sisters, one a historian in Virginia, the other an artist in California. Their identity is a closely guarded secret . . . unless someone really wants to know.

SIGNET   (0451)

TAMAR MYERS
PENNSYLVANIA DUTCH
MYSTERIES—WITH RECIPES!

"As sweet as a piece of brown-sugar pie."
—*Booklist*

"Rollicking suspense."
—*Washington Post*

Available wherever books are sold or at
penguin.com